The HERetic's DaughteR

The
HERetic's
DaughteR

A NOVEL

KATHLEEN KENT

LITTLE, BROWN AND COMPANY

New York Boston London

Little, Brown and Company
Hachette Book Group USA
237 Park Avenue, New York, NY 10017
Visit our Web site at www.HachetteBookGroupUSA.com

First Edition: September 2008

Little, Brown and Company is a division of Hachette Book Group USA, Inc. The Little,
Brown name and logo are trademarks of Hachette Book Group USA, Inc.

The characters and events in this book are fictitious.
Any similarity to real persons, living or dead,
is coincidental and not intended by the author.

Library of Congress Cataloging-in-Publication Data
Kent, Kathleen.
The heretic's daughter : a novel / Kathleen Kent.— 1st ed.
p. cm.
ISBN-10: 0-316-02448-1
ISBN-13: 978-0-316-02448-8
1. Witchcraft—Massachusetts—Salem—Fiction. 2. Salem (Mass.)—History—Colonial
period, ca. 1600–1775—Fiction. 3. Trials (Witchcraft)—Massachusetts—Salem—
History—17th century—Fiction. I. Title.
PS3611.E674H47 2008
813'.6—dc22   2008001887

10 9 8 7 6 5 4 3

RRD-C

Printed in the United States of America

Book design by Jo Anne Metsch

This book is dedicated to
Mitchell and Joshua

And to my parents, John and Audrey,
for giving me the stories

In 1630 Governor Winthrop of the Massachusetts Bay Colony took a small group of men and women from the old England to the new. These Puritans, so they were named, would make a place in the colonies by surviving war, plague, and the work of the Devil in a small village called Salem. One woman and her family would stand against religious tyranny, suffering imprisonment, torture, and death. Her outraged and defiant words were recorded by Cotton Mather, who called her "The Queen of Hell." Her name was Martha Carrier.

Letter from Colchester, Connecticut,
November 17, 1752

TO MRS. JOHN WAKEFIELD
New London, Connecticut

My dear Lydia:

I have only just received word of your marriage and I thank God he has delivered to you a husband who is worthy of your hand and has the means to begin family life with all comfortable effects. I do not have to tell you, my dearest, that you have always had the greatest share of a grandmother's love.

So many months have passed since I last saw you and I ache to sit with you and share your joy. My infirmities have too long kept me from my loved ones and I hope I will again be able to travel to see you. I know you are a woman fully grown but in my mind you are still a girl of twelve, fresh and lively, come to stay with me for a good while to lighten the press of years. Your presence always brought with it a fragrance of greening things that chased away the decay of my own rooms. I pray I may see you one more time before my death, but my hold on this world is gentle at best and I feel most urgently that now is the time to give you a gift greater than plates and bowls. What I give to you is a treasure which encompasses generations and spans the oceans from this world to the old.

Today is my birthday and, because of God's grace, I am seventy-one years of age. This is an astonishing amount of time to live even in an age of wonders and, dare I say it, magical occurrences.

As you must well know, in September of this very year minds wiser than ours decided that eleven days must be dropped from our calendars. For what reason, I cannot divine. I only know that I went to sleep on a Wednesday, the 2nd day of September, year of our Lord 1752, and woke up on a Thursday, the 14th day of September of the same year.

They call this new reckoning the Gregorian calendar. The Julian calendar is abandoned. We have been plotting time in the same way, or so I believe, since the birth of the good Christ. Where do you think these eleven days are supposed to have gone? As you are still young, these things may seem very like a part of the natural world. But I am still tied to the past and these happenings fill me with apprehensions. I have lived long enough to remember a time when progress of this sort would have been seen as sorceries and witchcraft and would have brought a terrible judgment from our Town Fathers for placing a hand too near the inventions of heaven.

And now I have hit upon the heart of my letter. You cannot have grown to womanhood without hearing the embittered whispers of Salem Village, and of me and my parents. But in your love for me you have never asked me to reveal the dread happenings of my youth. The name Salem even now causes grown men and women to blanch with fear. Do you know that a few months past, the councilmen of Essex County, Massachusetts, voted to change the name of the village to Danvers? It was a thing well done and done quietly, too, though I believe the memory of the Salem witch trials will last well beyond the few remaining living relics of that time.

As God in heaven knows, changing a name cannot change the history of a place. This history has for so long lived like a spider in my breast. The spider spins and spins, catching memories in its web, threatening to devour every final happiness. With this letter I hope to sweep away the terror and the sadness and to have my heart made pure again by God's grace. That is truly the meaning of the word "Puritan."

I believe this word is sorely out of fashion now. It brings to mind thoughts of an antiquated people steeped in superstitious beliefs and old-fashioned prideful practices. Puritans believed they were a people covenanted with God. Charged by Him to secure a fortress in the wilderness and make it sacred ground. There in those remote places they were to bend the course of the world to God's plan.

I say now, What arrogance. The Town Fathers believed they were saints, predestined by the Almighty to rule over our little hamlets with harsh justice and holy purpose. This holy purpose, like autumn brush fires, would swell and burn mightily through Salem Village and neighboring towns, committing scores of families in due course to dust. And beneath it all was greed and the smallpox and the constant raids of Indians, dismantling people's reason, eating at the foundation of trust and goodwill with our neighbors, our families, and even our belief in God. It was a terrible time, when charity and mercy and plain good sense were all thrown into the fire of zealotry, covering everyone left living with the bitter ash of regret and blame.

The Puritan faith turned every happening, a falling tree, a sickness, a wart, into a warning and a judgment from the Eternal Father. We were like children who quaked and shivered at the world we had been given. And it was through childlike distempers, selfishness, and slanderous voices that entire villages were brought low. I have seen firsthand,

God help me, more than one child bring a parent to the scaffold. "Honour thy Father and thy Mother," saith the commandment. This covenant was surely put aside in the black year of 1692, and many more commandments besides were broken as easily as limestone upon hard rock. I tell you all of this to show you the inner resources of the Puritan mind and to prepare you for what I am sending you by parcel.

What follows is my own written history, pieces of which may have been told to you from your earliest childhood. That you came to love me so deeply when others turned from me is God's miracle and perhaps my recompense for so many losses. My life is very like the bedtime fables a parent might tell an errant child to frighten him into obedience: the stuff of nightmares. But, oh my child, this nightmare was not drawn from the well of fanciful hearth tales but woven from the blood and bones and tears of your own family. I have set down my recollections and my involvement in the events surrounding the Salem Village witch trials, and as God is my witness, I have set them down as faithfully as I may. I pray that with this record you will understand, and come to forgive me for what I did.

The winter winds have come early and have blown tirelessly for weeks. Do you remember the great oak that grows hard by the house? It is very old and has lost many branches but the trunk is thick and sound and the roots are deep. There was a great span of time when I hated the sight of an oak tree. But I cannot blame the tree for a hanging any more than I can blame the ocean for a drowning. Once you have read this account you will know my meaning. I pray you liken your family to this venerable old tree, within whose branches you may find shelter and a connection between the earth and the heaven above, where we may hope to be one day united with God, and with each other.

Yours, in God's gracious care,
And ever-loving, Grandmother,
Sarah Carrier Chapman

Ah, children, be afraid of going prayerless to bed,

lest the Devil be your bedfellow.

COTTON MATHER,
from a funeral service

The HERetic's DaughteR

CHAPTER ONE

Massachusetts, December 1690

THE DISTANCE BY wagon from Billerica to neighboring Andover is but nine miles. For myself it was more than a journey away from the only home I had ever known. It was the ending of a passage from the dark fog of infancy to the sharp remembrances of childhood. I was nine years of age on that December day and my entire family was going back to live with my grandmother in the house where my mother was born. We were six in all, cramped together in an open wagon, carrying within my mother and father, two of my older brothers, myself, and Hannah, who was but a baby. We had with us all of our household possessions. And we were bringing, unbeknownst to any of us, the smallpox.

A plague of it had swept across the settlements of Middlesex

County, and with our crossing east over Blanchard's Plain, contagion and death followed with us. A close neighbor, John Dunkin of Billerica, had died within the space of one week, leaving a widow and seven children. Another neighbor brought us the news, and before the door could close on the messenger, my mother had started packing. We had thought to outrun the pox this time. My father had bitter memories of being blamed for bringing the pox into Billerica many years before. He always said it was because he was a Welshman and a stranger to the town, even after living there for so many years, that he stood accused. But the disease crept along with us like a pariah dog. It was my older brother Andrew who would be the first to succumb. He carried the seeds of sickness within him, and from him it would spread to our new town of residence.

It was deep into the season and so bitterly cold, the liquid from our streaming eyes and noses froze onto our cheeks like frosted ribbons of lace. All of us had dressed in every bit of clothing that we possessed and we pressed tightly together for warmth. The crudely hewn boards of the wagon had been covered with straw, and my brothers and I had wrapped it around us as best we could. The draft horse labored under his load, for he was not a young gelding, and his breath steamed in great puffs into the air. His coat was as woolly as any bear's and encrusted with a forest of icicles that hung down sharply from his belly. Richard, my oldest brother, was not with us. He was near a man at sixteen and had been sent ahead to help ready the house for our arrival, bringing provisions strapped across the back of our one remaining ox.

Father and Mother sat at the front of the wagon silent, as was their habit. They rarely spoke to each other in our presence and only then of weights and measures and time delineated by the seasons. The language of field and home. He often deferred to her, which seemed remarkable, as he towered over my mother. Indeed, he towered over everyone. He was close to seven feet tall, so it was said, and to me, being a small child, his head seemed to rest in the clouds, his face forever in shadow. He was forty-eight years of age when he married my mother, so I had always thought of him as an old man, even though he carried himself erect and was fleet of foot. Thomas Carrier, so the gossip went, had come from old England as a young man to escape some troubles there. As my father never spoke of his life before marrying, and for truth said hardly a word regarding anything at all, I did not know his history before he plied his trade as farmer in Billerica.

I knew only two things for certain of his past. The first was that my father had been a soldier during the civil wars of the old England. He had a red coat, old and battered and faded to rust, which he had brought with him from London. One arm was torn, as though slashed through with something sharp, and Richard had told me that, but for the padded lining in the sleeve, Father would have lost an arm for sure. When I pressed Richard for more of the story as to how and where Father had fought, my brother would purse his lips and say, "Ah, but you're only a girl and cannot know the ways of men." The other thing I knew was that men feared him. Often behind my father's back they would gesture secretly to one another a peculiar signal. A thumb passed over the neck from one side to the other as if to sever their heads from their bodies. But if Father ever saw these gestures, he gave them no notice.

My mother, who was Martha Allen before marrying, sat next to him, holding Hannah, only one year old. She was wrapped into a shapeless bundle and held loosely like a package. I remember watching my little sister with the cruel fascination of a child, wondering when she would topple out of the wagon. We had lost a baby sister, Jane, years before and my lack of close affection could have been for fear that this baby would die as well. The first year was so fragile that some families did not name their child until the child was past twelve months and more likely to live. And in many households if a baby died, that same baby's name would be passed on to the next born. And to the very next if that babe died as well.

At times I suspected my mother had no tender feelings for any of us, even though we were as different from one another as children could be. Richard was very much like Father: tall, silent, and as impenetrable as the rocks in Boston Bay. Andrew, the next oldest, had been a sweet child and cheerfully willing to work, but as he grew, he stayed rather slow in thought and often my mother lost patience with him. Tom, the third son, was closest to me in years and closest to my heart. He was quick and bright, his humors running hot and restless like mine, but he was often afflicted with attacks of labored breathing and so, at the times of seasons' changing, had not much strength to work in the field or barn. I was next in age, stubborn and willful, I was often enough told, and thus not easily loved. I approached the world with suspicion, and because I was not pretty or pliable, I was not doted upon. I often challenged my betters and was therefore often chastised vigorously with a slotted spoon we children had named Iron Bessie.

It was my manner to openly stare at the people around me, despite knowing how this discomforted them, especially my mother. It was as though my staring robbed her of some essential part of herself, some part that she held in reserve even from those closest to her. There was hardly a time when we were not eating or sleeping or working together, and so we were expected to give quarter in this regard. She loathed my staring so greatly that she would work to catch me at it, and if I could not look away before she turned to me, she would use Iron Bessie on my back and legs until her wrist gave out. And as her wrists were as strong as any man's, this took some time. But in this way, I came to witness so much that others did not see. Or did not wish to see.

It was not defiance only that made me study her so, although our cat-and-mouse games did become a kind of battle. It was also because she, with a deliberation bordering on the unseemly, set herself apart from what a woman should be and was as surprising as a flood or a brush fire. She had a will, and a demeanor, as forceful as a church deacon's. The passage of time, and layer upon layer of misfortune, had only worked to stiffen the fabric of her being. At first glance, one might perceive a comely woman of some intelligence, not young, but neither yet old. And her face, when not animated by speech or untempered passions, seemed serene. But Martha Carrier was like a deep pond, the surface of which was placid enough but deeply cold to the touch and which was filled beneath the surface with sharp rocks and treacherous choke roots. And she had a tongue, the sharpness of which would gut a man as quick as a Gloucester fisherman could clean a lamprey eel. I know I was not alone in my family, or amongst our neighbors, in fervently praying for a beating rather than having to endure the lacerations of her speech.

As our wagon moved slowly past fields covered in deep drifts of encrusted snow, I looked expectantly about for farmhouses or, better still, the sight of a garrison outpost or a gallows hill with the remains of ropes still dangling from broad-limbed oaks where the hangman had cut down the bodies. We speculated about how long the bodies would be left on the rope before public decency required them to be removed. In years to come children of a tender age would be kept away from the hangings, flailings, and public tortures of the honorable courts of New England. But I was yet in my innocence and thought such necessary instructions to be no more unpleasant than wringing the head from a chicken's neck. I had, from time to time, seen men and women in the stocks, and it had been great sport for my brothers and me to throw bits of refuse at their captive heads.

Crossing over the Shawshin River bridge, we entered the Boston Way Road, which would lead us north to Andover. We passed the houses of our new neighbors, the Osgoods, the Ballards, and the Chandlers, all to the west of us. And there, just ahead to the east, was the town's southern garrison. The garrison was a stout two-storied house with provisions and ammunition kept on the second floor. The stockades were of great necessity, as there were still violent Indian raids in the surrounds. Only the year before had there been a deadly raid on Dover. Twenty-three were killed. Twenty-nine children were captured to be kept or traded back to their families. We hailed the guard, but as the windows were frosted, the man posted on the lookout did not see us and so he did not raise his hand to us as we passed by.

Just north of the garrison, set off from the main road, was my grandmother's house. It was smaller than I had remembered and more homely, with a steeply pitched roof and an iron-cladded door. But when the door opened and Richard came to greet us, I remembered well the old woman who followed him out. It had been two years or more since our last visit. Her bones did not like to travel to Billerica by cart, she had said. And she told my mother she would not imperil her daughter's immortal soul by having us travel to Andover until my parents had started going to the meetinghouse on each and every Sabbath. We could be captured and killed by Indians on the way, or waylaid by path robbers, or fall into a sinkhole and drown, she had said. And then would our souls be lost forever. The years of separation from Grandmother were testament in equal parts to my mother's obstinacy and her great dislike for sitting in a pew.

The old lady lifted Hannah at once from my mother and welcomed us into a house warmed by a great fire and the smell of a cooking pot, reminding us that we had eaten only a few hard biscuits at dawn. I walked through the house, sucking my stinging fingers, looking at the things my grandfather had made. He had died some years before I was born and so I had never met him, though I had heard Richard say he was so alike my mother that bringing them together was like throwing oil onto a burning brand. The house had one common room with a hearth, a table hand-rubbed and smelling of beeswax, butter, and ashes, a few rush chairs, and one fine carved sidepiece for storing plates. I ran my fingers lightly over the designs, wondering at the cunning workmanship. Our house in Billerica had only benches and a rude trestle table with no pretty patterns to please the eye or the hand. The Andover house had one small bedchamber off the main room and a stairway that led up to a garret room filled with a lifetime of crates and jars and wooden trunks.

My parents, with Hannah, were given Grandmother's room and bed, while she took a cot next to the hearth in the common room. Andrew, Tom, and I would sleep in the garret, while Richard would have to make his rest with the ox and the horse in the barn close behind the house. He could stand the cold better than most, and Mother said it was because his inner heat was not diminished by an open mouth and a loose tongue. He was handed most of the blankets, as he would have no way of making a useful fire in the hay. Grandmother found for the rest of us a few old relics of batting for our covers against the freezing air.

The first night, the house was filled with the sounds of the walls settling against the layering snow and the warm animal smells of my brothers. I was used to sleeping in an alcove with Hannah at my chest as a warming stone. I lay on my pallet shivering in the cold, and when I closed my eyes I could yet feel the movement of the wagon. The straw worked its way out of the ticking and pricked the skin on my back, making me restless. There was no candle to light our room, and I could not see where my brothers lay sleeping only a few feet away. At long last a shaft of moonlight worked its way in between the boards at the window, and the long-necked jars made shadows of headless ghost-soldiers on the rough timbers, marching as though in battle with the moon shafts traveling across the walls. I threw off the batting and crawled across the splintered planks, feeling along with my hands until I reached my brothers' pallet and crawled in close to Tom. I was too old to be sleeping with my brothers and would be punished in the morning if caught, but I pressed myself close to his huddled form and, taking in his good warmth, closed my eyes.

WHEN I WOKE in the morning I was alone, my brothers risen, the objects scattered about the room looking gray and much used. I dressed quickly in the aching cold, my fingers as unbending as sausages. I crept down the stairs and heard the sound of Father's voice vibrating through the common room. The smell of cooking meat made my belly cramp but I crouched low on the stairs so I could see while not being seen, and listened. I heard him say "... it is a matter of conscience. And let us leave it at that."

Grandmother paused for a moment and, laying her hand on his shoulder, replied, "Thomas, I know of your differences with the parson. But this is not Billerica. It is Andover. And the Reverend Barnard will not brook absence from prayer. You must go today in good faith to the selectmen, before the Sabbath, and give your oath of fidelity to the town if you are to stay. Tomorrow, on the Sabbath, you must come with me to the meetinghouse for service. If you do not, you may be turned out. There is much conflict with newcomers laying claim to land. There are jealousies and resentments here enough to fill a well. If you stay long enough, you will see."

He looked into the fire, struggling to resolve the conflict within — between compliance to the laws of the meetinghouse and the desire to be left entirely to his own devices. I was very young but even I knew he was not greatly liked in Billerica. He was too solitary, too imposing in his unyielding beliefs in what was fair and what was not. And there was always whispered gossip of a past life, supposedly unlawful but never precisely named, that created a space for solitude. Last year Father had been fined 20 pence for arguing with a neighbor over property lines. His size, his great strength, and his reputation caused the neighbor to give way in the dispute, allowing Father to plant the boundary stakes where he wanted them despite the fine.

"Won't you do this for your wife and children?" she asked gently.

Bowing his head to his breakfast, he said, "For you and for my children I will do as you ask. As for my wife, you must ask her yourself. She has a great dislike for the Minister Barnard and coming from me it would be taken very badly."

For all Grandmother was soft and gentle, she was also persuasive, and like water wearing down rock she worked on Mother until she agreed to attend services on the morrow. Mother said under her breath, "I'd rather eat stones." But she brought out her good linen collar to be washed nonetheless. Richard and Andrew would leave with Father that very morning for the north end of Andover. They would put their mark on the town register and pledge faith to defend it from all attackers, promising to pay tithes in good time to its ministers. I pinched Andrew's arm hard and made him swear an oath that he would repeat everything he would see and hear. Tom and I were to be left behind with Mother for the cooking and gathering of firewood. Grandmother said that a respectful visit should also be made to the Reverend Francis Dane, who lived directly across from the meetinghouse. He had been pastor in North Andover for over forty years and was greatly loved. He was to have given way in his ministry years ago to the Reverend Barnard but, like a good shepherd, he sensed there was enough wolf in the younger man to warrant his continued protecting presence. The two men grudgingly shared the pulpit, and their sermonizing, every other week or so. I stood at the door and watched the cart's progress as far as the bend in the road, until they were swallowed behind mountainous drifts of snow.

When I closed the door Grandmother was already seated at her spinning wheel. Her foot was on the treadle but her eyes were thoughtfully on me. The spinner was beautifully carved of dark oak with leaves twining their way round and round the outer rim. It must have been very old, as the designs were too fanciful to have been made in the new England. She called to me and asked if I could spin. I told her yes, well enough, but that I could sew better, which was a statement only half true. A camp surgeon would have had a better hand with a cleaver to a limb than I with a needle on cloth. She spun the wool through knotted fingers glistening with sheep's oil and wrapped the threads neatly around the bobbin. Gently probing, she teased out the story of our days in Billerica just as she teased out the fine line of thread from the mix and jumble of the coarse wool in her hands.

I did not think to tell her we lived a solitary life, as I did not know there was any other life to be had. Our plot of land in Billerica rested on poor soil and yielded little. And of late our animals seemed to sicken and die as though the ground itself leeched up the ill will of our fitful neighbors like a poisonous fog. Tom was my closest companion but he was ten years of age and worked in the fields with Richard and Andrew. My days were spent caring for Hannah and helping Mother within the dreary confines of the house. I cast about for something of interest to tell her, remembering a day last spring.

"One day," I began, "this May past, laying Hannah down for to sleep, I crept out of the house and ran to spy on Tom. I hid behind our stone wall, for I was not supposed to be there, y'see, and I saw Father putting the plow harness round Richard and Andrew. Tom was before them, rolling from the field rocks the size of his head. He was sweating and breathing something terrible. And all the while the ox was tied under the shade of a tree. At supper I asked Tom about the ox and he whispered to me that Father was saving the ox for easier work. We have only one ox, y'see, and he is very old. It would be hard on us should he die."

Grandmother's foot faltered and the wheel slowly ceased turning. She pulled me closer into the crook of her arm and said, "Life is surely hard, Sarah. God tests us to see if we will put our faith in Him no matter what may come. We must attend God's house and be guided by His ministers so that we may make our reward after death." She paused to smooth a strand of hair back under my cap. "What say your parents on this?"

I reached out, tracing the lines on her face, and answered, "Father has told us that ministers in the new England are no better than kings in the old."

"And your mother? Has she this opinion also?" she asked.

I told her what I had heard Mother say about a visiting parson come from the wilderness of the Eastward in the territory of Maine. She had asked him, "Are you the parson who serves all of Salmon Falls?" "No, Goody Carrier," he answered. "I am the parson that rules all of Salmon Falls."

I had thought to make her smile but she cupped her hands around my face and said, "Parsons are men and men will often fall short of Grace. But you could do no better than to put your faith in the Reverend Dane. He was my sister's husband and has looked after me since your grandfather died." She paused with her hand on my cheek and looked suddenly beyond me into the still-darkened common room. The sun had barely risen above the bottom window casing, leaving shadows pooled around the walls like draperies of black velvet. A barn owl at the end of his night's hunting gurgled out one last protesting song. Grandmother raised her chin and sniffed at the air as though a warning wisp of smoke had found its way from the hearth. Her arm tightened around me, pulling me closer to the warmth of her body.

I have come to believe that some women can see things yet undone. My mother surely had this gift. Often without a word she would straighten her cap and smooth her apron and stand looking down the empty road that led to our house. And before long some neighbor or journeyman would appear at the yard and be surprised to find Goodwife Carrier standing at the door waiting for him. Perhaps that thread of knowingness had been passed to her from her mother. But Grandmother must have known that seeing is not enough to change the course of things, for she released me, starting the action of the treadle once more. Picking up the string of wool she said, "Accept whatever comes as the will of God, no matter how harsh. But if you are ever in need, turn to Reverend Dane and he will find a way to help. Do you hear me, Sarah?"

I nodded and stayed awhile at her side, until Mother called me away. Later I would often think on her words and wonder that she could have remained so kind under the yoke of a God who caused infants to die in the womb, women and men to be hacked to death by stone adzes, and children to suffer and die from the plague. But then, she would not be alive to witness the worst of it.

"WE'VE BEEN GIVEN a warning," said Andrew, his voice high and brittle. It was dark but we could feel our breaths mingled together as we talked. Tom and Andrew and I sat on the sleeping pallet, our knees touching, our heads covered with the batting to mask the sounds of our whispers. Grandmother had prepared for the Sabbath with lengthy readings from Scripture before supper and it was hours before we could climb the stairs to our garret room for sleep. And so in the dark of the attic Andrew told us of Father's progress north up Boston Way Road to the meetinghouse, the farmsteads lying along the frozen banks of the Shawshin as many as cones in a forest.

Approaching the village center, they came upon the meeting-house, larger than the one in Billerica, with a full two stories with leaded-glass windows. It was the constable who unlocked the doors, letting them in to wait for the selectmen. The constable, John Ballard, had been positioned for fifteen years, though he was but thirty-two, and was a great bull of a man who lived less than half a mile from Grandmother's house. Andrew grabbed my elbow, saying, "Sarah, you should have seen this fellow. He had hair the color of brass and a face that looked like boiled wax. Surely the man was poxed to have such holes on his face."

It was another two hours before John Ballard returned with the selectmen, having left my father and brothers to shake off the cold below the drafty timbers. There were five patriarchs who finally gathered together in the meetinghouse, each wearing a thick woolen cape, none being turned or patched. They bore themselves with tight reserve and had names that were well known in Andover: Bradstreet, Chandler, Osgood, Barker, and Abbot. It was they who had the power to decide which families could stay and which families would be turned out. They sat together on benches facing my father, appearing as judges at a trial to which one was considered guilty until innocence could be proven. The most impressive, according to Andrew, was Lieutenant John Osgood, a severe and long-faced man who neither smiled nor made any words of greeting. The other men deferred to him in all things and it was he who asked most of the questions. A younger man, the town clerk, followed close by and made with quill and ink a record of the judgment.

Andrew said, leaning closer to me, "This Lieutenant Osgood

shuffled a few papers about, then looked Father up and down and asked him if he knew of the smallpox in Billerica. Father answered him aye, he did know of it. Then he asked if any of us was brought to Andover ill, and Father answered no, that all of us were fit. The lieutenant squinted hard at Father, shaking his head, and I thought we were in for it. And then, what do you think happened? The door flew open and there, standing like the Angel of Light, was Reverend Dane. He stood next to us, facing those five men, and spoke of Grandmother and her long good standing in the town and asked to let us stay. I tell you, they were blown over by his words as foxglove is by a summer wind."

"Then, can we stay? Yes or no?" demanded Tom, gripping my hand.

Andrew paused, savoring our tension, and finally said, "We may stay but are given a caution. We must follow all the town's laws and attend prayer service or we will be sent back to Billerica." With that, a violent shudder passed through his body and he coughed a dry, rasping cough. I placed my palm over his forehead, and it was like placing it on a burning kiln.

"I'm very tired," he said, dropping back onto the pallet, his eyes like two burnt coals in a blanket. Tom and I lay down and followed Andrew into our own dreams. Sometime later in the night, I woke thinking I had fallen asleep next to the hearth. I reached out in the darkness and touched Andrew's neck. His skin felt hot and papery-dry, and his breath smelled sour and thick. I moved closer to Tom and fell quickly back to sleep.

When I woke again it was the Sabbath, and I threw back my covers, eager to see the meetinghouse where the prayer service would be held. Tom was gone but Andrew still lay on the pallet, his back to me. His breathing seemed queer, halting and shallow. I reached over to shake him, and his body was warm. He moaned softly and mumbled but did not rise. I told him it was morning and he must ready himself for leaving. I was already dressed and on the stairs before he sat up, clutching his head. His color was high and the shadows under his eyes were dark like bruises. He slowly put a silencing finger to his lips and I went quickly down to the light of the common room. Soon after, Andrew followed, his fingers still fumbling to button his shirt and pants, as though his hands had lost their strength.

As soon as we were able, we left, bundled together in the wagon. Grandmother sat in front between Mother and Father and spoke to us at length of the warmth of the Andover fellowship. After a time Mother said, "I pray that may be so, for though I have not been there for some time, I remember well enough there is little fire to keep a body warm."

Grandmother said sharply, "Martha, you have always spoken for the attention it would bring you. You put your soul and the souls of your children at peril. You, and your family, have come back to live in my home, and it is by my rules that you shall live. The day of the Sabbath is for prayer, and prayer we shall have."

I looked with stealth at my mother's rigid back. I had never heard anyone speak so harshly to her without a quick answer in return. Father coughed into his fist but said nothing. The meetinghouse was larger than I had imagined it to be, and as we tied up the horse's reins, we saw a town full of people entering through the forward doors. Many faces were turned our way, some in curiosity, a few in open hostility. Just outside the doors stood an aged woman ringing with both hands a large brass bell. Grandmother nodded to her and told me she was the widow Rebecca Johnson, who rang the bell signaling the beginning of service. Many years before, she said, a man would have been selected by the town to beat a drum, marking the beginning of services and ending the day's toil in the fields.

The placement of the people for services was of solemn and inviolable importance. The wealthiest and most prominent families sat close to the front near the pulpit, and so backwards until the last rows were filled with the town's least fortunate or newly arrived citizens. Grandmother had a place of prominence on the women's side, and after much jostling and shaking of heads took place at our presence, space was made for Mother, Hannah, and me. Father and Richard sat across from us with the other men, and Andrew and Tom sat in the gallery above us. I could turn my head and see them clearly, Tom looking expectantly about, Andrew with his head cradled in his hands. I started to wave to Tom but Mother grabbed my hand and pushed it back into my lap.

The pews were set together close and I wondered how Father would fold his long legs to fit under them through the entire service. The building was as cold within as without, and so I was grateful for the number of bodies pressed together for warmth. There was a constant and frigid passage of air rushing past my legs, and through the long hour on the hard bench, my feet and my backside battled for prominence in discomfort. And then a collective sigh went out as the Reverend Dane swept forward past the pews. He seemed to rush towards the pulpit as though his eagerness for spreading the Gospel might overpower him and cause him to begin sermonizing before attaining his lofty position in front of the congregation.

The Reverend Dane was seventy years of age in that year, yet he had all of his hair and carried himself with great vigor. I cannot say in truth that I remember much of what he said that day but I do remember the tone of it well. My expectations were that we were to have a full measure of hellfire and damnation, as we had had in Billerica, but he read from Ephesians and spoke pleasantly of the Children of Light. I would later learn that one of the men sitting in the front pew, frowning, was his adversary, the Reverend Thomas Barnard. He had looked hard at us as we entered, pursing his lips and shaking his head at me when I did not drop my eyes in modesty. As I practiced rolling the name "Ephesians" round my tongue, I carefully moved my head so that I could catch a glimpse of Andrew and Tom. Andrew had his head nesting in his arms, but Tom looked transfixed upon the Reverend.

A dark figure took shape behind Tom and my mouth hinged open, knocking my chin against my neck. It was as though the very shadows in the gallery had taken on solid form. There, seated behind my brothers, was a child, a very lumpen and deformed-looking child, who was as black as the inside of a cauldron. I had heard of black slaves but had never before seen one. His eyes seemed to bulge out and his head twitched as though chasing away some stinging insect. I stared until he felt me looking. He made faces at me, sticking out his tongue, until I thought I might laugh out loud. But Mother elbowed me sharply so I would once again sit facing the Reverend.

When the service was over, after much rising and sitting and singing psalms, and rising and sitting again, we made our way soberly out into the snow. The day was brilliant with the noon-day sun, and I waited for my brothers to come down with the odd little shadow-boy. When Andrew walked out, he lurched about, unsteady on his feet, and Tom had to help him to the cart. Seeing the black boy, I rushed to Richard and tugged on his sleeve until he stopped and spoke to me. He told me that the boy was a slave who belonged to Lieutenant Osgood, one of the selectmen. I stood and stared at the child who seemed miserably dressed for such weather, even though he held a good heavy cloak for his master. We made faces at each other until the lieutenant came out, put on his cloak, and mounted his horse. The boy followed along on foot, his overly large shoes slipping in the snow. I strained to watch him until both the boy and rider passed beyond Haverhill Way.

BY THE TIME we had arrived home, Andrew's illness could no longer be hidden. Father carried him to the hearth and laid him down on the cot. Andrew was insensible, grasping at the covers and then throwing them off again as he was set upon by chills and fevers. Grandmother felt his face and knelt beside him, gently opening his shirt to reveal the first flush of a rash across his chest and belly. Mother came to stand next to the cot, her hand hovering just over the crimson patches.

"It could be any number of ailments," she said, her voice sounding defiant, even angry. But she wiped her palms against her apron and I smelled fear among the folds of her skirt.

"We will know soon...perhaps tomorrow," Grandmother said quietly as she laced up my brother's shirt. She carefully inspected each of us for fever or crimson patches and then, without another word, began to prepare food for us and a posset to ease Andrew's fever.

We ate our dinner in silence, broken only by the sound of the fire and the soft moaning coming from the corner where Andrew lay on his cot. Grandmother and Mother bathed his forehead and tried to force him to swallow whatever they could pour down his throat. Father sat as close to the fire as he could without climbing under the roasting spit and stared into the flames. The sweat poured from his face and he worked his hands together as though kneading beeswax between his palms.

Soon after, Tom and I were sent to bed, but neither of us could sleep. Sometime during the night I heard Andrew cry out as though in pain. I crept swiftly down the stairs in time to see him standing in the middle of the room, his arms outstretched, lit from behind by the fire that had burned low to embers. He had wet himself and seemed confused and wandering in his mind. Mother was trying to move him back onto the cot and he fought her as though drowning. Moving swiftly into the room, I took a rag and bent to clean up Andrew's mess. Grandmother grabbed my arm and pulled me harshly away.

"Sarah, you must not touch any part of Andrew now," she said urgently. She softened her grasp and stroked my face. "By touching him you may become ill as well." She moved me to a chair close to the fire and threw her shawl around my shoulders. She wrapped the rag on a broom handle and cleaned up the clouded water on the floor, then threw the rag into the fire. I fell asleep watching the dark shapes of the two women hovering above my brother's grasping, restless form.

I opened my eyes to the sound of Father's voice in the room. It was early morning, and though there was little light, I could see the drawn face of my mother in the gloom. They were speaking quietly but passionately and did not hear me pad on cold bare feet to stand next to my brother's cot. I looked at the blanket covering him and saw the faint movement of breath. I bent closer to peer at him and could plainly see on his face and neck the slightly raised pustules of the plague, rosy pink to deep purplish red; a pretty color on the petals of a rose or carnation. I took two, then three, steps backwards from his cot, and the thudding of my quickening pulse sounded like the drumming of hussars on horseback, sabers flashing through the air coming to sever our heads from our bodies. Many were the stories of entire families waking together in the morning but by supper all lying dead on the floor, festering in their seeping flesh. He coughed suddenly and I raised my shift in alarm over my face and turned away in fear. The shame over my disgust at his contagion was not enough to stay me as I raced with all the strength in my legs back up the stairs and into the safety of the garret.

ALTHOUGH IT WOULD cost us dearly, Grandmother insisted on sending to town for Andover's only physician. Richard went straightaway but it took him four hours to come back with the doctor, who stood a good distance from Andrew, careful not to touch anything in the room. Covering his face with a large handkerchief, he looked at Andrew for the space of three breaths, then made a rapid retreat through the front door. But not before being escorted out by my mother's voice, braying, "You're no better than a barber!" As he mounted his horse, he told Father that he would have to sound the alarm, post the Bill of Isolation for our family, and send the constable to read the bill to our neighbors. He said all this as he beat the ribs of his horse to ribbons making his escape. Grandmother did not let Richard back into the house but sent him away to stay for safekeeping with the Widow Johnson. As he had slept in the barn, there was a chance he would yet be free from contagion. He did not return that day, and we believed him to be in the home of at least one charitable Christian woman.

Grandmother, sitting at the common-room table, wrote a letter and called me over to her knee. She held my hands, saying, "Your father will be taking you and Hannah to your aunt Mary back in Billerica. You will stay there ... perhaps for quite a while." I must have stirred, for she quickly said, "You will be happy there with your cousin Margaret. And you will have Hannah to look after." It had been years since I had seen my cousin, who lived in the northernmost part of Billerica, and my memory of her was of an odd, dark girl who would at times talk to an empty corner of a room.

"Can I take Tom as well?" I asked her, and my mother answered for her.

"No, Sarah. We need Tom to stay and help with the farm. Richard is gone and Andrew ..." She paused, her meaning clear. Andrew would die soon or if he lived would be an invalid for months. It would be left to Tom and Father to carry all the weight of the fieldwork. Tom stood quietly by, regarding me with the eyes of someone falling down a hill made of powdered limestone. There came a hard knocking on the door, and a large, bristling man came in, announcing himself to be the constable. Holding the Bill of Isolation in one hand and a vinegar-soaked handkerchief in the other, he walked boldly to where Andrew lay groaning on his cot. His cratered face was as Andrew had described it and gave proof that some did survive the pox by the grace of God, or through protection by the Devil. He read aloud the posting that would be nailed on the meeting-house door for all to see so that we should not "spread the distemper through wicked carelessness." I looked about my grandmother's neat little room and saw no carelessness, only order and sober tranquillity. As he left our house he said under his breath, "God grant mercy . . ."

I SAT SHIVERING, hidden in the frozen straw piled into the wagon, and held on tightly to a restless, struggling Hannah. We were leaving against the quarantine and so must sneak out in the dark of night like thieves. If we were caught, the entire family could go to the jailer. If any of us were left alive, that is, after the pox had spent its fire. Mother's mouth was pinched tightly as she handed me a bundle of food and a few pieces of clothing. I had expected few words of comfort beyond caring for Hannah, but she straightened my cap with a firm grip, and her fingers lingered overly long at the laces.

Grandmother came with her knuckles pressed over her lips and, handing me a small bundle, said, "Now is the time to give you this." I unwrapped the cloth and saw it was a poppet fully clothed, with strands of wool on its head dyed in reddish tint to match my own hair. The mouth was made from the tiniest stitches.

"But she has no buttons for eyes," I said. Grandmother smiled and kissed my hands.

"I had not time to finish it. We shall sew some on when you are returned to us," she whispered.

Tom waved with a weak hand as Father shook the reins and we started south, back towards Billerica. We had gone but a short distance when we heard Tom calling out to us. He ran to the wagon and pressed something into my palm, closing my fingers back again so I would not drop it. He then turned and ran back towards the house. I opened my fist to find two small white buttons torn from his only good shirt resting in my hand like twin pearls. I would often worry during that long, cold season that the wind was finding its way up his open sleeves, making him feel the bite of winter all the more.

CHAPTER TWO

December 1690–March 1691

THERE ARE WINTER evenings in Massachusetts when there is no wind and the crust on the snow seems to hold in the cold. And if the moon is three-quarters full, its light adds a kind of warmth to the surrounding earth. The light was so sharp I could see the dark form of a hare rushing across the fields, braving the hooked death of an owl. The long, pitted barrel of Father's flintlock lay across his knees and I wondered if he regretted missing the chance at bagging such a prize. I had heard Richard many times brag that Father could shoot with deadly measure up to eighty yards and could load and discharge four rounds in a minute's time, whereas most men could load only three at best.

The silence of the countryside was absolute and we held our breath whenever passing a darkened house. The rattling of the horse's trappings was fearfully loud, and Father let the horse go at a slackened pace to ease the quaking of the wagon. Hannah had fallen asleep cradled in my arms, and I prayed she would not waken and cry, as a baby's mewling can travel a great distance in the night. We did not fear discovery once we had passed over the Shawshin bridge, for although the wagon jostled to wake the dead over the trestle, there were no settlers nearby to question us.

I lay back in the straw and watched the stars in a perfect black bowl, which made the sky look like curdled milk in Mother's dye pot. The trip would take three hours, enough time for Father to deliver us, then turn straight around to reach Andover before dawn. I fell asleep after a time and dreamt I was floating in a little boat, carried in the strong current of a river, my hand trailing next to the hull. There were dark, dimly formed creatures gliding beneath the surface of the water, the bright sunlight masking what swam below. A creeping numbness started in all my limbs and I could not pull my hand from the water. There soon came the tug of grasping mouths at my fingertips, mouths filled with the buds of tiny sharp teeth. I waited to feel the first stabbing pains drawing blood but woke instead with a start to feel Hannah sucking hungrily upon my fingers.

In the near distance was the dark silhouette of a house, dim yellow light shining from its open doorway. Standing on the threshold was the form of a man, his voice calling out in warning, "Who are you, then?" In his hand was the curved shape of a small scythe. My father's deep Welsh accent cut through the air like a bass viol. "Thomas Carrier. And I be carrying my two daughters with me, Sarah and Hannah." At that moment a woman's shape stood next to the man and she, pulling a cloak about her shoulders, walked out towards the wagon.

"Thomas, what is it? What has happened?" Without seeing her face I knew it was my aunt and could hear the fear in her voice. What else but misfortune would have brought her sister's husband and two nieces to her doorstep so late of an evening? She drew close to the wagon, but Father said, "Mary, do not yet come so near. I have a letter from your mother. Best you read it first." His long arm held out the parchment and Mary took it reluctantly, as though it were a serpent that could bite. She walked back to the light of the open door and read the letter, her fingers restless about her neck. She handed it to my uncle and waited for him to finish reading as she strained to see our faces through the darkness. Hannah, satisfied no longer with my fingers, began to cry in earnest. Her crying took on a queer jolting sound as I bounced her harder and harder upon my knees and we waited for a welcome or a turning-away.

Mary walked carefully back to the wagon, carrying a lighted taper, her every step dragging, like one following behind a funeral cart. She stood close by, looking at our white and shuddering forms, pinched from the cold and the late hour. I could see she was afraid, for in taking us into her house, she could well be bringing the means of destruction to her own family. But she held out her arms for Hannah and took her to her breast, covering her with the cloak. Then she said, "You must come in with me now, Sarah." I climbed stiffly out of the straw, carrying my small bundle, and began to follow her inside. When

I saw that Father was not following I stopped, uncertain whether to crawl back into the wagon or enter the strange house.

Father's voice came to me as deep as vibrating stones. "Be good, Sarah. Keep well." There was a pause and then a shake of the reins, and without another word he pulled the horse around and rode away. I stood watching him follow his own newly made tracks back towards Andover. The moon had begun to set behind the trees, so the roof of the house could not be seen, only the small rectangle of yellow light in a wall of blackness. I locked tight both knees and planted my feet in the snow, clutching my belongings to my chest. A twig rustled and snapped somewhere in the forest beyond the yard as though something had pawed its way closer to the clearing. And still the door remained open and still I stood outside the house. After a long while, a girl came to stand at the door. She was wearing a white shift and cap, her dark hair spilling over her shoulders. A soft voice called out, "Sarah, come in now. It's very cold." But I could not move. The air had turned thick around me and my body had grown rigid and fixed, like a splinter of oak spun in glass. Like a wraith she moved towards me, barefoot in the snow, her hand out, feeling her way in the dark. I saw it was my cousin Margaret, and though she was two years older than I, she was exactly my height. Her hair was crow's black and she was very slender with a pointed chin that gave her an elfin look. She did not smile or try to speak. She merely reached out for my clenched hands and pulled me gently, until we stumbled together over the threshold.

I stood inside the door, my skirt and shawl steaming in the warmth. Hannah had fallen to sleep in Aunt Mary's arms, sucking on a rag that had been dipped into a bowl of sugar water. I hoped that they had a cow, for the baby would be wanting milk in the morning. A straw pallet had been set close to the fire, and Margaret led me over to the hearth, which had been newly filled with kindling. I was soon tucked tightly inside thick blankets with Hannah nestled beside me. Sleep came with the sound of my aunt's voice whispering we would have to sleep and eat apart from the family for some days, until it was certain we did not carry sickness. She did not say what would become of us if we should show signs of the pox.

THE NEXT TWO days Hannah and I lived a half life in the home of Mary and Roger Toothaker. We were given food and a place by the fire but we were kept at arm's length. I tried to keep Hannah close by, even sharing with her my poppet, but she was restless and willful and would often test her legs in the greater household. In spite of her ban, Aunt would sometimes reach down to pat the top of her head, twining her fingers into the downy ringlets. And then would Hannah bounce about the room happy again. Her antics made Uncle laugh, and he would chuck her lightly under the chin before shooing her back to me.

As the day's shadows deepened into evening, I sat in my dark corner like an invading spirit and followed their movements about the house. From under my lashes I watched my two cousins, Margaret and her brother, Henry, studying us in turn. Henry was thirteen, slender and dark. To my mind he was furtive and a sneak, and often when Aunt was not looking, he would poke at Hannah or cause her to fall. Once, when he thought we were alone, he crept up behind me and pulled hard at the tender hairs on the back of my neck. My eyes watered but I said nothing and waited. The next morning he found the piss barrel upended over his shoes.

My aunt was also dark, as dark as my mother, but her face likened to my grandmother's. For where my mother's eyes showed an unyielding defiance, Mary's eyes showed, even in the midst of laughter, lines of sadness, giving her a softness and a sweet melancholy. Mother had said she had lost three babes in a row. They could not ripen in her womb and at the turning of the third month were washed away in blood and tears.

Uncle Roger was as unlike my father as any man could be. He was of average height, slender, with somewhat delicate hands for a farmer. He had a high forehead, the dome of which was prominent, for his hair was receding on top. He had more books and pamphlets than I had ever seen in one house. He had an old, well-thumbed Bible, works by Increase and Cotton Mather, almanacs for planting and sowing, and other tracts, printed on the thinnest parchment, telling of news of the colonies. He smiled often, which to me was notable. But the most remarkable thing about him was, where my father was silent, Roger Toothaker was ever talking. He talked from rising in the morning until he retired for bed. He talked through meals and around whatever chores he set his hands to doing through the long winter hours in the house. And it must be said that Uncle never seemed to sharpen an implement or tool a leather harness without handing it over to Henry to finish. It was as though the drudgery of handy-work crossed his ability to weave a story.

I remembered watching my father split a cow's hide and stitch it into the shape of a new plow harness in the time it took my uncle to fasten a buckle onto a brace.

That first evening at supper I sat in our far corner with Hannah heavy on my lap. The meat was so tough I had to chew it well to a pulp before placing small bits of it between my sister's lips. She yet had few teeth, and Aunt was out of practice making mash for a baby's mouth. The squash was well baked and Hannah sucked happily on a piece of it, the grease sliding down her hand onto my apron. Uncle had paused in his meal and, pushing his chair back from the table, stretched out his legs. Henry looked with slanted eyes over his shoulder at me before saying, "Tell us the story of the wandering soldier's ghost, Father."

"Oh, no, Roger. It is too late for such as that," said Aunt, her mouth turning down at the corners. She caught Henry taunting me with an ugly face and pinched his hand. Uncle sat looking at me beneath heavy lids, the grease on his mouth and chin glistening orange and yellow in the light of the fire. It gave him the look of someone baked in a furnace. Margaret had turned to look at me as well, her dark hair making a curtain over her face. But the tense arch of her neck like a strung bow signaled to me, Do not hesitate. So I spoke out, "I am not afraid. Tell your story."

Uncle slid his arm around Margaret's shoulders and said, "It seems you have a companion spirit in your cousin Sarah." He pushed his plate away and looked at the grain of the wood on the table as though a map had been spread in front of him.

"In the lowering twilight around some lonely and isolated village, much like Billerica, the dark gathers and gathers until the only light to the living comes from a few early-evening stars overhead. The light of a candle casts feeble shadows around a windowsill. The very air about the village fills with the terror of some yet unseen presence, the terror flowing like some rippling fog about the houses, the pastorage, the burial grounds. Soon every tree with its shattered limbs appears like some armed enemy. Every stump, a ravenous devourer.

"A thin and bony soldier appears from out of the purpled forests of oak and elm. He is dressed in torn and wretched clothing, wrapped in gory linen from ghastly wounds, going doorstep to doorstep through the village, begging something to eat. The only words he whispers at every door are 'Hungry, so very hungry.' A kindhearted woman hears his piteous pleas and returns with a plate of food, but he has disappeared from sight. Then, before going to bed, some foolish parent forgets to bolt and lock a door. A child, a redheaded child, who happens to be nine years old, like Sarah, wanders from the house carrying a sweetmeat for the brave soldier. In the morning the alert is sounded. The child is missing. After searching, the men in the village find only a shoe torn with sharp and jagged teeth, part of a petticoat matted and bloody, and a skein of bright red hair. Nothing more is ever found of the girl and it is many years before the hungry ghost is heard from again."

I had grown up hearing the lusterless warnings of old women to shy away from glens and bogs after dark, as these low places are known to be visited by spirits of the dead. But the pitch of my uncle's voice had been a kind of music. Not the dull, confining songs of the meetinghouse but a music both musky and dark. His words created a weighty tension in my chest as if

I were a small fish hooked through the breastbone and pulled against the current of some unnatural course onto a strange and dangerous shore. The rude and simple furnishings of the room seemed richer. The warmth of the fire and the cinders stirred up from the fire were like a golden wool. The little black panes of window glass had turned to garnets and topazes in a giant's ear. Hannah began to protest and struggle against my clasped hands and I let her slip to the ground, saying, "Why would the hungry ghost eat a child when offered village food?"

"Why, indeed," replied Uncle, laughing. "To question shows an active mind. But be careful, it is sometimes better not to ask, and be satisfied with a tale well told. Especially if you value the good opinion of the teller." He said the last in all seriousness but he winked at me and I felt as though his arms had embraced me.

Later, as I lay on my pallet, the rise and fall of Uncle's voice was fixed in my head, though he had long since gone to bed. I would sleep deeply and well through the night, but the cup of my imagination was not yet filled, for the next night my dreams would keep time with demons.

THE SECOND DAY I felt idle and cross with nothing useful to do and I wanted very much to open one of the small, leaded-glass windows and toss Hannah out into the snow. The only respite came after supper, when Uncle told of his adventures in King Philip's War, and then only after we had begged and begged him to tell it.

"King Philip," he said as he moved round closer to the fire, "was the English name given to Metacom, chief of the Poka-noket tribe. This chief was proud and haughty and believed he could drive out the English settlers. The war began in a village near Bristol in 'seventy-five. Indians had butchered a settler's cow and the settlers followed by killing an Indian. The Indians then revenged themselves by knocking over the head the farmers and their families, and so began a trail of murder that would destroy settlements for hundreds of miles." He ticked off the names of invading Indian tribes, sounding like a shuttlecock striking a wooden weaver's frame.

"Nipmucks, Wampanoags, and Pokanokets all began raiding villages and homesteads in the territories of Rhode Island and Connecticut and Massachusetts. A thousand men assembled by General Winslow marched as neat as you please into Indian territory, and it was with this group of men that I served as an officer's surgeon. A Narragansett camp was soon discovered in the woods by advanced scouts. Now, it's true that the Narragansetts had been a peaceable tribe until that time, but their great numbers caused the New Englanders much unease and it would only be a matter of time before they roused themselves to join their dark brothers. So, in the early dawn hours, a tree was felled over a stream and our forces swarmed quickly into their camp.

"The killing was swift and complete. Every last Narragansett brave in the camp was packed off to hell. By nightfall the ground was so slippery from the bloody matter of the shootings and the knifings that man and beast alike could not stand upright on the snow. I myself killed six or seven before the day was complete. The marvel was how easily they were dispatched. We placed their heads on pikes and left them in the ground to give fair warning to the other tribes." He stopped for a moment to light his pipe with a taper pulled from the hearth. His exhaled breath sent smoke from his nose down his cheeks, and he pitched a ragged, suffering note to his storytelling.

"A certain Captain Gardner had been mortally wounded in the head and chest during the battle and would allow no other physician but I to attend him. Blood ran down his face in rivers where his skin had peeled away from his skull like a soft-boiled chestnut. I lifted him up and called him by name. 'Captain Gardner, Captain Gardner, can you hear me?' He looked up at me, his life force flowing out of his veins, and thanked me for my service. He died in my arms. We carried him back to Boston, where he was buried with all due honors."

We all sat in silence and watched the firelight on white birch form dancing pictures of massacres in the snow. Henry then said, "Father, show us the scar from the battle."

Aunt frowned at this, but Uncle cheerfully opened his coat and shirt to reveal an angry scar that cut downward across his chest, just under the left nipple, to the tender part of his belly. As he tamped out the remaining embers of his pipe, he said in closing, "Only a year ago during the coldest months were Schenectady to Salmon Falls to Falmouth attacked by the French and Indians. Hundreds were killed and captives taken. Women with child ripped open, their babes dashed on the rocks. People think that the winter season forbids the stirring about of the Indian"—and here he looked up at me—"but it seems the snow and cold does not keep them from our door."

Suddenly Aunt called out, "Enough!" Her jaw quivered as

she hurried to draw the bolts on the door, and the look in her eyes spoke of days and nights spent in fear of such a raid coming to the Toothaker farm.

That night I lay staring into the darkened room, every sound, every shadow, turning to creeping horrors. I pulled Hannah against me as a shield until I thought my scalp would crawl off my skull with fright. After many hours I fell asleep and began to dream. I saw the terrifying faces of Indians, their skin painted as bright as any scarecrow, forcing their way into my grandmother's house, carrying with them impossibly long and sharpened butchering knives. It was to my family they had come, but I could not sound the alarm, for my body had been left many miles behind. I watched them gather around my brother Andrew's cot and saw the sheet pulled back from his head. He lay there unmoving, his pale blue eyes resting in the middle of a bloody mass that had once been his face. Every bit of flesh had been flayed from his muscles, skinned as neatly as an autumn hog.

When I opened my eyes, Margaret was kneeling next to me, her face solemn, her eyes wide and unblinking. I began to cry and she bent down close to my ear and whispered, "Come and sleep with me." Together we carried Hannah into my cousin's room and crawled into Margaret's bed. She held my hands between her own and breathed her moist, warm breath over my fingers. Her breath smelled sweet, like porridge with sweet-gum syrup poured through. Her lips curled up in a knowing way, her eyes slanted to a drowsy pitch. "No one tells stories like Father. He weaves them out of the very air. But I have stories to tell as well, Sarah."

Through the matted light I could see the delicacy of her, the smooth whiteness of her skin, as she talked. Her voice was low and strangely hoarse as she hummed some bit of nonsense. She placed her arm tighter around my shoulders and pulled my head to her neck like a piece of lump metal to a polished lodestone. We fell asleep, the three of us close together, Margaret's fingers wound tightly with mine. We woke to my aunt standing startled over us, saying, "Margaret, what have you done? You have put yourself in danger." We lay there, looking at her as if she were an intruder in her own home.

"There is naught to do for it now, God help us." She knelt down by the bed and said a silent prayer. I looked to Margaret, but she smiled and nodded, and I believed in that moment that Aunt and Uncle would come to love me as well.

From that time, there was not an hour that passed that I did not compare the fullness of my days with the dryness that was life with my own family. Where mine was reserved to harshness, Margaret's was lavish with praise and care. Where my parents were silent or sullen, hers were animated with talk and laughter. And even though Margaret's laughter was directed at me at times because of some slowness or ignorance on my part, I believed it made my own wit grow all the more, like a copper coin that is rubbed to greater brightness with a rough cloth.

Being with Margaret was like standing inside the casing of a lantern, one that kept the warmth in and the stinging insects out. I refused to think it peculiar if at times, gazing up at the tops of trees, she nodded to the air and said, "Yes. I will." Or if, in carving out little hollow places in the snow, she placed her ear close to the ground to listen to some music only she could hear.

I did not think it strange, because she was lovely and had claimed me. And because she was mine.

Once, when I was five, my mother had harvested a large crop of early pumpkins, more than we could keep without their rotting. We chopped them into fragrant pieces, salted them, and fed them to our cow. The milk and cream that she gave for many days was yellow-orange and tasted as though someone had ladled honey into the milking buckets. That was how it was in the presence of my cousin's family: their sweet and salty natures mingled themselves with my own, leavening my suspicious and prickly nature.

My cousin and I did everything as with one hand. Whatever work one of us was sent to do, the other would find some strategy to accomplish that same task, so that Uncle would often say with great relish, "Ah, here come my twins." And Margaret and I would laugh as we looked at each other, she with black hair and skin like potted cream and I with my flaming hair and spotted face. The only time we separated, waking or sleeping, was upon the Sabbath, when Uncle and his family went to the meetinghouse. Hannah and I could not accompany them, as we were meant to be home in Andover dying of the plague. My sister and I would wait, house-bound and bored, eagerly watching the road for the Toothakers to return to us again.

It snowed hard that winter, and the drifts often buried the house and barn within a few hours. Before sunrise every morning, we would clear a path to the barn with shovels and bowls or with our bare hands. Once a path was cleared, Margaret and I would walk hand in hand to the creek that ran hard by the house to get water. The snow was deep along the creek banks, waist high, and if we fell into the drifts our clothes were wet to our skin. Breaking through the crusted ice to fill our buckets blistered my hands, and however hard we tried, however big the hole, the following day the creek would be covered again with ice. Margaret always wore her mittens to save her hands from the snow, which made me loath to place my calloused palms into her own seamless ones. I would look at my hands and feel ashamed of their hardened places, the cracked and bleeding skin around the knuckles. But she, after kissing each fingernail in turn and slipping her own mittens over my hands until they were warmed to life, would sing in an odd, lilting way, "And thus I am you and you are me and I am you again, you see."

Drinking the water from the creek was like biting into a piece of metal that had long been buried in the snow, and it would sting the back of our heads if drunk too deeply. After taking water to the house we would with Henry's help lead the animals out one by one to the stream. I fear the animals suffered greatly from thirst as we hurried them, urging them back to the barn to save our frozen hands and feet.

Margaret's family had more livestock than did mine. Their barn was not large but had been well built with the help of the oldest son, Allen. Allen did not yet have his own farm but lived and worked in north Andover in the house of his friend, Timothy Swan. He came often during planting and harvest seasons to help work his father's fields and share in the yield. It would be Allen who would someday inherit Uncle's farm. In their barn was a milk cow, two oxen, a large hog, her belly swollen with a litter soon to come, three chickens, and a rooster.

Uncle also had a large roan gelding that he used only for the saddle. He said the horse was too finely bred for a cart. One of Henry's chores was to keep his father's saddle well cleaned and oiled. Once he showed me a place just under the horn that had been nicked half a dozen times by a sharp knife. Henry whispered to me that these marks were the number of Indians his father had killed with his own hands during King Philip's War. He ran his finger along the small gouges in the leather and bragged, "Someday this saddle will be mine, and there'll be a dozen marks on the horn before I turn twenty." I looked at him through slitted eyes and wondered how he was to accomplish so great a murdering task, because he had no great strength and no full measure of courage. Perhaps, as he had done with Hannah and me, he'd ambush them all from behind.

When Uncle came into the barn, he always brought some fine treat, a piece of dried apple or some kernels of corn, for his prized gelding, Bucephalus. It was the name Alexander, the Greek king, had given to his favorite war steed. An apocalyptic horse, for where the horse went, so went Alexander's troops, bringing the fire of battle. The name meant "Oxhead," which made me laugh, as the gelding had a very small, neat head. Uncle would wag his finger at me and say, "Ah, but there is the word and then there is the spirit of the word. Bucephalus is so called because I see in him the spirit of bravery. I see the world, Sarah, and call it by what I feel it should be, not by what others who in their dull reveries think it is."

"So, should I now call you Alexander, Uncle?" I asked slyly. He laughed but I could see that it puffed him up. I did not know then that Alexander had been poisoned by his troops.

MOST EVENINGS MARGARET and I sat side by side for many hours repairing torn winter clothing, watching Hannah play with the odd bits of yarn or thread too short for use. Margaret's fingers were very nimble and at times I pretended to drop a stitch or lose my place on a piece of cloth so that she would fold her hands over my two clumsy ones and guide them into an orderly procession of stitches once more. She never called me to my mistakes but always praised me for my own poor efforts. As we sat together, our heads bent, our lips scarcely moving, we told each other secrets. We thought ourselves clever and unde-tected, but once Aunt surprised me by saying, "How many times as girls have your mother and I sat as you and Margaret do, telling confidences, whispering our hopes..." She pulled impatiently at a tangled thread caught in Henry's shirt and smiled.

"My sister could tease out a knot the size of a raisin with more patience than I've ever seen." I mulled over for a moment who she might mean, for I knew she had only one sister: my mother. I could not imagine the gentle seamstress described by Aunt as the same woman who could see from the back of her cap my misdeeds at two hundred paces.

Without thinking, I asked, "Why do we never see you, Aunt?" Her smile faltered, and Margaret tapped at my foot for silence. Aunt called for Henry to come and put back on his mended shirt. He had been sitting at the fire shivering under a blanket, and, as she pulled the cloth over his head, Aunt said softly, "I will only ever say the discord is not between me and your mother. I love her well and would see her more if I could."

Towards dusk I followed Henry out to the barn and asked him about the chasm dividing our two families. He crossed his arms and sniffed. "*Your* father thinks *my* father cheated him out of some land. But that's a lie and I'll knock to ground anyone who says it's so." Whatever reticence I may have felt towards my father for his stern and distant parenting, I could not imagine him as dishonest in any way. But it was a charge against Father that would not be answered for many months. I shook my head and asked, "But what has that to do with Aunt and my mother?"

"Where the husband goes, there the wife is bound to follow," Henry replied with a huff. He said it with all the authority he could gather, but I knew he was quoting some homily he had overheard. "My mother takes her husband's lead. Something your mother will never do, which makes her trumped-up and loose —" He was greatly surprised when I shoved him backwards into the stalls. He was not stout but he was taller than me by a head and wiry. It was one thing for *me* to think badly of my family, but another entirely for my cousin to speak ill of them. I left him open-mouthed and swearing, and later, when he came in for supper, I fingered chicken droppings into his stew.

MARGARET AND I traded scandalous stories whenever we could. Whenever she caught us, Aunt would gently remind us that gossiping was a sin, and so our stories were traded with caution. Margaret's secrets were more interesting than mine, she being two years older and more experienced in the world than I. She seemed to know many unsavory things about her neighbors, but endlessly fascinating to me was her knowledge of the Invisible World. She knew how to tell a witch by the markings on her body. A witch's teat could be disguised as a mole or any raised pustule on the skin. A witch could not say the Lord's Prayer in full without stumbling over the words. A witch would not sink if thrown into a body of water but rather float upon the surface as though liquid could not tolerate the pollution of its element. And as I myself would sink like an anvil if thrown into the sea, I did not doubt her wisdom. When I asked her how she came to know such things, she responded that her father, being a man of science, had shared with her this knowledge, for where there are women, there are witches.

"And," she said, her eyes lost to the lengthening afternoon shadows, "I have felt them flying above the roof when the hawkweed root grows under the moon."

I wondered aloud if there were witches even now in Billerica. She leaned closer to me and said, "You can be sure of it."

I told her then what little I had heard in the marketplace or on the streets, and if I expanded upon the truth, it was only to bring piquancy to the tales, like cloves added to meat. I did not want my cousin to think of me as an infant who did not know how the world moved. It was my first taste of sharing and holding secrets with another girl. Through the many years since that time, I have learned that women show their true selves in a different way.

Sharing secrets is the way in which women tie themselves together, for it reveals complicity and trust. Holding secrets shows trustworthiness and a sort of quiet defiance. It is a natural thing for a female to hold secrets within her breast until the time is ripe to release them. Does it not follow the way in which her body is formed? A woman is made with that dark and mysterious recess that can grow a child safely until the child is ready to come out onto the birthing bed. And like birthing, secrets present themselves in many ways. Some slip easily into the world, others must be torn out, if the body is unwilling.

LATE IN JANUARY the snow stopped falling and the very air seemed to freeze around us. The drifts became fortresses of ice and the stream froze solid, so that we had to melt blocks of it in the fire for drinking and cooking. The animals could not be taken outside for long for fear of laming them and so became restive on their tethers. Margaret and I had come in early one morning for feeding but we were careful to stay away from the shuffling feet of the oxen and the cow. Bucephalus rocked to and fro in his stall, shaking his head and rolling his eyes. I had brought a bit of apple from the cellar to quiet him, and, as I drew near, I saw a man cowering in the straw.

I stood for a moment in silence as the man looked fearfully at me from beneath bundles of cloaks and shawls. He was a young man, his face ruddy from the cold. But the flesh under his eyes looked scorched, the fluid pooling in the bottom lids as with a fever. I thought of my brother's face flushed with sickness, the skin below his eyes gray and unwholesome. The man held his hand up, in supplication or in warning. Margaret had come to stand behind me, and I could hear the sharp sound of her breath. His lips tried to form words but he could not at first speak, as though his tongue were swollen to the roof of his mouth. Finally he said with great difficulty, "I pray thee have pity and give me water and food or I shall die." He groaned and shivered beneath the straw. We began to pull away and he reached out to us like a man drowning. "Please, I will not harm thee. I will take food and rest awhile and then I will leave."

Margaret moved closer to the man and said accusingly, "You are a Quaker." The man lowered his head, panting, but did not speak. "If my father finds you trespassing here, he will turn you over to the constable."

The man struggled to stand, pulling himself up by the stacked boards in the stall, but sank back down onto his haunches. I tugged on my cousin's cloak and I whispered, "Should we not bring him food? He looks very bad." Margaret pulled me away some distance so that we could speak without being heard.

"Father says that Quakers are heretics and are to be shunned. And besides, this one may be poxed."

"Oh," I replied, not knowing what a heretic might be. I looked over at the man and pitied his misery. Margaret suddenly grabbed hold of my wrists and, leaning closer in to my ear, said, "We shall help him. It would be our secret. We must not tell Mother or Father, for then we will surely be punished, and harshly, too." I smiled at her and nodded. I was more pleased by the prospect of sharing this dangerous secret with my cousin than of helping the stranger. "We shall have to be very cunning. Mother keeps a close watch over the larder."

After the noon meal, Margaret told some fable about forgetting to put out grain for one of the animals and I was amazed at how easily the falsehood slipped from her mouth. We managed to take to the barn bread and meat and a cup of cider without being discovered but took care to stand well away from the wretched man. He was so starved that he swallowed his fill without his teeth so much as touching the food. He drank the cider and then fell back into the straw as though dead. We watched him sleeping there for a while, listening to the coarse sounds coming from his windpipe.

Margaret asked me, "Isn't he handsome, though?" And I agreed, even though he looked to me like any other young man I had ever seen. We left him there in the stall, whispering to his sleeping form that we would return the next morning with more food.

That evening Margaret and I lay close together in her bed, watching the last of the light from our nightly stub of candle, our feet and hands entwined as tightly as two cold-water eels. Aunt had become so attached to Hannah that she took my sister to sleep with her every night. Captured in the crook of my cousin's elbow was a poppet that Aunt had made. It had black rope hair and a crimson skirt. The cloth had a soft sheen to it, so it caught the light, and the feel of it beneath my fingers was like the skin of a lamb newly shorn. Uncle had returned with the cloth from Boston, where many fine ladies wore skirts or bodices of such color. Aunt was too modest to wear such a fabric but took a small piece of it to make a skirt for the doll. Margaret whispered to me that her father had gotten very angry when he saw what Aunt had done and he took away the entire bolt of cloth. What was finally done with it, she did not know.

My own doll was much plainer in dress but I thought it more skillfully made. Margaret, with her own hands, had sewn on the buttons that Tom had given me. The button eyes somewhat ruined the beauty of the doll's face, giving it a baleful look, and they sometimes brought me anxious, terror-filled thoughts of my family dying of the pox.

As we closed our eyes for the night, the rhythm of our breathing paced like two horses harnessed to a sleigh, I asked, "Margaret, how did you know he was a Quaker?"

There was a gentle stirring next to me. "Because he said 'thee.' "

"Margaret, what is a heretic?" Next to the pleasure of tapping the wisdom of my cousin's head was the loveliness of saying her name.

"It is someone who goes against the word of God" came the answer.

"And why is a Quaker a heretic?"

Margaret did not answer right away and I thought she had not heard me, but soon I felt her breath stirring against my neck.

"A Quaker is a heretic because he makes himself answerable to no body of church, only to the voice of his own conscience. Quakers believe God resides within them like an organ of the body and speaks to them, causing them to shake and tremble as with ague."

"And does God speak to them?"

"Father says no." She yawned and her leg came to rest over

mine. "They are greatly persecuted. Would God speak to those so shunned by ordained ministers? Sarah, go to sleep now."

"Why, then, did you help him?"

She opened one heavy-lidded eye and the corner of her mouth turned up in a way I had seen her father smile, splitting her face into two halves — the lighter, smiling half amused with the changes of the temporal world, the darker half looking sunk into the insensibility of a madwoman, or a saint, close to tumbling into despair or enraptured seclusion.

"I wanted to help him, Sarah, because *they* told me to." Her hand stayed cradled next to my face even as her eyelids began closing.

" 'They' ... Margaret, who are they?" I blew gently against her face to rouse her and she opened her eyes once more.

She slowly lifted a forefinger so that it pointed over my shoulder. I turned my head and saw only the heavy chest where we kept our few clothes. She pulled me closer and whispered, "The little people in the cupboard, Sarah."

I watched her drop into sleep, her skin blue-white in the dark, her eyes moving slowly beneath the lids. The hair on my arms rose as with a cold breeze, and I glanced fearfully over my shoulder but heard and saw nothing save the wind outside our walls and the shadows draping themselves into the familiar, unmoving shapes of benign slumber. Her madness was a secret I would gladly keep, and, before I joined her in sleep, I moved closer into her warmth and kissed her.

The next morning we brought the man in the barn an apple and some bread. But he was not there. We searched every stall and climbed up into the loft but could not find him. And as

snow had fallen during the night, there was not one track leading from the barn to signify that he had been real and not a
straw man come to life through our imaginings.

LATE AFTERNOONS, JUST before the evening meal, Margaret
and Henry and I would have lessons in reading and writing and
history. This was done for the sole purpose of learning the
Scriptures. I could write only a few words, and Uncle asked me
if Mother had ever bothered to teach me. I told him she had
not, although the truth was that my mother had tried to teach
me to read and write but my defiance, and her lack of patience,
had combined to keep me ignorant.

Margaret could read very difficult passages from the Bible. I
would sit next to her, my chin resting in my hands, gazing at
the movement of her lips as she pronounced the tantalizing and
half-understood words of the prophets. The sound of her voice
was like a gentle scarf being drawn across my ears. In the evenings, after the dishes and cups were wiped clean and the fire
banked, Uncle would tell us stories of the first colonies and the
time before, with the early troubles in old England. Soon, the
shadows on the walls would become the murderous dancing of
Indians who held aloft their bloody scalps. A falling branch
upon the roof became the severed head of King Charles the First
as it bounced down the scaffold steps at Whitehall-Gate. And
with every telling Uncle's tales grew larger and more expansive.

He knew all sorts of hand tricks as well. He could perform
the secret manipulation of articles from one place to another, as
well as the misdirection of our attentions so that these move-

ments were not seen. He could cause a coin to disappear from his hand and make it reappear in a cup of cider at the far end of the table. He could pull a hen's egg from the top of Henry's head or a feather from the recesses of my ear. Once he clasped Margaret's and my hand together and with a great flourish of his arms pulled from between our joined palms a piece of lace. It never occurred to me that Margaret might have assisted him by hiding the lace inside the fullness of her sleeve.

Uncle spent many hours with us through the storms of January. There was nothing about which he did not have a strong opinion. It took only a few well-chosen questions for him to speak at great length on some piece of ancient history, point of law, the nature of man, or the mysteries of the divine. But as the month of February began and the cold hardened the snow on the roads, there was a tautness and a tension that seemed to grow within the Toothaker house. Uncle's usual good-naturedness was by turns taken over by impatience and moody silences. He would stand by the open door, shifting from foot to foot, until Aunt called to him to close the door again. He would pace restlessly about the common room, agitated and short-tempered with everyone.

Many mornings, Uncle left early astride Bucephalus and did not return until supper. At those times, after we had all retired to bed, the sound of Aunt's weeping would work its way through the walls of our bedroom. I had, at first, imagined that her agony was over the fate of my mother and grandmother, as she had often prayed aloud for their deliverance from death. But soon I knew it was over Uncle's continuing absences.

Aunt's only comfort at those times was in holding Hannah,

who would sit on Aunt's knee and call her Mama. The smile on Aunt's face made me long to share my sister's place on her lap, being stroked and coddled and made much of. In the mornings Uncle would sleep far past cockcrow, and Aunt's gentle sadness would deepen and solidify around her like a crust. Upon finishing her work, she would tightly wrap a shawl about her shoulders and sit and stare into the hearth for hours at a time.

Finally, in the first week of March, it seemed as though Uncle would not return at all. It was long past dark and we had shared a bleak and troublesome supper without him. When we had finished eating, Aunt perched at the edge of her chair, glaring at the door. Margaret, Henry, and I waited patiently for her to break her silence, sitting until our backs ached while trying our best to keep Hannah from fitful restlessness. The fire fell to embers before we heard the sound of Bucephalus shaking his harness as he approached the barn. Soon Uncle walked into the house and saw the garden of statues sitting at his table. His hair was lifted about his head as if he had ridden into a high wind and his clothes were stained with some dark liquid. He walked to the hearth like a man walking the deck of a rolling ship at sea, and the smell from his clothes was sickly sweet, like flowers rolled in spices. He drank deeply from the water bucket, spilling most of it onto his vest. He turned to face us and laughed, puffing air through a closed, dry mouth.

"It's time for us all to be asleep. Mary ... come now to bed."

Aunt stood up and, taking Hannah by the hand, walked to her bedroom, closing the door behind her. The click of a bolt-lock being slid into place sounded loud through the common room. The three of us, Margaret, Henry, and I, were left sitting at the table, speechless and tense. Uncle stood for a while, his head down, muttering to himself. He grasped the back of a chair as though he would fall without it, but after a time he lurched his way to the table and sat down heavily next to me. His breath smelled strong and sweet and the whites of his eyes were veined with red. Margaret and Henry sat staring at their hands, their heads bowed as though waiting for punishment. Until that time I had never seen Uncle other than smiling and in a good humor.

"Uncle, what is wrong?" I finally asked. "What has happened?"

He faced me, his head swiveling ominously on his neck like a falling capstone, and said, "Magic, Sarah. I've been practicing magic again." His words were indistinct and run together, as though his lips had lost their shape. He leaned towards me, putting one finger up to my mouth. "Husssshhhh . . . I'll tell you a secret, shall I . . . Sarah? I've been trying to . . . *disappear.*" The word at the last was all but lost in his soured breath.

I looked to Margaret but her eyes were down-turned, and Uncle tapped me on my head to mind his words. "I've been trying to vanish, but as you can see, I'm still here. Still here in Billerica. This desert of yeomen and yeomen's wives and their brats and pigs and dogs . . . I am a man of *letters,* Sarah! I served with Captain Gardner as his *surgeon* . . ."

He paused for a moment, his voice rising towards anger. His unsteady gaze searched the room as he sighed and slumped farther into his chair. I studied Margaret's still, passive face and was comforted by her calm. But it was Henry's face that set me to pity. From under his lowered lashes, tears streamed and scalded his sallow face to pink. His lips quivered and shuddered and, for all of his bullying of Hannah and me, for all of his cruelty, he was still a boy who lived and died on his father's good words. Uncle reached for me, fumbling for my hand, and said, "You are still Margaret's twin, are you not?" I nodded and he nodded in kind, painfully squeezing my fingers. "You are as much of a Toothaker as any of us. I'll be father to you now . . . a better father than ever a man with blood on his hands could be . . ."

Margaret stood suddenly, saying, "Father, it's time for us to go to bed." She grabbed at my apron and pulled me after her to our room. Very soon after came Henry, scratching at the door, asking to sleep on the floor next to us. For a long while we heard Uncle moving roughly about the common room, until with a groan he bedded down on the floor close to the hearth. I slept only fitfully that night, partnered with dreams of carnage. In my night visions I saw Father approach a hog's pen, his timber axe balanced over one shoulder. He picked out a grown, bristled hog, dwarfed in size next to his towering height, and dragged it screaming like a man into the shadow of the barn. There was a hidden scuffle, a sweep of whistling air, and then the slapping, meaty sound of metal severing flesh.

IN THE SECOND week of March, Margaret and I sat knee to knee, buried deep in the straw next to the sow's pen. The air was thick with a pungent smell like melted copper and something else. Like cured meat left too long in hanging. The wind outside blew hard against the planks, causing errant wisps of snow to filter in through the walls. The sow had just given birth to her piglets, and we were watching them suck noisily against the swollen teats, pushing one another away with their snouts. There were six piglets in all and we had made a game naming them after villains of the Bible. The fattest gray piglet we named Goliath. The greediest, a little spotted one, we named Judas. Then came Pilot, Herod, and Pharaoh. The last was a handsome banded female. We sat quietly together, my head resting on Margaret's shoulder, my fingers playing lazily with a strand of her hair fallen from her cap.

"I wish your father were here. He would know a proper name for the piglet."

Uncle had regained his more gentle spirits and had not returned to the house in a rage, though he still often traveled out at night, coming back with the odor of strong ale on his breath. Margaret's face remained thoughtful, but she didn't speak. To fill the silence I asked, "Where does your father go when he leaves us?"

I felt Margaret stiffen beneath my cheek and was readily sorry for my curiosity. She said, "Father goes to town to treat the sick." I knew by the way her eyes studied her shoes and not my face that she was not telling the truth.

"What about naming the piglet Harlot?" I ventured. I had heard the name from the Bible readings at night and thought it a dangerous name, like a rare perfume made of musk and lilies from the land of Ur. It made me smile to think of naming a pig in such an extravagant way. But Margaret frowned and pulled away, saying, "That's not a proper name. 'Harlot' is a kind of woman."

"What kind of woman?" I asked, sensing a new secret at hand.

"The worst kind. How can you not know what a harlot is?" She stood up and brushed the hay from her legs in a brusque manner. "A harlot is a woman who goes with men she is not married to." When I shook my head, mystified, she continued, "A woman who lies down with a man in sin."

"What kind of sin?" I silently ticked off the sins I knew of, gluttony, laziness, untruthfulness . . .

She leaned in close and whispered each syllable harshly, "For-ni-ca-tion. Do you know what that means?"

Margaret formed a circle with one hand and plunged a finger of her other hand back and forth through the circle in a gesture that even I could understand. I blushed, only just then realizing that what I had often seen done between the animals of the barn was being done between a man and woman.

She sat down again, pulling my ear close to her mouth, and asked, "Shall I tell you a secret? Do you know what these harlots are called?" She laughed bitterly as I shook my head. "Whores," she breathed suddenly. Formed with a sharp exhalation of breath, the word sounded ominous and final. "They live in taverns and keep vigil in inns and wayside hostelries to trap men. They press drink on the men and wear shameful colors, without a scarf on their bodice to cover their bosoms. They paint their mouths to match their cunnies and drench themselves in scent."

I thought of Uncle, his coat reeking of some sweet foreign fragrance, staggering about the common room, and blushed again to think of him in such places. I could not imagine where

Margaret could have gotten such knowledge, certainly not from Aunt. I asked gently, "Is that where Uncle goes of an evening?"

She idly plucked a strand of straw from my skirt and was quiet for a moment, as though doubtful of revealing more. Finally she said, "I followed him out one night. It was an evening last summer. I heard him leave long after Mother had gone to bed. They had argued about his absences. They thought Henry and I were sleeping, but I could not sleep. I heard Mother say to him that if he could not be a decent husband, he should go and live with his whores and be done with it."

A deep crease had formed between her brows, making her seem suddenly much older. "It is but two miles to the tavern, and when I crept up and peered through the shutters, I saw him. I saw Father at his cups and there was a woman seated with him. She was coarse, with rolls of fat and hair the color of old copper.... I heard things..." Two bright spots of pink showed through the opaque white of her cheeks but her eyes were vacant and staring. "Father would never have done such things, or said the things he has said, if the woman had not entranced him. So I set a curse on her that she would die before the year was finished." She turned to me then, her lips parted and unsmiling. "She caught the pox last November and died."

How often had I heard Uncle claim to work contrary magic on a witch. He had once said, "To kill a witch with conjuration is a service for the good." But the thing Margaret had claimed to do, even towards saving her father, made a trembling start up in my middle and I clutched at my own shoulders for comfort. If it was so, that the copper-haired woman had bewitched Uncle, her enchantment crept past the grave, for what else could explain his continuing slide into vice? Margaret reached out and I let her pull me into her warmth. She said softly, "You must promise me, Sarah, that you will not let Mother hear you ask where Father goes. It upsets her so."

She rocked me like a babe, my head on her shoulder, until my fearful quivering had stopped. That she had entrusted me with such a secret made me love her all the more. And if I in that moment also feared her, it only worked to add to her mystery and wonderful strangeness. By the time we had shut up the barn to return to the house, we had agreed to name the last piglet Jezebel.

THE END OF March is often the cruelest time in the year, as the air will of a sudden turn warm and moist and bring a promise of a great thaw. And no sooner are the doors opened and the heavy cloaks and woolen wrappings laid by than the cold, killing winds prick cruelly and drown the world again in snow. It was during such a false spring that Uncle announced we were to have as a guest the Reverend Nason of Billerica. The Reverend, so he said, was a man of great respectability and no mean intellect. He was to come in two days' time. Hannah and I were to be hidden in Margaret's room, where we would take our supper. The sight of us would bring too many questions.

Aunt was not a little anxious about the preparations. Between the frenzied movement of furniture and the airing out of linens, Margaret and I were put out a dozen times to collect water from the ice for cleaning and cooking. On the day the Reverend was to attend us, I was sent for roots for the pot. I sat in the cold-cellar, sorting through a basket of apples, my face long and dark. The open trap allowed only a little light into the hollowed space, the far walls receding into murky vapors.

I was bitterly disappointed to be banned from the evening's company for not only was the Reverend to be there but also Margaret's elder brother, Allen. The porridge I had eaten for breakfast soured and turned to goose eggs in my stomach. I looked again at the apple as it lay in the hollow of my apron. The pearly inside of the meat had remained unchanged for months, the skin darkening to a dull rust. But I had pierced the skin with my teeth and like a shadow stealing overhead, the whiteness had turned to yellow and brown.

Before dark Hannah and I were given food and sent to Margaret's room. Upon sunset the Reverend Nason appeared at the door. Margaret had shown me a chink through the wall for a spy hole, and, putting my hand over Hannah's mouth, I placed my eye at the opening. The Reverend was a man of prodigious size but with a remarkably small head. His skin was pale and glistening, as though brushed with the white of an egg. His eyes were settled deep into his face, and his ears were dainty for so large a man. He looked like an immense loaf of bread too well seasoned with baker's yeast. And yet I held my breath, for so keen was his gaze about the room that I felt surely he must see my eye pressed against the peephole. He took stock of every homely item, fingering the linen on the table, testing the joints on every chair, hefting the pewter mugs to test their weight.

Allen followed shortly after, and from the start I did not like him. He was dark with a high forehead like his father but with a face narrow like a ferret. His lips were full and out of proportion to his eyes, which were set too close together to be pleasing. The set of his face was of someone tasting bread soaked in vinegar, and I could well believe that he was a man who would find pleasure in the plaguing of small children or the needless hectoring of animals.

The Reverend praised Aunt's cooking, invoking the Bible in defense of his gluttony. "As you know, Goodwife Toothaker," he said, spilling food on the table from his mouth, "in Isaiah, chapter twenty-five, verse six, the Almighty's good graces are also brought about through the bread at table. Truly this repast is a worthy companion to the soul's feast of God's holy word." One would have thought Aunt had served up angel's bread rather than an aged and pungent spit of mutton. As he chewed, he pulled pieces of gristle and fat from between his teeth and wiped his oily hands on his trousers. In awe of the sound of his own voice, the Reverend closed his mouth only to swallow. And, as Uncle and Allen were eager to be heard, one would hardly finish speaking before the other would launch himself over the last word. At times the three would speak all at once, sounding like Dutch merchants on market day.

My eyes grew heavy until I heard the Reverend saying, "The pox has run its course, it seems. Only six people dead this past month. Three of them from a Quaker family, one of whom was a runaway. We can all thank God He has rid us of three more heretics."

"Have you heard how fare the neighboring towns?" asked Aunt, twisting the table linens in her hand.

"I have not, Goody Toothaker. The inclement weather has kept us prisoners in our homes. But I have recently had a letter from a fellow theologian in Boston. He said the smallpox has come. As well as an outbreak of . . . strange disturbances." He waggled his fingers about at the last, imitating a flock of scattering birds.

"Disturbances?" Uncle asked, the corners of his mouth turned down.

"Witchery. Spells and incantations. My colleague has taken the belief that disease follows a decline in virtue and brings a rise in witchcraft. In the same fashion that foul vapors arise from a bog. He remembers me the case in the south of Boston not two years past of an outbreak of smallpox at the same moment that a Mr. John Goodwin, mason by trade, and his entire family were plagued by stupendous witchcraft. I say 'stupendous,' as these were the very words used by Cotton Mather in his writings of a woman named Glover who was charged with these happenings."

Not to be outdone, Uncle motioned for Margaret to stand in front of the Reverend and said with pride that he had trained his daughter how to sight a witch. The Reverend gestured for her to come closer. "Now, here, sweet child. Tell me what you know."

She recited the signs, saying, "Firstly, a voluntary confession of the crime."

The Reverend responded, "As Perkins has written, 'I say not, that a bare confession is sufficient, but a confession after due examination . . .' " He patted the shoulder of her frock with a dirty hand and lingered there. A black crow despoiling a field of snow.

Margaret continued, "Secondly, if the accused will not confess . . ."

The Reverend squeezed and kneaded her shoulder tightly. "Then there is need of the testimony of two witnesses. Who must offer proof."

Allen leaned forward in his chair and asked, "What kind of proof?"

The Reverend removed his hand from Margaret's shoulder and counted off on his fingers. "The accused was seen in the company of the Devil by invocation or spell making. The accused has a familiar, such as a dog or some other creature, in the use of spells. The accused has put into practice spells or enchantments against the accuser's person or belongings. Also suspect are divination and petty forms of magic, such as moving objects about the room." I looked at Uncle, thinking of the feather he had pulled from my ear. Uncle waved Margaret back to her seat and said, "I myself have successfully broken the spell of a witch by boiling away the water of the victim."

The Reverend picked from the pocket of his coat a small worn Bible and said, "That, Dr. Toothaker, is using the Devil's shield against the Devil's sword and will go very hard on you should you be called to account. There is only one way to conquer witchery and that is to invoke the holy word of God. And that, mark you, is the only legitimate course of action." He threw the Bible down on the table. "This is God's hammer, which will forever break the Devil's sword. Boiling piss in a pot, no matter how well meaning, will only bring trouble." He looked pointedly at my uncle, who sat silent for the rest of the meal.

The Reverend took his leave late, crumbs following behind him like a cloud. I crept out of hiding and stood before my eldest cousin, watching him scowl at me. He crossed his arms and cocked his head to the side as though listening for something, and I knew with a certainty that he disliked me as much as I disliked him. Something about him made the front of my teeth ache as though I had bitten into a hard summer peach that was mostly pit.

He turned to his father, saying, "It's a dangerous thing, don't you think, to take them in. After all, Thomas' family has been known to carry infection."

I could feel the red blush of anger creep up my neck into my cheeks and I dropped my head to hide my true face. Father and son lit their pipes, and when the smoke was thick enough, Allen leaned his arm upon the chair where his father sat and said to me, "Your father brought pox to Billerica when first he came. As well as a bad history."

"My father is every bit as good as the next man," I replied, feeling a hatred like black ice form in my heart. In that moment I wondered if this was what Uncle had meant by saying Father had blood on his hands.

Allen bent down so that our eyes were on a level. "One would think he believes himself better than most, as he has taken over our grandmother's house." If I had been a boy, I would have thrown seed to the Devil and planted my fists over his nose.

Uncle put a hand on Allen's arm and said, "You must remember, Sarah is our family, and while she is here we must try to be kind." But he said nothing in defense of my father, and the shadowy smile behind the pipe smoke stung deeper than the insults.

Later that night I lay with my back to Margaret, stewing in rancid juices until she coaxed me to turn and face her. "Do not be angry, cousin," she said. "You will love my brother as I do when you have come to know him better. You will love him as I love you."

I lowered my head and tucked it into the hollow of her throat. Not because I was ready for sleep but because I wanted to hide the thought that burned my face. The thought, the prayer, that in that moment I would be made an orphan so I could forever stay in my cousin's house. Roger as my father, Mary as my mother, and Margaret as the sister of my heart. I think God must have damned me then for my thoughts, for the next day Father came to take me home.

MARGARET AND I returned the following morning from the barn, our arms about each other's shoulders, lingering in the watery light of the sun that played in and out of blue-gray clouds. We squatted down to look at the spongy ground and at the ripening tips of bulbs stabbing their way through the thinning layers of snow. The churning engine of spring was massing, bringing a sharp smell to the air as from a blacksmith's stable. There would never be a time of an early melt when I would not think of my cousin braced by the gathering warmth, the clouds racing behind her smiling and enraptured face.

I did not know my father at first. I had come into the common room to find a giant sitting at the table, my aunt sitting across from him with her head in her hands. She was sobbing loudly and Uncle stood behind her with his hands on her shoulders. The giant looked up at my approach but did not speak. It was Margaret who spoke first and made me know my father again.

"Uncle, what has happened?" Her hand found mine and squeezed it painfully. Uncle Roger beckoned for me to come closer. I took tiny steps towards the table, trying to multiply the distance and increase the time before hearing what I did not wish to hear.

Father stared into his lap and said, "Your grandmother has died."

"And Tom and Andrew and Richard?" My hands crept to my ears to blot out the words.

"They are alive."

"And now must I leave?" I would be the last in the room to comprehend that I had not asked about my mother.

"The ban has lifted. It is time for you and Hannah to come home. We will leave at nightfall."

Margaret led me to our room, where I lay on the bed until it was time to leave. She whispered to me again and again that we would never be parted. That she was the sister of my heart, now and forever. Aunt tied together a bundle of food and clothing for our journey. She promised they would come to Andover in the spring, but I would not be comforted. Hannah screamed and struggled and had to be torn from Aunt's arms. I believe that losing Hannah was more painful to her than the death of her mother. Even as a swaddling babe, Hannah had been sober and quiet, as though she sensed from the beginning my mother's intolerance for plaintive neediness. But my sister had come to know the fawning attention and gentle caresses of the Toothaker family. That Henry had come to adore her as well raised him in my estimation and made a sort of peace between the two of us. Hannah would soon be sent to other families and other households, and not all of them would be so kind. It was this separation from her truest mother, though, that would leave her forever fearful and grasping.

Margaret and I held back at the last and exchanged poppets. She lifted the crimson skirt of her doll and showed me where she had left a needle so I could practice my sewing and not lose the skill. From the cart I watched Margaret grow smaller and smaller until she looked like the poppet I held in my hands. Father had said to me as he lifted me into the cart, "Your mother is alive." I set my jaw and looked away, giving him no cause to think me happy about the news. I would return to a cold house with no certainty of when I would see my cousin again. I gripped the poppet tightly and felt the needle prick my finger.

A needle is such a small, brittle thing. It is easily broken. It can hold but one fragile thread. But if the needle is sharp, it can pierce the coarsest cloth. Ply the needle in and out of a canvas and with a great length of thread one can make a sail to move a ship across the ocean. In such a way can a sharp gossipy tongue, with the thinnest thread of rumor, stitch together a story to flap in the breeze. Hoist that story upon the pillar of superstitious belief and a whole town can be pulled along with the wind of fear. Perhaps I should have seen the needle prick as a sign. But I was very young and the wound had stopped bleeding long before we arrived in Andover.

I looked at the sky but saw no stars, only clouds that would bring many weeks of snow before winter would end.

CHAPTER THREE

April 1691–August 1691

THE STRUGGLE AGAINST the smallpox had left its mark on my family in many ways beyond a pitting of the skin. Only Father retained his vitality and continued to press himself in caring for the livestock and hunting for days at a time in the surrounding woods. On those early mornings when he moved across the fields alone, his flintlock strapped to his back, the world leeched of all colors save for white and black, he looked like a towering elm walking upon the snow. He would return in the evening with a hare or fox hanging from his belt. At times he returned with his belt empty and we went to bed with our stomachs gnawing at our backs.

I don't know what my mother must have thought the day Hannah and I were returned by wagon to Andover and she was greeted by my hard-set face and Hannah's fright over seeing this now-forgotten woman. But there was little time to brood, as my first days home were filled with bringing the house to rights, boiling rags and clothes in vinegar and lye to kill the evil humors lurking in the folds of the cloth and behind buttons and clasps. The sickness had taken what little patience my mother possessed and, however much I scrubbed or boiled or swept, she found in me shortcomings to shame a pope. I did not yet know that, like fermenting ale left too long in its keg, restrained sorrow will turn towards anger.

I had promised Aunt that I would be a good and compliant daughter, but within a few days, there were Lucifer sparks between my mother and me. I searched the house for signs of my grandmother's presence, but her dress and bedclothes had been burned, her cot by the fire broken into pieces for kindling. She had left me her shawl and, after it had been boiled and scrubbed, I wore it round my shoulders like an embrace. I cried for her goodness lost to me so soon, and it was at these times that Mother took pity and left me to mourn her passing. At night in my bed, I held Hannah close and imagined Margaret's breath, warm and moist, on my neck. The rancid smell of sickness still cloaked the house, and to my regret, my first thoughts on seeing my brothers' wasted bodies brought shame. Watching my father escape into the brilliant cold wash of snow made me wish to be a boy and leave the fear of contagion behind.

MAY CAME FIRST with storms and then with a great heat all at once. On the first of the month I sat in the shadows of the house, holding a skinning knife in one hand and waving away with the other flies that hovered over the corpse of a bear Father had felled earlier that morning. He had killed it with a clean shot through the neck, leaving the head intact. The brown milky eyes remained open in death, and his fixed gaze seemed to regard me thoughtfully, as though he did not begrudge our use of him. Another hunter would have bragged about killing a bear weighing twice that of a man and shot at a distance of twenty feet. A charging bear can run the distance of twenty feet in the count of ten. And knock a skull from its backbone in the count of two. But as Father hoisted the bear to a brace for the bleeding, I heard him recounting the story to Richard as though he had bagged a pair of geese.

It had taken my father and brother most of a day to take the wagon to Falls Woods and return again with the bear. Father stood close by, feeding the flames under the giant pot he would use to render pounds of fat from the meat. The meat would be dark and rank but it would dry better than beef and last longer than buck. When we had scraped the skin and combed the burs from the fur, it would make a warm winter coverlet for Mother's bed. Father strongly believed in the curative powers of bear fat and would use it for everything from greasing the cart wheels to a poultice for Tom's chest. Mother would add mustard seeds to the fat, heat it until it bubbled, and spread it on my brother's chest before covering the stinking mixture with lamb's wool. The blisters soon turned to scars but his breathing would ease.

I lifted my head to spy on Hannah playing nearby in the shade and saw Tom and Mother broad-hoeing the garden. They were planting corn, beans, and squash all in the same mounds together. The corn would grow tall and straight as a pole. The beans would vine the corn towards the sun and the squash would grow in the shadows below. Tom looked up at me and smiled, but his eyes had the look of Abraham's son upon the altar, full of trust but somehow knowing the blade of sacrifice must come. He had grown bent and stooped in the space of months and was pitifully thin, the bones of his wrist jutting out at odd angles. Had it not been for the Reverend Dane and the Widow Johnson laying food at the doorstep, my family would have starved.

Andrew followed slowly behind, placing the precious seeds on the mounds and pushing them in with an unsteady finger. As he planted he sang in a voice reedy and thin a song he had heard Mother hum in the garden many times before.

> *One for the squirrel, one for the crow,*
> *One for the cutworm and one to grow.*

He had been much affected by the smallpox that kept him near death for three months. His face would forever be scarred and it would signify to the world that he would never again be at risk in falling to the disease. But his mind, which was reluctant to thoughts before the illness, had slowed to a crawling pace and would scatter like a flock of birds before completing a sentence. He would often stop speaking mid-word and walk away, leaving the listener unclear of his meaning or intentions.

I sat staring at my hands, shining and slippery with bear grease, thinking of Margaret's hands over mine as we sat together sewing. Father called out to me to stop gathering wool and finish my work. I brushed away the biting flies and made a deep cut across the bear's corded muscles to pull out another bit of fat. Seeing the fur stripped away from the bloodied flesh brought back the dream of the Indians bending over Andrew's bed. And in that moment I knew with a certainty that it was Andrew who had brought the breath of contagion to Andover. Thirteen people, my grandmother among them, had died wearing to the grave the Devil's rosy bridal bouquet on their flesh.

The selectmen had ordered that we leave Andover at the end of our isolation, but the Reverend Dane spoke passionately in our favor, as it was Grandmother's last wish that we stay and care for the Allen farm. Because the Allen name was one of the oldest in the settlement, and because Reverend Dane begged for it, the selectmen bowed reluctantly to his wishes. But we stayed in Grandmother's house mainly because my mother refused to go. Mother's stubbornness would be deeply resented by our neighbors and, in particular, the new young minister of Andover, Reverend Thomas Barnard. He had for some time waited impatiently for the older man to step down and was thwarted as, year after year, Reverend Dane ascended the pulpit and preached to the congregation, taking half of the younger man's salary. If ever there needs to be proof that a minister is a corruptible man and not a glistening saint, take away half his pay.

At Grandmother's burying, Reverend Barnard had said to Mother, "Goody Carrier, it says in Romans that he who rebels against the given authority is rebelling against what God has ordained and those who do so will bring judgment upon themselves."

And without a pause my mother coolly responded, "And does not First Peter say rid your selves of hypocrisy, envy and slander lest it bring to ruin the defiler?" From that moment Reverend Barnard would wish us gone forever.

I carried the heavy bucket of bear's meat to the fire, where Father poured it into the cauldron for rendering. We stood for a moment near the flames as he stirred the mass of flesh and fat until the smell rose up, making my stomach growl with hunger. His face was deeply lined but ruddy, the sickness passing him over without so much as the kiss of fever. I slipped my hand into his, and though he squeezed my fingers with a calloused palm, his face looked as remote and guarded as ever. Since my return I had not seen him shed one tear for my grandmother. But it was not my father I resented. It was my mother I blamed for bringing me back, separating me from my cousin.

I gave her long hateful looks even when she put Iron Bessie to my buttocks until I screamed. Living with the Toothakers had softened me, and so, at first, I bleated like a lamb at slaughter when she hit me. In time I learned to make a jail of my teeth for I would rather have died than cry out to her. The only truce to my feelings came late at night when I stood alone, running my fingers along the carved rim of the spinning wheel, wishing for my grandmother's gentle touch.

As the days passed I tried to bring the Toothakers alive to my brothers. I told them the stories I had heard in Uncle's house about Indian raids and the battles of militiamen, but my recounting lacked the richness and magic of Uncle's telling. Richard would sit and smirk and Tom pretended to listen, but he often fell asleep after the evening meal. The stories gave Andrew nightmares and he would wake screaming in the night, his arms and legs waving about. Mother made me stop then, saying Uncle could run a forge with the air from his lungs and fill a well with curdling nonsense. In the space of a few months, I had become a stranger to my family, my only companion a demanding Hannah, two months shy of her second birthday, who balked at being held or fed by anyone but me. We had been told to stay within a gunshot's distance of the house, as the Wabanakis had been sighted in settlements south of Cambridge. The Reverend Dane had come with the news that the smallpox was ravaging whole tribes and the braves had come looking for young colonists, boys and girls, to fill their ranks. Grown colony men were knifed and bludgeoned, as were women past childbearing age. Old grandmothers, infants in arms, and children too weak or young to keep pace with the retreating warriors were cut down and left for the ravens.

In Andover and Billerica in the space of a few days, colonnades of sharpened pikes were built around manned towers to defend against stealthy and silent attacks. One guardsman, so unnerved by the thought of a raid, shot and killed his own son as he gathered firewood not twenty paces from the tower. Father shook his head and said the miracle was that such a blustering farmer had been able to hit the boy at all. Young women carried sharp blades within their bodices and aprons, not to kill a raider, but to open their own veins rather than submit bodily to their abductors. Young children were tied with string to their mothers so they couldn't wander off, and boys of serviceable age were given over to the practice of deadly combat using only sticks, wooden hoes, and scythes.

The only salvation left for the captured was to be ransomed by barter by the relatives left living. There was no forced rescue ever, for the Wabanakis had been born of the fomenting wilderness and knew every mountain pass, every river, and forest as well as the hairs on their own arms. The few who were brought back after living for a time in those dark, obscure places were wild and strange even to their own families. One young woman, returned to her kin in Billerica, had to be tied to her bed, so often did she try to escape back to her abductors. When no family was left, a redeemed captive could only be indentured to those who paid the ransom.

Mercy Williams had been born in Topsfield and had moved with her family to the so-called Eastward, the wild territory to the far north and east of the colonies. Her parents and all her brothers and sisters had been killed by the Wabanakis and she had been taken captive into Canada. Governor Phips ransomed her along with a dozen others and sent them back to their families or as indentured servants to the homes of strangers. With the exchange of twenty muskets she had become a laborer and would have to work for five years to pay back her rescuers.

Father had wanted a manservant to help on our farm, but we could not afford to pay the indenture for a man, so we settled for an orphan girl nobody else wanted. It would soon be apparent why Mercy Williams' indenture came on the cheap.

Grandmother had owned a comfortable bit of land in Andover, close to four acres on fertile ground, and we would need help in the spring, rendering the fields ready for planting. Mother had earned a small inheritance, a bag of coins placed into her hands at Grandmother's deathbed, and with it a chance to buy more seed. We would plant on the first warm days a half acre of hay and an acre each of corn and wheat. With a sturdy plow and an ox, two grown men could plow an acre in one day but the land of Essex County was peppered with stones as plentiful as the mussels at Casco Bay. The rocks could defeat the sturdiest plow, and furrowing could be done only after more trees had been cleared with a felling axe, the brush cleared with a billhook and fire. Then the heaviest stones, half buried, could be pulled from the dirt.

The first week of May, Mercy arrived at our house, following Father as he bent his tall frame to clear the door. She stood with her arms crossed, giving us as much of a once-over as we gave her. Mother took one look at her and ordered her outside to wash and sent me along to check her head for nits. I filled a pot with stream water while she sat on the ground like a man, watching me, her knees bent and spread far apart. She fanned herself with her apron and I was shocked to see she was not wearing a shift beneath her skirt.

Her legs were as brown as her arms, and when she caught me staring, she pulled her skirt higher over her thighs. Father had spoken of her as still being a girl, but she had corded muscles like a boy and a gaze that raised the hackles on the back of my neck. Like Lazarus come back from the dead, she had seen what I had only imagined through the stories of Uncle. She had survived the long march to Canada as well as her own memories of the journey. My curiosity at that moment was greater than my decorum over her shame, and I asked her, "How old are you, then?"

She looked at me and smiled a crooked smile, as though one

side of her mouth was palsied, saying, "Seventeen or so." She turned her head and spat through her teeth, mouthing words that did not sound to be English. I handed her the washing pot and a lump of harsh lye soap, which she sniffed and put aside. She rolled up her sleeves and roughly scrubbed at her arms and face, using only the water. The skin on her face was pitted with pox scars, and, despite the washing, she had a smell about her of something sour, like milk gone bad or calfskin poorly tanned. The hair on her scalp was sparse and there was not much to comb through for the lousing. I thought she had been scalped, but when I later asked Richard about it, he told me that had that been so, she would have been missing the top part of her skull as well.

As I teased out the tangled hair, looking for crawling things, I asked, "How long were you with the Indians?"

" 'Bout three years' time, mebbe more," she answered, scratching the back of her neck. The comb caught and pulled at a knot and her fingers wrapped round my wrist as quick as a corn snake. She took the comb from me and set it aside. She then reached out and fingered a bit of my own hair that had spilled from my cap. I felt pity for her at that moment and smiled to show my compassion. She smiled back at me in a one-sided grimace and said, "But now I am home, aren't I?" I followed her back to the house and she whistled some bit of song. I remembered Mother once saying a whistling woman and a cackling hen come to no good end, but I was lonely and looked for friendship wherever it was offered.

That evening at supper we watched with fascination the way she funneled food into her mouth. She ate with her hands without spilling one crumb and guarded her plate as though it would be taken away at any moment. When we cleared the table, she dropped a plate and broke it. Mother gave her the eye that we had all come to fear, but Mercy picked up the pieces without seeming to notice. Afterwards we were sent to bed. Father had built a separating wall in the common room so that Mercy and I could have our own little room. Richard, Andrew, and Tom slept in the garret above, and Hannah slept on a low cot beside Mercy and me. Father had also built a new rope bed for himself and Mother with a longer frame, as Grandmother's bed was painfully short for his legs, and had given us the old bed. The first night we lay together, Mercy, without asking, grabbed Margaret's poppet out of my hands and looked at it as though it were a piece of sweet bun. She roughly turned the doll this way and that, holding it with fingers chewed down to the quick.

I asked, "What was it like to be captured? Was it horrible?"

The needle hidden under the doll's skirt must have pricked her skin, for she yelped and suddenly thrust the doll back to me. "Not near so bad as being knocked over the head." She abruptly turned from me and fell to sleep. I moved away from the unpleasant smell of her body and studied the doll to make certain she had not split the seams. I stroked the red cloth and wondered if Margaret was even then thinking of me as well.

Although Mercy was to my cousin as a grackle is to a dove, she did have her winning ways. At times she seemed cumbersome and plodding on her feet, but at other times she would appear behind me without having made the slightest bit of noise.

I would turn to find her standing at arm's length, studying me in a way that made me want to cover the tender part of my belly. She did her chores well enough, for she was strong and never complained, but there was an air about her as though she submitted to her labors only because it suited her to do so. She had been with us a short time when she pulled a face behind my mother's back. Mother had given her a chore to do in her usual cast-iron manner, and when she turned around, Mercy puckered her lips up in a mocking way. I clapped my hand over my mouth to keep from laughing, feeling at last that I had an ally. She soon made a habit of being compliant to my mother's face while making fun of her when she was out of the room.

One night after supper I told the story of Uncle's battle with the Narragansetts. I had hoped to grease the spokes of Mercy's memory so that she would tell me something of her captivity. When I had finished, I was startled to hear the rumbling voice of my father coming from the far corner of the room. He had been braiding rope, and while he talked he twisted the strands sharply together. "The village attacked by General Winslow's men had women and old people in it. The braves had gone into the woods for hunting. They had never once attacked an Englisher. But their children were all butchered as fawns are butchered in a pen. Their bodies left to the crows and the wolves. The Narragansetts fought then with King Philip, and there was bloody murder on both sides before it ended."

"But I saw the scar he got fighting a brave . . . ," I said, thinking him to be jealous of Uncle's courage.

Father wound the finished rope between his elbow and hand, making neat coils, saying, "That scar he sports was made by a squaw who split him open with a troweling knife before her head was hacked from her body."

I heard Mercy snigger as she turned away to bank the fire. I felt bruised that she should laugh at my expense, but she shrugged her shoulders when I caught her eye.

The days passed and we planted the acres of wheat and corn and hay easterly in the direction of Ladle Meadow. Even Hannah was given a small sack with seed, and she helped broadcast the kernels into the ground, her little legs tripping over dirt clods and the hem of her newly lengthened shift. We made slow progress, as the ground was heavy with rocks, but the weather was fair with a few good rains. Mercy proved to have as strong a back as any youth, and she easily pulled from the ground stones the size of a calf's head.

I would have thought she would not be eager for such hard labor, preferring instead to cook at the hearth. But wherever the men were working, there she was content to be. At times Robert Russell would come to help us with the planting. His homestead was southeast of ours, between Ladle Meadow and Gibbet Plain. He was tall and well seasoned and had come with Father from the old England many years before. Robert was the only man that my father took hunting, and when they left for the woods together, we knew them gone for days. The first day Robert appeared in the fields, Mercy jabbed me sharply with her elbow and whispered loudly, "Has that man a wife?"

I answered, rubbing my bruised ribs, "No, but he lives with a niece named Elizabeth."

"How old is she?"

"About fourteen or fifteen, I should think."

She put on a knowing face but beat a ragged path to Robert, bringing him water at every opportunity. He wasn't the only man to receive fair treatment from her hands. She had started shadowing Richard about, offering to do his chores in the barn and serving him larger portions of meat at the table, until Mother finally took Richard's plate away and gave it to Father.

IN THE SECOND week of May, Mercy and I were doing the washing together. We had added lye to the boiling water and were placing shirts in the pot with long sticks. The cast iron smelled of bear even though we had worked for most of an hour scrubbing it with sand to clean it. She was still maddeningly thick to my questions about her life with the Wabanakis and was unimpressed with Uncle's stories. Father and my brothers were out in the fields broadcasting seeds from their sack aprons, and Mercy would often raise her head from the steam to look at them.

"Mercy, I have heard that Indians are devils. And that Lucifer himself appears as a brown man."

She looked at me, squinting her eyes against the slanting light. She snorted air out through her nose and said, "An Indian is a man like any man." She raised the long stick she was holding until it jutted straight out from her loins and said crudely, "And all men are designed in like fashion." I laughed to show I understood her meaning but inwardly felt an uneasy clenching.

"Your brother Richard is a ready man. He will need a wife soon, I think."

I had never thought of my brother as a man and no longer a boy. I had never given him much thought at all, except for the times he was being quarrelsome. Mercy walked away from the heat of the fire and laid herself down under the shade of an elm tree that threw its branches over the roof of the house. She picked up a blade of grass and, cupping it in her hand, made a high-pitched whistling noise through it. I sat next to her and, pretending to study the laces on my shoes, looked at her face and thought that Richard would never take such an ugly girl to wife.

After a few moments she said, "You asked about devils. Do you know what the Indians do to those trying to escape?"

I shook my head and she said, "There was a man from Salmon Falls who was taken captive to Canada with the rest of us. His name was Robert Rogers. He tried to escape but he was caught." Here she looked at me and blew through the sliver of green held between her fingers, making it sound like the scream of a woman. "He was stripped naked, tied to a stake, and scorched with burning brands. This went on for some time. Then they pulled him from the stake and danced around him and cut pieces of his flesh from his naked body and threw the bloody pieces in his face. When he finally died, they tied him back to the stake and burned him until he was charred to a lump of coal."

I felt my breakfast rising to meet my tongue.

"After that I was content to stay in Canada awhile." She looked at the pot and said, "It's time to stir, I think." But as she made no move to stand, I hurried away and finished washing the shirts alone.

ONE UNEXPECTED CHANGE in my mother was the return to the rituals of the Sabbath. Grandmother, knowing she was soon to die, had made Mother promise to attend the meetinghouse faithfully once the ban had been lifted and all of us were well and whole. So on the 24th day of May, we were dressed with all the grim haste of a garrison being fired upon by French troops. We were forced to scrub at our necks until they were scarlet and put on stiff aprons and shirts. This Sabbath exercise meant that Mercy and I were washing the whole of Saturday and our hands were chafed and raw from the lye.

That Sunday morning, Mercy had crawled into the cart with me until she saw that Richard would be walking behind us. She gave up her place to Andrew and walked next to Richard the whole way into town. I thought, uncharitably, that even with a fresh cap and apron she looked unkempt and not too very clean. Richard might as well have been walking alone, though, for all the attention he gave to her chattering mouth. After a few miles her breath gave out and they continued their walk in silence. Mother glanced over her shoulder a few times and, had her looks been barbed arrows, Mercy would have been dropped to the dust like a Norman at the hands of a Welsh bowman. I wondered what sparks would fly if Iron Bessie were applied to Mercy's backside, as she was every bit as large as my mother. She told me once she would knock senseless anyone who mishandled her.

Walking into the meetinghouse was a cold and cheerless affair. The insistent buzzing and clacking about of our neighbors ceased the instant we passed from the sunlight of the yard into the dark of the sanctuary. I looked about and saw many pairs of eyes turned to us. The silence was so great I could hear the mourning doves nesting in the rafters. The Reverend Dane, sitting at the front, turned and with the briefest of nods bid us enter and be seated. I wondered if Mother would find a place in the back, but she walked with the pride of a queen to the place where her mother had sat for many years. At first the row of women would not yield. But my mother placed her foot in the pew and it was either part to give us a place or be sat upon.

The last time I had attended the Andover meetinghouse, I had heard the welcoming voice of the Reverend Dane. It was a different matter when the Reverend Barnard let loose his dark visions upon the people, for though his voice was like creek water over soapstone, his message was ominous. Friend to the great theologian Cotton Mather, he was a minister of ferocious and unshakable belief that God was as hard as bedrock. He often used Mather's sermons, his favorite being the vengeful Deuteronomy: "Their foot shall slide in due time." On that day he began with Joel, chapter 2, and the promise of "a day of darkness and gloom."

He finished sweetening the sermon with the story of Job and his running sores. It would have taken a fool not to see the thread he was trying to weave. The suffering of Job and the horrors of smallpox. There were many, hearing these words, who threw hooded and disapproving looks in our direction, making my palms damp and chilled. A hunted rabbit, finding no warren or cover, will run itself to ground and die before a fox can catch and devour it. But, if the rabbit turns and faces the fox, the rabbit will become rigid with fear and die fully aware of the jaws closing around its head, the fox's eyes doing the hunting before his teeth. I followed Mother's lead and stared at a place on the wall above the minister's head.

At the end I walked out into the light and stood looking for Lieutenant Osgood's little black slave. I did not see him but did spy Mercy whispering and tittering to another girl near her age. Their heads were close together, and when I approached, they pulled apart and looked at me with blank faces, as though I would not know they had been talking about me. The girl's name was Mary Lacey, and within the space of minutes, she had told me of all the young men vying for her favor. I did not miss the look Mercy threw Richard, and when she told me in a bold and bossy way to leave, I planted my feet and locked eyes with her. With a shrug Mercy continued her gossiping, which had in the main to do with all the unmarried men in the village.

"Oh, look," said Mary, averting her eyes suddenly. "There is Timothy Swan and his brothers."

I saw a smallish man talking to three younger men. He was bowed at the shoulders with a sallow cast to his skin.

Mary said, "Robert Swan is married now, but Timothy and John are not. Timothy has been ill of late." And here she bent to whisper something in Mercy's ear. They covered their mouths to stop up their laughter, but the sound carried and several of the old women coming out of the meetinghouse frowned. I looked back at the men, and there stood Allen Toothaker among them. The look he gave me brought back the dank air of his father's cold-cellar. Mary grabbed at Mercy's sleeve and, lifting her chin back towards the men, said, "And there is Allen Toothaker, come from Billerica to live with the Swans until he can get his own homestead. He thought he had one" — and she looked pointedly at me—"but it seems someone got there first. He is your older first cousin, isn't he, Sarah?"

I felt a tug at my elbow and heard Tom at my shoulder say, "It's time to leave. Mother is waiting." He pulled insistently at my arm until I followed him back to the cart. It took Mercy a while longer, for she had hoped that Allen would cross over to speak to her, but he had walked away through the sloping, clover-filled mounds of the burial grounds. On the way home Mercy walked close to Richard as before, but, trying a new tack, she feigned injuring first one ankle and then the other. Richard aided her by handing her a stout stick and a water skin and continued his wordless, dogged march behind the cart.

THE WORLD THAT spring looked a continuous freshening color of green, as if it had been made from some vast limitless bolt of linsey-woolsey. The trees bloomed in delicate laces of pink and white, and ivy crept beyond the shadows of the hawthorn bushes. Wild violets bloomed on the banks of Roger's Brook, and tall grasses bowed double in the wind. On such a morning Tom found me hoeing in the garden, and after he had tortured me for a time with his sighing and restless toe tapping, I asked him what the matter was. I knew something worrisome had been catching at his thoughts, but Tom often ruminated over little things far past the time of their usefulness.

He finally said, "Do you remember Sunday last when we were to town and Allen Toothaker was there?" I had remembered Allen's skulking movements through the cemetery as he left the meetinghouse but thought it an attempt to keep from Mercy's company. Tom moved closer as if wishing not to be overheard and said, "I'm afraid of him." His face was pale, as though his breath had been pinched off. I tore loose some clods of dirt with my hoe and thought of Allen's close-set, hateful eyes near mine when he said Father was to blame for bringing the pox. And of how we had usurped the Toothakers' right to Grandmother's house. I said carelessly, "Allen is a jackdaw, full of more swagger than sense."

Tom shook his head, saying, "In March, when you were with Margaret, Allen came to us to speak to Mother. He said his mother, Mary, was the oldest of Grandmother's children and by rights should own this homestead. But Mother accused him of laying claim to the house for himself." Tom took the hoe from my hands and pulled me to hunker down in the rows of corn, not yet knee-high. The memory of the visit agitated and un-nerved him to the point of tripping over his own words. I gave him the hem of my apron to wipe his face and calmed him for a moment before letting him continue. "There was a terrible row. Mother clapped her hands in front of his face and told him he would get nothing by it. And that he would get the house only over her corpse. Then Allen said, as angry as I've ever seen a man, 'That may well be.' "

"Where was Father?" I asked, imagining Allen would have gotten more than a hand in his face if Father had been near.

"Hunting with Richard. Mother chased Allen out with a broom. I had gone to the yard to escape the shouting. I was holding the reins for Allen's horse, a fine roan gelding, thinking to do him service." The beautiful red coat of Bucephalus came to mind, and I knew that Allen could only have ridden him with Uncle's blessing.

"When Allen came to mount his horse, he grabbed the reins and balled up his fist. He hit me hard, knocking me to the ground. He told me he would see all of us driven from the house if he had to burn it down. And, Sarah, I believe him."

"What did Father say when he came home?" I asked.

"He said that Allen's tinderbox was too small to start much of a blaze. And then Mother did a strange thing.... She laughed."

I had begun to hate Allen all the more for thrashing down a boy half his size, but I smiled to think that my parents saw fit to ridicule his threats. I gave Tom a push to give him courage and said that such a coward would never dare do us harm when Father was about. And for a time we believed it.

JUNE LAY FULL and heavy on us, and the heat in the garret at night drove Richard to sleep in the barn. Andrew welcomed the heat. He seemed always to be cold, as though his illness had put out his inner furnace. Tom slept as one dead and could have drowned in his sweat before waking. Mercy became restless as well and would often slip from our bed, thinking, I suppose, I wouldn't wake to her large feet fumbling about in the dark. She would be gone for an hour or more, and I wondered if she was stealing food from the larder as I had seen her do before.

One day found us all in the garden, bringing buckets of water from the well to the tender vines and stalks that had grown sparsely through the dry soil. Large purple clouds could be seen in the east, but the wind was moving from the southwest, blowing rain into Salem Town and then out to sea. The hot air had made us all prickly and short-tempered, and Richard, in particular, was being unpleasant. I had learned to respect his black moods, giving him wide berth whenever possible. He was sixteen, with a quick temper, as though he had been born with too much powder in his firing pan. Mercy had been teasing him that morning and I tried to warn her to leave him be, but she only smiled her crooked smile and continued to torment him. Their bantering voices continued up one row and down another, and I heard Richard say rudely that if she didn't shut her hole, he would shut it for her. I was shocked by his language and looked around to see if Mother was close by, for she would surely bend Richard's ear for it. Mercy did not seem threatened but rather put her bucket down and said, laughing, "Come here, then, and shut it."

Richard threw down his bucket and walked swiftly towards her, thinking to make her cower. She stood calmly with her hands at her sides, and then a remarkable thing happened. As he approached her, she took a few steps as though to pass to the side of him. In so doing she grabbed his shirt, hooked her left foot behind his heels, and pushed him backwards with some force. He fell as hard as a locust tree under the axe and lay on the ground, staring upwards. I believe it took him the space of a few breaths to understand why the sky was in front of his eyes and not the horizon. Mercy stood above him, smiling, with her hand out to help him to his feet. At first he would not take her hand, but soon he was hoisted up on his legs, and I waited for the thunderstorm to erupt.

But instead he said to her, "How did you learn that?"

"The Indians are a small people, but they can fell a larger man in just that way and open up his ribs before his heart stops beating."

"Teach me that," he said, and so she did. Once our watering was done we moved behind the barn so we would not be seen. She spent most of an hour showing Richard how to sweep a man's feet out from under him, indifferent to the direction and manner of the attack. I thought that Mercy's hands lingered overly long on Richard's arms and chest, and after a time they rolled around in the dust until the sweat poured in muddy rivulets down their faces and arms. I left, disgusted with their play when Richard sat upon Mercy's chest, her legs bent upwards, her skirt up around her thighs. Tom's eyes would have started from their sockets if I hadn't grabbed his arm and made him leave. I could hear Mercy's laughter even after I had returned the buckets to the well on the far side of the house.

MOTHER HAD AN unsettling ability to foretell the weather. It was the dregs of July and the sky had been dark for days with a blanket of low, roiling clouds. We were close to harvesting the wheat, and Father watched the sky carefully, as too much rain would ruin the crop. She assured him that the clouds would not release their water, though she believed there would be winds and lightning. We feared the summer lightning, as there had been little rain and it could bring fire enough to consume a barn, or a field of crops, within the time it took to fill six buckets of water from the well. There had been stabs of lightning in the far distance, and after supper Tom and I ran to Sunset Rock just to the north of our house to watch the march of heavenly fire crossing the Merrimack River to the west.

There was a greenish, sickly light within the clouds and a sort of leadenness to the air that made the hairs on our arms stand on end and the backs of our necks ache. Mercy had climbed the boulder with us and stood for a short while wringing her apron like it was the head of a chicken. Her breathing was rapid and shallow, and within a few moments she hurried away back in the direction of the house. I danced up and down to the music of the advancing thunder. Soon the lightning could be seen jumping over Bald Hill, making white fairy lights over Blanchard's Pond. Then there was a pause, and the sky darkened until I could barely see Tom standing next to me. I felt his hand creep into mine, and we waited and waited, until a ragged arm of blue and yellow light jumped from the sky and spread like poured mercury over Blanchard's Plain, only a few leagues away. My teeth were knocked together with the sound of it and my ears at first were deafened and then clicked rapidly like a stone caught in a miller's wheel.

The air turned still of a sudden, and a much colder puff of wind at my back caused my shoulders to seek each other for comfort. I turned around to face the east and saw the front of another storm coming fast to meet its twin. There were cascading ripples of light over in the direction of Salem Town, as though a flash of arms was being presented before the battle would be joined over Blanchard's Plain.

The coming storms had made me reckless and I felt myself being raised up on my toes as if the winds were trying to enlist

me to their ranks. I said to Tom that we could better see the
lightning from the hayloft in the barn, but he was shivering and
pale and he answered me by pulling my arm from its roots,
climbing down from the rock. I went to bed that night but
could not sleep, my ears trained to the retreating sounds of
thunder that rolled by diminishing fits and starts into our little
room. That is how I knew that Mercy had slipped out of bed a
few hours after Mother and Father had gone to sleep. She stood
at the foot of the bed listening for any change in my breathing
and then crept barefoot from the room. I counted to ten and
then rose to follow her. Pulling my skirt quickly over my head,
I carried my shoes for stealth. As I stepped from the house, I
saw the white form of her shift struggling against the wind to
open the door of the barn, and then she was swallowed by the
black inside.

I walked the short distance to the barn, careless to the sound
of my shoes, as the winds were still high and struck at the larg-
est trees, making them creak and groan. I bounced the door
until it parted enough to let me pass, then stood in the blackness, listening. I could hear the gentle milling about of the cow
and the ox in their stalls and I let them settle before feeling my
way forward. It came to me then. The sound of mewling and
sighing, not from the stalls but higher up, in the loft. I inched
my way towards the ladder and froze as a flash of light illuminated everything, enough for me to see the rolling eyes of the
aged draft horse jerking against his tether. The mewling stopped
for an instant and then resumed with greater force. I found my
way to the ladder and climbed slowly upwards, minding the
hem of my skirt, until my head cleared the last rung. At that

instant, there was another flash of light, this one revealing two people wrestling and fighting together as though each would commit bloody murder on the other. When the dark returned, I could hear them rolling about in the dried billows of hay and then I heard Mercy laugh and Richard's voice say, "Hold still, then, you bitch." The words were coarse but there was laughter in his voice as well. And then there was silence but for the strangled sounds of their breathing. I slipped one shoe from my foot and brought it behind my head, aiming for the tangled shadows a few feet away. The lightning soon came, and I threw the shoe with all my might at Mercy's head. Blackness fell again, but not before the gratifying sounds of Mercy yowling and cursing. I was down the ladder and out the door, running before they could think of following me.

I crawled back into bed and kept my back to her when Mercy shadowed her way in. I could feel her eyes on me and then felt a sharp weight as she dropped my shoe upon the bed. The ropes beneath us shifted as she settled her head on her arm, but I knew she would not easily fall into sleep. A strong, raw animal smell came from her body. I rolled the word around and around in my mind before parting my lips and whispering, "Whore." The sound of it mingled with the rising storm and so I did not know whether or not she heard me say it. Margaret came to me in a dream that night. She stood on the far side of the Shawshin River and called out to me something I could not hear over the roaring of the wind. She cupped her hands around her mouth but still I could not hear her words. I ran back and forth on the embankment, looking for a way to get across, but there was no boat and no bridge. She pointed to a place beyond my shoulder, and the words floated to me. "Fire, Sarah. Fire."

I woke to Tom shaking me frantically by the foot. He was shouting, "Fire, Sarah! The fields are on fire!"

Hannah opened her eyes then and, seeing the terror in Tom's face, screamed like something dying. She clutched tightly to my legs, threatening to trip me as I struggled to pull a skirt over my head. I picked her up and ran with Tom to the edge of the fields. Mercy was running with Father towards a wall of smoke, and the world to the east of the barn was made of yellow, low-surging light. I could see Andrew running as fast as he could, bringing buckets of well water to Richard, who had climbed to the top of the barn to dampen the roof. There was a slight rise behind the barn and as I crested it I could see where the fire had started. A lone elm that had stood for generations had channeled the lightning as easily as a gutter channels rainwater. The split trunk lay blackened and dead and the fire was consuming the outer fields of hay on the far side of the path running along the crest from north to south. The wind buffeted first to the west and then to the east as the twin storms combined. I saw a man working next to Father, both desperately trying to make a space between the fields of hay and the tender shafts of wheat, their hoes rising and falling in rapid succession.

Mother grabbed at my shoulder and thrust me back in the direction of the barn, shouting, "Bring the scythes, Sarah, and there is another hoe just within the door. Hurry, for God's sake, or we will be burned to the ground."

I ran until my lungs ached, wondering what I was to do with Hannah. I could not bring her into the burning fields, and my brothers would be needed to keep the flames at bay. Her nails drew blood when I pulled her from my neck, and as I tied her to a post with a leather strap, she kicked and cried piteously. Her fear of being abandoned made her feral, and the whites of her eyes showed as she bit at the strap. I shouted to Andrew to remember to rescue Hannah if the barn should catch fire and prayed he would remember her in the confusion. I gathered up the needed tools and raced back to the fields, hoping I wouldn't trip and cut off my legs, falling on the newly sharpened scythes. Mother and I worked next to the men as they dug their shallow trench, scything away the stalks to make a path the fire could not jump. But the fire raged on towards us and into the wheat, and I could feel the heat of it on my cheeks, curling my hair. I stopped for a moment to rest, but Mother pushed me and said hoarsely, "Don't stop. Keep working." I could hear Tom somewhere behind me as he lay down buckets of sand over the fallen shafts of grain.

The heat was terrible, but worse was the billowing smoke that found its way into every opening, until our eyes and ears and throats blistered and watered. I pulled my skirt up around my face to breathe, and suddenly I was standing alone in the tortured field, lost in a wall of smoke. I felt panic rising in my throat and turned to see a tongue of flame flowing like a runnel of silk towards the sole of my shoe. I cried out but could see nothing beyond the gray mass and would have run but did not know north from south, east from west. I sank to my knees and felt a creeping blankness in my head, like a drawstring tightening within a gray felt bag. There was a pain at my shoulders as fingers clamped around my arms. Strong hands lifted me up, and we ran through the fire clouds until I could see the sky and the fields again. Mercy clapped me harshly on the back as we coughed and spit foaming ash from our lungs. I looked up and saw the bruised knot my shoe had left on her brow, large enough to show through the blackened soot covering her face.

She said to me, without malice, "It seems we may both be homeless soon."

My family and some of our close neighbors gathered on the crest, expecting to watch the burning of the remainder of the wheat. Robert Russell stood next to Father, as well as Samuel Holt and his brother Henry Holt from the farms near Ladle Meadow. A growing light came from the eastern horizon and the wind changed course and blew suddenly from the west, rushing to meet the dawn. The fire stalled for a moment, the heads of the flames licking at the air like tracking hounds. And then the fire turned and flowed east, churning and fast, as though it would throw itself into the sea. The Holts raced back to their farms, and with them ran my Father, his long hoe braced over one shoulder, its heated metal head sending up wisps of steam. A cold splinter of thought shifted in my head as I remembered Allen's threat to burn us out. But our fields and house remained. It would be many more hours of work with a bucket and hoe before I could fall into bed, my skin and hair bathed and perfumed in acrid smoke. When I finally re-membered Hannah, left tethered in the barn, it was in the full light of morning. She had fallen asleep, her first and last fingers pressed wetly into her mouth, but woke as soon as I lifted her to take her to the house. She would demand to be carried for days afterwards, eating and sleeping only in the circling embrace of my arms.

THE FIRE HAD burned the hay but left the wheat. The flames had come close to the corn, wilting some of the silk tassels and puckering the husks. The kernels from those ears at summer's end would have a scorched taste, as if they had been dragged through the ashes in the hearth. The loss was disappointing but did not compare with the loss of some of our neighbors. The Holts suffered far worse, losing most of their yield. The fire stopped only when it came to the waters of the Skug River after sweeping across the whole of Ladle Meadow. When Robert Russell came to the house days after for the harvesting of the wheat, he said there were hardened feelings from the Holts, as our crops had been spared and theirs had not. I could see that Robert's sandy brows had been burned quite off, and one cheek was oozing from raised, seeping blisters. His leather doublet was cracked and blackened from the heat, and I pitied him as he had no wife to bind his wounds or mend his vest. He had been widowed for many years and would have to marry again soon or be thought scandalous.

He turned to my mother and said with a smile, "Susannah Holt said she saw you dancing on the crest before the wind turned direction." Robert could often play with her in such a way, and where the rest of us would have been singed for it, she would only dip her chin and smile. Sometimes the color in her cheeks would flare, if only for a moment. Had I been older, I might have sensed that she, though a married woman, was not above being seduced by a winning, handsome man. Rattling some pots at the hearth she said, "I cannot help that their fields were burned. I am sorry for it. They are decent enough folk. But Susannah is old and half blind, and if I was dancing about, it was to put out the fire from the hem of my skirt." Later, when we had milled the wheat into flour at Parker's Mill, we would send four bags of it to Susannah Holt, but the bread she made from it was not enough to soak up the bitter juices of resentment.

Mercy and I made a peace of sorts, and as we worked scything down the shafts of wheat, she taught me a little song she had learned from a French trapper who traded with the Indians. The words were foreign to my ears and, as I did not know its meaning, I decided it must be a lullaby, for the words were soft and lisping. But then she told me with a twisting of her upper lip that the song was about a butterfly that goes from flower to flower to flower before drowning blissfully in the weight of the pollen.

Once the wheat had ripened, we had at most eight days to finish harvesting before the heads shattered and released their kernels. All the stalks were bound and shocked in three days. The mounds of sheaves were plentiful, perhaps a hundred or so, and they were dry and would be easy to flail and winnow. I liked best the winnowing, and I matched the bouncing movement of my basket to Mercy's. We made a game to see who could be the first to separate out the chaff from the kernels. It was at such a time that she first spoke of her family, which was lost to the Wabanakis. She had had a mother and a father, two older brothers, and two sisters, the youngest being but four years of age. The Indians had crept in at first light and set the roof of the house on fire. As each one of her family left the house to escape burning alive, they were knocked over the head and left for dead. She was taken captive along with an older brother who later died along the long trail to Canada. Finishing her story, she smiled her crooked smile, and snaking her fingers about my wrist said, "But I shall get a new family soon, I think."

But that was not to be.

MERCY AND MY mother stood facing each other, arms folded at their chests, both throwing knives with their eyes. It was August, and though the day had just begun, the heat from the cooking fire was near unbearable in the common room. Sweat poured from Mercy's red face, soaking through the front of her apron and wilting the corners of her cap. Mother's dress had large damp stains under the arms, but her face in profile was as smooth and cold as a gravestone. From the back it looked as if the laces of her bodice would burst from the arching of her rigid spine. I held my breath, making myself small, for I did not want to be remembered and sent from the room.

The morning had started peaceably enough. Father had gone hunting at first light with Andrew and Tom. Richard had left with a few bags of ground wheat for barter in the town's market. The three of us had risen early to do the baking for the week and I was shredding greens from the garden, sifting through sprigs of rosemary lying in fragrant bunches upon the table. A pot of rabbit for the day's dinner was already beginning to bubble as it swung from the lug pole under the flue. As the men were not present, Mother and Mercy had tucked up their skirts and aprons into their waistbands, giving them easy movement about the hearth. Mother had just tested the heat of the baking niche with her arm and found it ready. The skin on her right arm was forever as smooth as an infant's bottom, for all the hair had been burned off by the heat. Hannah sat below the table at my feet, playing happily with a wooden spoon that she spun dizzily across the wooden planks of the floor. Mother was in a brighter mood that morning, for she had nursed the milk cow back to health. The cow's udder had become swollen and painful with the damp heat and had been giving less milk. Mother had made a poultice of some mossy herbs in warm water that she bathed over the cow's teats every hour until the swelling had gone and the cow could once again give her full measure. Mercy said she had never seen a cow with such an illness heal so quickly.

The clouds made good on their promise of rain. The wheat had been harvested and the corn swelled and grew hearty. The yield from the corn would be plentiful, bringing greater opportunity for trade. Mother had spoken almost cheerfully about the tallow she would get for candles and the wool she would have for spinning in the autumn. She talked of getting a young heifer and a sow for more milk and meat. Mercy must also have thought that this day was a good one to do some bartering with my mother, trading the scandal of a bastard child she said was to come for the respectability of Richard's name in marriage. But Mercy made a bad show of it and bleated out the news like a stranded goat. When she finished, there was a great crash as

Mother slammed down the lid for the oven, making Hannah start and cling to my legs in fright. And there they stood, both of them working to master their emotions, my mother tempering her anger, and Mercy, I believe, stuffing down her fear. Richard had turned seventeen in July and by all accounts was a man and could take a wife, but only with the consent of his father.

Suddenly Mother pushed up her sleeves and said, "Very well, then. You say you are with child, so let me see with my own eyes if that be the case."

Mercy was so surprised that her mouth fell open and she watched wordlessly as Mother swept every bit of greens off the table into my apron.

"Good God, girl, don't open your mouth to me. I've been midwife a dozen times and have seen full well what's under your skirt. Do you think I'll give my son up to one such as you without proof you are in the family way?"

Mercy stood rooted to the spot and her eyes searched me out for help, but I was useless against Mother's fury and could only watch her go to the slaughter. She started to protest by saying forcefully, "I am with child, and Richard must marry me now or I am ruined."

Mother did not answer but waited ponderously by the table. I could see the thoughts chase themselves across Mercy's face, some of them cunning and some of them tinged with terror. Perhaps she thought that enough play had gone on with Richard to fool her inquisitor, and so she climbed up on the boards and lay on her back. Mother briskly pulled Mercy's skirt and shift up over her thighs and pulled her knees apart. I backed

away from the table but not so far as to not see what she had
between her legs. For everything that Margaret had told me, I
had no picture in my mind of what a woman fully formed
looked like. I watched with equal parts fascination and horror
as my mother quickly examined her and then pulled her skirt
back down to her ankles. Mother stood up from the table saying, "Your maidenhead is still intact. It would be a fine trick to
pass a child through your birth canal without having had a man
pass through it first."

Mercy sat up, screaming loudly, "I am with child. I am with
child." The last word was said in a long protesting wail, but
Mother was unmoved. Mercy sat on the table for a while, crying
and whimpering until she saw that there was nothing to be
gained by it. She then scrambled off the boards, smoothing
out her rumpled skirt and apron. She drew herself up as best she
could and said, wiping her streaming nose on her arm, "It's because I'm indentured that you think I'm not fit for your son. But
no matter what you say, he by rights should marry me and buy
in earnest what he's already used. You think I'm nothing now,
but my family had better than this in Topsfield. Enough to
make this farm look like a dung beetle's pile."

I think my mother had begun to pity her until she insulted us.

"You could not help your state. Misfortune has placed you in
servitude, but that's not the reason you'll not get my son as a
husband. It's because you're a sneaking thief and a liar that I'll
not have you any longer in my family. I took you in and clothed
you and fed you, and you thanked me by stealing the food from
my children's mouths. Don't think I don't know about the food
you've taken, and the bits of wool and the bottoms you've shaved

off the candles. You'd have stolen the spinning wheel if you could have gotten it up under your skirt. For all that you stole, I might have forgiven you, but worst of all is your lying. I will not abide a liar."

"You're the liar," Mercy screamed, her white skin turning blotchy and liverish. "You and your useless son. He promised to marry me and I gave him a roll to bind the deal, but your son and his puny wick couldn't find his way into a woman even when it was thrust in his face. If you turn me out without a promise of marriage, I swear I'll tell the whole village your family is filled with whoresons." The rising sound of her voice was cut short by Mother slapping her hard across the face. A thin sliver of spit ran down the corner of her mouth while she cradled the reddening cheek with her hand.

"I turned a blind eye while you made moon eyes at Richard and shamelessly chased him about the place. But had I known you were putting yourself out with him under our roof, I would have dragged the rest of your hair out by its roots. At least Richard had enough sense to keep his rod in his pants with a girl so homely and rummy that even the Indians wouldn't have her."

I have never since seen the enormity of hate on a woman as that which filled the face of Mercy Williams in that moment. She looked at the both of us, and I was soon clinging to Hannah for comfort. She gathered her few things and walked out the front door, and it was days before we heard that she had been taken in by the Chandlers. They lived close by, across Boston Way Road, and had a travelers inn and were happy to buy from Father the remainder of her indenture. What story she must have told them I do not know, but Father was honest with William Chandler and said that Mercy had been a good worker. After Mother spoke to Father that evening, he beckoned ominously to Richard and they were out in the barn together a good while. When Richard came back into the house, he could barely walk from the welts the strap had left on his legs, but he seemed much lighter in spirit.

Lying in bed alone that night, I hummed the French trapper's song but soon gave it up as I had already begun to forget the words. I held Margaret's poppet close to my lips, but, not feeling the needle within, I lifted the skirt and found it to be gone. I sincerely hoped that it would soon break in Mercy's thieving fingers, giving her lockjaw and a slow, painful death. Sometime during the night, Hannah crawled into my bed, and, as I pulled her round little body to me, I whispered, "Mercy is gone now. And as you are two years old, and a big grown girl, you shall sleep with me in my bed from now on." I could smell the rosemary still clinging to my fingers and was grateful for its fragrance covering over Mercy's musky odor, which had sweated into the sheets: an odor of hidden thoughts and furtive womanly desires. I fell asleep thinking of swift-burning fires and forested paths that traveled nowhere but north.

CHAPTER FOUR

September 1691–December 1691

OFTEN DURING THOSE first days of September I would hide myself away in the cool and rustling stalks of corn growing in the house garden. The beans and squash had begun to ripen and I took time filling my apron, knowing that other less pleasant tasks waited for me in the torpid heat of the house and barn. We had nearly eighty bushels of corn from the harvesting of the outer field, and there was hardly a meal that didn't have the hard little kernels ground or mashed or soaked into the game Father had shot. We had them as roasting ears pulled from the embers, as hominy soaked to mash in wood-ash lye and baked with beans and squash. Later, in the new year, when the sap rose in the maples, we would have cornmeal mixed with syrup and flour to make Indian pudding. It would take a goodly amount of the syrup to disguise the gritty taste of corn that had been stored in bushel baskets for many months.

I moved deeper into the shade and came upon the scarecrow, his head and shoulders peeking above the corn's silken tassels waving in the wind like citizens hailing their protecting king. He was in fact a lengthy baking paddle with a hickory branch lashed to the pole to make two arms. We clothed him with a pair of Father's aging breeches and coat, so ancient they had been worn on the crossing from old England. The jacket was a faded red woolen with turned-back cuffs of blue and a mended tear across the sleeve. Weeks before, I had come upon Father staring at the stick man as though at one long thought dead. The day had entered the long-shadow time that Father loved best, and, as he was at his ease, I braved asking him what he was thinking. Unmoving, he had answered, "I am remembering what I would forget. But a man's past is like his own shadow." After a time he felt my wondering gaze on him and nodded. "Go on, Sarah, ask your question."

"Is it a soldier's coat?" I asked.

"Aye," he answered quietly.

"Where did you fight that you received such a tear in it?" I asked, moving closer.

"Ireland." His answer surprised me, for I had thought him only a soldier in old England. "I went with Cromwell to fight Catholics."

I had heard enough in the meetinghouse to know that Catholics were idolaters and blood drinkers and were as evil as Lucifer himself. With a growing excitement I asked, "And did an Irish soldier give you that wound?" I pointed to his arm where I had seen the raised, puckered scar running like a snake from his elbow to wrist.

He shook his head, saying, "No. He was only a man defending his hearth and family."

Disappointed at the homeliness of his answer, I frowned and considered what else to ask him. When I raised my head to speak, he had already turned away, moving into the corn. The green stalks swished and crackled as they first parted, and then came together again behind his retreating form.

Strings of rattling shells hanging from the scarecrow's arms moved with the breeze and brought me back to the moment. Mother called the scarecrow a murmet, which had a more secretive sound. A scarecrow was a thing of bold-faced tactics, out in the full light of day. A "murmet," the "r" softly rolling against the tongue, spoke of murmuring stealth, as though it hunted marauding crows in the darkening twilight. It was the name that people who came from the south of England used. Places such as Devon, Basing, and Ramsey, where the old tongue was spoken.

I caught a glint of light and turned to see a giant web collecting dew like strung beads along its woven wheel of spider's silk. It must have taken a very long time to make such an intricate pattern, but though I looked long and hard, I could not find the weaver. Slowly and gracefully the beads of water slid downward along their silken paths, gathering for a moment at the bottommost part of the wheel and then dropping, forever lost, to the earth. It was like some wizard's hourglass counting off the minutes and hours of my days. For the briefest moment I thought I could catch the drops of water in my hand and stop the passing of time. I could stay in the sanctuary of this garden, my grandmother's garden, forever safe. I would not have to face days filled only with tasks that were never enlivened by laughter or the quick embrace that a whispered confidence would bring. A red wasp crawled across my hand and I froze lest he bury his stinger in my flesh. He was beautiful and frightful with his soulless black eyes and quivering barb and it came harshly to me that this garden was the world and from the world there could be no hiding.

I heard the striking of hooves on Boston Way Road but could not see the rider over the towering stalks. Following the sound, I picked my way back to the house, my apron sagging and ribbed with squash. When I came to the yard I saw Uncle riding Bucephalus and dropped the squash to the ground to wave to him. He was studying the fields, one hand cupped over his forehead, hiding his eyes against the light. The corners of his mouth pursed and turned downwards, as though he had chewed on something bitter. But when he saw me, he smiled cheerfully and called out, "Here, then, is my other twin."

I held tight his fingers and led him into the house like a prized captive. Mother had been stripping corn and stood quickly, shedding silk from her skirt in a storm of green and yellow. She did not like work-a-day surprises.

She frowned and asked, "What brings you to Andover, brother?"

Uncle replied, smiling, "Sister, it's been a long, hot ride. A glass of cool water would be welcome." When she turned her back for a cup, he winked at me. He drank quickly and said, "It appears you have prospered at your mother's house. How fares your homestead in Billerica?"

"You would know better than I, brother, as you have probably only just come from there. And as you see, we have been here in Andover working."

There was silence as they took the measure of each other, and then Uncle said, taking a different tack, as a ship will do when facing an imminent squall, "Mary sends her loving regards and hopes to visit soon . . . when the climate is not so heated."

"The weather here may stay hot for some time. But my sister is always welcome. It seems, though, that she may be the last one of your family who will come."

Uncle said, shaking his head, "I fear my son made bad a visit that I had hoped would bring us to greater felicity as a family."

Mother laughed through her nose. She stood at the table, her arms crossed below her chest, and said nothing.

"I was hoping," he continued carefully, "that we might come to an . . . agreement. Perhaps some sort of recompense regarding your mother's property. It was to Mary, and in turn to Allen, that the land was to go."

"All that has changed. On her deathbed my mother placed in our hands the care of the land. And this house."

"Be that as it may, as a physician I know full well what delusions may be brought about by a fever of the brain. It may be that your mother was not in her proper mind when she made those promises. Or perhaps her intentions were . . . misunderstood." He said the last without adding extra weight to the words, but it hit the mark nonetheless.

Mother uncrossed her arms and took on the look of a river mink poised over a trout bed. "It is of note to me that you would recall your claims as a physician. We could have put it to good use during the fourteen days I spent caring for my mother. Wiping the pus from her weeping sores and changing the bedclothes at every hour when she had the bloody flux. In truth, it surprises me you didn't hear her screams all the way to Billerica."

"Sarah," Uncle said, turning suddenly to me, "I have brought something for you from Margaret. Go and fetch it from my saddle."

I ran from the room into the yard and let Bucephalus sniff at my arm so that he would know me again. I reached into the saddle pack and pulled from it a small square of muslin. It had been cross-stitched in neat rows of letters surrounded by a colorful border. I brought the small bit of cloth to my face and breathed in Margaret's scent. She had only just touched the muslin, perhaps a few hours before. I read the letters carefully, teasing out the words from Proverbs. "A friend loves at all times." Of course she had not finished the verse, for it reads in sum, "A friend loves at all times, and a brother is born for adversity." A remembrance of Allen's sour face came to mind along with the smell of charring wheat. I sat on the doorstep with Margaret's sampler tucked into the bodice of my dress and listened to the muffled voices coming from the house. I could not hear the words but I could feel the thrust and weight of them, Uncle's placating voice countering the more strident tone of my mother. He worked like a potter trying to cool a hot mold of sand and potash into a vessel for use. But sometimes even the most careful of handling will bring the fiery vessel to shatter. I sat with my hands over my ears and waited for the inevitable sound of breaking glass.

Father then came from the fields, a large axe carried over one shoulder. He had been stockpiling wood, and his shirt was soaked through with sweat, his hair hanging damp and limp around his neck. He saw Uncle's horse and hurried his pace to the house. He gave me a glance but did not pause to set down the axe at the door frame as was his habit. As he passed through the door, the head of the axe caught the wood, cutting a deep gash in the frame. He had been inside for the span of a few breaths when all talking within ceased. Soon Uncle rushed out the door, stumbling over me in his haste to leave.

I followed him, calling out, "Uncle, please stay awhile. Uncle, please don't go," but he did not turn to answer me. I had had no time to gather up a present for Margaret. What would she think of me when her father returned to her empty-handed? I had not plied my fingers to sewing as I had promised, for the needle she had given me was gone, stolen by Mercy, and I could do no patching without it. The only needle left to me was a coarse one made of bone that was used to mend our woolens. Uncle mounted Bucephalus and snapped sharply at the reins. I ran at his boot heel, panting out, "Tell Margaret . . . tell Margaret . . ." But soon he outpaced me, and as I reached for the stirrup, I cried, "I am not like my mother . . . I am not like her!"

I watched him on the road until Mother called for me, but I dragged my heels until she appeared at the door, her eyebrows forming a line of warning beneath the furrows in her brow. When I came into the kitchen I saw Father's axe lying heavily on the table, the sharpened edge of the head pointing to the place where Uncle had stood.

THERE CAME A morning in September when Andrew, Tom, and I were together in the barn. I had been house-bound, smoking and drying meat for the winter, and had spent hour upon hour turning the spit. I became careless and singed the bottom of my skirt on the embers and could have within the span of a thought become a burning brand. Mother snatched me from the hearth, saying, "God's apron, Sarah, will you smoke us all out!"

She sent me to the barn with Hannah to set out a tray of milk for the mice that were eating our precious store of grain. The mice would come to drink and the cats that lived in the loft would have a breakfast of fur, teeth, and tail. I amused myself by watching both the tray of milk, hoping to see a bloody battle in miniature, and my sister's struggling form. I told myself I had tied Hannah to a post to save her from being kicked by the horse, but closer to the truth was my impatience with her clinging to me and the endless calling of my name. She thrashed against her tether but I drew a hard line and ignored her pleas to be lifted up and held once more. I could hear Tom working in the stalls, laying down new straw. With every forkful lifted, minions of dust devils spread through the air, making him sneeze in rapid pulses. He bent over double, hands on his knees, spewing spittle in cascading waterfalls. I numbered each successive fit, counting to nine, before hearing the outraged sound of my mother's voice coming from the edges of the cornfield. Andrew had just finished the milking and almost dropped the bucket from fright. Most times such vocal fury meant that someone was to get a beating.

The three of us ran from the barn, Tom carrying with him his pitchfork, sure that Mother was being set upon by Indians. As we followed her voice, we could not see at first what had angered her so. Her back was to us and she stood with her hands knotted on her hips. Then she turned and we saw a fawn-colored cow in the corn, calmly trampling down the stalks to get to the kernels. Behind her, looking shyly from large liquid eyes, was her calf. They had been in the field a good while, perhaps most of the morning, for they had broken down the remaining ears. The cow looked at Mother contentedly, the little brass bell on her ear tinkling faintly, and continued her chewing despite Mother's shouting and hand clapping. On the bell were carved the letters "S.P." Over the sound of the gently threshing hooves came the sounds of Hannah crying. Mother turned with pinched lips and a raised brow and said, "Sarah, go back to the barn and, after you have untied your sister, bring me the tether. And be fast. We will be paying a visit to Goodman Preston this morning."

Hurrying to the barn I gauged the time to sneak back to the house and take up a biscuit. We had not yet eaten, and my stomach had folded in on itself. I untied Hannah and, giving her over to Andrew, ran to the kitchen and tucked a biscuit into my apron. After a moment's thought I took yet another, as Mother's biscuits were hard to break in even parts and if I was clever and quick, I could eat a biscuit in secret while generously encouraging Mother to eat the whole of the other. The cow came willingly enough, as there was no corn left in our garden to eat, and I walked behind, using a stick to keep the calf apace with Mother's rapid stride. Samuel Preston was our neighbor to the south, below Chandler's Inn and Thomas Osgood's house on Preston's Plain. He was long established in the town, having ten acres, but he was careless with both family and livestock alike. In July Father had found one of Preston's cows in a bramble pit, her legs and udder torn to bloody ribbons by thorns. He worked her free and spent days salving her wounds with small beer and bear fat. She was returned to Samuel Preston whole but with her injured bag empty of milk. Goodman Preston gave little thanks, accusing us of keeping the cow those few days to take her milk for our own uses.

As we walked I broke small pieces of the biscuit hidden in my apron and put them into my mouth, keeping a close watch on my mother's determined form marching in front of me. The evening had been cool, laying a fog on the fields, but the sun was raising the billowing mists much as the swelling harbor tide effortlessly lifts an armada of ships. The trees and meadows were still a deep green, but here and there I could see tips of burnt yellow on the outermost branches of the oaks. Elm and ash arched and grew together tangled above the road, blotting out the light like the inverted bowl of a dark green cauldron. Cardinals and crows perched high in their waving green tents, rasping out warning calls. The fragrant air was like a warm, wet flannel on my skin, and I slowed my pace, dragging my shoes in the road to make dust angels. The sound of Mother's voice, humming a rare tune, rose up warm and throaty, and soon her pace slowed as well. She looked at the crisscrossing bower of branches and at the grasses underfoot and once glanced at me over her shoulder and smiled. Not a smile of unfettered joy, but a smile of pleasure nevertheless. She waited for me in the road and said, "Do you know what day it is, Sarah?"

I thought for a moment and answered, "It's a Tuesday. I think."

"It is the first day of autumn. The end of harvest. Ended sooner than expected," she said, patting the cow's hide. "What say we have a pudding for supper. There are eggs and a cone of sugar and you shall have licking rights. Would you like that?" Without waiting for an answer, she gave my chin a gentle cupping and then turned from me. It had been a very long time since we had had a pudding, and Mother almost always gave Father or Richard the dregs left inside the bowl. Some hardness within me loosed its grip, and had I been able to see my own face, I am sure I would have seen astonishment and gratitude in equal measures. She walked down the path at an easy pace and motioned with her hand to follow.

I watched from a distance her graceful form moving under the trees into shadow and light and shadow and light. There for an instant and then swallowed up by the darkness, seemingly disappeared from the world. My tongue swam in my mouth as I thought of scraping and licking the pudding bowl, and I decided to give some to Tom for a share of my chores. A jay called out from a lower branch, jittering and fluttering, his tail close enough to touch with my finger. The branch shifted and swayed with a breeze, veiling my face from the sun, and a feeling of dread touched the crown of my head. It poured itself down my brow, my neck, and shoulders, into my chest. My heart beat out fearful humors, enough to lift a tonnage of grain or scale a stone wall, and yet I could not move or call out.

The day had been so very lovely, the summering shades of plant and rock and sky showing the goodness, the reasonability of order, from the Master's hand. And yet with a shifting of sunlight, I had seen, as though looking into a killing pond, that beyond the restive landscape of the living, the Master stood poised, razor in hand, to cut and scrape away our delicate flesh, leaving only bone and weathered shell. My mother, as strong and hard as any young pine, was suddenly smaller and immensely more fragile. She walked purposefully onward, her forceful nature entwined with her very ribs. But what was that to the awesome power of a God who would at year's end slaughter off multitudes of the living to begin anew in the spring. And with that thought came the certainty that Mother would soon present herself to Samuel Preston and demand recompense. They would cross words, as the man was mean-spirited and argumentative, and she would give no quarter until she was paid in full, in barter, or in pieces of Goodman Preston's hide. And as certain as I was of my own name, I knew that he would somehow exact the final payment.

I beat the flanks of the jolting calf so it would move ahead more quickly. Remembering the biscuit in my apron, I thrust it out to her and said, "Mother, here. I brought this for you."

She looked at me with surprise but took the biscuit. She brought it to her lips but paused and, breaking it into two pieces, handed me half.

"I am not hungry," I said. "You must stay and eat. Please, can you not sit awhile?"

She shook her head and moved on, saying, "That was kind of you, Sarah, to remember me. But I can eat a biscuit and walk." She smiled and tossed over her shoulder, "Just as you have done this morning. Now, brush the crumbs from your face or our neighbor will think us unruly."

Goodman Preston refused to make good the ruined corn,

saying that he was no fool and that our crops were already harvested. His wife came to the open door of the house to listen, and I could see that her right eye had been blackened and was swollen, so that the lids were shut together. His children stood about, all white of hair, all dirty and wild-looking. Mother called him "a mean, tightfisted badger who would try to pass a Dutch pound of grain for a hundredweight and who would melt down the lead cover to his well to make a profit even if it meant all five of his children were to fall in." Having never before encountered my mother's play with words, he was made speechless for a time.

But he soon recovered and called her "a black-faced waspish harpy in the shape of a woman whose breast must be filled with bile to flail an honest yeoman so and who would just as soon fry up and eat a man's liver as stay at home and eat maple sugar."

When he saw he could not drive her away with the sound of his voice, he clenched his fist as though to strike her. Mother then raised over her head the long thorny stick she had used to prod the cow. I don't think, until that moment, a woman had ever met his anger without a bowed head and a curved back. It so disturbed his expectations that he took a few steps backwards. I reached down to pick up a stone and, judging the distance to his head, stood nearer to Mother. She simply waited until he had paused to breathe and then said sharply, "Samuel Preston, the next cow that wanders onto our land will be ours in recompense. And from the look of things, we won't have to wait long before you lose another one." She gazed into the one good eye of his wife, still standing at the door, and said, "Take heed to take better care of what's yours or what's yours will sicken and die."

She turned and walked away, leaving the cow and her calf standing in the yard. I carried the stone the whole of Boston Way Road and would have carried it into the house but for Mother barring the door. She reached out for my fingers and saw the stone clenched within. Placing one hand beneath mine, she bounced it slightly as though measuring the strength of it. Then, with her other hand, she gently closed my fingers back over the glittering weight of the stone.

IN EARLY AUTUMN, there came a cooling at night. The fireflies, their mating done, danced crazily about the fields, much as people will do during the bonfire nights of the Plague, knowing that a black wind is soon to come to kiss them with an unremembered death. There was ample rain, and at dawn the garden mists yielded crops of pumpkins, turnips, and onions. The lentil pods swelled and spilled their seeds over the ground. Bunches of purslane grew close by, their reddish stems and yellow flowers showing like the sun against the drab gray of the house. The wild game were so plentiful, they seemed to throw themselves into the pot. Father would often return from hunting with his belt heavy with quail or heath hens. Once he dragged into the yard a turkey as big as Tom, and it took Mother and me an afternoon to pluck him naked. Within one week Father brought down two deer. The meat was cut thin and salted over a slow fire to cure. And during the long winter months, the strips would be soaked in water with berries and cornmeal and made fit for the tongue with savories gathered from the woods.

Father warned us never to go on our gathering walks without Richard following behind with the flintlock. But I often found ways to escape through the surrounding meadows and woods alone or with Tom, if I could persuade him to come. The safety offered by Richard's aim was a poor exchange for his dull talk and surly looks. He had no patience for our adventures and made us keep to the path.

We picked Queen Anne's lace along the banks of the Skug River and traveled farther east to gather apples from an old orchard. The apples were little and dry, and Mother called them Blaxton's yellow sweetings after the man who had brought them from England many years before. There were a dozen pips in every core and Richard told us if we swallowed any of them, an apple tree would sprout from our heads. Poor Andrew, who since his illness believed everything he was told, would always, if he swallowed a pip, spend hours feeling the hollows of his ears for branches. All through October the animals wild and tame grew fat and sleek as did we from our stores of food. The bounty of our larder, the clement weather, the surplus for barter should have given me peace. Yet I could not rid myself of pestering violent thoughts. The wind would blow down our roof, or the well would turn to poison, or one of us would slip and fall on the axe. And I could not forget the blanket of doom that had fallen over me the day we returned the cow to the Preston farm. It was with no satisfaction that I met my brutal expectations in the person of Mercy Williams.

I had seen her every Sabbath at the meetinghouse. She now

sat with Phoebe Chandler, the innkeeper's daughter, but she never looked at us or acknowledged us in any way. Phoebe was eleven years old and comely in a bland sort of way. Her sight was weak, though, and she often lifted her chin and squinted her eyes to better see. Her two top teeth stuck out past her lips, causing her to look like a beaver crossing a high creek with a stick in its mouth. One Sunday the Reverend Dane gave us the 19th psalm, "The law of the Lord is perfect, reviving the soul." His kind eyes took in every face seated before him, no doubt believing in the goodness of his congregation. Upon the closing prayers we poured out into a day made perfect with honeyed light and a brisk wind tempering the heat of morning. I was closed in among the press of women when I felt a sharp little jab in my back and then again quickly in my right buttock. I cried out and turned to see Mercy, her hands crossed in front of her stomach, her face an empty page. Phoebe standing next to her stifled a fit of laughter with one hand held over her mouth. I wanted to wrestle Mercy to the ground and pry from her fingers the stolen needle she had used to stab me. I gave her an evil look and pushed my way rudely past the women in front of me, then stood outside waiting for Tom and Andrew, as Mother walked ahead with a crying Hannah, to climb into the cart.

Soon Mercy and Phoebe came into the yard, whispering and casting me glances. I moved away from them and into the shade of the trees growing around the burying grounds, which fronted the meetinghouse. They followed me into the shade and came close enough that I would not miss their words.

Mercy said, "Don't you think red hair an ugly color on a girl?" Phoebe hiccupped a small bit of laughter, and Mercy continued. "I've always thought it so. The Indians would kill outright a redheaded girl, so ugly did they think the color."

I crossed my arms over my chest and pretended not to hear, but something in her tone made my heart beat faster. At that moment Mary Lacey appeared next to Mercy and knew in an instant who was predator and who was prey, like a hound that late joins a chase.

Mercy turned to Mary and said, "I have only just said to Phoebe that redheaded girls are too ugly to live."

"You would know ugly, Mercy, as you have lived in that house all your life." I said the words carelessly but knew at that instant I should have better governed my tongue.

Mary and Phoebe turned first to look at Mercy and then, without a trace of pity, turned to me to wait for the gathering storm. Mercy glanced briefly over her shoulder and saw that most of the congregation had returned to their wagons. The four of us were a good distance from where my family waited. She then moved towards me and, remembering her ability to toss Richard to the ground, I stepped backwards. I did not see anger in her face; only a calm deadness that made me want to turn and run and signaled more danger than any amount of scowling or puffing about. I began to walk quickly around them but Mercy grabbed me viciously by the back of the neck and pulled me down onto her lap, holding me tightly about the arms so that I could not move to stand. Her broad back rested against a burial stone for leverage and Mary and Phoebe came to stand behind us, spreading their skirts much as a curtain is drawn to hide something unpleasant. Mercy bent close and bit my ear, not enough to bring blood but enough to hurt.

She whispered to me, "Cry out and I will bite it off in earnest." I had no doubt that she would not only bite it off but swallow it whole.

I said loudly, "You smell like a sump hole."

She tightened her grip on me and said to the others, "Best be careful of this one. The Indians say a redheaded girl is a witch. Her mother is a witch. It's true. I heard her conjuring down lightning. And she changed the course of the wind carrying fire from her fields and onto Henry Holt's fields. And she cured a cow's festering udder faster than you can say 'teat.' "

"The only witch in Andover is you," I said, trying to free myself. Her arms squeezed harder, bruising my ribs, making it difficult to draw a breath.

Mary spoke up eagerly, "Timothy Swan says he was given a foul look by Martha Carrier upon her first visit to the meeting-house and has not been well since."

Phoebe put her toe in the water by saying, "My father says that Roger Toothaker has been to the inn many times and that Goody Carrier has cheated him out of the house meant for his son. He says that she cursed at him and has since had an old scar on his belly open up and fester."

The words stung me as though I had fallen into a field of nettles. Mary leaned farther over the stone to whisper loudly, "I have spoken with Allen Toothaker about this very thing. He lives now with Timothy Swan as he has no place to call his own. Allen says that his aunt is the foulest woman to draw a breath."

Now Phoebe had the course of the stream and she jumped in with both legs. "I heard my father just these weeks past talk of

Benjamin Abbot. He has a house on the far side of the Shaw-shin. Well, Goodman Abbot crossed words with Goody Car-rier. He was putting up a stone fence, minding his own business, when she assaulted him, saying he would soon wish he had not meddled with that land so near her house. She shook her fist at him and said she would stick as close to him as bark on a tree and that he would repent of it before seven years came to an end. Furthermore, she said she hoped he would fall so ill that Dr. Prescott could never cure him." One would have thought her tongue was licking honey off a stick the way it waggled about.

"What should we do with this one, do you think?" Mercy craned her neck up at the girls hanging over the gravestone like a pair of gargoyles.

"I say we stuff her mouth with dirt," Mary offered, all but jumping up and down and clapping her hands.

"Tie her fast to the stone first," said Phoebe.

Mercy dug her nails into my shoulders, drawing blisters, and said calmly, "I say we bury her in one of the graves."

I heard my name being called from the meetinghouse yard. Mary hissed to Mercy, "Here comes the Reverend Dane. Best let her go."

My name was called again, closer this time. Mary called out, "She is here, Reverend Dane. She is with us." And then to Mercy, "For heaven's sake, let her go."

Mercy bent to my ear again and whispered into it as softly as any lover, "Remember the story of Robert Rogers and the Indi-ans who skinned him? How they tied him to the stake after he had died? I lied. Robert Rogers was alive when they burned him. Speak one word of this and I will come to you some night and burn you alive in your bed." Then she pushed me roughly off her lap and stood brushing the leaves from her skirt. She faced the Reverend and smiled, saying, "Sarah fell running through the stones. We were helping her upright."

She extended her hand to me, which I ignored, but I did not miss the look that followed like a fiery tail trailing a comet. The Reverend walked back with me to the waiting cart and stood waving to us until we had passed beyond the bending oaks gating the old burial ground. Behind him at a distance were three skirted figures who did not wave but stood close together, impassive and watchful.

TRUE AUTUMN CAME at the end of October, and while the days were yet warm, the evenings grew cooler until the earth put forth an old moldering smell like a sodden blanket or the sharp tang of mint crushed in a glass. The sky in early morning and late afternoon would darken with the passing of carrier pigeons, too numerous to count, on their way southward. Their departure left me sad, as though my true namesakes were abandoning me to another season of cold and unbearable gravity. The waxing and waning of dying embers in the hearth at eventide brought about wakeful visions of places dark and primitive. In my dreams at night I slipped my earthly bonds and flew to those same places, waking in the morning with a cramped and yearning pain in my chest. The visions filled my head until I grew agitated and restless and wandered sullen about the house. The only respite I found was to stand on Sunset Rock, sniffing at the air blowing westerly the thirty miles from Boston Bay, inhaling the last bits of sea foam descending over the salted wastes of Cat Swamp.

I found a shard of crude pottery in the garden near the well and held it in my hand, marveling at the painted markings snaking their way across the length of it. It was very old, worn by years of weather and the action of the earth over its curved form. It was striped with tiny grooves, and I scratched my fingernail over them, hoping to bring forth the sound of its maker from the clay, much as a finger will pluck the strings of a fiddle to bring music. I looked for Father and found him oiling with bear grease two sprung beaver traps that had belonged to my grandfather. He would set them on the southern fork of the Shawshin and harvest any pelts for a new cone of sugar, enough to last us the winter. When I showed him the piece of clay, he held it for a moment and said, "This was not made by Narragans or Abanak. They have no wheel to make such."

"Who made it, then, Father?" I asked, feeling the chill of holding a thing ancient as the dirt below my feet.

He rubbed his knotted fingers over the pitted face of the clay and said, "Some as came before the Indian and are no more. The history of the world is such, Sarah. To build upon the bones of those who have come before. Thus it will ever be."

That night as I lay in bed, I knew I would give the shard to Margaret. I could not make a gift fine enough to match hers. But I could give her something that was strange and wonderful and rare. I closed my eyes to sleep and dreamt I was wandering lost through a cornfield. I could hear Margaret calling to me, but wherever I followed the voice, it retreated into the stalks.

The voice at last led me to the lip of a well and called up from the depths of the water below. Lying on the lip of the well was the glistening fragment of clay, wet as though risen up from the shaft. The voice floating from the well shifted and changed. It was no longer Margaret but some other girl, calling and calling. I walked to the very edge of the well and peered into the violet shadows and saw, reflected in the dark pool below, my own face. I woke, my face slick with tears, my chest an empty cask.

From that morning a growing resentment started to swell in my chest. I formed a hard and embittered resolution that my mother was responsible for all my losses. Because of her selfishness I was taken from Uncle's family. Because of her ungovernable anger Uncle would not return to our house, perhaps refusing his family to visit as well. Because of her acid tongue our neighbors talked ill of us and gossiped freely in their homes and in Chandler's Inn. I even worked my mind around Mercy's towering deficiencies of character, overlooking her scheming and stealing and bullying, to blame Mother for turning the girl out of the house. Darkest of all were the grudges for the loss of my grandmother, as though my mother through neglect contributed to her death. And when I could no longer hold in my fury, I let out a long, despairing cry. So astonished was she by my wailing, she dropped the braided bunch of onions she was hanging over the hearth to dry. I stood facing her, my fists balled tight at my hips, and screamed, "Why must you take everyone I love away from me?"

Without a word, she picked up her cloak and beckoned for me to follow her out of the house. Expecting a beating, and a short return to the house, I did not wear my cloak, and the cool morning breeze licked at the sweat on my lip like a dog licking a salt wheel. Now it comes, I thought. She is finally to murder me and leave my bones in the fields.

With a glowering face I followed her, walking up and over the elevated path behind the house and through the long har-vested fields towards Robert Russell's farm. Then I thought, She is going to leave me with Robert Russell, and I will be made servant in his house. But we at length passed by his house and turned south into the forest of pine surrounding Gibbet Plain. I could hear a cardinal calling out, "Quit-it, Quit-it, Quit-it-now," and I suddenly regretted leaving without my cloak, as the wind had turned cooler, ruffling the hair along my arms. I trudged behind Mother, picking her way confidently through the spaces between the trees, and wondered if she would walk all the way to Reading with me in tow. We broke through some branches of thinly spaced fir and entered onto Gibbet Plain. It was a giant meadow, graced with clusters of trees watered on three sides: the Skug River to the east, Foster's Pond to the west, and a swamp to the south that no one had named, as it was believed to be haunted by those who had been hanged there. I looked at the vast spread of green and yellow grasses, some growing knee high, and my mood lifted despite my efforts to anchor it down with crossed arms and a clenched jaw.

Mother said, "I used to come here with Mary when I was a girl." I realized that she meant Margaret's mother, Aunt Mary, but it was hard to think of my restrained mother as a girl gam-boling through a field. "The first time I saw the meadow," she continued, "was when your grandmother brought me here. I was

about your age, maybe a bit younger. I had been for a while angry with her, over what I cannot now remember, and I had made
myself ill from it. I could not eat nor sleep and would pace the
house just as I have seen you do. My mother brought me here
and said to me, 'This one time, until you are grown, you may
say whatever you wish to me. Whatever anger you have stored
against me or the world you can speak it to me and I will not
chastise you or punish you nor reveal to another living soul
what you have said.' "

She paused here and turned her face to the light of the sun,
closing her eyes to its warmth. "She told me that hoarding anger
is like hoarding grain in a lidded rain barrel. The dark and the
dank will cause the seeds to sprout but the lack of light and air
will soon force the grain to spoil. So I told her my resentments
and my complaints, such as they were, and she listened to me.
When we left this field, she was good to her word and we never
again talked of those things. But I was unburdened and it brought
more harmony between myself and my mother."

She opened her eyes and her gaze turned to me in a questioning way. For a moment we looked at each other without speaking, but I knew for what she waited. She waited for me to reveal
all of *my* angry thoughts, but I did not open my mouth to speak.
I did not believe she had enough of Grandmother's sympathies
to be kind to my disappointments or painful losses. And if
there had been such harmony created, what had happened all
those years later to cause Grandmother to lock her daughter out
of her own house for a time? But there was something else as
well, something deeper that I could not confess: my fervent
prayers to be returned to Margaret and her family. As much

rage as I had felt in my mother's presence, I could not admit to her that I had wished her dead. So I continued to stare off into the waving grasses, making my back as rigid as my mother's ever was. She sighed in a way that was both tired and accepting and she said, putting equal emphasis on each word, "You are so very hard."

"You have made me so," I said bitterly.

"No, Sarah. This hardness is native born." She placed herself in front of me and said softly, "But I have done little to tender it." I turned my back to her, unbalanced by her sudden gentleness, and the grasses swam like kelp through the tears I would not let fall.

"Do you think I don't know what it is that you want?" she said impatiently, and I expected the burn of her fingers on my arm, but she did not touch me. She kept her distance and then said tightly, "And so we are to keep our disharmony a while longer. Then you and I will talk of petty things." She started to walk about, aimlessly, I thought, looking down at the ground, kicking away bits of scattered limbs or piles of fallen leaves. She knelt down, her dark skirt pooling around her legs, and uncovered something white growing under a bit of bark. She called for me to come, and I walked reluctantly to stand at her shoulder and saw that she had found a mushroom. I had been mushroom hunting many times with her before. Hunting morels in May in the wild-apple orchard, gathering chicken mushrooms growing in stacks upon the trunks of elm and ash during the hot summer months, and picking devil's snuffbox along the banks of the Skug River. Mushroom hunting was a slippery task, though. You had to know the differences between the healthful mushrooms and the unhealthful ones. Some of the differences were slight indeed. A bit of carelessness, and death could come hiding under a milky dome or a purple gill.

"Do you know what this is?" Mother asked, taking off her cap to let her black hair blow free.

"A meadow mushroom," I answered, trying to sound as uninterested as possible.

"Are you certain?" To which I nodded, crossing my arms again.

I released a short, impatient breath. Meadow mushrooms could be eaten fresh from the ground. They had a strong musk-like flavor with a dense flesh. A dozen or so could be boiled together with a bouillon of dried fat to make pocket soup, and meat lacking for the stew would not be missed. The white cap was about three inches across, dry and smooth, and it had a short stem.

"Yes," I said, "a meadow mushroom."

"Eat, then," said Mother, gesturing for me to take it.

The well of my mouth overflowed as I squatted down to pluck it from its shallow root. A weak amends, I thought as I opened my mouth to receive the offering. The iron grip of her hand clamped down on my wrist and held my hand a few inches from my tongue. Her face was close to mine and for the first time I saw that her hazel eyes had equal shares of blue and amber coloring in them.

"Sarah, look underneath the cap," she said as she forced my wrist around, exposing the underside of the mushroom. The gills were white and the mushroom had a white skirtlike ring on the stem just below the cap. "It is called a destroying angel. If you were to eat this, you would surely die. Not today and perhaps not tomorrow. But after four days of spitting every bit of water from your belly and your ass, you would welcome your death."

She released me and I threw the mushroom from my hand as I would have released an oiled rush torch. I wiped both of my hands on my apron.

"The signs are varied and subtle. You must look carefully, not just at the top of the thing but at its underside, where the poison often gathers. The meadow mushroom when early has pink gills that turn to brown upon maturity. If you didn't know the lore, you would liken the dark underside to unwholesomeness and the light underbelly to goodness. The morel can be dark but it is always pitted, whereas the false morel is dark but smooth. That which is scarred and pitted in nature can mean sustenance and life, whereas a smooth and pretty skin can mean destruction and death. People, too, are not often what they seem, even those whom you love. You must look closely, Sarah."

The warmth from the sun, the gentle cooling breeze, the velvet moths floating past my head all seemed at odds with my mother's words. My wrist ached from her touch, and I wanted her to let us go home. But she would not stop her lecturing.

"You love your cousin and my sister and that is the natural course of things. But you also have a great love for your uncle, and he is a man not worthy of that love. He is one who appears outwardly all smooth, all right with his fellows, when inwardly his heart is filled with poison. If he could, he would turn you out of your house in the time it took to take off his boots, and where he goes, his family follows. He has done it before, long ago, when he cheated your father and me out of land that was rightfully ours. Your uncle talks from two sides of his mouth and works even now to destroy our standing in Andover."

Thoughts of Uncle's misdirection performing his bits of magic rose up in my head, but I would not be put off him and said under my breath, "You need no help in that regard." I steeled myself, waiting for the slap to my face. She rocked back on her heels, her arms about her knees, as though *I* had slapped *her*. In that moment of surprise, with her widening eyes and parted lips, she appeared somehow younger, more unguarded. But her gaze darkened, the amber in her eyes consuming the blue, and she looked at me for so long a time, it made me lower my eyes and bite the inside of my lip. A cardinal sounded again his "Quit-it, Quit-it" and was answered in kind across the field. She opened her mouth once to make a sharp retort but closed it again, and I could see that it stung her to swallow her words, like swallowing a thistle that had been stirred into a plate of greens.

"There is an old saying," she said as she idly plucked at some weedlike runners about her skirt, "and it is as true now as ever it was. It goes 'If not for king, then for county. If not for county, then for clan. If not for clan, then for my brother. If not for my brother, then there is naught but home.' Do you understand what I am trying to tell you?"

"If you mean that I am to give up my love for Margaret because you have a quarrel with Uncle, I will not do it. And you cannot beat it out of me. Margaret is everything to me." My voice had risen, and I realized that against my wishes she had worked me around to speaking my mind.

Mother looked away as one would do coming upon a naked stranger and waited until I had tucked my despair behind my anger again. Then she said strongly, "Loyalty to your family must come first. Loyalty always to your family." She stared at the mists burning themselves off the swampy bogs to the south and spoke softly. "You will be ten years of age come November and are leaving the age of childhood for womanhood. But it is not as easy as stepping over a threshold. It is more like traveling a long corridor. I had hoped today you and I could . . . come to a place of understanding. Still you and I stand at odds. So be it. But there is one thing I must tell you. Something that is painful."

Her words had taken an interesting turn, and I hoped to be initiated into a deeper understanding of the bit of business that had come close to making Mercy a shamed woman. She had chosen the time and the place well, for I knew that a mushroom was often likened to a man's root. I had seen such a root on my brothers and was unimpressed. Tom and Richard were too modest to reveal themselves willingly to me, but tight quarters make for revelations. Andrew had lost his modesty along with his wits and so he did not try to hide himself when he made water in the fields or behind the barn. Upon observing the poor, pale thing, I could not imagine such an organ could bring much pain at all to a woman or hold much interest beyond its ability to provide the spark for growing a babe in her belly.

But what she said, to my great disappointment, was "Life is not what you have or what you can keep. It is what you can bear to lose. You may have no choice but to give her up."

"No." I stood up, the tendons in my legs cracking with the

tension of wanting to escape her insistent harping. I blinked a few times, waiting for her to continue, but she had fallen silent. The sun shone full on her face, and I could not mistake the look she gave me. More cruel than anger, more terrible than pride, more painful even than regret, it was the look of pity. Without another word she rose to her feet, put on her cap, and started walking. The sun had slipped behind a bank of rolling clouds and the air suddenly chilled and moved the grasses about.

I saw at my feet a lone birdfoot violet quivering in the wind. The violet was a spring flower but would sometimes, if the days were kind, bloom again in the autumn. Soon the flower would wither and die alone in the coming frost, its beauty disappearing under the first snowfall. I hurried after her, not wanting to be left behind so close to the swamp. The next time I would see Gibbet Plain with my mother would be under the dark of a new moon, and the surrounding earth would be in the full bloom of spring. The day would be a Monday, May 30th, 1692, and the trout lily, nodding and speckled, would be growing in the forests, and the stargrass, with their winsome yellow blossoms, would be growing on the great meadow. But the day-blooming bloodroot flower, one of my mother's favorites for its beauty and healing powers, would be shut up tight, as though it feared to hear my mother's secrets.

NOVEMBER BLUSTERED IN, wet and full of gloom. The days had been too warm to force the leaves to brilliant color, and so the world turned to gray. The weather became cool enough for Father to build a large smoking pit to cure the game he had killed. A long trench was dug in the ground for cold storage of late autumn apples and wild berries. Straw would line the pit, then a layer of apples, then more straw, and finally dirt to cover it. Andrew had been charged with planting markers so that when it snowed, the fruit could be easily found. With great care he stuck in a dozen or so crosses until Mother made him replace them all with simple pikes, as she said it made the mound of dirt look like the aftermath of some bloody battle. Andrew cried and carried on, confusing the fruit buried under the dirt with a buried corpse. He had counted and recounted all of us, certain that one of his family was dead until we gently reminded him to count himself, giving him the comforting number of seven living souls. The yearling hog that Mother had bartered for had grown fat and was slaughtered without too much complaining on his part. Indeed, at first I was sorry to watch him butchered, as he had been docile and showed himself to be clever by coming to us when called to be fed. But if truth be told, my mouth watered when I thought of a portion of his fat little hindquarters finding its way to my mouth.

Robert Russell was to come and share with us a meal to honor the end of the autumn fieldwork and the hopeful beginning of a winter without want. He was to bring with him his niece, Elizabeth Sessions. In the ancient manner of things, he had helped us through the plowing and harvesting, and Father had in turn helped Robert with his. It was then that I learned of Richard's inclinations after he returned one afternoon to the house, dripping water from his hair and skin like a dog from a dousing. When I asked him if he had fallen into the Shawshin, he scowled and told me to go away. Tom whispered that Richard had actually bathed himself, stripping off his shirt and breeches and jumping into the river wearing only his short hose. This was potent ammunition for teasing him about his affections for Elizabeth and worth the bruises I received on both arms.

On the morning of the feast day Mother sent us all from the house so she could sweep and scrub the dirt from the floor. Tom had fashioned a bow out of pine bough and catgut, the arrows from stripling hardwood, and feathers from an eider duck. We hid behind the barn, not because his bow was forbidden but because the bow's objects surely would be. He had mastered the primitive targets we had drawn on a wooden plank and all of the smaller animals had long since found a nesting place underground. What was left for us to practice on came in the persons of Hannah and Andrew, who would wear on their heads a kind of straw tower, tall enough to draw the aim of the arrow away from the top wearer's head. I counseled Tom to imagine the tower as the neck of a deer raising its head to test the wind. A well-placed arrow in the neck could bring down a buck of any size better than a wound at the ribs or rump. We quickly discounted Hannah as she could not hold herself quiet and kept stooping down or moving away from her place, toppling the tower to the ground. Andrew proved much more cooperative and even willing to stand very still and straight, patiently waiting for Tom to take aim. Tom nocked his arrow and pulled back a bit, saying to Andrew, "Now for pity's sake, don't dare move 'til after I have hit the target or you'll be wearing that tower for all eternity."

At that moment Mother called for us to come back to the

house, and I think Andrew would be standing there even now had I not taken his hand and told him it was time to go in. In the kitchen Mother gave me a bucket and bid me go to Chandler's Inn for small beer. She tied a few precious coins in a little bag and knotted it tight to my apron. William Chandler would take barter for his room and board but not for his spirits. He had to pay coin to the shipper in Boston and so demanded payment in kind at his door. Most times it was Father who went to the inn for the beer, but he had left before dawn to check his traps at the river, and if we were fortunate, we would have fried beaver tails with pork for our supper.

As I walked the short distance down the main road to the inn, I remembered hearing Richard say to Father that in Boston, there was a new drink from the Caribee sold in the taverns to sailors who made port there. It was called "rum" and was wickedly stronger than beer. Father then told Richard that the surest way to awaken on a ship far out to sea was to drink this rum until you were made senseless, easy pickings for the impress men. I matched my steps to the little marching tempo I sang, "rum, rum, rum, rum . . . rum, rum, rum, rum."

Within a short while I entered the yard at the inn and saw Phoebe Chandler struggling to lift a full bucket of water just drawn from the well. I stood by for a time, enjoying the wrestling and jerking about of the heavy ropes, hoping she would fall in before she cleared the bucket over the lip of the well. She was resting on the edge of the stones, catching her breath, when she looked up and saw me. It must have seemed that I appeared from out of thin air and she started with fright. With an ugly look she ran to the inn, slamming a side door as she entered.

I followed, entering by the front door as if I were queen of the world. Inside all was dark, the smell of roasting meat feathering my nose as well as the fruity ripeness of a tripe gone over, or a fish poorly smoked. Goody Chandler was a thrifty cook and would throw back into the pot any entrails or head soup left on a patron's plate. In this way she would ensure enough food to feed her visitors from Sabbath to Sabbath.

The common room was like a small cavern, smogged and musty, with a generous fire burning in the hearth. Men sat about the few tables, eating their noonday meal, and seated closest to the hearth was a figure I knew well. His face was in profile, the high domed forehead etched in sharp relief by the glow of the fire. And leaning over him to give drink was Mercy Williams. As she poured beer from a pitcher into Uncle's cup, one of his fingers brushed lightly over her bodice where her nipple would be. The gesture could have been accidental, the chance collision of flesh against wool. But I saw the crooked smile on Mercy's face and knew that she had invited it. Phoebe slipped into the room from her mother's kitchen and looked about with eyes squinted against the murky light. As Mercy straightened to stand, she tucked the pitcher onto her hip and looked directly at me, as though she had known all along I had been standing in the shadows. Goody Chandler came into the room with a rag in her hands, and from the way her lips pursed and her eyes narrowed, I could see that Mercy had been making batches of her own fermenting noisome brew.

Men are always the last to ken what women know by sniffing the air. That's why God gave bodily might to Adam, to balance the inequities in strength. For if Eve had been given the power to serve her cunning and cruelty, there would have been a terrible reckoning for all mankind, and the archangel would have trod on Adam's heels to escape paradise unsinged. The three of them stared me down for a time, until one of the men remembered his empty belly and called for more food. Uncle turned to me, his face red from drink and the heat of the fire, and his smile disappeared. He raised a finger and pointed at me, jabbing the air like a sword, and said, "I am watching you. I am watching you all."

Mercy took a few steps closer and said, "What do you want here?" A corner of her brown dress had worked its way up, showing the tiniest bit of crimson underskirt. As she walked nearer, I saw that the dress had been pinned up with the needle she had stolen from me. The needle pinned back the darker fabric, holding the overskirt aloft as if it had been raised by some little breeze or some misstep as she paced the common room floor. I had seen the likes of such red drapery on Margaret's poppet. And I knew then what Uncle had done with the cloth he had taken from his wife.

I held up the bucket and said to Goody Chandler, "I have come for small beer." She took the bucket and the coins and disappeared into the kitchen. Mercy drew her arm around Phoebe's shoulders and, whispering into her ear, pulled her to the back of the room, ignoring the men's calls for service. Goody Chandler soon returned with the bucket filled with a rich soapy broth and held the door for me as I left. Most likely to lock it behind my back.

Low, skittering clouds had started a misting rain and I pulled the lid tight over the bucket, pulling the shawl closer about my head. Passing the yard, I saw Phoebe standing at the side door, Mercy hanging about her neck. I turned my back to them and had walked no more than twenty paces when a piece of the sky fell on the back of my head, knocking me to my knees. The bucket dropped without breaking, and lying next to it was a stone the size of my fist. Had it grazed my naked skull, it would have peeled away part of my skin and with it a braid of hair. They stood motionless next to the well, Phoebe still holding a stone in her hand. I reached behind my ear and felt a tender knot rising beneath my hand. The spiced and gummy air, filled with rain and dust, turned to the flooding coppery tincture of blood. I had bitten my lip and drops of red spackled the ground in gentle wavering patterns. My fingers closed around the soaking leaves littering the yard like remnants from a pagan wedding, and I remembered from Uncle's stories that every pagan ceremony ended in sacrifice. I also remembered my mother's words, "If not for my brother, then there is naught but home." Uncle had given me up for a lathered and slatternly whore, and I felt the hope of seeing Margaret again diminishing to a thing as small and hard as the shard of pottery I had found in the garden.

I heard Mercy say, "Go on . . . go on . . . ," and Phoebe walked closer, squinting and grimacing to better see, expecting the vague crouching form in front of her to cower and cry, as this was what she would have done. What she did not expect was a raging creature in the guise of a child, shawl flying behind it like the wings of some predatory bird, spitting and foaming. Startled, she dropped her only weapon and had but a moment for a squall of protest before I dragged her to the ground and raked my nails across her bland and milky face. I grabbed at her cap, pulling savagely, and parted her from clumps of her hair before Mercy came from behind and boxed my ears. I threw myself then at Mercy, kicking and biting, inflicting as much damage as I could, knowing she would soon throw me to the ground. I kicked both her shins and bit the web of her hand so deeply that she carried the half-moon scar for the rest of her life. What saved my head was the ample bulk of Goody Chandler tearing us apart as though she would cleft sin from salvation.

She screamed as she pushed me away, "You are a devil to fight so. Look, see what you have done to my daughter!"

Phoebe lay on the ground, her arms flung over her head, squealing like a titmouse caught in the jaws of a black snake. Some of the men had come to the door to witness the thrashing, and among them was Uncle, holding a cup in his hand.

Picking up my bucket, I said to Mercy, who was sucking on the wound in her hand, "I hope it rots until every finger on your thieving hand falls off."

I turned to go, but the folds of wool wrapped around my neck were not enough to stop the sound of Mercy's voice, hard and carrying. "You all heard," she said. "She cursed me. She has a witching way. But why else? She is her mother's daughter."

Before I entered the house, I sat in the yard, rubbing my head. The skin on my skull knocked painfully with the rhythm of my heart, and one shoulder felt bruised and tender. The palms of my hands were scraped from falling and I gently brushed at the dirt in the wounds. Perhaps it was true that I was like my mother, as everyone seemed to think so. Perhaps the very desire to set myself apart from her proved that I, in

fact, had her contrary nature. I was not pretty and quick like
Margaret or bland and pliable like Phoebe Chandler. There
was a glittering hardness about me like mica and I thought of
my fingers wrapped around the rock I had carried against
Samuel Preston. Camp dogs will fight and tear at one another
for days until a stranger comes too close to the fire, and then
they will turn as one and attack the intruder. And the world
was full of intruders.

But I did not yet want Mother to know what had happened.
I could not bear the knowing look that said, "You see, I was
right about your uncle." I looked down at the bucket and saw it
had not spilled much. My dress was torn under the arms, but I
could say I had slipped and fallen and so pass scrutiny. I had to
calm the beating of my heart, for just as Mother was keen in
knowing the changes in the weather, so was she clever in finding
out my hidden thoughts. The best way to escape notice was to
stay close to my brothers. I would lose myself in the mix and fray
of their clattering movement and become like a board piece in a
game of Nine Man Morris, a game that my father loved well.
The goal was to line up three pins in a row, jumping your opponent's pins quickly and with a great show of confidence, confusing
and weakening the other player. The winner was the one to remove all of his opponent's pieces first. It was a game of cunning
and forethought, but the key to winning was to keep moving.

No one that night regarded my torn dress, although Mother
asked me, as she scrubbed at the wounds in my hands, if I had
fallen into a ravine. But I was soon forgotten in the press of
welcome as Robert and his niece appeared, and from that time
until late we stuffed ourselves with suckling pig and flat cakes.

Father had trapped two beavers, and we had their tails on a cast-iron platter, shimmering and bubbling in rivers of their own fat. We ate ribs of smoked venison, cracking open the bones with our fingers to suck out the rich marrow. And when we were full to bursting, Mother brought out a pasty she had made with sugar and wild rhubarb that was both sweet and sour together. Richard sat awkwardly with Elizabeth on a bench by the fire, both too drowsy and shy to speak.

I fell to sleep with my head on the table and was carried to bed, my hands sticky and red from the rhubarb. I woke once during the night and remembered it was the 17th of November and that I was then ten years old. I felt under my pillow for Margaret's sampler wrapped around the pottery piece. I crept out of bed and softly climbed the stairs to the attic, careful not to wake my brothers, and placed both the cloth and the shard in the bottom of my grandmother's trunk. I closed the trunk and felt my way, shivering, back to bed.

Winter came in hard and fast towards cock's crow. I could hear the rising wind rushing in like a maid late for her own wedding, the snapping and rustling hem of her skirt scattering snow and ice across the frozen ground. Sleep soon found me, and when I woke again, the drifts of snow were so deep as to shrink the boundaries of our world to house and barn.

It was one of the coldest winters in many years, and it spread from our new world to England and from there to the countries of the Dutch and the French. The Belgians and Prussians alike shivered in their beds while the Papists in their northern countries danced a jig to keep their feet from icing to the ground. The Indians stopped their warfare and for the whole of December left the Boston Colony at peace, and the frontier towns let down their guard to celebrate quietly and soberly the birth of the world's savior.

But in the next village of Salem some young girls, in the comfort and warmth of their minister's home, banished the boredom of their confinement by creating a forbidden Venus glass. With the help of a West Indian slave they told one another's fortunes and answered to their satisfaction such little questions as Who will be my sweetheart? or Who will marry me? The eggs were dropped into the glass, the water was stirred, and the spin within that fragile vessel would form a vortex into which the good and the evil alike would be sucked down and drowned. And from that time, I would often think of hell as a very cold place.

CHAPTER FIVE

January 1692–May 1692

ON THE 25TH of January a messenger kicked the flanks of his horse bloody as he rode south towards Boston along the Ipswich Road. In his saddlebags he carried a packet of parchment edged in ash and smoke. Forty miles to the north in York, Maine, one hundred and fifty Abanaki Indians had attacked settlements along the Agamenticus River. Hundreds of families were burned from their beds, most still wearing their nightclothes. The Reverend George Burroughs of Wells, a neighboring village, gave the Town Fathers of Boston nightmarish descriptions of the slaughter, with pillars of smoke, raging fires, and the hacking apart of some fifty souls, among them the town's minister. At least eighty young women and men were taken away by the Abanakis into Canada. Some were later redeemed, some were never heard from again. Reverend Burroughs knew well the Town Fathers, having earlier been the minister of Salem Village. He felt it his duty to write of the attack, as many of the dead had relations there. It would be these same relations who would later arrest him, try him, and hang him for witchery.

But we would not hear this news of attack until February. January was spent in isolation, and, despite the hillocks of snow and ice blocking the pathways to town or to our neighbor's door, we all felt a creeping sense of well-being in spite of Mother's firm belief in tempering exuberance over good fortune. Whatever she tended, whether at the fire or at spinning, she had a distracted, calculating look on her face, and I knew she was mindful of spring. We had meat and wood to last many months. And in the attic hung hard little seeds, dry and suspended in their muslin sacks, sleeping their Lazarus sleep.

Late in the month Hannah pulled down a pot of soup from the edge of the table, where it spilled onto her neck and chest. The skin curled and bubbled up, and if Mother had not ripped the smock from her body I think she would have been forever scarred. Hannah lay on our bed for most of a day and night, crying and twisting away as Mother and I soaked rags with water and chamomile for her burns and forced teas of mint and lavender down her throat. She cried and cried, and nothing I did could calm her until Mother and I lay down next to her. Towards dawn she drifted into exhausted sleep, holding my poppet in her blistered arms.

I must have fallen asleep as well but woke when Mother got up to stir the coals for the breakfast fire. My brothers and Father were yet sleeping, so I watched quietly from my pillow, my arm still cradling Hannah's damp and fevered neck. After the coals were fed Mother walked to Grandmother's oaken sidepiece, the carved vines appearing as ogres' faces in the dark, and pulled from a drawer a quill, a pot of ink, and a large red book, one I had never seen before. She leafed through many pages filled with a dense and flowing hand and settled on a blank sheet at the end. She dipped the quill into the ink and began, in tiny letters, to fill the page. Her writing hand was her left hand and very fine. It turned and flexed on her strong wrist like the delicate head of a Moorish mare above its muscled neck. Her fingers were long and tapered and the bones beneath the flesh made me think of a story Uncle had told me last winter of a young woman drowned in a millstream, her bones coming to rest on the shore by the great wheel. The miller's son made a harp from her breastbone, stringing the frame with her raven hair and anchoring the strings with pegs made from her long white fingers. And whenever he played the harp, it spoke in the drowned woman's voice and sang of how her sister had come to push her into the river. The story gave no hint why the murder should have been, but Aunt later whispered, out of her husband's hearing, that the reason must have come in the form of a man.

Mother's black hair, graying only at temple and crown, spilled down her back and blended seamlessly into the shadows hanging hooded and dense from the rafters above. I wondered what kind of music my mother's bones would make. I had no doubt the words would be as strong and relentless as a booming surf over tidal rocks, the music as weighted and cold as the easterly ocean. Perhaps, I mused, if I could learn the music, I could hear her deeper thoughts, just as a fisherman trains himself to the sounds of the incoming swells, which tell him of crashing waves or a calm, welcoming sea. Carefully sliding myself from the bed, I tiptoed softly to where she was sitting and asked, "Mother, what are you writing?"

She had been at her ease until that moment but started at the sound of my voice and right away closed the book. Placing it back into the sidepiece, she said, "It is only the counting book. Go to sleep, Sarah. It is early yet." As she turned away I knew she was being untruthful about the book. It held something more than the number of barrels of corn or baskets of potatoes stored in the cellar and, as it was filled to its last pages, had been her companion for a very long time. We sat in silence, waiting for the cock's crow, when we would begin the baking. Her face was ruddy from the fire, a fine sheen of sweat like a beaded diadem on her forehead, her deep-set eyes on the firewall beyond the hearth. She seemed so collected in her own skin, so separate and apart from me, not needing or wanting the small exchanges of family comfort. Her outer life was as circumscribed and homely as any villager's in Andover, and yet I wondered what surging restless thoughts pressed behind the expressive bones of her brow, enough to fill the pages of a book. In a whispering voice I said, "Will you teach me to better write?"

She looked at me, surprised, but said, "If you want. We shall start today, before supper."

I ventured cautiously, "Why do we not see..." I stopped, waiting for some warning word or gesture that I was not to talk of Uncle's family. But she reached out with one hand and smoothed flat the skirt over my lap, brushing away all the shadows hiding in the folds.

She said, "You mean to say, 'Why have we seen so little of Margaret?' " I nodded and she cradled her elbows in her palms and looked away. "Your uncle has been made shameless with hard drink and has neglected his wife and children. The elders of Billerica have given him more than one warning to better tend his family. We have offered help many times but were refused, and resentment grows where help is not wanted."

"But why should he refuse us?" I asked.

"There is great enmity between your uncle and father." She paused but did not say why this should be. "And now," she continued, "there is greater reason for Roger Toothaker to hate us. We have been given this house because your grandmother came to know the worth of your father over a man who calls himself a healer and a man of God but spends his days with a cup in one hand and a bawd in the other."

Now I had a new word for Mercy and I said teasingly, "And all of this is in your great red book?"

She took my elbow forcefully and said with an edge, "You must never speak of the red book to anyone. Promise me now that you will keep this one thing a secret, even among your brothers. Promise me."

The only secrets I had ever kept were girlish confidences with Margaret. But here was a different thing. My mother was demanding of me to keep a secret about a large leather-bound book of which I knew nothing. Her face was backlit by the growing flames from the hearth, and though her eyes were in shadow, I could feel her questioning gaze. It was the first time she had asked me for anything beyond the labor of my two hands. I nodded and whispered, "I promise."

She raised a forefinger to her chest, tapped it several times, and then pointed to me, the movement of her finger forming the illusion of a thread connecting us, breastbone to breastbone. She said, "Someday I will tell you what is in the book, but not today. Come, it's time to start the baking. I hear your father stirring."

She turned away but I could yet feel the glint of fear in her, like a flame inside a hooded lantern. I did not see the red book again for the whole of the winter, but I kept my promise not to speak of it.

We started our lessons that day as Mother had promised, and, as she was patient with me, the scratchings of my quill soon grew into passable letters. Sometimes as we sat at table side by side practicing some tiresome Bible passage, she would place her left hand over my right and guide it from chaos to order, and I came to seek out the closeness of our bodies. What I dreaded most was copying from a catechism book by the great Cotton Mather, passages such as "Heaven is prepared for pious children; Hell is prepared for the naughty" or "What a sad thing 'twill be, to be among the devils in the Place of Dragons."

When my fingers could no longer write she would read to me so that my head would increase in knowledge, much as a pillow casing will swell, the more goose down is forced into it. She had a little tract of poems by a woman named Anne Bradstreet whose works had been published by an Andover pastor. Late into evening the words became a boat on which we floated, out past the cornfields covered over with snow, out past the murmet unclothed and barren but for the drifts wrapped round it. Out beyond great marbled stones that slept under ice until the warming action of the earth in spring forced them tumbling to the surface.

> *To sing of wars, of captains, and of kings,*
> *Of cities founded, commonwealths begun,*
> *For my mean pen are too superior things;*
> *Or how they all, or each their dates have run;*
> *Let poets and historians set these forth,*
> *My obscure lines shall not so dim their worth.*

With her reading done we would sit in silence, perched together on our bench, our minds wandering far away, and I would rest my head upon her shoulder and she would let it lie there for a while.

THE LAUGH WAS a childish thing. It burst out loud and injurious over the reverently meditating parishioners. The stunned Reverend Barnard was poised at the pulpit, his mouth open as if to call back into his throat the pious words he had only just released. His eyes searched me out but he did not know me at first. Some goodwife sitting in front turned her head around and hissed at me as one would hiss at a yowling cat.

I had not meant to laugh. I had been sitting quietly listening as the Reverend repeated a sacrament-day sermon given two Sundays before by his colleague Samuel Parris in Salem Village. The daughter and the niece of this Reverend Parris had begun having strange fits, and it had been given out that the girls were under an evil hand. I had listened with delicious fearfulness as he told of the girls' torments as they twisted and cried out or fell motionless upon the floor. At times they were bitten or pinched by unseen agents and at other times they raced about their rooms, leaping into the hearth as though they would fly up the chimney. I had looked up into the rafters, wondering if the invisible world was even then gathering to make mischief in Andover as well. Reverend Barnard had called for a day of fasting and quoted from Psalms, "Sit thou at my right hand, till I make thine enemies thy footstool." And with those words I had pleasant thoughts of propping my shoes up on Phoebe Chandler's backside. My eyes wandered to the gallery above and I spied sitting there the little black slave boy. He was looking at me as though he had been waiting only for my gaze to meet his. The orbs of his eyes crossed and he stuck out his tongue, the tip of it passing beyond his chin. I smiled at his antics and he started mimicking the Reverend as he preached his sermon, exaggerating every movement of his face and body. Just as the Reverend would lean into the pulpit and point to some member of the congregation, so would the boy lean forward and point his finger at me. And when the Reverend's eyes gazed heavenward to invoke the Almighty, the boy rolled his eyes upwards in the thrall of a palsied fit. And so I laughed.

The silence following my exhaled breath built slowly, every member following the gaze of every other until finally resting their eyes on me. They were like a den of foxes so surprised at finding a hen dropped into their midst that they were stunned into motionless waiting. It would take the rumbled growling of their leader to bring them round to their true natures. I looked up at my mother holding a sleeping Hannah but her expression

was unreadable, caught somewhere between caution and disbelief. I looked back at the pastor and his eyes had narrowed, his
face set into satisfied indignation. He shifted his weight slightly,
setting his feet as though approaching a battle, and started
drumming the text with his fingers, stabbing the words, prompt-
ing them to leap from the page and flood over my head like rain
from the sky. And though his voice raked the whole of the congregation, his words were meant for me.

"The Church is separated from the world and the Devil's
main purpose is to pull down the Church. In the world the
Devil comes in many forms. He comes with disease and pes-
tilence. He comes in the allure of carnal desires. He comes in
spells and incantations. In unseemly conduct such as pride-
fulness and hot rebelliousness" — here he looked briefly at
my mother before returning to me — "and, sometimes, sometimes in the form of a child. The Devil preys on the weak
both as his victim and as his instrument. It is therefore left to
all of us to watch for these instruments. To root them out
where necessary and purify them with prayer, with punishment, and, when necessary, with the fire of the Word . . ." His
voice had reached such a pitch that had I not been holding to
the bench where I sat, I would have crawled over twenty ma-
trons to escape.

There came a loud and prolonged clearing of the throat from
the men's pews. Scrutiny lifted from me at the rasping sound,
like a vast shifting of stones, and men and women turned in
their seats to stare at my father. He sat with his long legs pulled
up at sharp angles, his eyes calmly regarding the prayer book
made tiny in the giant splay of his fingers. He continued to

read, his lips moving slightly, turning the pages as though he was alone at home, deep in spiritual contemplation, undisturbed even by a bothersome clot of phlegm in his throat. The fox had lost the scent and the Reverend continued his planned sermon, but I did not hear any of it for I was blinded to everything but my hands twisting in my lap.

When I followed Mother out, I hung my head and let the cape cover my face lest I see the censuring looks. I had no doubt that this day, the 28th day of February, would prove to be very black and that Iron Bessie would have her say against my thighs once we had returned home. I could see Father and Robert Russell standing close to the cart, deep in talk, but they stopped their speaking as we approached. Mother passed Hannah to me and was mounting the wheel step when something in their manner made her pause.

"Robert, your face is very long. Has Reverend Barnard's strong message curdled your breakfast?" she asked.

He smiled slightly but his brow knitted together and he said, "There is very bad business in Salem Village these past few weeks. The Reverend Parris' niece and daughter, and some others, have cried out upon three women, one a slave and two village women, for bewitching them. There may be a formal complaint made to the magistrates, which will mean a trial."

"There are always cries and whispers of witchery, Robert, especially in winter, when idleness marries with fearfulness and superstition. You heard our good Reverend, the Devil is every-where to be found, but, God willing, he will stay in Salem Vil-lage. From what I hear they are a contentious lot, and their quarrels will make a pretty stew for him to feed upon for some time to come." She stepped into the cart and reached down for Hannah. Father placed a restraining hand upon her knee and nodded to his friend to continue.

"Contentious people live here in Andover as well. The winter months are indeed giving more time and opportunity for mischief and for gossip. I have heard quite a bit of it here and around. At the meetinghouse and at Chandler's Inn. Your brother-in-law is still singing his song of displacement to any-one who will listen."

"A song that no doubt grows a verse with every telling," she said lightly. But the men did not smile and so she set her shoulders and said, "Go on."

"Gossip abounds that you have used witchery and cast spells. I myself heard Samuel Preston say that soon after you returned a cow to him this September past, it sickened and died. He said you cursed him after he refused to compensate you for some imagined injury and foretold that it would die and so it did. Your nephew Allen has been fanning the fires of the property dispute you had with Benjamin Abbot last March. He and Ralph Farnum both say they heard you lay a curse on Benjamin, and soon after, he grew a swelling in his foot and in his groin that had to be lanced by Dr. Prescott."

I looked over at the burial stones peeking above the snow in the church graveyard, some leaning so close to the ground they seemed to be listening to the voices of the dead, and remem-bered Phoebe's eager retelling of the argument between my mother and Benjamin Abbot.

"And now," he continued, "Timothy Swan is joining the chorus, saying that his illness is brought about by malcontented spirits."

"The only malcontented spirits Timothy Swan has encountered are his own shadow and my nephew who shares his house." My mother's amused listening was giving way to restlessness, and a barbed tone had crept into her voice.

But Robert pressed on. "And that is only the men. There is much talk among the women as well. Susannah Holt has put it about that you charmed the wind to carry away the fire from your crops and onto hers, and Mercy Williams has told so many stories about your foretelling storms and the healing of animals that she is like the town crier before a plague."

He turned and called to his niece, Elizabeth, who was standing at a distance by Robert's horse, speaking in hushed and furtive tones to Richard, both of them trying to ignore the gentle taunting by Tom and Andrew. Richard was not yet as tall as Father but he had to stoop down to match his height to Elizabeth's, as she was very small. She walked over to us and stood meekly in front of the cart, her hands clasped and her head bowed as she had been taught to do. She was not so very pretty but she was clean and neat, her face and hair pale, her eyes so light a blue as to lack almost all color.

"Elizabeth, tell Goodwife Carrier what you have heard from the other women." When she paused he added then very gently, "Go on. Tell her."

Her breath quickened and her eyes sought out the group of women still standing about the yard talking. Among them was Mercy Williams, red underskirt nowhere to be seen, only the respectable dark gray of her cloak. Elizabeth's voice barely raised itself above a whisper and her lips fought to move not at all. "I have heard Mercy Williams and Phoebe Chandler tell Mary Lacey and others that Goodwife Carrier practices witchcraft against them and that she goes nightly to Blanchard's Pond to have meetings with other witches."

"That's a neat trick. And just how am I to walk there and back in the span of one night?" Mother asked, her hand knotted on one hip.

"They say you fly there, mistress. On a pole."

For the second time that morning, there was sharp laughter, and it drew many looks to my mother. Heads came together, hands were raised to mouths to mask the buzzing of voices, and men and women widened their circles away from us, as though to avoid an overflowing cesspool. Elizabeth twisted her body from us, longing to walk away with the others, and her eyes searched about for somewhere to land. When her gaze crossed over mine, it lingered for a moment, and I caught my breath, for I knew that she had heard stories of me as well. The dread that had poured over me on the way to Samuel Preston's farm returned to lick its way from my eyes to my neck. It congealed and tightened there like an insect caught in an amber necklace.

Mother notched her head over her shoulder towards the parishioners still gathered at the front of the meetinghouse and said, "Just what am I to do with such nonsense? What answer should I make to people who are so foolish as to believe that someone who is of this earth, certainly no angel with wings, can fly on a pole in the dead of night to make sport at Blanchard's Pond?"

Robert moved closer to the wagon, placing his hands upon

the wheel, and when he looked up into her face, I saw a passion that was greater than the sentiments of neighborly concern.

"These days are very harsh, Martha. There are still smallpox and Indian raids not two days' ride from here. People are very much afraid, and fear makes fools of us all. The best answer is no other answer but calmness and"—here he paused, tightly gripping the wheel—"most of all restraint."

She looked at him, her mouth twisted into a half smile, and then at Father, who continued to stare at the ground, his brow shadowed by the brim of his hat. Expelling her breath sharply, she pointed her chin in the direction of home and repeated the word "restraint." But I knew she was dismissing all the talk as easily as she would have dismissed a whaler returned from the sea, recounting tales of monsters from the deep. Mother tapped my shoulder to give Hannah to her and I crawled into the back, finding my place between Tom and Andrew. As Father climbed onto the driving board, she said in parting to Robert, "I hear you have been courting the Widow Frye. I hope that we are to have a wedding soon or people will start their gossiping about you as well."

He did not answer but only signaled good-bye as we rolled away across the snow. I looked at Mother and saw that she was unmoved by Robert's words and it lessened my own fears. Father's face was more difficult to read, for his mouth neither smiled nor frowned, and the flesh surrounding his jaw clenched and unclenched. I turned and waved to Elizabeth, but she did not return the wave.

We had gone only half the distance down Boston Way Road, when the horse came up lame and everyone was forced to walk home except for me and Hannah and Tom. Tom would have walked as well but for the tightening in his chest from the bitter cold. He lay with his head in my lap, pale and gasping, but I pestered him until he gave me, with fits and starts, the story of the massacre of York he had heard from the older boys. And with the retelling of so many missing scalps, so many hacked-off legs and arms, so many captives taken away and traded from Abanaki to Narragansett, we made our way slowly, slowly to the house. The welcoming warmth of our fire was made all the sweeter for the carnage of a massacre left outside our door.

THE OLD WOMEN used to say, "When the days begin to lengthen, the cold begins to strengthen." But in the first few days of March the glow of the afternoon sun warmed the ice and snow enough to form little rivulets and streams between each embankment, and we watched Father eagerly to give us a sign that it was time to take up our buckets and venture into Billerica Meadow for the mapling. When it was time, we wrapped ourselves in cloaks and shawls, stuffing straw into our shoes, for the ground was still frozen where the shadows lay, and followed him single file into the woods. We went in order of age and height, first Father, then Richard and Andrew, then Tom and myself, looking like the last of some children's crusade returning through a blackened forest from the land of the Turk, our only weapons a mapling rod, a hook, and a little tin bucket.

We cut west across Preston's Plains and then south along the snow-blown shores of the Shawshin. We walked over the southern fork of the river, pausing only to look at the silvery remains of frond and fish rigid in motionless sleep. Richard, awkward in his emerging height, went down hard on the ice, and when we laughed at him, he grabbed at us until we all slipped and tumbled into the snow. When Father reached out his long arm to help me up again, he scolded us for our horseplay, but I saw him smile and push Richard back onto the ice. The maple grove was very old, many of the trees forty or fifty feet high. Father told us that the Indians would come there to make their gashes in the trees, collect the sap in hollow logs, and thicken the sap by dropping heated rocks into it. Father chose the best trees, feeling carefully around the crags and fissures with his fingers, never tapping below a lower limb or close to a defect in the bark at the northern exposure. When he chose his site he gently hammered into the bark, in an upward motion, the concave rod, allowing the sap to flow downwards from the inner recesses of the tree. It would take hours to fill the buckets, and so Father headed into the woods to check his traps, leaving Richard behind with the flintlock. Close to the maple stand we had seen the ghost of tracks in the snow. Not a square-toed Englisher's shoe but a rounded soft-heeled slipper. Father said that an Indian had passed the grove only a few days before us.

We sat all together in a small circle of sunlight, our backs to the northeast, facing towards the forest, and whispered stories that made the hair on our necks stand on end. We spoke of the newly arrested women in Salem. One of them was an old woman so greatly loved by the men and women in the village that they cried in the streets when she was carried from her sickbed to the magistrates. Having never seen a magistrate before, I fancied them as creatures with the heads of men and the bodies of crows who perched on their long benches and tapped their talons impatiently, waiting to flay their captives muscle from bone. Though Salem was near to Andover, we knew no one from that village, and I believe it never entered our minds that, like the pox, witchcraft honors neither border nor boundary.

On the 26th of March the weather turned cold again and we knew the mapling was done. Mother rendered the last bit of syrup from our tins of sap and we were allowed the best of winter meals. We were each given a small measure of hot syrup, which we poured onto the drifts to make sugar-on-the-snow. As I poured my portion onto the frozen white of the yard, the brown liquid hardening to a coppery crust, it suddenly looked to me like blood seeping through a shroud. My hand stretched out trembling before me, and, even though my mouth watered for its sweetness, I could not pluck up the taffy crust from the ground. Losing all desire for it, I gave my portion to Tom. Mother, seeing this, felt my head for fever and quickly gave me a strong physic against illness, making me retch for an hour. Within the week, we would hear from Richard that on that day, on that exact hour, a four-year-old girl, Dorcas Good, was examined by three judges in the Salem Town jail. Her little feet and hands were bound by iron manacles so she could not send her spirit out and torment further the girls who were her accusers. They would later return Dorcas to her underground cell, where her mother had been sitting chained in the dark for many days.

At the end of March it snowed steadily and then suddenly stopped. I was wakened in the dark on that last morning of the

month by Mother, who said we must go to the barn and lance
the horse's leg or risk losing the horse. A hard nodule had grown
to the size of a small fist on the inside of one knee and was hot
and painful to the touch. Richard had lanced it once the night
before, but the kernel was not pierced and did not seep properly.
It was dangerous business and I was warned to stay away from
the horse's hooves and told to only observe and learn. Richard
would brace the horse's head with both arms, holding one long
and twitching ear gently between his teeth. When the lancing
cut came, he would pull the head down and bite hard on the ear
so that the horse would kick back with his hind legs instead of
rearing up and striking with his forelegs.

I was cold and cross from being awakened so early and was
only half aware of my surroundings when we left the house for
the barn. The world was all of white and blue and black so that
Richard's form moving in front of me turned as dark and shadowed as the trees on the horizon. Our footsteps were muffled by
the snow, which is why Allen never heard our approach. We
were but twenty paces from the door of the barn when it opened
just enough for a slender mannish figure to slip out from inside.
At first we could not make out his face, but he was so startled to
see the three of us appearing as if sprung from the ground that
we could see the whites of his eyes as they widened with alarm.
If Allen had been at all clever he could have tried any number of
stories to explain his presence in the barn. But he only stood
staring at us until at last he bolted and ran, leaving footprints of
guilt in his wake.

Richard with his long legs quickly caught him and pulled
him by his hair down to the ground. Allen struggled to his feet

and with arms flailing tried to land a balled fist in Richard's face. He made high-pitched, excitable noises like a woman as he breathed through his mouth, spittle flying in a spray from his lips. Richard leaned in and, as Mercy had taught him to do, swept his right leg under Allen's feet and knocked him to the ground again. Richard then sat on his chest, pinning both arms beneath his knees so he could not move.

Mother rushed out of the barn, holding some bit of straw in her hand. Her shawl had come loose from her head, and from the set of her jaw, I felt something close to pity for my cousin. She knelt near Allen's head and shoved into his face the straw, which we now could see was blackened and smoldering, too wet from a leak in the roof to catch proper fire. Some of the straw fell onto his cheek and must have held a spark, because he yelped in pain.

"Did you think that burning down our barn would be enough to drive us away?"

"Get away from me, you howling old bitch." Allen was struggling furiously but Richard ground his knees further into his captive's arms and cuffed him about the jaw. Mother leaned her face nearer so that Allen could look her in the eyes.

"You're going to have to do a better job of it to get rid of us. You're going to have to burn us out of the house, but then what good will that do you? You'll still be homeless and you'll still be a coward, Allen Toothaker. Just like your father. And I'll tell you something else, if Thomas catches you about the place, your head will have to look for a new home and your shoulders will be wearing your hat." At this he blanched, his face turning to the color of the snow beneath him. She stood and motioned for Richard to follow. Allen rolled to his feet and started walking away as fast as his quivering legs could carry him. When he had gotten far enough, he turned and pointed at us with a shaking finger. "This is my land and my house and you stole it from me, but by Christ you will burn for it if I have to go to Hell myself to get the brand to do it."

Mother showed him her back and he stood for a moment longer, his thick lips shiny from spit, his close-set eyes mean and pinched. There was a large red welt on his cheek from the spark in the straw, and it blossomed on his face like the mark of Cain. He looked at each of us in turn, and when his eyes found mine I crooked my nose at him. Whatever else he may have forgotten to hold against us, he would never forget that last insult. He walked away through the brightening snow and it was months before we saw him again. But as I followed Mother and Richard back to the house to begin the morning fire, I looked behind me and saw a bit of straw still smoldering in the snow. One small ember winked wickedly at me like an oracle's eye foretelling some disaster.

FATHER RETURNED ONE day to the house with a black, cross-haired lurcher on a short chain. He was a noisy beast, of middling size, and Father put him in the barn to give warning when intruders were about the place. Mother said the dog would do his best to mangle the cats, but Father said we would just have to do with a few more mice in the barn. Once the days had warmed everything into a proper thaw, we chained the brute at the side of the house facing the road so that everyone who passed that way could see his menacing teeth. Father was the only one to feed him so he would learn who his master was. And we were warned to stay well away from the ground circumscribed by the length of his chain, as he was snappish and quarrelsome over his food.

Our days entered the plodding rhythms of the yeoman. The sun came up and over and down again like the arc of the seeds we sowed from our grain sacks, or the rise and fall of the prodding stick plied to the back of the ox to make him plow faster. Andrew turned fifteen on the 7th day of April, and even though his body had continued to grow, it remained pale and soft, his mind as gentle and cradled as a child's.

Robert Russell married the Widow Frye and came to our house for the wedding feast. The new Goodwife Russell was plump in the face and broad across the waist but she was settled and kind and was young enough to bear Robert the sons he had never gotten with his first wife. That she was kind and motherly to Elizabeth, Robert's niece, when the gossip went that Robert had bedded the girl, showed her true good nature. She would brook no ill words about Elizabeth from anyone and kept her within the house when most women would have turned her out. Soon her good opinion restored Elizabeth's virtue so that my mother remarked dryly, "Remarkable that with a few words maidenheads become like reputations. Easily broken, easily mended."

Robert Russell was our source of news, as he often bartered in Andover and as far away as Boston. At the end of April he told us that twenty-five more men and women had been arrested and were held in Salem Village for consorting with the Devil.

Among those arrested was Elizabeth Proctor, a midwife and brewer of simples, and a few days later her husband, John Proctor, was taken to Salem Town jail for coming to her defense. Some arrested were old and nettlesome women. Some were well-to-do, like the Bishops, man and wife, and Philip English, who later bribed his way to freedom. Some were slaves, and one was the former minister of Salem Village, the Reverend George Burroughs, who had been brought back in chains from Maine. The arrested were from surrounding Topsfield, Ipswich, Reading, Amesbury, Beverly, Salem Village, and one from as far away as Boston. Yet not one soul from Andover. They were all alike in being chained and manacled to bring relief to the misery of the group of young women who had been bewitched. But soon, so said the young women, more witches were about, sending their invisible bodies forth to bring fresh torment to the innocent. The accusers renewed their screeching and rolling about, and the best minds in theology and the law that Salem could produce proclaimed that there were more witches yet to be found.

SUNDAY, MAY THE 15th, brought a sky full of clouds, but so high were they in the bowl of the heavens that the gray seemed uniformly painted there. I sat in the cart on the way to the meetinghouse holding on to Hannah's skirt with one hand as she leaned over the side, her fat fingers reaching and straining for the turning spokes of the wheels, and with the other hand I held on to the corner of an oilskin that Father had spread over us to save us from the misting rain that started as we pulled from the yard. The air was by turns hot and then cold, and I struggled with my shawl as I sweated and shivered beneath it. Mother had been cross and short with us all the whole of the morning, for she, like the rest of us, dreaded going to the meetinghouse. The air about the congregants the previous two Sundays had been heavy and punishing as the Reverend Barnard peppered his sermons with the names of townsfolk accused in Salem for witchcraft. For the Reverend it was a sign of a greater battle to come. One that could spill over at any moment into Andover. His lurid predictions had taken precedence over the sermons of the Reverend Dane, and, like an angry ship captain upon the foredeck, he cried out warnings of the evils to come.

We arrived a full quarter hour late. The Reverend was at the pulpit, and he paused in his invocation to follow us with his eyes as we found seats at the very back of the room. There were no open stares from our neighbors, just a ripple of sly nods one to the other and a cascade of knowing exchanges, "you see, you see, you see . . ." As we settled quickly into our seats, I searched the front pew for the Reverend Dane and was surprised to see the Reverend Nason from Billerica along with the other elders seated facing us. He was more grossly fat than ever, but his gaze was keen, his eyes within their restricted field squeezed into sharp focus like a narrow spyglass. He stared at me for a moment, as though he had seen into my hiding place as I peeked at him through the hole in Margaret's bedroom wall, and then looked sharply away.

When the psalms had been sung, Reverend Barnard began in a clipped, bitten-off way, "Many this day are tormented. Most of them children. Innocents. Christians. Saints. . . . I myself was witness to this witchery a fortnight ago when I gathered with others of my calling in the home of the Reverend Parris in Salem Village. I saw with my own eyes the work of the Devil as he strove to separate those tortured children from their salvation. My brother pastor, the Reverend Nason, who sits before you, has seen this struggle as well. He has been moved, as I have, to work day and night to stop this spread of evil, and believe me, my faithful followers in Christ, it will spread as contagion is spread without our diligence and scrutiny. But we will find out this black work through prayer and through testimony. Yes, testimony. For it is not enough to fear evil or to pray against evil. It must be dragged into the light of day so that it may be carved out and cleansed and made pure with fire and with the sword if necessary, for does it not say in the Scriptures, 'Thou shalt not suffer a witch to live'?"

And here he stopped for a moment to calm himself, to swallow, to compose his face, which had twisted itself into ticks and grimaces. He pointed to the Reverend Nason and continued quietly, confidentially, as though sharing a secret. "He goes on the morrow to Salem Village to give testimony of a man from Billerica, a physician by calling, who not only claims to have killed a witch but boasts he can foretell a witch at any place. Not through prayer or fasting or by the consultation of his minister but by the use of charms and spells. He has even taught his little daughter this charm making and has boasted of it in taverns in Billerica and here in Andover as well. This is devil's work. You see how it spreads? How it crosses borders and roads like a rolling fog?"

My breathing had stopped, forcing the blood to beat against

my skull like a clapper vibrating inside a bell. I saw in my mind's eye Margaret, standing all clean and straight in front of the Reverend Nason, reciting her catechism on finding a witch, and recalled Uncle's claims to be able to break the spells of witchcraft.

"This man works to pollute his own children. See how it spreads? Who may know how he works to pollute others of his family. See how it spreads?" And he began to repeat the last phrase over and over again, catching the eye here and there of his parishioners, making a final chorus to his psalm of retribution. Heads started to turn back and forth ("See how it spreads") first in our direction, then to Reverend Barnard, and then back to us again, like so many county banners snapping in a cross breeze ("See how it spreads"). There was not a person in the meetinghouse who did not know that Roger Toothaker, doctor by trade, was related by marriage to the Carriers. At the last, his gaze fell heavily upon the Reverend Dane as he sat in the front pew surrounded by his sons and wife and daughters. And there was not a person there who did not know that the Carriers were in turn related to the Danes by marriage.

Upon hearing the last "amen," I strained to stand to be the first out the door, but Mother's fingers closed over my arm, keeping me seated next to her as one by one every member of the congregation passed us in solemn and silent procession, as though viewing bodies at a laying-out. She sat and stared ahead, looking neither to the right nor the left, making her face all smooth, all cold and proud. The only sign of her anger was a blue vein beating fast and hard at her temple. When all had left the sanctuary, she released my arm and I followed her out. The mist had turned to heavy rain and she pulled her shawl over her head with one hand and half walked, half dragged Hannah with the other to the wagon, where Father stood waiting for us. One of my shoes had come off in the wet ground and as I struggled to pull it out I heard a voice licking at my ear, soft and malicious.

"Witch," it said. I looked up and saw Phoebe Chandler. Standing behind her were Mercy and Mary Lacey and some other girls I did not know.

"Witch," she said again as I pulled the shoe from the sucking mess and, taking no time to place it back on my foot, walked with it in my hand as best I could through the mud. They followed close on my heels and chanted "witch, witch, witch, witch..." The yard was silent except for the hissing sounds of their voices and the soft pattering of the rain. Our neighbors stood about as motionless as stones, letting the rain soak their coats and skirts, their mouths unmoving but their eyes bright and attentive. I stumbled and fell to my knees, covering my apron with black mud, and heard laughter behind me. My face was pointed to the dirt but I could feel the press of bodies at my back and I flinched, remembering well the feel of a rock on the back of my head. Phoebe bent over me and continued in a high, ringing voice the same words, faster and faster, "witch-witch-witch-witch..." I did not see at first what made the others take two and then three steps backwards. Phoebe could not have seen, for she hovered over me, chanting to the crown of my head like a chattering squirrel. The soiled hem of a skirt was fast approaching as well as the tips of well-worn shoes, which flung pellets of clay in every direction. When my mother grabbed her shoulders and shook her, Phoebe's voice was cut off as neatly as new bread cut through with a knife.

"Here, here. Where do you suppose you live? Were you raised in a cellar to behave so badly?" Mother's hair had come uncoiling out of her cap and her color was high around her cheekbones.

"Go on now. All of you."

The girls had started to leave until they saw Mercy fold her arms and stand with one hip jutting out, her upper lip curled. Then they all stood and watched as Mother helped me to my feet and held my hand, the mud making a glue between our two palms. Father had been sitting all along in the wagon, and I had two thoughts as I crawled into the straw. The first was that Mother had come to my aid. And the second was that Father had not. The ride home was quiet as we huddled under the oilskin, but I could feel my brothers watching me. I started to shake with the wet and cold and from a lagging fear. Tom put his arm around me and wiped the dirt from my hands with his scarf.

When the wagon bogged down in the road, Father gave the reins to Mother and he and Richard pushed the wagon from behind. Father looked at me once and asked, "All right, then?" I nodded my head but I was bitterly taken down that he had not flung himself from the wagon as well, scattering the girls like a flock of ground hens. I turned my back so he would not see the tears but Andrew saw and he patted me on the shoulder and said, "All gone. All gone." And the whole way back he sat close to me, his moon face beaming, saying, "All gone, Sarah. All gone."

ON THE 18TH day of May, Uncle was arrested in the early morning and taken to Boston Prison. When the Salem constable, Joseph Neall, arrested him at his home in Billerica, Uncle was so much in his cups that he was halfway to the jail before he became aware that he was going not as a physician to practice medicine upon one of his neighbors but as an accused practitioner of the black arts. There were by this date thirty-eight men, women, and children in the jails of Salem and Boston in common cells that were meant for half that number. On the 24th day of the month the new governor of Massachusetts, Sir William Phips, ordered that the Court of Oyer and Terminer be formed to hear and determine the outcome of the witchcraft trials. Nine judges were appointed to stand as guardians between the sanctified world and the damned.

Goodwife Easty, the sister of the sainted Rebecca Nurse of Salem, was arrested, released, and arrested yet again when the tormented children of Salem Village cried out with renewed vigor that she was sending out her specter to pinch and bite and choke them. On the 28th day, there were more warrants from Salem Village, and, as such things go, even secret things, word was spread of the impending approach of the constables. The news went from neighbor to neighbor to neighbor until Robert Russell appeared at our door and told us on the evening of May 30th that Mother was to be arrested at first light on the morrow and taken to appear in front of the magistrates in Salem Village.

We all stood about the common room, the remnants of supper strewn on the table, stricken blind and deaf as one would be after a thunderclap. Mother looked up at Robert as if he had just told her our ox was nesting on our roof, but when he begged her to consider fleeing as others had done, she shook her head and continued clearing the bowls and cups from the table. He turned to Father and said, "Thomas, speak to her. Make her see." But Father said, "She does see. It is her choice to stay or go." My anger jumped over my terror, pounding it harshly down, to hear Father speak so weakly on her behalf. Did he care so little for her, did he care so little for us, that he would not urge her, as Robert had done, to hide herself away until she could be safe again?

Richard, his face dark, his lips pressed tightly together, walked from the room and made his way to the barn, where he would stay until the constable came. Andrew walked round and round in ever tighter circles like a piece of wood caught up in some fearful eddy, until Tom took his arm and seated him at the hearth. Tom's ragged breathing filled the room as he tried to keep from crying out and he finally sank to the floor-boards as his knees buckled. I stood and looked from Father to Robert, unable to understand the cessation of blunt action, wanting to shriek into the silence or throw myself against something hard and unrelenting to keep my mother from the prison cart.

Some movement at the table made me turn to see her staring back at me, not in fear or in condemnation or even in sadness, but in a kind of furied understanding. She looked at me so long and with such complete recognition that it was as if we were alone in the room, shrouded together in silent speaking. Or in an enveloping cocoon made of mother's milk and kettle iron. But it lasted only until Hannah started her crying. Robert told us that Aunt Mary and Margaret were also to be arrested, and then he left us with promises that should Mother change her mind and flee, or if she was detained overly long in Salem, he and his wife would do their best to care for the rest of us.

Mother stayed at the hearth long after my brothers and I had gone to bed. I turned and thrashed and shook Hannah's arms from around my neck but could not sleep. Finally, I crept from my room and saw that Father had joined her at the fire and they sat facing each other, speaking in whispers.

"They are like dogs sniffing their own asses," Father said. "There's no' so sweet a smell as the corruption you put forth yourself." Mother exhaled a laugh and moved her head closer to his, and I knew they had been speaking on Mother's warrant.

"I will speak reason to them. They must listen," she said. "Then these girls and their stories will crumble and fall like so many cards on a tilted table. They've had so many shambling, half-witted women in front of them that the magistrates are starting to harken to this nonsense. Well, I am not confused and I am not afraid of them. They are lawyers and judges and must rule by law."

He reached out and took her hands in his, resting his fore-arms on her lap. His thumbs worked the inside of her palms and he said, "Martha, they will not listen to reason. How can they, when all they have built here is to keep themselves propped up on the backs of others? You do yourself credit to believe in your own strength and courage. But they will not hear you. They cannot."

She took one hand from his and stroked his head where the hair hung long and ragged and said, "If I do not do this thing, then it may go on and on. 'Nothing of the greater good comes without struggle and sacrifice in equal measure, be you man or woman, and in this way are we freed from tyranny.' Those are your words."

He made an impatient gesture and said, "They are not my words but words of those who gained from them by being murdered and put to rot in unmarked graves."

She laid a finger to her lips and said, "Would you give me this light and then put it out again? Would you have me run away? And then what am I? I am only a servant with a boot on my back. And what am I to my children or to you? Can you love me as you have when I abandon what I know to be true? I am not afraid, Thomas."

And Father answered, "Aye. That's why I am afraid."

The floorboards beneath my feet shifted and Mother saw me hiding in the shadows. She rose and told me to get dressed quickly. I threw on my skirt without its apron and shoved my feet into shoes without their stockings, thinking all the while that she had changed her mind and would leave, taking me with her. But my hopes were ended when she said to Father, "I'll return in two or three hours' time. There is something I must give Sarah."

The night was very dark as the moon had waned to nothing, but the weather was close and warm and soon the shift under my arms was damp with sweat. She walked so swiftly that I ran to keep pace with her, a canvas sack she carried bouncing heavily against her thigh. We walked along the pathways leading to Robert's house but soon cut south into the forest of oak and elm and I knew we were going to Gibbet Plain. I thought of the mushrooms and flowers, the bloodroot and violets, that must be growing in every corner of the field, but I could see very little of it through the dark. About a hundred paces into the meadow, Mother led me to a small hillock where a lone elm grew, and then she stopped and turned to me.

She spoke with such intensity that I blinked against her breath. "You know where I go tomorrow?" I nodded. "Do you know why?" I nodded again, but she said, "Say it, then." I opened my mouth and said in a small voice, "Because they say you are a witch."

"And do you know why Mary and Margaret are arrested?" she asked. And I responded, "Because they are believed to be witches also."

And here she put her hands on my shoulders so that I could look nowhere but into her eyes and she said, "No. They are arrested to make Uncle confess and in the hopes that they will in turn cry out against others for practicing witchcraft. They will come for me tomorrow, but I will not confess and I will not cry out on anyone. Do you know what that means?"

I started to shake my head no, but a terrible idea was forming in the back of my mind and my eyes must have widened, so that Mother nodded her head grimly and said, "When they cannot make me confess they will come to my family and it will not matter that you are a child. There are children in Salem Town jail even now." She saw the look in my eyes and knelt in front of me, holding me tight in her arms.

"If they come for you, you must tell them anything they want to hear to save yourself. And you must tell Richard and Andrew and Tom to do the same."

"But why can you not do the same . . ." My voice had started to rise plaintively but she shook me and choked it off.

"Because someone must speak for the truth of things."

"But why must it be you?" She ignored my question and pulled out of the sack the red book I had seen her write in so many weeks before.

"This book..." She paused for a moment, fingering the worn leather. "This book has in it the history of your father in England before he came to the new colonies."

"That is all?" I asked, disappointed.

"Sarah, there are men who would walk over your breathing body to possess it, and it could mean the destruction of every one of us. You must promise me two things. On the heads of your family. First you will guard this book. We will hide it tonight but you must take it back again when the time is right if I should not be able to. And the second promise is that you will not try to read it until you have come of age." I looked at her, confounded. How was I to make such a promise when I didn't know what I was promising to keep?

"Give me your hand." And as I held it out she took it and placed it over the book as one would take an oath on the Bible. She said forcefully, "Promise me, Sarah."

"But I don't understand," I cried. I didn't care if she shook me until my teeth rattled in my head. I didn't care if my voice traveled south over the swamps and woke every sleeping farmer beyond the border in Reading. But she didn't shake or strike me, she held on tightly and let me cry until the saltwater soaked her dress down to her skin. Then she pulled away and, taking off her cap, wiped the tears from my face, saying, "Sarah, time is very short. Someday it will all be made clear to you. But tonight I must have your promise. When they come for you, tell them what they wish to hear and they will be satisfied and let you go. Even if you have to say you fly to Bald Hill on a pole and dance a jig every night. Even if they ask if I am a witch, say aye and let it go."

I started to shake my head again but she said, "My fiercesome, fuming Sarah. This is a heavy burden but you are the only one who can carry it. Richard can hardly bear the weight of his own brooding nature and would collapse with the knowledge of it. And Andrew, poor witless Andrew. He cannot find the door for looking through the window. Tom is good-natured but he cares too deeply for the feelings of others and would make the wrong turn through wishing to please. This book is our history and a family's history lasts only so long as there is someone left to tell it. And so in you will we be carried forth, and even if I should die, we will not be forgotten."

"And Father. Why can he not keep the book?"

I heard the slow intake of breath and a pause before she answered. "He does not know of it."

I stood in disbelief that such a secret could be kept, wife from husband, and that she had shared this secret with me. She moved away, the darkness hiding her expression, the sound of her voice muffled as though speaking through her hands. "I have never told him of the book because in telling his life to me he hoped to put it behind him, to be forgotten and never again relived. But I could not let it stand. There are recorded within the sacrifices of many lives. Much blood has been shed to bring the story to these frail sheets, and it will all be for naught if it is forgotten."

She took my hand and kissed it and placed it over the book,

saying, "No more questions now, Sarah. All will be answered in time." I gave her my promise then and we buried the book in an oilskin at the foot of the elm, using our hands to pull up the damp earth. She made me mark it well so I could find it again and we walked back with no more words between us.

In the early morning hours of May 31st a cart approached the house and we heard the lurcher strain against his chain and bark viciously as John Ballard walked to our door. I knew that Father had just lengthened the links, and the dog was caught up only a hair's breadth from the constable's boot heels, startling him and making him curse. He walked into our house and read the warrant and Mother stared him hard in the face as he tied her hands with a rope. She did not cry out for consideration or beg for more time; she only looked at each of us in turn and called me to her side. She tapped a finger to her breast and then brought it to mine, creating the invisible thread of understanding and complicity. Of secrets well kept. Hannah cried and struggled at Mother's leaving and I held and rocked her as best I could, the sound of the cartwheels grinding ever more softly on the road to Salem Village.

CHAPTER SIX

MANY YEARS AFTER I was married and my children grown, my own dear husband, John, paid a costly sum to have a clerk sent from Connecticut to Salem Village to transcribe the documents recorded at the time of my mother's trial. A great portion of the documents had been destroyed over time, some by the judges themselves and some by the families of the judges who had grown to fear the turning tide of sentiment against them. The remaining documents had been sealed against scrutiny for the passing of decades, until they lay near forgotten in the back of a wooden press that housed the birth and death registries of Salem Village.

I had no desire or thought to revisit the past in such a way. But one night, when the weather had turned to the cool of autumn and the smell of decaying things lay about, I had a dream. And in the manner of dreams, I knew that I lay heavily in my bed next to my husband, surrounded by the sleeping forms of my sons and daughters and their sons and daughters, and yet my spirit-self had flown to a place at the edge of the cornfields by my grandmother's house.

It was night and there were long shadows in the field, and I stood listening to the swelling and rustling of the tassels on the corn. The murmet twisted on his pole with the wind as though he were looking at me, not with malicious intent, but with a calm waiting. The moon was full and it had a haze of silver around it, foretelling a sunrise filled with rain. But in that moment the sky was bluish black and clear of any clouds. The air felt liquid against my skin and warm, like the breath of a child. The murmet moved to and fro, pointing north and south, and then east and west, and soon there came a quivering and a shaking at the edge of the field. A little foot emerged from the corn, wearing a worn, overly large shoe with a silver buckle that flared in the moonlight. Then there appeared a hand wearing a black glove, then an arm, a little crooked body, and finally a dark head, the eyes saucerlike and glimmering against the green. And then I saw that the figure had not been wearing gloves; it was the black hand of Lieutenant Osgood's slave boy.

He looked at me, very sad, and we gazed at each other for a while. His other hand was hidden in the corn, and when he brought it out, he was holding a small scythe, the kind one would clear bracken with, too small to trim a field. The edge was rimmed with a dark stain of red turned to copper. The boy shook his head as if to say, "It is a pity what I must do," and then he pulled back a few stalks of corn, making a path for me, and pointed into the opening with his scythe.

I was very afraid and could not lift my feet to move. Dark forms flitted about within the corn, figures of men and women that were tantalizingly familiar but never fully revealed through the shadows. Then the little black boy opened his mouth and spoke to me in a sweet, childish voice. "Sarah, come into the corn."

"But why, why must I come in?" I cried, my voice sounding loud and peevish in the still night.

And in spite of my desire to remain fixed where I stood, I moved forward as though dragged on a sled until I came to rest next to the boy. He whispered into my ear, this time speaking in the voice of Margaret. "Can you keep a secret, Sarah?" she asked. I nodded, remembering all our secrets shared together in her mother's house, and she said, her breath hot in my ear, "You cannot harvest the corn until you go into the corn."

I awoke with tears on my face, my hands clutching at the ribs around my heart. I had for more than forty years kept the past behind an impenetrable wall of my own devising. I thought that to move beyond this wall and revisit the past would scorch my reason and make me mad. But then, as I lay sweating in bed, restless and prickly, it came to me that to harvest a field of corn one does not wade into the dark middle of things and cut the stalks from the inside out. It is best done starting with the outside ears and working inward, stalk by stalk, keeping the light of the sun always at one's back so that its rays can illuminate each ear of corn, be it whole and sweet or black and blighted.

And in this way does one make a meal that feeds a starving body back to wholeness.

What follows are the records of the witchcraft trials brought to me from Salem Village. Upon receiving them I started to remember. And with remembrance came healing.

The Transcribed Documents from The Tryal of Martha Carrier Resident of Andover Massachusetts 1650 to 1692

The Complaint

Complaint v. Martha Carrier, Elizabeth Fosdick, Wilmot Reed, Sarah Rice, Elizabeth Howe, John Alden, William Proctor, John Flood, Mary Toothaker and daughter, and Arthur Abbott

Salem May the 28th 1692

Joseph Houlton and John Walcott both of Salem Village, Yeomen, made complaint on behalfe of their Majesties against Martha Carrier of Andover, wife of Thomas Carrier of said Towne, husbandman, et al, for sundry acts of witchcraft by them and Every one of them Committed on the bodys of Mary Walcott, Abigail Williams, Mercy Lewis, Ann Putnam and Others belonging to Salem Village or farmes lately, to the hurt and injury of theire bodys therefore Craves Justice.

JOSEPH HOULTON
JOHN WALCOTT

The Warrant

Warrant for Arrest of Martha Carrier, To the Constable of Andover

Salem May the 28th 1692

You are in theire Majesties names hereby required to apprehend and forthwith secure, and bring before us Martha Carrier, the wife of Thomas Carrier of Andover, on Tuesday next being the 31st day of this Instant month of May about ten of the clock in the forenoon or as soon as may be afterwards at the house of Lt. Nathaniel Ingersall in Salem Village who stands charged with having Committed Sundry acts of Witchcraft . . .

JOHN HATHORNE

JONATHAN CORWIN, ASSIST.

The Depositions

John Roger v. Martha Carrier

The deposition of John Roger of Billerica aged 51 yeares or thereabouts, saith, that about seven yeares since, Martha Carrier, being a nigh neighbor unto this deponent, and there happened some difference betwixt us. She gave forth several threatening words as she often used to do and in a short time after this deponent had two lusty sowes which frequented home daily that were lost. And this deponent found one of them dead on the night he was found at the Carriers house with both eares cut off and the other sow I never heard of to this day . . .

Samuel Preston v. Martha Carrier

Samuel Preston aged about 41 yeares, saith, that . . . I had some difference with Martha Carrier which also had happened sever-all times before and soon after I lost a cow in a strange manner being cast upon her back with her heels up in firm ground when she was very lusty, it being in June. And within about a month after this the said Martha and I had some difference again at which time she told me I had lost a cow lately and it should not be long before I should lose another which accordingly came to pass . . .

Benjamin Abbott v. Martha Carrier

The testimony of Benjamin Abbott aged about 31 yeares, saith, last March was twelve months, then having some land granted to me by the Towne of Andover near to Goodman Carrier's land, and when this land came to be laid out Goodwife Carrier was very Angry, and said she would stick as Close to Benjamin Abbott as the bark stuck to the tree and that I should repent of it afore seven yeares came to an end and that Doctor Prescott could never cure me . . .

Allen Toothaker v. Martha Carrier

The deposition of Allen Toothaker aged about 22 yeares, saith, . . . about last March Richard Carrier and myself had some difference and said Richard pulled me downe by the hair of my head to the ground for to beat me. I desired him to let me rise, when I was up I went to strike at him, but I fell down flat upon my back to the ground and had not the power to stir hand nor foot. . . . One time she, Martha Carrier, clapped her hands at me and within a day or two I lost a three year old heffer, next a yearling, and then a cow. Then had we some little difference againe and I lost another yearling. And I know not of any naturall causes of the death of the abused Creatures, but have always feared it hath been the effect of my Aunt and her malice ...

Phoebe Chandler v. Martha Carrier

The deposition of Phoebe Chandler aged 12 yeares, testifieth that about a fortnight before Martha Carrier was sent to Salem to be examined, upon the Sabbath day when the psalm was singing, said Martha Carrier took me, said deponent, by the shoulder and shaked me in the meeting house and asked me where I lived, but I made her no answer (not doubting but that she knew me, having lived some time the next door to my father's house, on one side of the way). .... And that day that said Martha Carrier was arrested my mother sent me to carry some beer to the folks who were at work in the lot and when I came within the fence there was a voice in the bushes (which I thought was Martha Carrier's voice, which I know well) but saw nobody, and the voice asked me what I did there and whither I was going, which greatly frightened me ...

CHAPTER SEVEN

May 1692–July 1692

THIS, THEN, WAS my mother's trial.

Richard, who had been watching Mother's arrest from the hayloft in the barn, followed the constable on foot the few miles north up Boston Way Road and then south along Salem Road at the meetinghouse juncture. It was not yet seven of the clock, but as they rolled over the common green, a small group gathered to stare at Mother as she passed by. No one spoke. Not one person called out with curses or warnings or even pleas of leniency for pity's sake. And until they came to Miller's Meadow, men and women stepped out of their homes or stopped working in the fields to watch and give testament to their neighbors that they had seen the witch of Andover.

The day was warm, and the constable, being a porous beefy man, drank often from his water skin, though he never once offered a drink to his prisoner. Richard had not thought to bring a water skin, and so when the cart crossed the little bridge over Mosquito Brook, he dipped his hat into the stream and ran to give Mother some water. John Ballard growled and showed Richard his fist and said that if he came close again to his prisoner, he would be tied hand over hand and thrown into the cart as well. Richard followed the cart the whole of the seventeen miles into the quiet, fearful streets of Salem Village.

Through Richard's telling of the examination we heard only the scaffolding of events. Later, we would all see for ourselves the place where judgments were rendered. The Salem Village meetinghouse was squarely built on a raised stone foundation with narrow doors on three sides that had all been opened to allow the coming and going of the accused, their victims, their neighbors giving depositions, and the sundry curious citizens who came from towns and villages across Essex and Middlesex counties.

Mother was lifted down from the cart and brought into the meetinghouse, her hands still tied, and though Richard tried to enter, he was warned by the constable to stay in the yard and not to interfere with the judges. Richard stood at the back of the press of people, but as his height was well above six feet, he had a clear field to the inquiry. As soon as she was taken in, the judges motioned to the constable, and he led her forward to stand facing the three men whose names were well known in Salem and beyond: Bartholomew Gedney, John Hathorne, and Jonathan Corwin. John Ballard signed the warrant receipt, took the rope from Mother's hands, tipped down the brim of his hat to the judges, and left her in the charge of the court.

Standing to her left, separated by some men and women in chains, were Aunt Mary and Margaret. Mother tried to speak to them but she was cautioned to silence. In the pews at the front, a group of young women and girls sat hanging on one another's shoulders, talking quietly, and looking keenly at the gathering of the accused. Whenever the judges called before them one of the prisoners, the girls would pitch forward or scream or fall to the floor and roll about like a serpent shedding its skin. Richard said that Mother stared steadfastly at the judges and ignored the girls as one would ignore the tantrums of a hobbled child.

Finally the name Martha Carrier was called, and Richard said that one of the girls, named Abigail Williams, immediately stood up and pointed, not at Mother but at Aunt Mary. As soon as Mother stepped forward, she quickly realized her error and changed the direction of her pointing, like a weather vane in a shifting wind. Then the other girls whipped themselves into frenzy, and it was several minutes before there was enough quiet for the judge to speak. One of the judges faced the accusers and asked the pointing girl, "Abigail Williams, who hurts you?"

And Abigail answered, raking her nails down her face, "Goody Carrier of Andover."

Then the judge turned to another girl and asked, "Elizabeth Hubbard, who hurts you?"

And Elizabeth, clasping her arms around her stomach, said, "Goody Carrier."

Turning to yet another girl, he asked, "Susannah Sheldon, who hurts you?"

And Susannah responded, turning to the onlookers as though she would enlist their help in fighting her tormentor, "Goody Carrier. She bites me and pinches me and tells me she would cut my throat if I did not sign her book."

There was another great outcry, this time among the general witnesses, who said to one another, "The Devil's book . . . she asked them to sign the Devil's book . . ." At that moment a girl named Mary jumped up, crying that Mother had brought the Devil's book to her as well and tormented her while she slept. The judges waited patiently for the room to settle and then they pointed their eyes at Mother. The chief judge then asked Mother, "What do you say to this you are charged with?"

Mother's voice sounded loud and clear through to the back of the room, "I have not done it."

Then one of the girls leapt up, pointing to a place on the wall behind the judges, and screamed, "She looks upon the Black Man," and another girl squealed out that a pin had been stuck into her thigh. The shortest of the three judges asked Mother, his eyes searching anxiously over his shoulder, "What black man is this?"

And Mother responded, "I know none," but her voice was all but drowned out by the crying of the two girls. "He's there, he's there, I see him whispering into her ear . . ." And "See how I am pricked again."

Mother crossed her arms over her chest but continued to ignore the writhing girls, and the chief judge asked yet again, "What black man did you see?"

And here Mother answered coolly, "I saw no black man but your own presence." Out of the momentary quiet came a soft, sniggering laugh from the back of the room. The chief judge blinked his eyes a few times as though peering into a bright light and frowned as he pointed to the girls. "Can you look upon these and not knock them down?"

"They will dissemble if I look upon them," she answered, but the judge stabbed his finger again at the girls, and when Mother turned her head to them, they fell to the ground, shrieking and clawing at themselves and moaning as though they were being drawn and quartered. Now the judges had caught a chill from the winds of hysteria, and the third judge, who had all this time been silent, stood up and said, "You see you look upon them and they fall down."

Mother stepped closer to the judges and said loudly to be heard over the din, "It is false. The Devil is a liar. I looked upon none since I came into the room but you."

Then the girl named Susannah seemed to go into a trance, her body rigid and trembling from some soul sickness and she pointed to the rafters and cried, "I wonder that you could murder thirteen persons." The other girls looked to the rafters and pointed and began crawling over one another to hide themselves under the pews and called out, "Look, there are the thirteen ghosts.... See how they point at Goody Carrier.... She has killed thirteen at Andover...." The men and women who had gathered inside the meetinghouse all looked to the rafters and swayed as one body outward towards the doors. Richard heard one woman standing close to him turn to another and say, "It's true. She killed thirteen people with the smallpox last winter.

I have heard she brought it with her from Billerica. It is much talked about."

Mother walked a few forceful steps towards the girls and so stunned were they by her advances that they for a moment fell silent. She turned and faced the judges, saying, "It is a shameful thing that you should mind these young girls that are out of their wits."

The girls howled with renewed vigor, saying, "Do you not see them? The ghosts." The judges shifted anxiously in their seats and moved their chairs about as people will do sitting under a tree, avoiding the droppings of birds. Some of the men pushed their way out of the meetinghouse in terror for their lives, and women grew weak and had to be held up in the pews. Hands pointed upwards to the shadows that lingered in the cross-beams, and heads swiveled about on necks made stiff with fear, and even Richard was moved to search the rafters for ghostly traces. The short judge asked Mother, almost pleadingly, "Do you not see them?"

"If I do speak, you will not believe me," said Mother, and it was then that Richard knew there would be only one ending.

The girls shouted at her with one voice, "You do see them. . . . You do . . ."

Mother pointed at them forcefully as any judge and said, "You lie. I am wronged." The fits grew and bubbled over and became so violent that the chief judge called forward the Salem sheriff for the touch test.

The sheriff held out Mother's arm, and the girl named Mercy Lewis came forward and was immediately made calm by touching it. Then the judges ordered that Mother be tied hand and foot, and as she was being bound with a stout rope, the girl named Mary told the judges that Goody Carrier had revealed to her in dreams she had been a witch these forty years. At these last words Mother cried out as she was being dragged away, "A neat trick that, as I would have been only two years old upon becoming a witch. Do you suppose I rode then upon my rattle?"

Once she was removed from the court, the girls became calm and peaceful until the next man or woman was brought forward for examination. Richard saw the sheriff put Mother in another cart and turn south for the Salem Town jail. She lay on the rough boards, as there was no straw beneath her, but when Richard tried following the cart, she shook her head and there was nothing left for him to do but walk back to Andover. He returned to the house before supper and after telling us of what he'd seen, we sat without speaking through the slanting light of dusk. Before the light had left the sky completely, I walked out of the house, and though Father called to me, I did not answer but ran as fast as I could to Chandler's Inn. I had thought to scorch their smokehouse, or cut off all of Phoebe Chandler's hair as she lay sleeping, but I had no burning taper and nothing sharp to cut with. But as I approached the yard, I saw three men finishing their work on a small outbuilding, and in the distance walking towards them, carrying buckets of food and beer, was Phoebe Chandler.

I quickly crossed the road and, hidden in full by the evening shadows, slipped into a stand of stunted pines that circled behind the inn on three sides. I waited for the men to finish their supper and, after packing away their tools, they parted company, leaving Phoebe to gather up the remnants of food and drink. I believe I could have walked up and tread on her toes and she would never have seen me because of her weak sight and because the moon was still empty in the night sky. But I stayed concealed in the trees and called out to her, making my voice low and threatening, "Girl, what are you doing there?" So startled was she that she shrieked and did not so much drop the buckets as fling them away. She stood twisting and turning about, looking for a body to put to the voice. And when she finally bent to pick up the scattered plates and bowls, I called out again. "Girl, whither go you?" She screamed again and, gathering what she could, ran for the inn.

Chasing her through the shadows, I made my breath harsh and ragged as though some desperate and hungering wolf were at her heels, and stopped only when she threw herself against the kitchen door. I watched her struggle mindlessly to push the door open, forgetting in her frenzy that the door was hinged to swing outward. I stood and laughed silently as she pounded and screamed and begged to be let in. Finally her mother, standing on the inside and fearing impending murder, flung wide the door and in so doing knocked Phoebe, with no little force, to the ground. She screamed and cried into her mother's bulky breast, gibbering that some ghoulish force had hunted her through the yard. In the beginning, the walk home brought feelings of satisfied vengeance. But, like a frightened mule treading over my heels, my dark, disheartened feelings soon overwhelmed me. Throwing Phoebe Chandler down a well would not have brought Mother back from prison and no childish pranks would change the opinion of the courts.

It was full-on night before I returned home, but no one had gone to bed, and though Father looked long at me, he did not ask questions. There were some dried bits of bread and meat still on the table but I had no strength left to clear it properly and so let it lie. I picked up Hannah and took her to bed with me, grateful for once to have her arms wrapped tightly and possessively about my neck. I lay for hours without sleeping, the images of Mother's inquest growing more grotesque and threatening as the hours passed. I thought of all she had said to me the night before and wondered how soon it would be before they came for the rest of us. I thought of Mother's book and the bloody deeds recorded within and the testimony of the girls saying Mother had told them to sign the Devil's book. All through the night I fell in and out of sleep and burned as if with a fever and wondered if the red book buried under the elm was filling the air with the scent of burning hemp and sulfur.

AND SO WE passed into June, and as the seed was in the ground, it was decided that Richard and Father would by turns make the daily walk to Salem to bring food to Mother while she awaited her trial. We could not risk further injury to the horse on such a journey and it was just as well for, truth be told, Father with his bounding stride could walk faster than any horse at a walk. In the space of a day, it was twelve miles there and back again, taking the shorter, southerly route through Falls Woods. On occasion Robert Russell lent us his horse and we could carry by cart enough food to feed Mother as well as those prisoners who had no family to provide for them. Once a week Father brought Mother a clean shift for the soiled one she had worn for seven days, and salve for her skin, swelling and chafing under her irons. The first week when Father brought back the dirty linen, it was crawling with lice and crusted at the edge with her own, or someone else's, waste. She had had her monthly courses and there was a large rust-brown shadow where she had bled onto her shift. I boiled it twice in lye to kill all the vermin and cried enough salt into the pot to bleach it white, but it would not come clean again. I folded it in such a way as to hide the stain and tucked lavender into the folds so that she would have the scent of something wholesome within the walls of her prison.

Father had to bring coins those first few days to pay back the Salem sheriff for the cost of Mother's manacles. Everyone held in chains had to recompense George Corwin for this and for any food brought into the jail by his wife. We had heard that when John Proctor and his wife were arrested, they had no coins, and so the sheriff had taken everything from their home that could be carried out, draining beer from a barrel to cart away the wooden stays and even spilling food from the cook pot left for the Proctors' children, made orphans with their parents' imprisonment.

Our days settled into a steady, predictable rhythm, and we each moved forward in our tasks as best we could. Much like a dog that has lost a forelimb but can still hobble to hunt, to eat, to move about from here to there. In spirit it was more like a starfish stabbed through its middle, its disparate parts moving and writhing but in opposite directions, as though its only reason for unity was destroyed when its center was pierced.

We did our share of work, made twofold because of Mother's absence, but we finished every task as though we were completely alone in our endeavors. Both Father and Richard remained mute on what they had seen and heard in the Salem jail, and the rest of us were left to thread together the shape of things from those few left in Andover who would come near us: Reverend Dane's family and the Russells. Their reticence soon infected all of us, and all bantering talk ceased, all teasing, all play with words. Even complaints came fewer and farther between, until silence seemed to settle over our house and fields like a steady, drizzling rain. Richard's quiet reserve darkened and settled harshly into a bitter, implacable wordlessness, and any attempts to plead with him or pester him into revelations would be met with a shove or a backhanded swipe.

Andrew, confused and distressed over Mother's absence, began to moan for hours at a time, until his turbid thoughts made a connection between his keening and Richard's knuckles upon his head. He perhaps worked the hardest, as his time was spent running from the field and barn to the kitchen to help me move the lug pole for the cooking pot or pull Hannah from under my feet. Hannah, though she had never fully settled into my mother's care again, became ever more brittle and fragile in her mind after Mother's arrest. The littlest disruption would send her into a frenzied crying and she would cling to my legs like ivy to brick. My own worry and exhaustion had made me short-tempered and mean, and more than once I pinched her arm hard enough to bruise. At those times, when her howling pricked my conscience, I would give her my poppet and after a time she would be silent and watchful again. Or I would give her a handful of June strawberries, little and sweet, and watch as she wiped her soiled hands on her skirt, the red jellied pulp smeared like blood on the cloth.

Many times at night, when I was awake long enough to form any thoughts at all, I would make a silent promise to talk to my brothers and warn them that the sheriff could come at any time to arrest us and take us to prison. Night after night I formed a resolve to make them promise on the morrow what I had promised Mother: to tell the judges whatever they wished to hear and in so doing save ourselves. But the days peeled away and I could not bring myself to speak of those things, as though by my being silent, our confinement would not come to pass. I came to believe that Mother, by remaining steadfast in her innocence, would soon be made free.

One day, a few weeks after Mother was arrested, I said as much to Richard as we worked at the well, trying to retrieve the bucket that had fallen into the water. The rope was old and had finally split and, as Richard worked with an iron hook and a length of rope, I leaned over the lip, holding a lantern. The well had been dug in my grandfather's day and the stones were slick with green and black lichen, punctured with vining tree roots. The level of water was low, for Blanchard's Pond, which fed the well underground, had shrunk from the heat of the season.

The day was dark from low-riding clouds and we worked to fish out the bucket before the rain came. It was quiet as the world often gets before a storm, the air close and oppressive, the lantern lighting our faces from below as we leaned into the mossy cavern, giving our skin a gnomish green hue. His hands moved my arms impatiently here and there, turning the lantern about to better see the bucket floating in the black water. His face was close to mine and I saw that he had not shaved with Father's razor that morning and his chin was peppered with dark whiskers.

I said, "I think Mother will be coming home soon." He looked at me oddly but did not answer. After a while I prompted, "There is no one as determined as Mother when she sets her mind on a thing. She will wear them down with her talking."

Richard had been retrieving and throwing down the hook in a lackluster fashion but with my words his throws became more forceful. He said quietly, as though to himself, "You don't know what you're talking about."

I had been looking for some reassurance, some encouragement, but his careless remark cut me and I said, "Richard, you don't know everything. I know a thing or two. Mother told me . . ."

"You don't know anything," he said, raising his voice to me as though I were standing across the field and not shoulder to shoulder with him, his breath hot in my face.

We pulled back from the lip of the well and stood angrily facing each other. I was furious with him for his arrogance and roughness, but more than being angry I was frightened. Richard's face in the lantern's half-light, the ragged stones of the well behind his head, made him appear to be walled in by a prison and I reached out to him, grabbing hold of his arm. He shook off my hand and said, "They have hanged Bridget Bishop." I looked at him without understanding and he said, bending close to me, "They have hanged Bridget Bishop as a witch. She was condemned at Salem court and taken by cart to Gallows Hill and hanged with three fathoms of rope."

"When?" I asked, my mind filling with questions I did not want to ask.

"Last Friday past. On the tenth of June."

"But if they hanged her —"

"You mean if they hanged her, she must have been a witch. She was a spiteful, razor-tongued tavern keeper who kept poppets in her cellar. But she was cried out against because they said she was a witch. She was brought to trial and convicted because they said she was a witch. And she was hanged because they said she was a witch." Richard had grabbed both of my arms and was shaking me with every word as one would rattle a gourd. Suddenly he let go of me and sank down against the stones of the well, putting his hands over his head.

"You don't know what it's like. They are but ... girls. But they cry and carry on and point their fingers at this one and that one. They're listened to and believed and another man or woman is thrown into Salem jail. And anyone who stands against them is cried upon as a witch. Sarah, I've been to the trials. I saw Bridget Bishop condemned, and it was like being full-blown mad to stand in that meetinghouse and see every eye turn savage."

"And what about Mother? She is no witch. She must be believed," I said, my body shaking.

"Goody Bishop protested her innocence even as they were putting the noose around her neck." He must have taken pity then, for he said, "There is a sort of quiet in Salem now. There are no new arrests. And every mind is turned toward the Indian raid at the fort in Wells. We must hope that one or all of the judges will come to good sense before the next session."

A soft dousing rain came at that moment, soaking us through, and I said, "They will come for us next. Mother said it would happen. She said we should tell them everything they wish to hear even if it means we are to say we are all witches. If we do, she says they will let us go."

A small movement over my right shoulder snapped my head around and I saw Tom hunched in the rain, his face pale, his lips a bluish tint, as he struggled to breathe. I don't know how long he had been listening but it must have been a good while, for he could not have been more panicked had my own fingers pressed hard about his throat. He wheeled around and lurched off into the fields, disappearing into the growing stalks of corn made soft and insubstantial by the warm and rising mists.

THE INCIDENT AT the well moved my two brothers in opposing directions. For Richard, his outburst had loosened some hard wall within his breast and he seemed, if not at peace, not as troubled as he had been. He was reluctant at first to tell me of the conditions in the jail because Mother had made him promise to keep what he had seen to himself. But I pestered him until he described the day-to-day life, the crowding, the filth, and the fear, and he soon took to Salem little scraps of notes I wrote to her. I spent most of a day torturing out the letters for a message that read, "Deare Mother. Wee are all missing you. Wee are all clean, but for Hanah, and are fed well as theire is meete for the pot." I received back a message from Mother written on the bottom of my parchment with some bit of charcoal. "Dearest Sarah. Practice your letters more. Yours, and ever faithful."

I pored over the note, disappointed in its brevity, searching for deeper meanings of sentiment within the message. Never once did I think of the cost to my mother, searching through the dark of her cell for the blacking to carefully inscribe the letters she could barely see. There were smudges where her hand marked the paper, and there would be many times I wished I had kept that note. The delicate swirls and ridges of her fingers imprinted in the paper with the filth of her captivity had been her truer message to me.

For Tom, the knowledge he received at the well shriveled and weighed down on him like a cider press until he looked as spent and knobby as a dried pear. His eyes were the worst, and when they lit on you, it was with the pleadings of a drowning boy. He daily struggled to work, but one day out in the fields, his shoulders harnessed to a leather strap wrapped around a stump, he threw off his harness and without a word walked away, climbing the stairs to the attic and lying down on his pallet. He did not answer Father's calls, he did not come down for supper, and when I climbed the stairs later to feel his head and threaten him with a physic, he would not look at me or talk to me. The next morning after breakfast Father climbed the stairs and was with Tom for a long time before they came down together. And though Tom continued to walk in the shadows, he ate his meals and worked and talked when spoken to and so remained among the living.

On Thursday, the 16th of June, Uncle was found dead in his Boston cell. His death was ruled suspicious, and so an inquest was called by the King's Coroner of Suffolk County. The findings from the fifteen men who viewed the body and who signed the Coroner's Return were that Uncle had died of natural causes. We received the news from Robert Russell the following Sunday evening while sitting at Sabbath supper.

Though we had stopped going to the meetinghouse after Mother's arrest, I had tried following her custom of roasting meat saved for that day. I had scorched the shank, and the bread was coarse and gritty, but no one complained as we sat quietly together in the common room, the early evening breezes sifting through the open doors, lifting the day's sweat from our arms and necks. Watching Robert cross the yard, his face long and solemn, I grabbed my head in my hands for fear it was to do with Mother. But when he told us Uncle was gone, it seemed to come as no surprise to Father, who only looked at Richard and nodded as though some private pact between them had been settled. Robert walked with Father to the yard, where they spoke together for some time. Richard sat with his head turned sharply to the door, marking the men in the yard as closely as one would mark an elk in a clearing. His breathing was shallow and rapid and when he turned back to his plate his gaze met mine.

My eyes had filled with tears and Richard said savagely, "Don't you cry. Don't you cry for that man."

I shook away the tears and went to my bed, pulling the coverlet over my head. It was no secret that Uncle had been weaving false stories against Mother from his prison cell, no doubt in the hopes of saving himself. Or with the hope of being recompensed with Grandmother's farm if he should be set free and the Carriers all arrested. He had even said that Mother's spirit came to Aunt Mary and tortured her with terrible dreams that the Indians would kill her unless Aunt signed her name in the Devil's book. We all knew of Aunt's great fear of raids and it was cruel and unjust to advance her longstanding terrors as the result of witchcraft. He put about that Aunt would freely testify to these spectral visitations if given the chance. I had thought I had little love left for Uncle, pitying more Aunt and Margaret brought to prison through his scheming. But I cried for him then, my pain made all the greater knowing that Father had only just been to Boston to visit him in his cell.

In the early morning hours of Wednesday, the 15th of June, the day before Uncle died, a stranger had come to the door and told Father that Uncle wished to see him as soon as was humanly possible. The man was a physician returning to Haverhill from Boston and had, as an act of charity, attended to those who were imprisoned there. He told Father that Uncle was well enough in body but that he was heartsick and desired for Father to come to Boston. He gave Father a sealed bit of parchment to read and left us before we had even thought to offer him food or drink. Father read the note and then threw it into the fire. Before it had been reduced to ashes, he had taken up his coat and hat and was on his way to Robert's farm to borrow his horse.

When he rode past the house going north towards Boston, Richard ran after him, following insistently until Father dismounted and spoke to my brother at length. Soon Richard trudged back to the house, but when I questioned him he would say only that Father had gone to visit Uncle. And though he would speak no more on it, his eyes were hard and glittering, almost triumphant. Father was gone the whole of that day and the next, returning to us on Thursday evening, the 16th day of June. The day that Uncle would have died.

I thought, as I lay suffocating under the covers to hide my tears, of something Mother had once said. "Happy accidents come to those who have the mettle to hatch them." I thought of the resolute knowingness that had settled around Father's eyes at Robert's news and I was overcome with a terrible feeling that death had come to Roger Toothaker most unnatural.

IT HAS BEEN said that the days of a child pass very slowly, as they are at the beginning of things and old age and death are a distant dream. But the days following my mother's arrest passed by at such a pace that I sometimes imagined I could feel the winds from the sun and the moon as they hurtled themselves across the sky. And every day I watched the world with two pairs of eyes and ears. One pair on my work and another watching and listening for the approach of the constable's cart.

On the 28th day of June the Salem Court of Oyer and Terminer began its second session. Rebecca Nurse was found not guilty by the court's jurors, but there was such a hideous outcry from the accusers and the judges that the jurors were sent back to reconsider, and when they returned she was convicted as charged. Over the five days of that second session there were twelve men and women brought to the court, my mother being one of them. On July 1st Father went to Salem to attend her trial. He woke me up before dawn on that morning to make his breakfast and fill a sack with food and he left, saying only, "If

I'm going to a dogfight I want to be there to hear the first growl."

At the trial, my mother was indicted for two spectral attacks by young women she had never seen before coming to Salem. It seemed that Uncle's death did not stop the accusations or the crushing slide towards a final justice. When Father returned to us that night, he told us that Mother was taken back to jail and that her sentencing would not come until sometime in August. What he did not tell us then was that five other women, including Rebecca Nurse, had been convicted and were to be hanged before the month had ended.

The month of July flew on and grew unbearably hot as Mother had predicted it would be. We rose each day to put on steaming, dirty clothes, we chewed our flattened bread and moistened it with water so that it would not catch in our gullets, we wiped the sweat and chased the flies, and ate our soup at noontide, and pounded our fraying implements against post and stump, shredded our meat for supper, and laid ourselves down again at evening-tide to wrestle against our dreams and our fetid sheets. I had made myself my father's shadow and the house could have burned down for all the care I gave it in order to be at his side in the barn and in the fields on the days he did not go into Salem.

My dress was torn under both arms from lifting and hauling heavy loads, and the skin on my knees was torn and scabbed over from the scratches I received on my bare legs, but I gave no thought to stockings or sewing, preferring the safety and comfort of standing close to the towering figure of my father. Hannah had grown so dirty and her clothes so threadbare that had

I the strength for shame, I would have hung my head to see her trailing flies like a yearling stoat. She never seemed to mind, and as long as I was within her sight, she played happily in the dirt of the fields or the hay of the barn. Her playthings were whatever came to hand: a stick, a bottle, a spoon, for we had no time or desire to make her the simplest of toys.

On the 14th of the month, Father and I were working to right the murmet that had fallen over in the cornfield. The stalks were by then over the crown of my head but Father's head was so far above the silk that, had he been a hundred yards away, I could have found my way back to his side. I held the lug pole while he wrapped birch whips around a sturdy branch that would make the murmet's arms. We mostly worked in silence but for the chattering of Hannah as she braided some corn leaves together to make a wreath for her head. I felt cocooned within the wall of corn and the comfort of it loosened my tongue and I asked, "Father, did you have such a murmet when you were a boy?"

"Aye," he said and I thought he would leave it at that but he continued, "But that's your mother's word. We people from Wales called him a boogan."

I stumbled over the word a few times, the Welsh harsh in my mouth. I knew that Father had grown up speaking a language that was not like the English we spoke but he rarely used it around us. He turned the murmet around to face the east and molded my hands over the pole to make it stand firm while he planted it again in the ground. "Some of the north folk call him a scarecrow," he said. "But the English have better ways to make scarce the crows." He said "English" in such a way that sounded scornful, and, though his face was placid enough, his mouth was frowning and troubled.

"And what is that, Father?" I asked, coaxing him to talk more.

"They put pikes all round the perimeter of a field. The pikes are sharpened to a razor's point. And on every pike, pierced through the breast, is a blackbird. Some yet live and flapping. The crows don't like it. And as long as any part of the black-birds cling to the poles the corn stays whole. That's the English way."

As Father knelt down to tamp new earth at the base of the pole, I looked to the outer edges of our little field and imagined it ringed with sharpened sticks all tipped with wilted, quivering bodies. His voice came close to my ear. "It's how the English run their courts. They sacrifice innocents, thinking to keep evil at bay, and call it a kind of justice. But they are no more just than this pole is a man." When I looked back at him he was still kneeling, his eyes close to mine, and the strength of his gaze made my throat tighten. He said with a sudden passion, "I would move the earth to save your mother. D'ye hear me, Sarah? I would tear down the walls of her jail and carry her to the wilds of Maine, but it is not what she wants. She will throw herself at her judges because she believes that her innocence will show through all the lies and deceptions."

He looked away, sweeping his eyes across the horizon, and said softly, as though speaking to the wind, "She humbles me with her strength." I studied closely the granite features of his face in profile. I saw the dirt lining the pores of his skin and the curved lines of pitted canals encircling his eyes and lips and saw the stamp of years of struggles of which I knew nothing.

"Is there nothing we can do?" I asked him, my hands closing around his arm.

He looked back at me and said, "It is in her hands and the hands of her judges."

It was not what I wanted to hear from his lips. I wanted him to hatch some black and fatal plan to release her. I wanted to shout out to him, "But what about Uncle? He was against us and now he is dead." I wanted to cry, "If you love her, let loose the dogs, Father. Burn down the jail. Bring a cudgel down onto the head of the sheriff, grease the locks, swing wide the door, and in the dead of night lift her from her prison and carry her away." And then, I thought, then the rest of us might be saved as well. But I said nothing. I only looked at him, my eyes burning in their sockets, my grip tightening around his forearm, and I remembered it was Mother who had come to my rescue that day at the meetinghouse when Phoebe stood over me, whispering "witch," and he only sat in the wagon.

He said, "I have talked with her by the hour these many weeks. But the stones in her cell will change their course before she will." He grabbed me around my shoulder and pulled me closer to him, saying, "I would shame her by begging her to lie or speak falsely of another. Do you understand what I'm saying, Sarah? We, all of us, must be left alone to make good on our own consciences. And no county magistrate or judge or deacon can separate us from the truth, for they are only men. You would say to me, 'Father, if you love her, save her.' But it is for love that I will not seek to sway her away from the truth. Even if it means she will die for it."

His eyes as they met mine were desperate and searching like some Celtic king who has launched his queen's funeral bier into the river and in his grief would swim after it and in so doing drown himself. I remembered my mother gently stroking the side of his face as they spoke in front of the fire those many weeks ago, and for the first time in my young life I had a presentiment of womanly feelings and I knew then that he loved her. But from that time on, I would never think of the love between them without the partial taste of flint in my mouth.

I said weakly, "You are saying that she is lost to us."

He bent his massive head to one side as though he would rest it on my shoulder and he said softly, "I am saying that she is not lost to herself."

Suddenly we heard the frantic barking of the lurcher from the yard. Father stood up, almost knocking me over, and, dropping his shovel, ran towards the house. I grabbed for Hannah and ran stumbling after him, my legs weak and shaking, thinking, "They have surely come for us." When I cleared the field, I saw that a wagon had stopped in the road in front of the house and in it were a man and two women. They were as any other villagers of Andover and about, wearing their drab workday clothes, the women in their starched caps, the man wearing an old felt hat. But they sat so queerly still and quiet, watching us as we approached them from the yard, that for a moment they looked carved from stone. The breath caught in my throat, as I thought that our warrants had come, but as I got nearer I saw that the man was not the constable but the constable's brother,

Joseph Ballard. Joseph was a close neighbor who lived just to the north a quarter mile on Boston Way Road. His wife had been gravely ill for several months, and Mother had sent herbs for her fever in the spring before she was taken to Salem. Goody Ballard had only worsened and it would surprise no one if she died.

Father hailed the wagon but something in their silence made him wary and tense, the muscles in his forearm flexed and tight. They did not greet us or smile or even nod. They said not a word but stared at us until Hannah buried her face in my hair, tangled and loose without a cap to keep it neat. The young women whispered together and then one of them, a heavy, raw-boned woman with a scarred lip, whispered to Joseph. She pointed to me and Hannah, and in that one small gesture the earth pitched and rolled beneath my feet. Father, seeing them point to us, walked with a set jaw towards the wagon. Joseph quickly jostled the reins and urged his horse away from the yard. We stood and watched them retreating north up the road and never once did they turn to look back. I would later learn that the constable's brother had gone to Salem Village to fetch the witch finders Mercy Lewis and Betty Hubbard, who had uncovered more than a dozen witches in their own town. He had long feared that his wife was ill because of maleficence, and since Mother's arrest he had come to believe that she was the cause of their family's misery. The young women would later give further testimony against my mother.

On the 15th day of July, Robert Russell came to us with the news that in four days' time Sarah Good, Elizabeth Howe, Susannah Martin, Rebecca Nurse, and Sarah Wildes, women from four different towns, were to be hanged by the neck until dead at Gallows Hill in Salem. He had meant to tell Father alone, but Father called us all into the house and seated us together at the table. We did not weep or cry out to one another or reach out for any comfort, for there was no comfort to be had. I thought of Mother in her cell and I said a silent prayer that we would be arrested soon so that I might see her before her sentencing. I remembered Dorcas Good, Sarah Good's little daughter, who had been imprisoned and in chains with her mother. I asked Robert if she would be released upon her mother's death, and he paused before saying that she had been left motherless in her dark cell. She would not be released for another four months. It would take that time for her father to raise the bail to release her. That night in bed as Hannah slept, I gave myself over to my tears of misery and anger. I tore the pillow with my teeth and stretched the blankets between my hands until the seams came loose, and sometime deep in the night I dreamt of blackbirds pierced through the breast, struggling against the pike.

IF WE COULD see the fullness of our tomorrows, how many of us would take desperate action to change the future? What if our far seeing showed us the loss of our homes, our families, our very lives, and to save it all we would need only to barter away our most precious souls. Who among us would give up what we cannot see for what we can hold in our hands? I believe many of us would peel ourselves away from our immortal selves as easily as the skin from a boiled plum if it meant we could remain on the earth for a while, our bellies full and our beds warm and safe at night.

My mother would not and she would pay the price for her resolve. She was too singular, too outspoken, too defiant against her judges, in defense of her innocence, and it was for this, more than for proof of witchcraft, that she was being punished. Which made it all the more remarkable that my father was not. In all of the months of the witching madness, my father, a man of preternatural size and strength who against custom hunted and fished alone and who said hardly a word to his neighbors, was never questioned, deposed, tried, imprisoned, or even cried out against, and the jails held men aplenty who had supported their suspected wives.

What was it, then, that kept my father walking free among his fellows? There had been widespread rumors among our neighbors of his life in old England. Was it his reputation as a soldier that kept people at a distance? I would have worked my way to asking Robert Russell about Father's soldiering, as they had been comrades in old England, but I would not get the op-portunity. After Robert told us of the hangings, Father put his hands on Robert's shoulders and said with great sorrow, "My friend. My old friend, you put yourself and your family in peril by keeping company with us. You must not come here again until all this has ended." At first Robert protested strongly, but he soon saw the wisdom of it and left, promising to do what he could to help us.

Mounting his horse, he said to Father in parting, "Salem Village isn't the only town where rumors and gossip of the dead can be resurrected to wreak havoc." And with those queer words he rode away and I was made more alone than ever.

Alone except for my sister, my brothers, and Father. And to my father I had always been a kind of stranger. I had rarely ever been in his company except to bring him food or a drink of water. Father's silent and purposeful work about the farm had been so ever-present, and at the same time so distant, that I came to view his movements as unremarkable as a field horse or an ox. But while the days without Mother passed, I molded myself to his rhythms, rose when he rose, slept when he slept, and flayed muscle from bone to lift and carry and dig as much as my brothers could. And in that time, I watched him and I watched others who came across his path, and I saw that they were, almost without exception, in great fear of him.

The day after Robert's last visit to us I went with Father to Thomas Chandler's iron mill for a small bag of nails and a blade sharpening for one of our scythes. Thomas Chandler was brother to William Chandler, the innkeeper, and was one of the most prominent men in Andover, his mill a kind of gathering place for the men of the town. Father at first told me to stay and look after Hannah, as Richard had left early to bring a sack of food to Salem jail, leaving only Tom and Andrew to mind the farm. But I had grown a mortal fear of being without his protecting presence, and my fear made me immovable. I threatened to throw myself under the wheels if he did not take Hannah and me, so he finally relented and lifted us up to sit with him on the driving board. The way to the mill was as to the center of town but for the sharp turn west on Newbury Road before reaching the burying grounds. The mill sat on the western side of the Shawshin River, and the morning we pulled over the little bridge to approach the ironworks, there were four or five wagons with men coming to repair, sharpen, or buy new tools for the harvesting that was fast approaching.

The men had been standing about in small groups as we pulled up, no doubt trading village news and waiting for their turn at the forge, but when Father climbed down from the wagon they stopped all their talking. They stared at us for a moment and then turned away as though from a chilly wind come off the water. They stood awkwardly hunching their shoulders, making dust motes in the air and islands in the dirt with the toes of their boots. Now, Father never ambled or shuffled and rarely slowed his gait through furrow or field, and when he was in his full loping stride I had to go at a dead run to keep to his heels. He pulled his large harvesting scythe from the wagon and walked towards the men at such a pace that the wind from his swinging arms could have filled a small sail. A ripple went through the small group, and they looked at first to stand firm and make him go around them. But as the rusted and sharply upturned blade of the scythe swung its way ever closer, the group parted wide and Father passed through them unmolested.

Once he had entered the forge, the men came into a group again, like flesh cleaving together after a sharp wound. They turned to Hannah and me to steal a look now and then, but I met each eye with a straightaway stare, which I think made them bold. After a time one of them, a man I had seen only in passing on the Boston Way Road, said loud enough for me to hear, "So the mother goes, there the children will follow."

Another man laughed and said, "By the looks of the older one, they'd better send for the constable quick before we're struck down with black looks." My fists tightened, bunching up my skirt into twin hillocks on my thighs. The other men had turned and were looking at me speculatively, their eyes wary, amused, hostile. Hannah crawled beneath the driving board and went silent, like an animal run to ground.

Then another man said, "They say there is one true test for a witch. You throw 'em in the river. If they drown, their innocence is proved. If they float, they're a witch and you take 'em out and hang 'em."

They made a great show at being at their ease but they edged closer, inch by inch, to Father's wagon. I think had I been alone, they might have drowned me in the river and been done with it. But at that moment a deeply resonant voice rumbled out from the forge, saying, "Who'll be next at the fire?"

The men wheeled around as if one body and I saw Father standing in the shadow of the forge, his old scythe blade sharpened and polished, and as he passed into the sunlight, the blade winked wickedly at the men. He stood a full foot and a half taller than the tallest of them, and when the sun struck his face his eyes were black and obsidian-like. The heated sweat from the forge had soaked through his coarse-woven shirt, his long hair looked lank and oiled, and a fire-smudge banded his nose. He must have looked to the men standing in the yard as the lime-washed druids looked to the Roman soldiers standing on the other side of a Welsh river.

Father called out, "Who, then, is next? Is it you, Granger, who lives on New Meadow?" His arm made a slight swinging motion, bringing the scythe along with its arc. "Or is it you, Hagget, that lives on Blanchard's Pond? Or maybe it's you, Farnum, who lives at Boston Hill?" And so he went, calling to the eight or so men that stood in the yard, naming their names and their farms, harvesting the air with his scythe, and putting them on notice that he knew them all and where they lived. He said the words not with a threatening tone, but as simply as a county tax collector will call the next man in a queue to make good on his debt. But there was something else beyond the words my Father said, something in the set of his face and the way he held his body at the ready, that washed the air with urgency and tension. The scalp on the back of my head tightened and I knew from the way the men buried their heads in their collarbones and hurried for their wagons or to the forge that there had already been some seed of fearfulness placed in their hearts.

Father laid the scythe as lovingly as a babe in the straw and, climbing into the wagon, hitched the reins around to return us home. I looked at him from the corner of my eye on the journey back, but he said nothing more to me, as though scattering a group of seasoned yeomen to the winds without a blow given or any harsh curses traded was an everyday occurrence. It was this incident at the mill that caused me to study my father in a new light, for not only had he raised himself in status in the pecking order of men but his actions left me in no doubt that I was in his protecting care. Not the strident and crackling interventions of my mother but a quieter, more subtle kind. It was our last visit to the Andover meetinghouse that revealed to me, at least in part, the fear and dread that most people felt for my father.

A dread that went beyond a natural temerity in the presence of brute force.

Reverend Dane came to us that evening, bringing food and some clothing but not even a small measure of hope. He told us he had visited Mother in her prison cell and that she had made peace with God and would accept whatever judgment came from the magistrates. He had it on good authority that we, the children, would be brought soon to the magistrates in Salem Village and because of this he begged us to come back to the meetinghouse on the morrow, as it would go better for us all if we showed publicly our faith in God. Father listened to him respectfully but when the old man finished speaking, he got up and brought down Mother's Bible from the carved sidepiece next to the table. He opened to the Gospel of Matthew and, stabbing a verse with his finger, walked from the room and didn't return until the Reverend took his leave. Later, searching through the pages in Matthew, I found the dark smudge of his forefinger over the verse that said, "But when thou prayest, go thou into thy room, close the door, and pray to thy Father, who is unseen." But Father did take us to the Andover meetinghouse on that last Sunday of our freedom, the 17th day of July, because if there was any chance of swaying our judges in our favor, he would take it.

We could not have created a greater furor had we appeared naked in the center of town. When we walked into the meetinghouse, there was no masking the animosity towards the Carrier family. Father, Richard, Andrew, and Tom had no real trouble finding a place with the men, but there was no pity shown from the women, who would not move an inch, forcing me to stand in the aisle with a squirming Hannah in my arms. Phoebe Chandler raised her chin to look at me down the long barrel of her nose, but then she caught sight of Richard's thundering looks and quickly put her attention to the pulpit. She would later say in her deposition for the Salem court that Richard's look caused her to be struck deaf for the whole of the service. It was only a pity that she wasn't struck mute as well. Father looked over at me once, and to make him proud I raised my head and squared my back, glaring at the Reverend Barnard, who by this time had taken the pulpit entirely for his own, banishing the Reverend Dane to the pews below. It was no surprise, then, that his sermon would come from First Peter: "Thine enemy, the Devil prowls around like a roaring lion looking for someone to devour . . ."

Hannah soon became impossible to hold, so I tried tethering her with my hand round her wrist, but she pulled and protested, so I dragged her outside, and as the day was hot, I sat with her under the nearest wagon. I kept her content, letting her dig in the dirt, not scolding her for making piles of it in her apron. She looked every inch an orphan, unwashed and unkempt. Since Mother had left, we had all grown dirtier and shabbier, and I looked at the grime packed under my nails and thought with a twinge of Margaret's smooth, clean hands.

We had stayed under the wagon for most of an hour when I heard the doors open and two men walked to the wagon carrying a third man, who was coughing and wheezing in the extremis of old age. They had left the service early to give the old man some air. As they approached, they began speaking, and before I could make my way from under the wagon, they had lifted the grandfather into the straw at the back. I could not then, without terrible embarrassment, show myself to them, and the longer they talked, the more difficult it became to come out like some lizard crawling from under a stone. I could only see their lower legs but I could hear their voices clearly and I hoped Hannah would be still and not give us away.

The first man said as he clapped the old man on the back, "What think you of them coming bold as ever to the meeting-house?" He had recently switched his square-toed boots around left to right but they had not had time to form themselves to their new occupants, so his feet looked put on crossways.

The other man, shorter and stouter and with the lingering burr of a childhood spent in Scotland, said, "The children are fey, no doubt about it. But it's him that makes my blood thicken." He put a great weight on "him" and I knew he was speaking of Father. He continued conspiratorially, as one would tell a ghost story to a child. "What kind of a man hunts alone? In these woods. Filled with Indians. A dead shot that one. He felled a bear as big as a house with one shot to the neck. I saw the car-cass, passing up the road. Biggest I'd ever seen. They say the Indians are even afraid of him."

Then Goodman Crossways said, "I was told a few years back, in Boston he killed a man with one blow to the head."

"No," said Goodman Stout, "it was fifteen year ago if it was a day, and he knocked the man down in Billerica. Near killed him. But didn't. He was fined for it, though."

The old man had stopped coughing, and I heard the wagon creak as he lay back on the straw to rest. The two pairs of legs came closer together and their voices lowered to near whispers.

Said Crossways, "Don't worry. You can speak. The old man's as deaf as a post. They fined Carrier because who would have the bones to put chains on that giant? He was a trained soldier in the royal guards, you know. Some say bodyguard to the King, until he switched sides to Cromwell. It's not many men who could have a witch to wife and still remain at liberty. Have you heard the worst, though?"

Said Stout, "Aye. Between us two, and God grant the second Charles a long life, being a Scot I have some fond remembrance of Old Oliver. But killing a king is something else entirely."

Crossways shushed him and said apprehensively, "It'll never be known for sure but that rumor of taking an axe to the first Charles has followed him for near thirty years as closely as hide on a dog. The man must be charmed to have escaped the King's justice for so long."

Then Stout spat on the dirt and said, "Charmed? An executioner's always masked, so who's to say? Besides, even if it could be proved he killed the King, who's going to serve the warrant on him? You? Robert Russell, who has his ear to the ground, has put about that there is a secret society of Cromwell's old army living as plain as a tit out of an ol' bawd's blouse. Here, right here in Andover. They look after one another and are sworn to avenge any of their own that are captured or mistreated. Russell says that they would come to the traitor's house in the wee hours before morning and cut off the offending head, put it in a black bag, and plant it in some bog, just like they did to Charles the first. Oh yes, quite a charm. One with an iron point at the end."

Crossways said, "Merciful Jesus. It's not enough that we have witchcraft to fear, but now we must lock our doors against avenging guardsmen."

Then Stout rested his foot on the wheel, brushing the powdery dust from his boots and clucking his tongue over Cromwell's hidden army. Hearing Robert's name made me wonder if he was working quietly as our murmet, shaking to life the breeze of fear-inspiring gossip to chase away the crows.

Stout continued, "And what about Roger Toothaker dead in his Boston cell? The jailer said that a tall man came to visit him on the day of his death. The tall man went in. The tall man came out and a few hours later Dr. Toothaker is stone dead without a mark on him. I tell you, there are secrets in that death. No matter what the inquest said."

At that moment, the meetinghouse doors opened and the congregants, hot and restless to catch a bit of breeze, spilled out into the yard. In that moment I grabbed Hannah and we crawled out from the far side of the wagon, but as I stood up I turned, and the stout Scotsman caught sight of me. It must have appeared to him that we had formed ourselves out of the vapors in the air, for his eyes widened as he awakened from surprise to fear, the realization growing that I had overheard his gossiping. I felt his eyes burning into my back as I walked to stand at the wagon, waiting for Father.

On the way home we were all quiet, suppressed by the leaden, hateful stares that had followed us across the green and down Boston Way Road. I pressed myself closer to my brothers, despite the wilting heat, and held Hannah's damp and drowsy body tightly in my arms. I looked at each of their faces and thought, here is Richard, a young man with a dark and moody nature. And here is Andrew, who is made a simpleton through ravaging illness. And there is Tom, whose sweet, enlivening nature is diminished daily by fear and uncertainty. I knew the composition of their inner selves, not just because it was revealed to me through their actions day to day, but because it was written plainly upon their faces. There was nothing hidden or contrary to give a lie to the face they gave to the world. And I had believed until that morning, as a child believes, that the intent and worth and very history of a person is stamped like a maker's mark on a silver chalice.

But when I looked at Father dressed in yeoman's clothes, the bones and muscles and tendons formed in opposition to rock and tree and dirt, his forehead crimped by months and years of staring into a planter's sun, my understanding of him was shattered. I thought of Father's old crimson coat hanging on the murmet's back, the coat with the saber's slash across the arm. Of the many times he had left us to go alone into woods where no other sober-minded fellow would venture. Of the deadly accuracy of his long-barreled flintlock. I thought of the tale-spinning of the two men at the meetinghouse and wondered how stories of a soldier's life and the death of a king could be fashioned from the body of a man who to all of the new England shouted, I am Farmer, Husbandman, and Toiler.

But if what they said was widely believed, it made all the more sense for Uncle to have run like a hare from Father's axe laid across our table. And for Allen's face to drain to the color of snow when Mother warned him that he would lose his head if he tried to chase us from our home. I remembered her warning me of the men willing to walk over my living body to get to the red book, the journal of our family's history. My desire in that moment to dig it up and read it burned a hole in my stomach. And finally, I remembered the stories Uncle told us as we crouched around the fire. Stories of the execution of King Charles I of England, who was taken up the steps of Whitehall-Gate, bent over a block, and separated head from neck by a tall, hooded executioner who held the head aloft for all of London to see and proclaimed, "The King, tyrant, and despoiler of the people, is dead."

As we left the meetinghouse yard, the only one to bid us farewell was Lieutenant Osgood's little black slave. He was standing off away from the crowd of the men and women of the meetinghouse, small and twisted, his shoes still immense on his bare feet, his coat more threadbare and ragged than ever. It was fitting that this boy, ignored, shunned, and despised, should be the only one to stand and wave to us until we'd disappeared from sight. I would never see him again, but I would often dream of him, and in my dreams his coat was new, the buckles on his shoes silver, his black face as sad and timeless as the dark half of the moon.

ON JULY 20TH Mary Lacey, Mercy Williams' friend who had taunted me in the Andover burial grounds and who had only just been put into Salem prison, gave testimony that she was indeed a witch, as were her own mother and grandmother. She told her inquisitors that Richard and Andrew were also witches and that Goody Carrier revealed to her at a midnight gathering of witches that the Devil had promised that she, my mother, would be Queen in Hell. On the 21st of July, John Ballard brought his cart for my two oldest brothers.

He waited until Father had left for his long walk to Salem and then strode as bold as anything into our house with the warrants. I had to call Richard and Andrew from the barn and stood alone with him in the common room while he smirked at me and told me with a crooked finger, "You'll be next, little miss." When Richard walked in and saw the master of warrants, he looked for an instant as if he might make a run but he thought better of it when John Ballard clapped his hand roughly on my shoulder and said to Richard, "If you don't come I can just take this one here."

Richard submitted to having his hands tied in front, and Andrew, following his brother's lead, willingly held out his hands to his captor. He shrank back only when the bonds were tightened hard around his wrists. They climbed into the cart, and as the constable adjusted his reins to depart, I whispered, "Richard, remember what Mother said. Tell them whatever they wish to hear."

But my heart tightened into a fist when he said, "There's nothing they can do to make me give a false statement. If Mother can hold fast, so can I."

The cart pulled away and I followed after, saying, "Richard, think of Andrew, then. He will take your lead and do what you do and say what you say." The cart was pulling away faster than I could walk, and I ran after them for a quarter mile crying out, "Richard, please, Richard . . ." He looked at me defiantly, braced with the pride of a young man who is strong and stubborn but who, until that day, has only shed his precious blood onto the edge of a shaving razor. He had turned eighteen on the 19th of the month, two days before his arrest.

When I returned to the house I found Tom curled up next to the hearth, rocking back and forth on his haunches, his face streaked with tears that had washed away the grime in pink bands down to his chin. I had no words to give him, so I sat next to him in the ashes and waited for Father to return. Upon arriving in Salem Town, five miles east of Salem Village, Andrew and Richard would be locked into the basement of Thomas Beadle's Inn for the night, as the constable did not want to take the chance of meeting my father along the road to the prison. The next morning they were taken in front of the magistrates, and among them, to see for himself the growing tide of spectral evidence, was Cotton Mather, spiritual advisor and exemplar to half of the ministers in the colonies. From his own mouth he gave instructions to Richard and Andrew to offer truthful testimony to the court. He told them that God and their earthly judges would be merciful to them if they offered up a full confession of their witchcraft. Mary Lacey, who had admitted freely to being a witch and spectrally torturing some of the girls of Salem Village, then entreated Richard to repent and admit his guilt to all. She accused him of bewitching the long-suffering Timothy Swan, the young man with whom Allen Toothaker had lived in Andover. She said Mother had killed seven people using a poppet that she stabbed with needles.

Richard had seen these judges at work at Mother's trial and the trials of others, and he did little to hide his contempt for them. To every question he answered them a curt "No" or "I have not done it." The chief magistrate, John Hathorne, then turned to Andrew, but to every question put to him he answered the same. When the magistrates could not get the compliance they had grown accustomed to having, they ordered Richard and Andrew to be taken into another room to reconsider their answers. The high sheriff and executioner of Essex County, George Corwin, waited for them in the anteroom with two lengths of rope. Richard was told to lie facedown on the floor, where his wrists were tied behind his back and his feet were bound together. After the rope had been wound round his ankles, it was then yanked up short and looped around his neck, arching his head back to meet his feet. This was called "the bow," and even with the strongest of men it took only a little while for the back to weaken, the legs and head to lower, and the rope to tighten around the throat. The strangling was slow and agonizing and, unlike with a drop from a tree branch, the neck was not broken quickly to end the victim's suffering. The tender flesh at the neck would crimp and bruise and burn, the eyes would bulge from the head and soon the blood would first trickle and then course through the nose in a torrent as the vessels burst from the pressure. The path for air would be inexorably shut off, and if the prisoner fainted, all would be lost for the laxity of the limbs would cause the rope to completely crush the airway. And although it was a departure from the usual methods of extracting a confession used in the new England, it was nevertheless called English torture because it was not considered as cruel as branding, burning, or racking.

Richard, being very strong and determined, looked to die rather than confess, so the sheriff threw Andrew down onto the floor and tied him so brutally that he bled from his wrists and neck where the rope cut into his skin. Richard later told me that Andrew cried like a little child and begged and pleaded to be released. He said over and over again, his words barely squeezing past the grip of the rope round his throat, "I'm sorry, I'm sorry, I'm sorry . . ." It was Andrew's suffering more than the danger to his own body that made Richard agree to tell his judges whatever they wished to hear.

When they brought my brothers back into the gathering room of the meetinghouse, Richard told the magistrates that he and Andrew were indeed witches but they had been so for only a little while. When asked who had made them turn against God, Richard told them that Mother had held their hands to the Devil's book and made them swear their allegiance to him. He gave them the names of other witches but named only men and women who were in jail already accused and awaiting trial or who had been found guilty and hanged. Andrew said not a word but clung to Richard's shirt and it took Sheriff Corwin and another man to separate them when their chains were brought to bind them for transport to Salem jail.

WHEN FATHER RETURNED late that afternoon and found Richard and Andrew gone, the look on his face was truly terrible. He stood and stared at a point beyond our heads and I thought the stones of the hearth would crack or the dying embers of ash and oak beneath the flue would rekindle to a raging fire. He ran into the yard and paced about and pulled at his hair and tore his hat between his hands. I could hear his voice as he hatched aloud desperate plans to rescue them but in the end he returned to the house and sat at the table, his long arms dangling between his knees. Tom and I clung together as we had done atop Sunset Rock the night of the lightning storm, and waited for Father to find his way back to us from whatever blasted and empty place he had traveled to. Hannah, hungry and afraid, cried herself to sleep under the table, a piece of dried corn bread crumbled within her hand.

Finally, long after evening had filled the common room, his voice called to us out of the shadows and he brought us each to his side, his arms encircling us with his strength and raw-boned comfort. And for the first time in my life my father held me and let my tears mix with his. In the morning we would all rise from our beds to face the slanting light, our desperate hope partnering with us as we began the summer harvesting. Most of the field would be left to rot, as there were only three of us to cut and bind and shock the staffs of wheat. But we worked side by side up and down the dusty rows, our mouths cottony from the heat and growing despair, our arms sore and trembling from the endless swinging of the scythe, and our eyes dry from searching the northern horizon for the approaching relentless crawl of the prison cart.

CHAPTER EIGHT

July–August 1692

AUGUST IS THE month for mad dogs but it was in the last days of July that we saw the cur come trotting south down Boston Way Road. Tom and I had been left alone to work in the barn since early morning. Father had gone on the long walk to Salem, carrying in his sack scarcely enough food for one person. Food that must now be shared amongst three. He made the trip erratically every few days, fearing that the constable would be watching and would come and take the rest of us while he was away.

We had all cinched our waistbands ever tighter, and hunger was a song that played in our heads morning and night. The heat had dried the Shawshin to a little stream, starving Ballard's Pond to a muddy pit and draining our well down to the smooth and mossy stones at the bottom. We had harvested whatever wheat we could, and while Tom worked from the loft to spread new straw for the animals, I thrashed and winnowed small piles of grain. The mice were the only living things in abundance in the barn, but the cow had given so little from her udder that I was loath to put out saucers of milk for the snakes. The cats, fearing the lurcher, had long since disappeared. As I watched the mice boldly eating the grain, I wondered how we could manage the back end of winter with no bread. It had been quiet in the loft for some time, the dust still settling from the last forkful of straw thrown down.

I called to Tom to stop idling and finish up his work but I got no answer. The heat had made me peckish and mean, and Hannah kept a safe distance from me, fearing more slaps than tickles. I could see her playing in the straw, pulling what was left of the yarn hair from my poppet. I had no reserves of strength left to bully her, so I called out to Tom again and saw his face appear above the ledge.

He threw down a jagged whisper, "Sarah, come up here. Right away." His face was at all times a mask of concern, but there was something to the pitch of his voice, a fearfulness, that made my chest cave in on itself.

"Is it him? Is he coming?" I asked, feeling suddenly light-headed and panicked. After all of the waiting it had come to this. That we should be taken without any ceremony or family left behind to give us a final farewell. I heard a low, wet snarling from the yard as the lurcher signaled an intruder, and while I climbed the ladder to the loft I wondered why he wasn't giving his usual frantic barking. I stood next to Tom at the open loft, and when he pointed up the road, I saw the dog. He came towards us, drunkenly weaving his way from one side of the road to the other, his head matted with the froth around his mouth, his tongue hanging down from between his teeth, and panting feverishly as though he had been running a great distance. The lurcher pulled backwards against his chain and his growls turned to a whistling whine. The cur continued his staggering walk towards the lurcher until he came to a stop about twenty or thirty yards from the front of the barn. He lowered his head until it touched the ground, the drippings from his mouth staining the packed dirt to a black mud, and bared his teeth all at once.

There is a space of time before a mad animal charges, a space that may last a few heartbeats or a few minutes, as though the sickness thickens the brain as well as the blood and makes the course of thought sluggish and interrupted. I looked down to the open doors below the loft and knew that once past our lurcher the cur could charge the barn and savage Hannah before I could climb down the ladder.

"Tom," I whispered, afraid to look away, "where is the flint-lock?"

He pointed down below to the stalls, and when I looked I saw it propped against one of the beams. The lurcher, at the very end of his chain, had thrown himself belly down and was lying motionless, no longer whining, no longer twisting against his tether, his lip curled up over his fangs. I could hear Hannah talking and singing to herself and I took a chance and shushed her. The cur moved his head slowly towards us and stared through the open doors with bloody weeping eyes. He took a step and another and then stopped. A low grinding sound came from his throat and he sneezed mightily, spreading the foam from his dewlaps for yards around. Every moment that passed I feared to move lest I bring the dog charging into the barn, but with every breath that he did not move I cursed myself for not running to lift Hannah to safety. The dog took another few steps and I tensed to turn and make a grab for my sister.

Tom held my arm and said softly, "There isn't time." He took from his pocket a few small objects which clicked together as he palmed them. He drew his arm back smoothly and let loose a stone, which flew in a high arc, landing twenty feet behind the cur. He did it without hesitation and with the surety of a boy standing on a riverbed, hitting his target on the far shore. The dog startled and wheeled around towards the noise. Tom let fly another stone, which landed ten feet beyond the first. The cur growled and charged the dust kicked up by the stones and then stood wavering on unsteady legs, searching for his prey. Then something, perhaps the shadow of a passing bird or a foraging squirrel or a leaf rattling in the wind, led him stumbling down the road away from us. For the rest of that day as we bent and reached and sweated our way through barn and garden, I watched the slight, hunched figure of my brother and wondered at his coolness and presence of mind. After the cur had wandered away like a fever breaking on a summer flux, my trembling legs gave out, and it was Tom who helped me to my feet and guided me down the ladder. It was Tom who picked up Hannah and to her great confusion held her rocking to his chest. It was Tom who picked up the flintlock with steady hands and walked the forty or so yards down Boston Way in pursuit of the dog, taking careful aim and bringing it to its end with one shot to the head.

Late afternoon as we sat on the threshold of the back door waiting for Father's tall form to appear from the simmering bracken of Falls Woods, Tom turned to me and said, "I'm not useless."

I looked at him with surprise as he wiped the damp grit from his forehead with his sleeves. The sleeves that had given up their buttons to make the eyes for my poppet, or rather the poppet I had given to Margaret.

He continued in a pinched voice. "You're not the only one on this farm who can take care of us when Father's away."

I started to protest but he cut me off, saying, "It's the way you look at me. It's the way you dismiss me and pity me with your eyes. Up there, in the loft, there was not once that you thought to ask for help. But I am just as able as you. I can work as hard as you. And I can take care of us as well as you can." He looked at me defiantly, his brows knitted together, his dark hair curling around his ears and I thought of the stones stored in his pocket and carried around for who knows how many days and weeks. The ammunition of every boy used in the chasing of birds and for skimming across the smooth surface of a pond. The ammunition he had used with calm assurance to save us from calamity.

"I miss her as much as you," he said, making knuckles of his hands between his knees, tightening and stiffening his back, forbidding the tears to come. But once he had said the words, I saw the misery that rested in purplish bands like bruises beneath his eyes and that pinched his lips into a perpetual frown.

I took my thumb and wiped a small circle of dirt from his cheek that his sleeve had missed.

"I'm the oldest now on the farm when Father's gone. I can take care of us," he said, reaching out and tugging at my apron to move me closer. I thought he would hold my hand or put his arm across my back but he didn't move to touch me save where his knee pressed into mine. Even so, there was a shifting away of something weighty and grasping about my shoulders, and we sat together for a long time, the sun behind us casting furlong shadows across the fields leading to Ladle Meadow.

ON JULY 30TH Aunt Mary was arrested again in Billerica and taken to Salem Village for questioning. She had been released to go home after Mother's examination but Mary Lacey cried out against her and so she was taken along with Margaret to face the judges. After a lengthy and punishing examination, she finally admitted to afflicting Timothy Swan and others and said that she had attended witches' meetings with my mother and two brothers. My mother had told her at these black Sabbaths that there were no fewer than 305 witches throughout the countryside and that their work was to pull down the Kingdom of Christ and set up the Kingdom of Satan. She said that the Devil had appeared to her in the shape of a tawny man and had promised to keep her safe from the Indians if she would sign the Devil's book. When she was asked if she looked to serve Satan, this good and gentle woman answered that, because of her great fear, she would follow him with all her heart if he would deliver her from the Indians. Two days later, on the first day of August, while she and Margaret were in prison, a small party of Wabanaki attacked homes close to theirs in Billerica, killing every man, woman, and child. The Devil had kept his bargain with her and perhaps for this reason Aunt never changed her testimony of guilt, as some would do once the prison doors were locked.

The third session of the Court of Oyer and Terminer began on Tuesday, August 2nd, and would last for four days. Mother's sentencing lasted the better part of two days. Appearing to give verbal testimony to the court against her were Mary Lacey, brought from her prison cell, Phoebe Chandler, and Allen Toothaker. And even though Richard and Andrew had given sworn statements against her, Cotton Mather moved to strike such admissions as there was so much spectral evidence offered from other sources. This, the one kindness from the man who would later call my mother, the only woman in the colonies to face down and challenge her accusers, a "rampant hag."

She was condemned to hang on the 19th of August along with the Reverend George Burroughs, formerly of Salem Village, John Proctor, who wrote to the governor of my brothers' torture, George Jacobs, an old rambling man of Salem, and John Willard, a young man who had nursed one of the girls who was bewitched and who woke one morning to find that the hand that worked to heal was often the first bitten.

ON AUGUST 10TH I woke with a great calmness. The heat of the day was as thick as ever but the evening before had turned suddenly cool. So much so that before retiring I had climbed the stairs to the garret room and pulled an old quilt out of Grandmother's trunk. Beneath the blanket lay the cross-stitch piece that Margaret had so lovingly made for me and within it was wrapped the ancient shard of pottery. I tucked both into my shift and lay under the quilt with Hannah in my arms, feeling the pottery's sharpness press like an accusing finger into the skin over my ribs. When I rose from bed, I dressed with great care, tearing out the knots in my hair with my fingers where the comb would not go and tucking the strands neatly into my cap. I put on my stockings, so little worn, and took a rag to my shoes, giving a glimpse of the leather beneath the dirt. I made whatever breakfast I could for the four of us and then I went to stand at the front of the door, my head turned to the north, waiting for my visitor to come. Knowing that he would come today, just as my mother had known when a neighbor was sure to appear for an unannounced visit.

He appeared soon after with a warrant for me and for Tom, and I believe he was more than a little shaken to find such a tiny sentinel poised and at the ready on the threshold of our house. He held the warrants up to Father's face, but Father's eyes never let go of the constable's and soon I could smell the sour essence of fear come off the man in heady waves. He spied the poppet in Hannah's arms and dragged it from her, saying only, "I am to take any poppets found to the court." She continued her steady, sharp wailing even as we were led out to the yard and placed in the cart. We had been tied, but loosely, and it would take only a little while before we were free of our bonds and could sit holding each other's hands.

As the constable was climbing onto the boards and taking up

the reins, Father took hold of the horse's halter and held it so tightly that the horse could not lift his head. "You know me, John Ballard."

The constable answered beneath his breath, "Aye, I know you."

"And I know you as well. And my children had best arrive in Salem the way they left." Father then let go of the halter and stood back, reaching down to grab hold of Hannah's shift and pull her from the wheels of the cart.

As John Ballard flicked the reins he said, "It's not me that will harm the children. But once I deliver them it's out of my hands."

We pulled away up Boston Way Road, Tom and I sitting close together, Hannah running behind, screaming and calling for us to come back, terrified to be left without us and in the company of Father, who stood in the yard, towering and still.

THERE WERE NINE judges in the meetinghouse-turned-court on that Wednesday, August 10th, along with jurors, plaintiffs, witnesses, and lookers-on, so many in fact that grown men sat upon each other's laps in order to watch the inquisition of such young children. We were the youngest among the accused, apart from four-year-old Dorcas Good, and every eye, every gesture, every breath was turned in our direction as we were led through the crowds and planted a few feet in front of the assembled magistrates. John Ballard handed to the chief judge my poppet and when his receipt was signed he left us without so much as a backwards glance. There was much rustling and sorting of paper and quiet sober speaking between the judges, and I looked through lowered lashes to the right and to the left of me to see their faces. My heart was a pick hammer in my chest, and dark particles danced in my vision as though the very air were disturbed by its beating. I felt Tom move closer to me and stand with his arm touching mine.

The poppet, worn and mangled by Hannah's rough play, was handed from judge to judge to judge, and the solemnity with which they studied it seemed so out of place with their calling that a quivering smile started to form on my lips. I felt its mate, a nervous bubbling laugh, start to rise with my terror from my belly, and to keep it from spilling forth I clamped my palm to my mouth. The same unwanted laugh that had erupted over the antics of the black boy in the Andover meetinghouse threatened to make me a chittering monkey in the faces of the men who could with a word end my life. I heard a loud commotion to my right, and when I turned my head I saw a group of young women and girls standing in tortured agony, their hands clapped over their mouths as if they were nailed there, cawing and moaning and straining to speak through their fingers.

One of the girls managed to spit out, "She tries to silence us. To keep us from giving testimony. Oh, my tongue, my tongue burns..."

I looked back at the judges and the chief of them, John Hathorne, the very same judge who sentenced my mother to be hanged, said to me darkly, "How long hast thou been a witch?"

For a moment I could not answer or take my hand from my mouth and so he asked me again, lowering his head and speaking slowly and carefully as one would speak to an idiot child, "How long have you been a witch?"

I lowered my hand and said, "Ever since I was six years old." There was a collective sigh from every bench, but all talking was shushed into silence so that no words would be missed.

"How old are you now?" John Hathorne asked.

"Near eleven years old." I could feel Tom's eyes on me and so, for his sake, tried to quiet the quivering of my face.

The judge paused some to let the clerk scratch my answers onto paper and then he asked suddenly, as if to befuddle my senses into revealing the truth, "Who made you a witch?"

I looked at him, my eyes wide with fright, my lips parted to suck in the air that seemed to elude my lungs, and I could not speak. I had been ready to give them any story they wanted about my own guilt. That I flew on a pole, my toes curled into the wind, that I baked bread for the witch's altar, that I danced on the graves of their mothers. But here it was and so soon. I knew what answer I had to give them but I could not speak. I was like one who stands stranded on a cliff over the ocean, unable to climb the wall behind them and too afraid to jump for fear of landing in the swirling eddies below. The moments stretched out and I could hear the restless stirring of the girls next to me, who would be all too willing to throw out a name, or two, or three, if I didn't give them one to write in jet ink on the waiting parchment. I felt Tom press something into my palm and felt the smooth hardness of a small river stone and my fist closed tight around it. And then I gave them the name they wanted. The name of the woman who was already imprisoned, waiting to die.

I took a step off the ledge and said, "My mother."

There was a satisfied nodding all around and then one of the lesser judges asked John Hathorne in a forced whisper, "How was it done?" and the chief magistrate turned to me and repeated the question loudly, as though I were deaf.

"She made me set my hand to a book." The outpouring of breath from the bench was as pleased and expectant as if I had pulled out of my apron a loaf of bread freshly baked. I looked across the faces of the men before me and saw in their eyes interest and enmity, curiosity and fearfulness, but to a person I saw nothing that could be called in good faith compassion or pity or even reserved judgment. I heard a small animal noise behind me and turned my head to see one of the bewitched girls make a mewling noise like a cat. She was dressed in dun homespun wool like me and wore a simple cap like me, and her hair was the same color of rust, so we could have been sisters. But in her eyes I saw only spite. I felt suddenly sick, a dark curtain drawing itself around the edges of my sight, and I reached out for Tom's arm and held it tightly.

Then Judge Hathorne said to me, "Go on," and his voice seemed swathed in bolts of rough batting and any meaning was severed from the sounds formed by his lips. My knees lost their hold and I felt Tom's arms go around me, lifting me up, forcing me to stand. Then the chief judge motioned for the clerk to cease his writing and he said to me, folding his hands tightly together, "Do you know where you are?" I nodded my head and he said, "Do you know whom you address?" and I nodded again.

"Then you know that we will have the truth from you. You

must answer every question put to you, completely and willingly, or it will go very badly for you. Do you understand what I am saying to you? We make no promises for leniency because of your tender years, and if you do not reveal to us your involvement fully in this witchcraft, you put at risk your immortal soul. The body can be sacrificed, but once the soul is lost it is lost forever."

The words worked their way through the batting, and the silence after was like the silence between the laying down of the fowl and the descending axe upon the block. And when the axe finally falls, hindered by flesh and bone, it makes a dull, muffled sound like a weighted latch forever bolting a door, or a mountain of paper being moved from one magistrate's table to another. Judge Hathorne motioned to the clerk to ready himself and asked me again, "How were you made a witch?"

"My mother made me set my hand to a book." I knew they were thinking of the Devil's book but in my mind's eye I saw Mother's red diary buried at the foot of a lone tree on Gibbet Plain. The diary I had sworn to hide and protect from men such as these.

"How did you set your hand to it?"

"I touched it with my fingers. The book was red. Red, the color of blood. And the pages were white. Very white like the color of . . ." My voice trailed off and I saw the clerk straining to hear me, but when I looked at him he lowered his gaze and reached for a clean sheet of parchment, as though my last words had rendered the first page untouchable.

One of the other judges asked me, "Have you ever seen the Black Man?"

"No," I said, wanting to answer, "None but you," as my mother had done.

A third judge asked me, "Where did you touch the book? Who was there with you?"

I gave them a near-truth by saying, "Andrew Foster's pasture, next to Foster's Pond. Hard by Gibbet Plain." After a pause I continued, "My Aunt Mary was there. And my cousin Margaret."

I had pulled Margaret down into the pit with me but only a little ways, as she was waiting even then for me in prison. The sharp edges of the pottery shard shifted beneath my bodice, and I pressed them deeper into my flesh in penance. I would finally have the chance to give it to her myself, as we would soon be sisters in confinement. So the questions went and I gave them the names of those who had already been arrested. With each answer my imaginings grew wilder, and the wilder my answers, the more in sympathy seemed the judges to my words. I danced with a black dog and sent my spirit out to pinch and torment others and talked to my mother's spectral form that came to me as a cat. When they were finished with me, they asked Tom the same questions, and his answers were in sum the same as mine. Our mother was a witch and we were made Devil's fodder through her. Our only salvation would be through equal amounts of contrition and imprisonment.

Once our testimony was recorded, witnesses were brought forward to give more evidence against us. Phoebe Chandler was called first and told the judges that I had cursed her and caused her to fall ill. Her fear was so great that she could hardly speak above a whisper and had to be asked repeatedly to talk so that the judges could hear. But it was not of the judges she was terrified, it was of the young women of Salem Village standing and whispering loudly at her back. Then came Mercy Williams, looking downcast and demure and fat as a partridge. She said that I had stuck pins into her, using the poppet, and she drew out from her apron one of the offending needles, the needle she had stolen from me. Judge Hathorne held out his hand, and to her dismay he kept it with the court. When she turned to go, she looked into my eyes for an instant and I knew with a certainty that she was in the family way with someone's bastard. The rounded flesh of her cheeks, her dimpled hands, one still wearing the moon-shaped scar from my bite upon it, her pasty skin for once flushed and damp, told a story of a red underskirt lifted one too many times in the quiet of some dark space.

The last to give testimony was Allen Toothaker, who said that when he had fought with Richard last March outside our barn not only had Mother's spirit gone out to render him motionless but mine did as well. He said that he was frequently tormented by spectral visitations in my form and that it had caused him much grief. He was dismissed and as he passed me he raised his thumb to his face and raked it slowly and deliberately down from the bridge of his nose to the nostrils. He had waited a long time to give me back what I had given him after his drubbing with Richard. There was some small comfort in knowing that his cheek was marked with a crescent scar, still angry and red, from the cinders that were meant to burn down our barn. The crescent shape of the letter "C"; "C" for coward, or for calumny.

As we were taken from the court a young woman was being led

before the judges, and I recalled seeing her in the Andover meeting-house. She was the granddaughter of the Reverend Dane and she would be the first of many in that family brought to the Salem trials. Her eyes were fixed and staring as though she walked while she slept, and behind her trailed a yellow stream, her body's water that could not be held against the growing heat of her fear.

Tom and I were placed in another cart and taken the five miles into Salem Town, east down the main street, the smell of brine and tidal pools coming sharp off the South River. As we passed each street and house of note, the sheriff, George Corwin, would call out, "Here is the house of your judge Jonathan Corwin." "Here is the house of your judge John Hathorne." "Here, then, is the meetinghouse," as though we were only lost and asking the way to be brought home again. Just before we turned north to go up Prison Lane he pointed and said, "Yonder is the house of the Governor-that-was, Simon Bradstreet," and the memories of reading with my mother the poems of his wife, Anne Bradstreet, came flooding back. But I could not remember the passages of hope won, only those of loss.

> My pleasant things in ashes lie,
> And them behold no more shall I.
> Under thy roof no guest shall sit,
> Nor at thy table eat a bit.
> No pleasant tale shall e'er be told,
> Nor things recounted done of old.
> No candle e'er shall shine in thee,
> Nor bridegroom's voice e'er heard shall be.
> In silence ever shall thou lie . . .

When we are babes newly born and the midwife pulls us through the passage from our mother's womb into the world, it is the sense of smell that awakens us first to our new realm of living. Babes are near blind and without strength to govern their limbs, but one not five minutes old can turn its head towards the waiting breast that is filled with milk, its nostrils twitching and wrinkling all the while. When Sheriff Corwin walked Tom and me down the stairs towards the waiting cells below, it was the smell of the place that first welcomed us to our new home.

It was like crawling headfirst into a midden that had been rained upon and then sealed with a tight canvas under a baking sun. The smell of rot was so sharp and so far-reaching that my eyes ran over and the furthest recesses of my nose and throat felt as if they had caught fire. But it was not just the rot of human waste that was so powerful, it was the sweetly sour rot of badly turned food, and perhaps something still living that was only partially dead: musty and coppery and bog-laden. The smell of decaying cattails and rushes being pressed into peat moss.

The stones of the stairwell were cold to the touch, and my feet slid treacherously from side to side as I felt my way down the steps, holding to the guide rope with one hand as I held my apron to my nose with the other. I heard Tom retch and pause behind me, but the sheriff pushed his shoulder and told him to move on. It was dark as we descended the last steps, and quiet. So quiet that I at first believed we were the only three to be in the cellar. Soon I could see little pinpricks of light through iron bars, where the few ends of candles sputtered weakly. I heard the rasping sound of a man coughing and then another answering sound of a woman clearing her throat. There was then the sound of rustling, bodies shifting in the straw, moving closer to us.

When my eyes had widened to the feeble light, I saw that we were standing in a narrow corridor with one long cell banded with bars to my right and, to my left, two smaller cells. Between the bars appeared the gripped knuckles of many hands. The sheriff's lantern light illuminated the hands in sharp relief while the darkness from the cells within severed the arms at the wrist, making the hands look unattached to any living body. He took out a ring of keys from his coat and unlocked the wooden door to the longer cell, swinging it outward, and pointed for us to go inside.

He said to Tom, "Boy, you'll be in the women's cell. The men's cell is full now. But if you pester the women, you'll be taken to the stocks. D'ye hear me, boy?"

The foul odor coming from inside the cell was even stronger than it had been on the stairs and the air was cold and dank. I took a few steps backwards, treading on the sheriff's toes, but before he could push me in, Tom took my hand and led me into our cell. The door was quickly closed and locked and we could hear the retreating footsteps of Sheriff Corwin as he climbed the steps to the room above. We stood together, clutching each other's arms, not speaking, afraid to move until the light coming from the small open slits in the far walls gave us the height and breadth of our new home. The floor was covered in straw and we could hear the continual rustling of people moving about. Slowly we saw them. First the feet and then the legs and then the bodies and faces of women, dozens and dozens of women, lying or sitting or standing throughout the cell, staring at us, their eyes looking nowhere but at our faces. I searched the shadows for a familiar face, any familiar face, and then I opened my mouth and called out hoarsely, "Mother?" At the sound of my voice several women groaned or shook their heads and one, a young woman at my feet, started crying. But there was no answering voice to say "Here I am."

I took a few steps towards the back wall and called out again, "Mother?" But there was no answer, and as I moved again I stepped on an old woman I had thought was a pile of rags at my feet. She shrieked and pulled herself up, holding her hands in front of her face as if to ward off blows. I moved my head back and forth, looking, looking for my mother, hugging my arms around my chest, trembling and shivering against the cold and the fear. Every eye was on me and yet no one had spoken, and the silence became more unbearable than the stench. I backed up the few steps to stand again next to Tom and then I heard my name being called. It was faint, as though it came to me through a blanket or from a great distance, and I called out again, "Mother?" I heard the voice again from the direction of the corridor and I ran the few feet back to the bars. There were outraged yelps and rude protests as I climbed over the women resting against the short stone wall into which the bars had been set. But I did not care. I would have walked over a hundred bodies to find the source of the voice. I clung to the bars and brought my face as close to them as I could and called out, "Mother, where are you?"

"Here, Sarah, I am here." And I saw from the far cell across the corridor an arm reach out. The hand was strong and beckoning, the palm turned up as if to catch rain or the sound of my voice. The wrist was strong and supple like the neck of a power-ful mare, and on it were a manacle and chain.

"Mother, Mother, Mother, Mother...," I must have said a hundred times and she, answering me. And so we called back and forth to each other until the sheriff shouted out from the top of the stairwell, "I'll have quiet or you'll know why." We lowered our voices to whispers and then I heard the sound of Richard's voice coming to me from directly across the corridor. He was with Andrew in the nearer small cell, the men's cell, and the three of us talked in whispers of small things: that Tom was with me, that we were for the time being safe. Richard told us of the wounds on Andrew's wrists, received during the torture ten days before. But he did not say that Andrew had begun to fever from the poison festering in the torn flesh. We did not speak of the trials or the sentencing or what was to come, but when Mother asked about Hannah I had no answer to give her. I had not given my sister a thought from the time I approached the Salem meetinghouse. Soon the women against the wall re-claimed their places and I was forced back towards the center of the cell, where Tom sat in wretched silence waiting for me.

A woman crept her way slowly towards Tom and me, her dress dirty and worn and rust-stained from the chains that rested against her apron, and said softly, "Children, come sit with me. You are in the good cell. Not the other one. Come and find a place with me and rest easy." Her face was very kind and her hands gentle as they found my resisting fingers. I looked around at the women, unbathed, unfed, and all of them mana-cled, even the youngest of them, and wondered what she could mean by the "good" cell. I did not know that most of the women in the far cell were condemned to die and that my mother had found fellowship with fifteen other martyrs in a cell made to hold six or seven.

We sat with the kind woman for a few hours, until the blacksmith came and fitted us with manacles, manacles that Father would have to repay the sheriff for. The man was curt and brusque but he knew his craft and did not miss his mark when the hammer came down for the final closure. Many an arm or ankle could be shattered with a careless blow. Some of the women, the women who had been longest in the prison, had their chains passed through a ring bolt attached to the floor or the wall, but because we were so young, our chains were left free. Soon after came the time for the sheriff to let into the corridor, one by one, the families of the imprisoned to pass food or clothing through the bars. The time spent in the corridor was only as long as the number of coins or barter that could be slipped into the hands of the jailer. Most everyone had no coins and so were given only a few moments for comfort or prayers or for saying good-bye.

The doors to the cells were rarely opened for visitors, except for a minister or the few attending doctors who came out of charity. Or to remove the body of someone who had died during the night. It was late afternoon before Tom and I saw the corridor darken from the shadow of our father's crouching figure appearing at the bars to our cell. The ceiling was no more than six feet high, three feet down into the rocky ground, making a half cellar, and three feet built up with a stone foundation for the house resting above the cells.

He wrapped his hands around the bars and called to us.

When he saw we were manacled he bowed his head and said, "Dear God . . . ," but there was no time to linger, for he had to deliver food to Richard, Andrew, and Mother before he was forced to leave. He handed me a small loaf of bread, a leather water skin, a shawl for me, and a coat for Tom, and said hurriedly, "Sarah, listen to what I say. Drink what's in the skin first and only from the open barrel when you must. This bread must last awhile. If you chew it long it will seem to be more. I will try to bring meat when next I come, but it may not be for days yet. So you must harken to me." He reached through the bars and pulled me closer to him and said, "Do not share this bread with anyone but Tom. There are women here who are starving and who will beg from you, but you will sicken and die if you do not do as I say. D'ye hear me, Sarah?"

I nodded, tucking the bread into my apron, and he said to Tom, "Tom, remember what I told you that day? After you threw down the harness in the field. Remember?" When Tom nodded, Father said, "It's to you now. I will return when I can."

He started up to leave, but, remembering my sister, I called out to him, "Where's Hannah?" He ducked his head for a moment and answered, "She is with the Reverend Dane's family. They will take good care of her." The Reverend's wife was a kind woman, but austere, and I wondered what she would make of Hannah, only three years old, wild, unclean, with an endless need for attention. For many months I had been mother to her and now she was torn away from yet another family. For all the times I had been unkind to her or impatient or cruel, I wept.

Father crossed the corridor to give Richard, Andrew, and finally Mother some small bit of food. When Mother's hands came through the bars, he pressed her knuckles to his eyes and said some soft words to her. Then the sheriff called down, and when Father left us, the afternoon had dimmed towards dusk. Our cell, our "good" cell, faced west, and the light of the setting sun flashed briefly through the high slits in the walls, turning our skin red and yellow, as though the straw had been set aflame and was burning us all alive in our prison.

IT TOOK ONLY a few hours for the vermin to find their way into my hair, and I woke in the night with my scalp on fire. I started scratching and tearing at it with my nails, feeling the tickling on my skin as the lice danced around my fingers. A woman somewhere on the opposite wall had started an ago-nized moaning, and with every breath she said, "Oh my God, my tooth. Oh my God, my tooth . . ." She continued her wailing even when she was accosted with pleas for silence, and some vio-lent curses as well. The night had turned cold and I wrapped the shawl more tightly around me. I turned to look at Tom but the rhythms of his breathing told me he was yet deep in sleep. The haggard crying continued for an hour or so until another woman tipped a flask of some liquid into the moaning woman's mouth. Soon her noises quieted into whimpering and she drifted off into oblivion.

I could hear tiny rustlings all through the straw and once saw the shine of a pair of dark, liquid eyes set narrowly over a pointed snout. He watched me, sniffing at the loaf of bread hid-den in my apron. I kicked out at him and he crept deeper into the straw but did not move away. I kicked at him more forcefully and he melted into the darker rushes below the straw. I dozed fitfully until the murky light from the morning filled the cell enough to see more clearly the features of the women surrounding me on all sides. One by one they opened their eyes, some to pain, some to desperation, some to prayers for deliverance or acceptance, but all of them to the renewed horror of their confinement. And in common to all of these wives and mothers and sisters who had worked and prayed and midwifed in good faith with their neighbors was the searching, confused gaze that they should be accused and imprisoned and seemingly forgotten by those same neighbors.

There were some so slatternly that they rolled over to the slop buckets, scratching and rubbing themselves without any attention to their dress, or their modesty, and took no time in straightening their aprons, lacing their bodices, or turning their stockings. But most tried to clean themselves, wiping their faces with their sleeves, or polishing their teeth with the edge of their aprons, in a way that was in equal parts noble and sad. And they shared whatever they had. A shattered comb was passed around as delicately and as solemnly as a holy relic. Some bit of ointment was given to whoever had wounds beneath her manacles. Many an undershift had been torn into pieces to bind open wounds. There was no lamb's wool or soft leather strips for the women of childbearing years who had their monthly courses, and many of the girls walked in shame with their skirts pleated together, held in folds at their backs, hiding the brackish stains.

And then there came the time when one woman went around asking for some share of food to be given to those women who had no family or had family too poor to come every day, or every few days, to pass through the bars even the smallest measure of bread. The woman's name was Dorcas Hoar and she had been arrested in Beverly and brought to the prison in April. She was old and walked with a rolling limp but carried herself with dignity, and when she came to Tom and me, her eyes were filled with compassion. But when she held out her hand, I dropped my eyes and said that we had nothing to give. I felt her eyes on me, and the blood rushed to my face with the lie. She reached down and placed her hand on my head and said, "God bless you and keep you, child." And then she moved to the next woman and the next and the next until she had a few crumbs to share.

I turned away to face the wall and sneaked my hand into my apron and pinched off a piece of bread, rolling it in my fingers to make it smaller. I held up my hand to my face as though to stifle a yawn and passed the ball of dough into my mouth. I chewed it until it turned to liquid and then swallowed it. My belly, brought to life, growled loudly, and so I ate another piece, all the while thinking that it might have been better to eat nothing than to eat a little morsel and feel the grinding pangs of hunger so keenly.

I tapped Tom and slipped him a piece of bread and then I stood up to visit the slops and stretch my cramping legs. There was a bucket at each end of the cell, and the one nearest to me was full to overflowing, the floor surrounding it dark and glistening. So I picked my way to the other end, the chains at my wrists swaying heavily, making my steps awkward. I looked at my feet, being careful not to trip on a leg or tread on a hand, and in so doing I did not at first see the faces of the women who had been hidden from me in the dark of the evening before. As I approached the bucket, I looked up and saw Aunt, sitting with her back propped against the far wall. And with Aunt, her head on her mother's lap, was Margaret.

The joy that I felt at seeing them was so powerful that my knees weakened and I uttered a sharp "Oh" that drew looks from the women around me. My eyes filled with tears and I said, reaching out, tripping over something or someone, "Aunt . . ." A woman reached up to steady me as the smile on my face faltered and faded. There was no doubt that it was my mother's sister, but the eyes that met mine were filled with anger and resentful purpose. I said again, "Aunt." I added, "It is Sarah," but her eyes only hardened more and the protective arm around Margaret tightened. The chains from Aunt's wrists draped in front of Margaret's face, casting ringed shadows across her cheeks. Margaret's eyes were not on mine, they were pointed at some distant place. Her mouth moved slightly, as though she were conversing with the air, and although she could not have failed to see or hear me, she never once looked in my direction.

I stood stupidly for another few breaths, staring at my shoes, and heard Aunt say, as though she were chasing a dog or a rat from her doorstep, "Whisht." I looked up and she gestured me away viciously with her free arm and said again, "Whisht." Her chains rattled in the silence and I turned around and walked, stumbling, back to my place next to Tom, my face wet with tears. I looked around, my chin tucked into my neck, my breath jerking and shuddering, and saw many pairs of eyes look away, as though my tears were somehow more revealing and shameful than had I been using the slops for all to see.

The morning passed into noon, and before the families were let into the corridor, the prisoners drew lots to see who would have the chance to empty the slop buckets in the yard above and in so doing have a few minutes to walk about and breathe in the fresh air. Two women from our cell would take up our buckets first, and then someone from the men's prison would take up their bucket as well as the bucket from the condemned women's cell. The condemned women were never allowed out of their cell for fear they would take to the sky and escape over the rooftops or cast out their spirits to further torment the people of Salem Village. Being so young and newly placed in the prison, Tom and I were not included in the drawing of lots. The few visiting families came and went and the afternoon sun warmed and dried out the stones, turning them from green to gray to white. They would be damp again come morning and moss would appear again like wet paint spread over mortar.

I watched the short wall under the iron bars at the corridor, and whenever a woman who rested there got up to walk about, I took her place and called out to Mother and to Richard. And every time we would speak, their hands would appear to reach out to me, and in this way I knew their voices were real, as real as the stones, and not a part of a fevered imagination.

Sometime in the afternoon the door to our cell was opened, and Abigail Faulkner, a woman of about my mother's age, was led into our cell. She stood blinking in the half-light, and several women from Andover gasped out, "It is Reverend Dane's daughter." Along with her niece Betty Johnson, Goodwife Faulkner would be one of more than a dozen of the Dane family, by blood or by marriage, who would be locked in chains.

She would be condemned to die on September 17th but would plead her belly and be reprieved. Her child would be born past its time in December, after she was released, as though the hardship of prison life had sealed her womb, preventing the babe from being born in that rank and hopeless place.

The day passed into evening, and when I lay down next to Tom, I ate another small piece of bread and hugged myself close to his body. And I counted Day 1 spent in my prison, the 11th day of August, 1692. There would be eight more days before my mother was to be taken out of her cell and hanged.

WHEN I WOKE the next morning, my head ached from lack of sleep; the moaning woman had cried for the longest time, until the Samaritan finally gave her whatever drink it was that made her sleep. After an hour of listening to her, I found myself wanting to shout out, "For pity's sake, give her the flask and let us rest." I struggled to sit up and took a drink from the skin that Father had left us. To my dismay I saw that the leather had been chewed almost through sometime during the night, causing drops of the precious clean water to seep out onto the floor. I would have to sleep with it tucked into my bodice to keep the rats from taking it all.

The women went through the same rituals of dress as the morning before and Goodwife Hoar soon made her way down the rows of women, asking for bread to be shared. When she passed me she did not stop, saying only, "God bless you children," before she went on. She would bless us every morning that we were in prison but she would never again ask us for food. I watched the short wall eagerly for a space to open up so that I could speak to Mother, but the women there were in no hurry to leave their places.

Footsteps on the stairs made everyone pause and grow tense and expectant. It was too early for the slops to be emptied and the visits from the families would not come for hours. There were two pairs of footsteps descending, the sheriff's rapid, heavy steps along with someone else's, and I wondered if there was to be an early trial. The door to our cell opened, and a woman, short and thick, walked in and started looking around the room as though searching for someone. I heard a whispered hiss, "The sheriff's wife." The door remained ajar but Sheriff Corwin's shadow stayed at the threshold. His wife strode confidently to Goodwife Faulkner and said, pointing to her shawl, "I'll give you bread for the shawl."

An old woman from across the room rasped out, "Don't do it, missus. You'll need it come September." She laughed unpleasantly but it ended in a barking cough. Goody Faulkner shook her head and pulled the shawl closer around her shoulders. The sheriff's wife shrugged and asked several other women, some who looked new to the cell, with clean hands and clean aprons, and a few desperate others who had been there awhile, to barter at a pittance pieces of their clothing. One of the women had been stripped down to her shift, but when she offered up a piece of the hem, Goody Corwin shook her head and moved on. She looked around once more and her eyes fell on me and Tom. She walked over and said, not unkindly, "Stand up and let me see you."

I stood up and she pulled me to her as though she would

embrace me. Her right hand held my shoulder while the left hand came to rest palm down on my head. She then pulled me back again and looked down at her left hand to see exactly where the top of my head had come to rest on her chest. She had been measuring me to see how tall I was, but I did not know the reason until someone called out with outrage, "For the love of Jesus. Leave them their clothes. Do you want to kill them with the damp?"

Goody Corwin did not acknowledge the speaker but said to me, "When you get hungry enough, we'll talk again." She gave my chin a squeeze and left us so that Sheriff Corwin could fasten the locks once more. When she had gone, I whispered to the woman next to me, "Why did she want our clothes? Is she so poor?"

The woman snorted, "Her? She's tighter than a tick with money. She's got more coin than all of us put together. She barters us with food for our clothes and then sells them at market for coin, saying the clothes are from the bodies of the unclaimed dead." I shivered deeper into my shawl, thinking I would never barter with the sheriff's wife, no matter how weakened I became from hunger.

The afternoon brought no visit from Father and I was able to get to the bars only a few times to speak to Mother. There was a growing flutter of fear within me as the day passed and the words "seven days, seven more days" ran again and again through my mind. Despite my earlier intentions, I made a promise to myself that when the sheriff's wife next came I would offer her every bit of clothing in trade for ten minutes in my mother's cell. When I called across the corridor to the men's cell, asking

Richard about Andrew, there was a long pause before he spoke. Finally he answered, "Andrew is bearing up. But he is worse today than yesterday. I fear his wound is festering and the poison has entered his body. Without proper care . . ." He paused, leaving me to imagine what was to become of Andrew without clean water to wash his wounds or salve to stop the poison from spreading.

NIGHT CAME AND Tom and I ate our hard bits of bread and finished the water in the skin. The air was warmer than it had been and despite all my worries I fell quickly into a dreamless sleep. Sometime during the darkest hours before dawn I heard loud shouts from the men's cell for the sheriff to come. The shouting went on and on but it was hours before we heard his footsteps lumbering down the stairs. He lived with his wife in the upper floors but would never come down before morning unless the cells had caught fire and smoke was rising from his floorboards.

I heard the men's cell being opened and pleading voices asking for help. Soon the door to our cell opened and there on the threshold, holding up a slumped figure between them, was Richard and an older man. They dragged the sagging figure further into the straw, and when they laid him down, I saw it was Andrew. I clung to Richard but he was pulled quickly out by the sheriff, who locked him back in his cell. When the sheriff returned, he said to Tom and me, "The doctor comes on Saturdays. If he's still alive by ten of the clock, he'll have a look. There's better light here and here he'll stay until then."

Several of the women came to help us bathe Andrew's face with a few drops of our precious water taken from the common barrel and loosen his clothing. His manacles had been pried open and removed, so his arms were free. They would not have been removed had he been expected to live. He had a raging fever, which made his face dark and livid like the raw liver of a deer, while his scars from the pox were pitted and white. When we pulled back the sleeves from his shirt I caught my breath, for on his right wrist where he had been bound and tortured was a festering wound that seeped with a yellowish matter. A band of bright red under the skin traveled up his arm from the wound. One of the older women put her nose to the wound and sniffed.

"It's poisoned," she said. "Once the red reaches past his shoulder..." She paused, shaking her head. "He'll die if the arm doesn't come off." Someone else whispered, "He will die if it does."

"Doesn't come off. Doesn't come off." The words rattled around in my ears but I could not make sense of them until I looked at Tom's face and saw the horror in it.

We stayed by Andrew's side until the doctor came in. He was a narrow, spindly man who shooed us away as though we were a brood of cottage fowl. He lifted Andrew's arm and studied the line of red, shaking his head all the while. He turned to me and said, "Your brother, the tall one in the cell across, said that I would be paid in coin for care tendered." I looked at him, not understanding, but Tom said, "My father will pay. When he comes."

"Very well," said the doctor. "I'll come back tonight. The

arm must come off and right away. And mind you, afterwards, I'll expect to be paid whether this one lives or not." When he stood up to leave, I looked down at Andrew's face and was startled to see his eyes open, looking at me. Eyes filled with pain and with understanding. For hours we sat with Andrew and tried to comfort him. He cried and shifted about and said over and over, "I'll be good. Don't take my arm. I'll be good." When I could stand it no more, I threw myself against the short bars and cried out, "Mother, what can we do? What can we do?" The answer came to me, escorted by the shadows from the condemned cell, floating insubstantial and piecemeal like a waving tendril of smoke in the corridor.

"Make your best good-byes to him, Sarah. Be with him. Help him to be strong. Give him comfort." I heard no more words from her, only the sound of weeping. The bitter kind that comes when a child is to depart the earth before the one who gave him birth.

Soon Andrew's crying stopped as he dropped into the sleep of the desperately ill and Tom and I took turns holding his head. Some of the women came to offer advice or to give us prayers in place of hope. Some of the women came only to look and be comforted that someone else was closer to death than they. When the noon hour arrived and the families of the jailed pressed into the corridor, Reverend Dane appeared, bringing bread and meat and a small pot of soup for us. The sheriff let him into our cell, and when he bent down to look at Andrew, I wanted nothing so much as to throw myself into the comfort of his arms and plead with him to take me with him when he left. He put his hands on our heads and blessed us with great tenderness. Then he pulled Tom and me closer to him and said quietly, so as not to wake Andrew, "Your father comes tomorrow with more food and with warmer clothing. He does not know how very sick is Andrew or he would have come with me this day. I fear that when he comes tomorrow Andrew will be gone from us." As though he had heard the whispers, Andrew shifted and groaned in his sleep.

The sheriff called out from the door, and as the Reverend rose to leave, he said, "Have faith in God, children. Andrew's pain is soon to be over." He reached out to place a hand on Tom's shoulder, but Tom pulled abruptly away. His face was dark with anger and with some stubborn resentment, and I wanted to cuff his ears for refusing a kind hand. But the greatness of the man was in his understanding of the human heart, and as he looked around the tightness and darkness of our cell, he said to Tom in parting, "Faith is what saves us from despair, son. But anger will do in its place for now. I will go and see your mother. Shall I pass some message to her?"

"Tell her . . . Tell her . . . ," I began but could not finish. How could I give words of comfort or ask for them in return with the sheriff standing at the door to the cell, beckoning impatiently for the Reverend to leave. It would be like trying to build a raft to ride a storm-ridden ocean with only a few sticks to lash together. My swimming eyes turned back to the Reverend's and paused there.

Squeezing my hands in his he said, "I will tell her, Sarah. I will tell her." He gave a bag of food to his daughter, Goody Faulkner, and prayed over the heads of the women despite the sheriff's harping. When Sheriff Corwin finally came to put a hand on the Reverend's arm to make him leave, the look the sheriff got was surely as scorching as the look Adam received from the Archangel when he was driven from Paradise. The hours stretched on into the afternoon and Andrew's fever continued to burn hot. He mumbled and murmured of things he saw behind his quivering lids. Sometimes he whispered and laughed. Sometimes he shouted and threw up his hands. But his words were not the words of a half-witted boy. They were clear and reasoned, as though the fire in his body had refined and sharpened his mind.

Around sunset, as the flickering light flowed through the openings in the walls, Andrew opened his eyes and looked first at me and then at Tom. "What day is it?" he asked quietly.

Tom answered, "It is Saturday."

Andrew drew his brows together as though calculating the days and said, "The doctor comes soon now?"

"Yes," said Tom, his voice grinding and choked.

"He'll take my arm," Andrew whispered softly as though hearing it for the first time. Alarm sprang into his eyes and he said, catching his breath, "He'll take my arm. Tom, he's going to take my arm." He grabbed at Tom with his left hand and held on tightly. "Don't let him take my arm. I'd rather die."

"Andrew," I said, cradling his head tighter in my arms, the tears falling into my mouth. "The doctor said you'd die . . ."

"No," Tom said, reaching for Andrew's good hand, "You won't die." He looked at me defiantly and said again, "You won't die, Andrew. I won't let him take your arm. D'ye hear me?" He looked down at Andrew. "I'll sit here all night and the next night and the next. I'll look over you, Andrew. No one's going to take your arm." He held on to Andrew's hand until Andrew fell back into his sleep and there he sat until the sheriff opened the door to let in the doctor. In one hand he carried a small leather bag and a belt. In the other he carried a small skinning knife and a cleaver.

He said loudly to the sheriff, "The light is going. I will have to work quickly. Stand here by the door in case I need you to hold him down." The cell had grown quiet but for the sound of whispered prayers and some fragile cloth being torn into bandages. As the doctor moved into the cell I saw several of the younger women put their hands over their ears to block out the screams. My hands went protectively over Andrew's eyes to shield him from the approaching doctor, and the anger that had plagued Tom came and bit me squarely behind the neck. The doctor turned to one of the women and said, "Bring me whatever water you have and then stand back."

He started to kneel to take his place by Andrew but Tom held up his hand and said, "No. We don't need you. You can go away."

"Don't be stupid, boy. Your brother is at death's door, and unless the arm comes off, he'll pass over that threshold for sure. Now, you can be brave for your brother's sake by holding his other arm."

"No," Tom said more forcefully, and the doctor rocked back on his heels, no doubt thinking of the coins he would forfeit by leaving his work undone. He picked up the belt and looped it together, forming a small noose, and motioned to the sheriff. I heard a woman call out of the growing dark, "Let the boy die in peace." The sheriff drew an agitated breath and, closing the door behind him, began walking towards us. I felt Andrew's hand searching for mine and the anger twisted in my spine. I said, forcing the words from deep in my throat, "If you touch him, I'll curse you." There was a stirring in the straw as bodies pulled closer, straining to hear the outcome.

The doctor turned to me, his brows drawn down, "What did you say?" But he had heard what I had said as clearly as if I had shouted the words. It showed in the way he tensed and looked over his shoulder at the murky figures standing in the lessening light, their hair wild and disarrayed, their clothing soiled with human filth, some torn into shroudlike tangles. He looked back at me with uncertain eyes and saw a flame-headed, remorseless child who had been thrown into a cell for doing the Devil's work. He began to gather up his things, but in all the world, there is no better whip against the diminishing effects of fear than the enlivening thoughts of coins in the purse, and so he paused and studied Tom again in a cautious manner. Tom sat poised with his fists balled in his lap, but for all his protesting he was only a boy. The doctor set his jaw and called to the sheriff to come so that he could finish up what he had interrupted his dinner to do.

I saw Tom look wildly around for something, some kind of weapon or stick, to keep the doctor at bay. His hand closed around the straw and he held it up to his face as though he had found some great treasure. The doctor had started to say to the sheriff, "Now, pull back these two and then grab hold of this one and be quick about it...," when Tom drew back his arm, his good throwing arm, and let loose the weighted straw, hitting the doctor square in the chest and in the face. It was as though

Tom had wounded him with a full measure of lead shot, so loud did the doctor swear and jump up and brush himself down. On his black great coat, the coat of his calling, and on his white linen shirt, were smeared dark and evil-smelling stains. All through the straw were the remnants of waste from women who, through illness or weakness from hunger, could not reach the slop buckets in time. Tom had only to reach a little ways to find it.

The doctor stamped his foot with rage and spit out, "You little bastard. Look what you've done."

"Aye, that shit will never wash out." We looked around, astonished at the strength in the voice and saw it was the old woman who had advised Goody Faulkner to keep her shawl from the sheriff's wife. She was feeble and bent and had a ragged cough but her eyes were sharp and amused as they looked on the doctor. She opened her toothless mouth in laughter and said, "It's the bile, you see? There's never so great a stain as that which comes from the outraged body of a woman wronged. No, you'll have to lop off a basketful of limbs to pay for a new coat such as that." The doctor pulled away from her abruptly as though she were wearing plague sores.

The sheriff swung the door to the cell open and said, "You'd best go now. You'll get nothing from this lot."

The doctor grabbed his tools and turned once to say, "Your brother will be dead before the sun comes up." We sat mute together over Andrew's huddled body, too dazed to speak, and so the only answer to follow him out was the sound of the key being turned in the lock. I slept badly, in and out of waking from hour to hour, but whenever I opened my eyes I saw Tom kneeling next to Andrew, holding his hand and smoothing his forehead with a small rag or spilling a few drops of water into his mouth. Andrew continued to shake with fever and fell back into his troubled dreams. Every so often Tom would gently lift our brother's sleeve and follow the progress of the red mark that crept upwards and upwards towards Andrew's heart. Close to dawn on Sunday I woke to the sound of Andrew's voice. I thought he was in his ravings, for Tom had leaned his head down to better hear. I crawled through the straw to be closer to them and I saw that Andrew's eyes were queer and clouded. His lips were cracked and bleeding but his words were calm and orderly.

He lifted his head slightly and said, "Richard promised that we shall all go hunting again in the autumn. And that I shall have a turn at the flintlock, if I'm careful. Now I'll have my arm to hold it and I will be as good a shot as Father."

"You shall have a turn. And you shall bag the biggest ground hen in the colonies." Tom smoothed Andrew's hair back from his forehead and he smiled and closed his eyes again. His head slumped to the side and his breathing coarsened until I felt faint trying to slow my breathing to his. Sometime before the dark turned to light I fell asleep saying good-bye to Andrew. I had tried to do what Mother had told me to do. To tell him that I loved him. That he would be missed. That I was so very sorry that I could do nothing to save him or lessen his pain. I had taken his presence as a dreary constant, giving him no greater attention than I had given the livestock: there to be led about to do my bidding or to share in my labors. I was sorry at the end that I had not been kinder or more patient. And he was always so with all of us.

As soon as I closed my eyes I began to dream, and in the dream I saw Andrew standing on a riverbank. It must have been spring, for the light was so bright and so yellow-hazing that all of the grasses and trees appeared indistinct and wavering, like melting butter. He was wearing Father's long flintlock strapped across his shoulder and he was poised with his arms around Tom and Richard. He looked up, his face good and moon-simple, and smiled broadly, as though he saw me standing on the other side of the river. He opened his mouth to speak, but before I could hear his words I felt my shoulder being shaken, and I woke to Tom's tearful face close to mine. I had fallen asleep slumped over Andrew's chest and I started to cry with the aware-ness that Andrew had gone.

I put my arms around Tom but he pulled my hands from his neck and said, "Sarah, look and see." But I did not want to see Andrew's face crumpled into death. Tom shook me by the shoulder and said my name again. I looked into his face, expect-ing to see my twin in mourning, but Tom's face was not closed in grief. His eyes were slanted with joy and his mouth was upturned, laughing in disbelief. He said to me, pulling up the sleeve on Andrew's shirt, "Look at his arm."

And I looked and saw that the red mark had begun its retreat back down Andrew's arm, down from the shoulder to the elbow and from there to his wrist. His breathing was deep and regu-lar, and when I felt his head, it was cool and covered with a fine sheen of sweat. When he finally opened his eyes, he had re-turned to the wit of a child, his smile foolish, his only request for soup and some bread.

When the sheriff came down later in the morning, he strode

into the cell to look at Andrew. He stared at me for a few surprised heartbeats before saying, "If that's not witchcraft, then
there never was." As he returned to the door, he told us that Andrew could stay one more day and then he would have to return
to the men's cell. As soon as his footsteps faded up the stairs, I
ran to the short bars and called out across the corridor to Richard and Mother, "Andrew is alive. He is alive." For the first time
in many days their answering voices made me feel enough joy to
press back the hopelessness of Salem prison. And for a few brief
minutes I could forget that there were only six days left for my
mother to dream or wake or feel anything at all.

The day was Sunday, and so a morning prayer meeting was
held in the women's cell. Goodwife Faulkner was asked to lead
us all in prayers of thanksgiving. When Father came at noon, he
brought us food and washed clothing and more clean water. He
grabbed the bars hard when Tom told of the doctor coming to
take Andrew's arm, and I thought he would pull them from
their casings. I propped Andrew's head higher into my lap so
that he could speak, and his first words in waking were "Father,
I can go out hunting with you now," and Father said to him,
"Son, you shall be the first of your brothers to fire the flint."
When his time in the corridor was finished, he told us he would
be back on Tuesday and every day from then on, until Friday.
Well into evening my brothers and I held hands, and our fingers
were folded together as strongly as the links in our chains.

PEOPLE WILL ASK those who have lived beyond terrible trials, "How did you come to get beyond your loss?" as though the

survivor who suffered the loss should simply stop up their nose until breath is starved from the lungs. It is true that some people will lose their desire for life and refuse food and drink after the death of a beloved, or if there is too much pain and injury to the body. But a child, so recently come into the world from the void of creation, can be more resilient than the strongest man, more strong willed than the hardiest woman. A child is like an early spring bulb that carries all the resources needed within its skin for the first push through the soil towards the sun. And just as a little bit of water can start the bulb to grow, even through fissured rock, so can a little kindness give a child the ability to push through the dark.

That kindness came in the form of Dr. Ames. When he entered our cell on that Monday, the 15th of August, I did not at first recognize him. He came in holding a kerchief to his nose and carrying a fitted calfskin bag. I thought at first he was a minister, as his coat was long and dark and he wore a sober, wide-brimmed hat. He soon put the cloth away into his pocket and I saw that he was a young man, perhaps no more than thirty, with a narrow, even nose and dark eyes banded above with thick black brows. He was greeted by several of the women, who reached out and swarmed around him, beseeching him for aid. He calmed them all with a few words and made his way around from woman to woman, stopping here to look at a wound and offer salve, or stopping there to hold a hand and talk for a while. With each supplicant, he would speak to that woman as though she were the only one in his presence, and more than a few would clasp his hand to her face and offer blessings for his gentle care. When he finally came to us, he knelt down and said kindly to Andrew, "Well, then, here is a miracle I can see for myself." He smiled at Andrew and Andrew returned the smile and held out his arm for the doctor to see more clearly.

As he examined the arm, he said casually to me, "You do not remember me, do you, Sarah?"

I was startled to hear my name and looked at him more closely. He turned his face to me and said, "I went to your home with the message from your uncle, Roger Toothaker." And then it came to me: the young doctor from Haverhill who had been to Boston to treat the prisoners there. He was the one who had brought the note to Father. The note Father had read and then thrown into the fire. He quickly unpacked dressing and ointment from his bag and wound it around Andrew's wrist. When he was finished with the binding, he treated Tom's chafed skin and then turned to my raw and burning wrists.

"I know your father," he said, wrapping strips of cloth around my wrists under the metal cuffs. "Or rather I should say I know of him. He is a person often spoken of in Boston. In certain fellowships."

I looked at him blankly and he continued, his fingers gentle and cool on my wrists. "Do you know how your uncle died?"

"It is said he was poisoned," I answered, uncomfortable with his question. "He was poisoned by . . . someone," I ventured, and I looked at his eyes with uncertainty.

He then held my hands in his slender ones and said quietly, "No, Sarah, not poisoned by someone. But by himself." When I started to open my mouth he said quickly, "I know what people have said about your father. It is true that he came into the cell the day your uncle died. It is also true that your uncle pleaded with him for forgiveness. He had been tortured by his inquisitors and knew that through his own weakness he would be forced to cry out against you, the children. He told me he repented of what he had said against your mother and that he would rather die than bring more harm. This was all written in the note to your father. But I do not believe your father was the cause of his death."

I stared at Tom, whose eyes showed me that I was not alone in harboring the belief that Father had done murder for our cause. I remembered Father once saying that Uncle had made good on a bad end, and I asked, "What do you mean?"

The doctor dropped his eyes and said, "Your uncle was under great distress and complained to me that his heart was failing. He asked of me to give him foxglove." I knew only that foxglove was a potent poison, and when I looked up at him, he said, "Foxglove in very small amounts is used for soothing an unsteady heart. In larger amounts it kills within hours, but unless you have a practiced eye, the death will often appear as though the heart stopped of its own accord. He asked for a large measure of it some days before his death, and because he was a doctor I bowed to his wisdom and . . . I gave it to him. But before I took my leave of him for the last time, I said to him, 'Be very careful to take only so much as you need.' And he replied to me, holding up the little bag of herbs, 'All that is here is what I need.' "

In my mind's eye I saw Uncle, cold and pale, lying dead in the dirty straw of his cell, and I found the pity for him I had lost while taking a beating in the yard of Chandler's Inn so many months ago. I looked down the length of the cell, trying to make out the forms of my aunt and cousin, but I could not see them through the murky light. I had no doubt that they yet believed what I had dared to believe: that my father poisoned his brother-in-law to save his own family.

"One of the doctors at your uncle's inquest is well known to me," he continued. "He saw the signs of poison and told me of it. I believe that once your uncle had seen your father, he took the only sure course to seal his own lips and in so doing protect the ones he loved."

The door of the cell opened and the sheriff rattled his keys loudly against the door. The young doctor gathered up his things and said, "My name is Dr. Ames, and though I live now in Haverhill, my family home is in Boston. I want you to give a message to your father, and you must remember it word for word. Can you do that?"

When I nodded my head, he continued, "Tell him that I and a few others are friends to your father. And tell him that we will do our level best to help him. Did you hear me, Sarah? Tell him we will do our *level* best."

I repeated the message, putting the emphasis on the word "level" as he had done, and he said in parting, "I will come as often as I can to look after you. You must know that this is not the world, and there are many who believe that this" — and he gestured about the cell — "all of this, is a shame to humanity." He smiled reassuringly at us once again and then left to see after the prisoners across the corridor. He had offered help and for that I had greater hope for myself and for my brothers. But he had said nothing about saving my mother. Later, before dusk, the sheriff came for Andrew, and it was only after Tom and I had struggled to walk him to the corridor and he heard Richard's voice calling to him that he stopped his crying and pleading to be left with us.

When Tom and I laid ourselves down that night, my last thoughts before falling to sleep were of Uncle. I thought of his quick and lively nature and remembered his ready laugh and the way the smoke from his pipe floated up beyond the prominent dome of his glistening forehead, curling up to the ceiling like a vagrant wish. And the way he delighted in calling Margaret and me his twins. I did not think much of the nights he came back to his home and family dizzy from drink, or of the late hours spent at an inn. Or of the tears Aunt had shed waiting for his return. I thought more of the stories he had told us by the light of the hearth. Tales of rampant Indians and wandering spirits and the deaths of pagan kings. I thought of him proudly astride Bucephalus, named after the war steed belonging to Alexander. The ancient king so beloved by his men until he led them off the face of their circumscribed maps into the lands of specters and strange men. The king who was given the cup of poison so that his men could return to the known world. But Uncle had taken up the cup of poison with his own hand in the hopes of returning those he loved safely back from the land of monsters, and for that I wept long and hard for him.

TUESDAY MORNING I woke with a start, a terrible panic seizing me by the throat. The wailing woman with the rotted tooth had continued her screeching throughout the night, giving me dreams of eagles falling headlong out of the sky to the earth. It was the 16th of August and I spent most of the morning pressed against the bars, speaking to Richard and Mother of the world outside our cells. We spoke only of the past. Of Mother's garden or the plentiful harvest we had had the year before or the enormous turkey Richard had shot early last spring. Mother's voice was weak and several times I asked her to speak out more clearly so that I could hear her words. The women at the short wall took pity on Tom and me and walked about the cell giving us more time to talk, but soon we were edged away from the wall and back into the middle of the cell.

I saw Mary Lacey come creeping past us to use the slops and my feeling of helplessness turned to rage. She was our neighbor from Andover and yet she had cried out falsely against my mother to try to save herself. She cut her eyes at me and I remembered sharply her face gawking at me over the village gravestones while Mercy Williams held me prisoner in her arms, telling me she would burn me alive in my own bed.

I rushed at her, pushing her hard enough to throw her to the ground. There were protesting words as Mary struggled over several of the seated women trying to rise to her feet again. But no one came to scold me, or to assist Mary. And there were more than one pair of eyes that glinted with satisfaction. She would not look me in the face but gathered up her skirt and stepped away deeper into the cell. I felt Tom's hand on my shoulder but I shrugged him off, too close to anguished weeping to allow comfort. I held my breath to slow my heart but its rapid beating was felt in every part of my body. My head throbbed and my eyes danced in their sockets, keeping time with the swirling, particled air, illuminated like mayflies in stippled shafts of sunlight. I looked around at the women scattered about the cell, sitting or standing slack-jawed and loose-limbed, and it enraged me. Where was the will to rise up and protest? To plan escapes or at least make demands upon our captors? Where was the outrage, the anger, the fury?

When Father appeared at noontide, bringing food, I could barely hear his promises that he would come every day until Mother's last day with us. In my panic I forgot all about the message I was to give him from Dr. Ames and would not remember it again for many days. I grabbed at his hands and pulled his ear close to my mouth and begged him again to try to save her. To take her, and us, away from this place. I told him I would from that day work day and night, that I would go without food, that I would go naked through the wilderness if only he would take action. When his eyes finally met mine, I imagined I heard the sound of an open book closing. A great book inscribed within with the resonant words of a lifetime. The forward binding arches up and over, the pages within whispering, "And then, and then, and then..." and then, just past the midpoint, the pages fall over, rippling and rustling towards the end binding, meeting a weighted closure and a last, unspoken "No."

From that point, after he had left us, I stood motionless in the middle of my prison like the needle in a sundial fixed and rigid, unable to join in the shifting currents of the living. The afternoon light worked its way through the window slits and brightened the cell for a short while. I watched with horror my changing shadow as the light first grew brighter and then dimmed again as night filled up our hollowed spaces. I was standing there even after the moon had followed the course of the sun, falling and disappearing into the westernmost horizon.

WEDNESDAY PASSED THE same as Tuesday, with the slops being taken up, with Father coming and going, bringing us some little bit of something to fill a small corner of our bellies, as well as the news that Andrew continued to heal and grow stronger. But the Reverend Dane did not come, and nor did Dr. Ames. The sheriff's wife did not come, as did very few of the families of the confined. On that day there were no new unfortunates to be tried and shackled and imprisoned within the jail. The voice from the Salem meetinghouse was stilled. It was as if time for us within the cells had shortened against the time that lay outside the cold and seeping walls of the prison. And like a smaller cog within a larger one, we were out-pacing the outer world in our rush towards our endless sleep. And try as I might to hold back its passing, by closing my eyes or slowing the movement of my limbs or shaking away immi-nent sleep, the day waxed and waned into evening and within a breathless span turned itself into Thursday.

I AWOKE CURLED against Tom's back and lay for the longest time pressed up against his warmth, my hands cradled at my chest. I could hear the sounds of stirring and rising all around me and I closed my eyes to bring back sleep. But my mind, once brought to awareness, would not be blanketed. I heard a woman close to me saying the Lord's Prayer and I followed the familiar words to the end. I wondered if this woman, who had spoken the passage without faltering and without hesitation, had tried to use this recitation as proof of her innocence, as it was said the Devil would confound the words in those he had sealed as his own. But even this device would be discounted, for when the former Salem Village Reverend, George Burroughs, recited the same prayer resolutely and without error as he stood at the hanging tree, a noose wrapped around his neck, Cotton Mather would say that the "Devil had often been transformed into an Angel of Light." George Burroughs was to be hanged on the morrow with my mother.

I tried to bend my thoughts to prayer as well. I wanted to believe that what was waiting for my mother was what I had been told in the meetinghouse waited for all its saints after death. But of course my mother had been excommunicated from the church as a witch with no hope of salvation unless she admitted her guilt before she died. The church said there would be no heaven for her, only the fires of damnation. But she was not a witch, no more than I. What middling place would there be for her, caught between the lofty reward of heaven and the tortures of hell? Behind my closed lids, there was only blackness, with pale and indistinct images floating at random in a narrow field. Would death for her be like that? Would it be like falling into sleep, becoming aware of place and purpose only in the grips of fragmented dreams? I suddenly jerked my eyes open against these thoughts of a darkly fogged existence stretching out beyond days and years and centuries.

The sound of footsteps shuffling carelessly down the stairs disturbed the early morning quiet and soon someone at the short wall looked into the corridor and whispered to the rest of us, "It's the sheriff's wife come a day early." We heard two pairs of footsteps walk to the end of the corridor to the condemned women's cell and soon the same woman turned and said, "She's gone inside the cell."

I rose quickly and found a place at the bars and waited to see her come out again. I could see the sheriff standing with his lantern in the corridor, impatiently shifting from one foot to the other. In a few moments' time Goodwife Corwin came back out again carrying something in her arms. She started back up the corridor and stopped when she saw my face pressed against the bars.

She said to me, "You'll be having a bit more to eat today." I looked down and saw she was holding the dress, now stained with the filth of the prison cell, that my mother had worn on the day she was arrested. I looked at her with dismay but she had started to climb the stairs again with her husband. Shortly before the noon hour the sheriff passed through the bars, first to Richard and then to me, a small loaf of bread and a lump of salt pork. It was all that my mother's dress could buy. I held half of the loaf cradled in my hands and rocked back and forth and back and forth until my tears had softened it enough to eat.

THE CONDEMNED ARE hanged early, and even before dawn the sheriff must descend the stairs, carrying his shuttered lantern in front of him, to read aloud the death warrant and call the names of those who must on that day die. On Friday, August 19th, there were five names shouted out over the waiting ears of the sleepless cells: John Proctor, John Willard, George Jacobs, Reverend Burroughs, and Martha Carrier. They would be taken at seven of the clock from the prison and carried by cart to Gallows Hill.

The night before, several black-coated ministers from Salem and its surrounding villages had come into the cells to plead for full and honest confessions of guilt. Not a one of the condemned recanted their claims of innocence. Margaret Jacobs, George Jacobs' granddaughter, stood next to me against the bars and begged the forgiveness of her grandfather, and of George Burroughs, whom she had also accused of wizardry during her trials. Reverend Burroughs, a man of unnatural strength who had outlived several wives, who could carry a seven-foot flint-lock in one hand like a pistol, as well as whole barrels of cider, and who went against the tide of custom and preached to the soulless Indians, forgave Margaret with tender grace. His voice, coarsened and tempered to fill the enormous spaces of the wilderness, overtook the voices of his fellow ministers and he drowned out their insipid prayers of condemnation with the trumpeted prayers of forgiveness.

The rebuffed ministers left, saying that before noon there would be five new firebrands burning in hell, and I watched their shadowed forms ascending the staircase like acrid smoke twisting up a chimney flue. The one exception was the Reverend Dane, who prayed with his small and miserable flock and left us, covering his face with his kerchief so that he stumbled up the stairs like a child who cannot find his way in the dark.

Then Father had come. Some coins had been found for the sheriff, bartered and sacrificed for, so that he could say his final good-byes. His bent form treaded softly to the end of the corridor, the back of his head grazing the rough wooden beams, to where my mother's hands came out to grasp his. He took off his hat and laid it aside and then, grabbing hold of the bars, knelt in the dirt and pressed his forehead against the pitted metal. Whatever words were exchanged were said quietly and went with her to her death. I saw her fingers cradle his face, her thumbs gently smoothing the channels under his eyes, wiping away the tears. He nodded a few times and once looked down the corridor in my direction, his eyes recessed and hollow. When the time came for him to leave, he spoke first to Richard and Andrew and then to Tom and me, saying that he would be there at the end. He would stand for all of us so that when she closed her eyes for the last time, there would be a counterweight of love against the overflowing presence of vengeance and fear. When he left, Tom and I sat together the whole of the night propped against the walls, dried into sand and bone.

Now it was morning and my heartbeat was the clock within my chest that counted out the minutes until the hour of execution. Tom and I stood at the short wall, our hands wrapped like summer ivy around the bars. Somewhere deep within my thoughts I became aware that the other women had moved away from us farther into the cells. Out of pity or fear I did not know. We heard the sound of the door at the top of the stairs being opened, and the sheriff came down, along with two men who were to assist him in his day's work. They approached the men's cell, and as soon as the door opened, the four condemned men walked into the corridor, the three strongest helping George Jacobs to stand, as he was the oldest, near to eighty years of age on that day.

They were taken up the stairs, and then the door at the top of the stairs was closed behind them. I saw Richard's face dimly appear at the bars across the corridor, his eyes feverish and darting. The door at the top of the stairs was opened again and the sheriff came back down alone to take up his last prisoner. I opened my mouth to call out to her but I could not find my voice. The door was swung open with a murderous rattling of the keys, yet the dark mouth of the cell remained empty for a long time. When she walked through the doorway, blinking into the illumination of the lantern's light, she was as insubstantial and weightless as the air she struggled to breathe through her cracked and bleeding lips. She was wearing only her shift and she hugged herself around her middle with arms that had been scraped away by manacles to raw flesh and sinew. Manacles that had been removed the night before by the blacksmith who had first hammered them closed.

She walked with great effort towards us down the corridor, and when she looked up into my eyes, she did not have to speak the words for me to know the feelings that she held for me and for my brothers. Her love was manifest within her starving body: the food that she had refused, perhaps for weeks, so that we could have the tiniest particle more of bread; the dress she had sold for a small pinch of meat; the cup she had passed over so that her children could quench their thirst, and live. She was not given the chance to linger, to touch or embrace her sons and daughter, but she sought out each of us with her eyes and lingered there in prideful silence. We had said all we could have said to her of love and sorrow on the evening before. Her last exhausted words to me, spoken as the cells quieted into the evening's rest, were "There is no death in remembrance. Remember me, Sarah. Remember me, and a part of me will always be with you."

As she passed closest to me, she raised a finger and tapped it to her breast and then extended it out to me, drawing the invisible connecting thread between us: the thread of hope, of continuity, of understanding. Her last act of will was to climb the stairs unaided, without stumbling and without crawling, and then the door above us was swung on its hinges and closed.

Cell-blinded and groping, she would have been placed in the cart with the four men, her hands tied perilously in front, so that she would have had to struggle to keep her balance when the cart turned sharply from Prison Lane to Main Street. The cart would have made its way past the houses of the judges, and of some of the jurors as well, and more than a few people would have lined the streets to watch the cart as it made its way west towards Gallows Hill. The cart would have crossed over the Town Bridge, which spans a finger of the North River with its sulfurous tidal pools, and then, where the road splits into the Boxford Road and the southerly Old Road, the cart would have struggled up the rutted path to the lower ledges of Gallows Hill. And there, gathered to watch, would have been dozens of men and women and children from Salem Town and Salem Village and other towns besides, their souls to be warned and chastened and at length profited by the lessons of the hangings. In the gathering would have been ministers and with them the greatest of his calling, the Reverend Cotton Mather.

Today there is only a stand of locust trees to mark the spot. But then there was one giant oak tree with sturdy branches that could have supported the weight of twenty, let alone a pitiful, strawlike few. A ladder was set up against the trunk of the tree and the sheriff, well known to all, would have donned his mask of office, not to hide his face but because it was the proper English custom to hood the executioner. To save his strength he would have taken the heaviest of the men first, leading John Proctor and then George Burroughs to stand on the ladder, slipping the noose around their necks and then pushing them out into the lessening air. John Willard would have been next and then George Jacobs.

Last would have been my mother, the frail body, already slackening into the embrace of a long-awaited release, carried, shoulder-borne, by the hangman to her place on the ladder. The splintering rope slip-tied around her neck. The push into the warm summer currents. The sky blue and cloudless as though God would watch with an open face and wide-awake eyes, no clouds to hinder the revealing rays of the sun. No rain like the shedding of tears, nor wind to punish the watchers in a tightening crescent of fearful expectation around the tree. The worn and cracked shoes, creased from years of treading the earth, now kicked free from struggling feet. The neck stretching, breaking; the gate to life closing and then collapsing. The eyes searching against the closing of the lids. Searching and finding the tall figure standing alone at a small rise behind the crowds.

The giant of Cardiff standing for all of us as he promised he would do, bareheaded and still, etched against the disappearing light of the world, the needle to the true compass that pointed north beyond Salem towards Andover and, beyond that, to her final home.

CHAPTER NINE

August–October 1692

I AM DREAMING and in this dream I am in Aunt's root cellar.
I know it is the cellar because it is cold and damp with the fusty
smell of things that have grown hard and bulbous beneath the
soil. Through the brown velvet darkness appear dimly the drying baskets Margaret and I used to fill in the autumn and then
empty again through the long winter. I can hear footsteps above
my head. Someone is pacing the length of Uncle's common
room and I hear the sound of voices in conversation, and laughter, too, soft and muzzy like carpenter's dust through joists
below the floorboards. There is life above me and light. But the
cellar door is closed and I have in my hand but one end of a
candle that has burned through most of its wick.

I cry out but no one hears me. I kick against the earthen

walls but can find no release. My ears remain sharp to the surrounding darkness, and a rustling, like voices sighing, comes
from every part of the cellar. It is not the skeltered scribbling of
a mouse or rat. It is softer, more faint. Somehow, more patient. It is the crackling of a beetle's wing, or the throbbing
carapace of a locust on a shaft of wheat. Or the dry, whispering
sound of root ends piercing through the earthen walls into the
cellar. Slender, attenuated roots, some as fine as spider's webs,
groping their way to the center of the cave where I sit. Drawn by
the warmth of my quickening breath, they wrap themselves
about my feet and ankles, wrists and hands. Then, with a delicate embrace, the roots weave in long tendrils across my thighs,
my waist, my chest. Tightening and clasping, holding me fast,
reaching upwards to wrap around my face as the candle flame
gutters and then goes out. And I am left in the last dimming
light of the cellar, my mouth shuttered and mute, my ears
plugged into silence, my blinded eyes wide and unseeing. And
then I wake. It is the dream that will come again and again for
many days after my mother's death, and always when I wake I
will be in a cell in Salem prison. And it will be raining.

The indigo summer skies had been swallowed up by roiling
oppressive clouds, drowning the lightning before it could spark
and smothering the attendant thunderclaps into hollow rum-
blings. The rain seeped through the crumbling mortar between
the stones and ran in rivulets through the open slits in the walls.
It stewed the rushes on the floor into a sour rotting mash and
soaked through the leather of our shoes. The days were spent
huddled together for warmth as far away from the leaking walls
as could be managed. For all the many witches in Salem jail,

more than sixty captured and manacled, the roof should have flown off its struts, allowing us to escape. But the nails lay rusting in their timbers, the bars at the windows stayed fixed, the locks remained bolted, and all, from the youngest to the oldest, still held the weight of eight pounds of chains in their laps.

Rain, wild and unpredictable, had swept in from the northeast, pounding its way down the coast from Falmouth to Wells to Kittery and then on to Salisbury like some black and nettle-fed mare. The battling currents off Cape Ann then pushed the storm clouds inland from Marblehead towards the Merrimack, and westward with the winds came the frenzied apparitions and malcontent of Salem Village. By September more than thirty women and thirteen men from Andover would be imprisoned, half of whom were in their minority. Young girls from Andover had begun to have strange fits, like their sisters in Salem Village, and the Reverend Barnard called for a touch test to be held during prayer meetings to find their tormentors. On the 7th of September many of Andover's first citizens were called to the meetinghouse to stand before the pulpit and be touched by shrieking, shuddering girls—girls who would suddenly be freed from their sufferings once they had touched the witch who had cast the harmful spells. The prison doors opened and closed and opened and closed, and soon seven of the Reverend Dane's family slept in the shadows within whispering distance of me. A grandson of the Reverend, only thirteen years of age, was placed in the men's cell with Richard and Andrew.

But it was not only the Dane family that suffered. Andover woke to find that witches inhabited every possible corner of its households and fields. A daughter drying herbs upon a corn crib was suspect. A niece marking a thumb print on an unbaked loaf was conjuring. The welcoming wife parting the sheets on the marriage bed was a succubus, draining the life's blood from her husband's body. A cross word, an unhealed argument, an oath or curse from half a generation ago was recalled, recounted, revealed. A man named Moses Tyler accused and had placed into prison his sister and five of her daughters, a mother-in-law of one brother, and the wife and three daughters of another brother. Such was the charity and generosity of spirit shown to women in Reverend Barnard's meetinghouse on that dissolute and shameful Wednesday. And thus it was that Reverend Barnard became the undisputed leader of a besieged town over his elderly and harried fellow minister.

FEAR WAS BROUGHT into the cells with the newly imprisoned like welts from a beating, and no one knew for sure if there were indeed witches sitting hand to foot with the innocent. There was no walking about now in the "good" cell. There was only room for shifting about. And only by mutual consent. There was never a time when it was completely silent. Many of the women had caught a rumbling cough from the damp, and the nights were noisier than the days. Sarah Wardwell, a neighbor to the north of our house in Andover, was imprisoned with an older daughter and a baby not one year old. The baby, sickly and small, wailed long and fitfully in the hours before dawn. Samuel Wardwell, the baby's father, lying in the men's cell, would be condemned and hanged before the month had ended. The woman with the rotted tooth cried in agony through the night and most of the day, finding no relief from the liquor that was poured in greater and greater amounts down her throat. Liquor that had been given to me, too, to stop my own screams of terror and agony as my mother was taken from her cell for the last time.

Upon hearing the end of Mother's footsteps upon the stairwell, I had pulled wildly at the bars, the rising shrillness of my voice cutting like a knife through the thick air of the corridor. I felt strong arms enveloping me, pulling me back, and heard a voice say sharply in my ear, "Hush, now. You cannot let your mother hear your cries. It will only distress her more. Hush. Hush and be brave for her sake." But I could not stop the wailing, the thrashing, and the grinding of my teeth as I fought the women who held me in their arms. I was a mad thing. No longer child. No longer reasoned. No longer restrained. I hit and kicked and bit until my jaw was forced open and a bitter, choking liquid was poured into my mouth and I was forced to swallow or be drowned. The liquid was poured a second and then a third time, and within a few minutes the beast retreated from the door and a spreading warmth spilled from my belly into my legs and then into my chest, my arms, and my head. My mind retreated from itself, and my tormented thoughts became like a twisted sheet beneath a thickly padded blanket. The restraining arms that held me loosened their grip, and someone, perhaps Goody Faulkner, whose belly was swollen with child, cradled my head in her lap and sang to me with a whispering, tuneless breath.

"Lulay, my little tiny child, bye-bye lulee-lou-lay,
Lulay, my little tiny child, sleep now until the day."

I stared at a low beam above my head and watched the rough
knots and channels in the wood become the grimacing faces of
men and women, some wearing half-masks and hats piled like
giant gourds on their heads. A splintered crevice became a horse
racing against the grain and a sworling crevice became a mer-
chant's ship that threatened to sail from the edge of that narrow
and rustic terrain. The beam was a world unto itself, fantastical
and somehow set apart from the surrounding indistinct haze of
my cell. Suddenly I had a clear and piercing thought that sup-
planted every imagining. Someday, after many, many tomorrows, the beam that straddled my sight would be the only part
of the cell left whole when all the stones had been carted away
and the rest burned to ash. The jail that seemed so impenetrable
and everlasting would fall like any cellar. The mortar would
soften. The beams would crack and sag. The rock would collapse. And the rubble would fill the gaping spaces so that no
passerby could stop and say, "Here and here was my great-
grandfather or grandmother or distant aunt kept in darkness
and in wasting despair." Before another hour had passed, and
before I closed my eyes to fall into the chasm of sleep, the
figures on the beam had begun to move.

THE RITUALS OF the days became as always. The slops to go
up, new straw to throw down. Visits from families with food.
Fridays brought the sheriff's wife. Saturdays the surgeons. Sab-

bath days, prayers all round. Mondays came the ministers to pray, to beg for a confession, or to harry with condemnation and excommunication. On the 9th day of September the fourth trial of the Court of Oyer and Terminer was held and six more women were condemned: Martha Corey, Mary Easty, sister to Rebecca Nurse, who had been hanged on the July past, Alice Parker, Ann Pudeator, Dorcas Hoar, and Mary Bradbury. They were placed in the condemned women's cell, and so I did not see these women well until they were taken out to be hanged. But often we could hear the coarse and winded voice of Martha Corey haranguing the ministers come to extract a confession from her. "I am no more a witch t'an you. I never have been, nor am I one t'day. You can close your book on me. But my deeds is already writ in God's book. And you and the Devil can take the hindest part o' me and be pleased wit' yoursels." The ministers would often leave the prison as quickly and as furtively as dogs from a dousing.

The early days of September also became a war waged against children. There were Abigail and Dorothy Faulkner, who were nine and twelve, the daughters of Goody Faulkner. Both shy and frightened, they never moved from the sheltering arms of their mother and clung to her desperately even when she rose awkwardly to use the midden. There were the nieces of Moses Tyler, Hannah, Joanna, and Martha, wild and uncouth-looking. The two youngest were twins, and though they were only eleven, they bullied the other larger girls into giving up what little food they possessed. When they entered the cells, we saw that these three girls wore the marks of old welts and bruises about their mouths and eyes. When they were asked with horrified concern if the bruises were from their judges, they only laughed and said they were a parting gift from their father.

In the beginning, many of the young Andover girls found their way to me in the cell, thinking no doubt that my long period underground had given me some kind of canny strength to survive the hardships of prison. But I had entered a place that shut out the world, and my apathy soon drove them away. The only person who could have stirred my spirit to rise never looked for me or sought me out and lay in Aunt's arms insensible to her surroundings. The days passed for me like the evenings, in a dull twilight between sleeping and waking. The voice of Tom or Father or Dr. Ames or the Reverend Dane had no deeper meaning apart from the rhythm and cadence of supplication. "Please eat, Sarah." "Please rise, Sarah." "Please speak to me, Sarah." "Please, please, please..." until I covered my ears and ground my head into the straw and forced the speaker to abandon his post. Hannah Tyler, thinking that my balling-up was a weakness, tried to work her hand into my apron to take a bit of corn bread hidden there. I pushed her hand away but she persisted and bent back my fingers to ease her theft.

I looked up and saw the pallid, avaricious face before me, the teeth protruding sharply from a meanly placed tongue, and I thought of Phoebe Chandler's ferretlike face chanting, "witch, witch, witch..." I sat up so abruptly that it unbalanced her, sending her back on her haunches. She squinted her eyes at me and looked set to try again, and it was that look that threw the final heated stones into the soup. Tom had crept up ready to put himself between me and Hannah, but I ignored him and said to her, "Touch me again and your fingers will rot off the bone."

Her jaw shifted from one side to the other with malicious intent, but she paused.

"You don't want to touch me again," I said, my teeth sharp against the words. "You're in here because you're low and ugly. I'm here because I'm my mother's daughter."

She drew back and from the edges of my vision I saw uneasy glances exchanged from woman to woman. I looked around the cell and saw that my warning had brought to life deep suspicions that even a child could harbor maleficence. Goody Faulkner, and the other women of Andover, gathered around her, lowering their eyes against my stare, but I heard a cautioning voice close by say, "Resist the Devil in all his works." The speaker had directed those words to me, but I, with a flash of anger, thought, I am not the one with my hands in someone else's pocket.

A dark shadow rose up against the wall opposite and crept towards us. The shadow was figured like a woman and layered over with the thick, steaming remnants of many different cloaks stitched together. I had seen her resting motionless against the wall week after week, her glistening black face passive and indifferent to minister and prisoner alike. Her mouth opening only to eat the meager shares of bread and gruel she had been given by her master. She had been one of the first of Salem to be tried and imprisoned and had remained in chains since the bitter winds of February. The Reverend Parris, the parson of Salem, who had taken her as a slave from her home in the West Indies, had beaten her into a confession, and she walked ever after with a crooked back. Her sorcery was as frail as the body she inhabited. As frail as the Venus glass she had used to help the village girls see their fortunes.

She stepped over the prostrate bodies of the women, as though crossing a shallow stream, and came to stop at the retreating legs and arms of Hannah as she crawled backwards to escape this first, dark witch. The black eyes swept around the room and she raised her manacled wrists like an offering and said, "You want to see the Devil's hand? The Devil's hands is wrapped around my wrist."

She stepped and turned and stepped and turned so that every eye could see the iron links beginning and ending the same, one to the other in a closed circle, encompassing birth and life and death. Then she dropped her hands and fixed her great, liquid eyes on me. She drew in a ragged breath and said haltingly, as though in great pain, "I am my mother's daughter, too." She moved away into the deep silence her words had carved and returned to her place at the wall. I never heard her say a word more. Her name was Tituba, and upon her release she would be sold again to another owner and disappear from the written deeds of men like a stone into a well.

From that moment on I was left unmolested. Apart from Tom, who tried his best to feed and protect me, there were few others in the cell who would approach me again. Save for Dr. Ames. And the sheriff's wife.

IT IS HARD to reckon the days underground. The only remarkable change of light came at sunset when for a brief time the sun worked its way through the high slits. It had rained steadily until mid-September, and for several weeks there was no sun to differ morning from night. Then the rain dried and the nights of a sudden turned bitingly cold. When the sheriff's wife came into our cell one morning, I knew it must have been a Friday. The evening before, a young woman of fifteen, Elizabeth Colson, had been captured and returned to jail following her indictment in May. She had fled from her home in Reading to relatives in New Hampshire but had been found by the local constables and dragged from her haven under the cover of dark. She was wearing good homespun wool, and Goody Corwin was keen to barter for the goods.

I was surprised to find that Elizabeth, hearty and well fed, was granddaughter to the old woman who had mocked the doctor from Salem, the doctor who had tried to hack off Andrew's arm. Lydia Dustin, so the grandmother was called, was so old and so decrepit that she seemed wholly cast from a children's tale of hags born from the bones and feathers of a crane. She put herself in front of Goodwife Corwin and said, swaying her spotted skirt back and forth, "Lay away, missus. You'll get naught off her. But I have a fine gown you can have for a small bit of bread." The sheriff's wife wrinkled her nose in disgust and picked her way across the straw, followed by the old woman's rattling laugh.

She stopped a short distance away and regarded me, her head cocked to one side as if reflecting on something many-sided. She tapped with the tip of her shoe an opening place between me and the woman sitting next to me and then squatted down, carefully pulling up her skirt from the muck. She dropped something onto my lap and said quietly, "Remember it was me who gave you this."

She got up and left the cell, and when I looked down again I saw it was a crust of pocket bread. Hard though it was, it looked to be stuffed with meat. I quickly tucked it under my apron but not before the woman next to me saw what I had done and gave me a look that was both envious and distrusting.

Several days passed with her coming into the cell and always dropping into my lap some bit of food. I tried to share the gifts with Tom but after that first day, he refused every morsel that came from the sheriff's table. I did not refuse. My hunger pains, which had been merely dull and aching before, came roaring viciously to life like a ratter that has tasted first blood. Tom did not begrudge me but many others did. The daily visits from the sheriff's wife were much remarked upon and gossiped over. I could see the same looks of displeasure and condemnation that had followed me in the meetinghouse. Quietly and relentlessly I was being shunned and I welcomed it, for it was the foil against which I could pit my growing anger. The anger that was the breastplate and armor against the deep and soul-shredding guilt grinding in my chest that I had, in good part, sent my own mother to be hanged.

On Saturday, the 17th of September, the judges tried and condemned another eight women. One of the women was Abigail Dane Faulkner, and she was returned to the cell before noon with her two daughters, who had been forced to testify against her. She walked, staggering, to her place on the wall, holding her daughters against her swollen skirts, and a new terror settled in upon us, hearing that a woman so far gone with child would be committed to the hangman.

The one man who had been tried on that day, Miles Corey, refused to speak, either to give confession or to deny his guilt.

He was husband to Martha Corey and was eighty years of age. When asked repeatedly to respond to the judges' questions, he crossed his arms and, setting his jaw, looked only at the floorboards in front of him. Because he would not speak, he was tortured to induce his tongue to be loosened. On the 19th of September, a gently wind-tossed autumn day, Goodman Corey was taken from his cell out to the prison yard, where he was laid prone in the dirt. His hands and feet were staked out and heavy stones were placed on a plank laid over his body until he could no longer raise his ribs to draw in a breath. He never spoke a word to his torturers except for the two words at the very end, when he said, "More weight."

His tongue was finally loosened in death. The crushing weight of the stones had forced it through his lifeless, protruding lips until the sheriff forced it back in again with the tip of his probing cane. The death of Miles Corey seemed to shift the winds over Salem, for Dorcas Hoar, already condemned to die on the 22nd, changed her mind and confessed that she was and had been a witch for many years. Also reprieved, in compassion for her belly, was Abigail Dane Faulkner.

IT WAS ON the fifth or sixth day of passing food to me that Goody Corwin told me the price she would exact. The morning she came in she looked distracted and out of sorts, wringing her hands upon her apron and then smoothing it down again. She approached me as usual, dropping the food into my apron, and said in a hushed tone so that no one else could hear, "My good husband tells me you may have the power of healing."

I looked at her without understanding until she said, "Your brother. Him that was to lose his arm. The surgeon said he was sure to die. But he lived and is whole again." She waited, and when I had nothing to answer, she continued, "I have a daughter. About your age." She looked at the top of my head and I remembered her measuring me with the palm of her hand. No doubt thinking my dress would just fit her own daughter.

"She is very ill and like to die. The doctor says there is nothing left to be done. Unless..." And here she left off and a dawning understanding made the skin on my scalp shrink. She leaned in closer to me and said in a forced whisper, "Heal her, and you will never lack for food. As long as you are here." I looked beyond her expectant eyes and saw an endless procession of days spent imprisoned, slowly starving or not, depending on the goodwill and whim of my jailers. She took my silence for consent and left me to the wondering looks of my cell mates.

In the early morning hours of September the 22nd the skies opened up and poured an ocean onto the houses and people of Salem Town. The water ran in streams and rivulets down pathways and alleys, pooling around casements and flooding into cellars and half cellars alike. The riven streets became ponds over which people and animals had to jump to cross, or find themselves wet to the knees. And when Sheriff Corwin opened the cellar door to walk with his deputies down to the corridor, a low cascade of water licked at their boot heels. The two deputies shook the rain off their greatcoats as the sheriff led Samuel Wardwell out of the men's cell. Sarah Wardwell was given a place by the short wall and held the baby up so that her husband could see his infant child through the bars. When he had been led up the stairs, the seven old women were brought hobbling and shivering from their cell. They made their way slowly and deliberately up the glassy steps, stopping only to assist the ones who faltered or stumbled, until they passed through the outer door, their footsteps washed over with rainwater.

Martha Corey, Alice Parker, Mary Easty, Ann Pudeator, Wilmot Reed, Mary Parker, Margaret Scott, and Samuel Wardwell went to their deaths claiming their innocence. But when the executioner's cart became mired in a rut on the pathway up to Gallows Hill, the onlookers cried, "Look, the Devil hinders the cart."

The day following the executions, Sheriff Corwin went with his deputies and seized property and goods belonging to the Parkers and the Wardwells. They were claimed for the Crown but the Corwins got the best of it. Mary Parker's sons were able to buy back their property, but Sarah Wardwell would return to her farm to find that every animal, every stalk of corn, every movable bit of furniture, including her husband's carpentry tools, had been taken and sold for coin. On that Friday, the 23rd, the sheriff's daughter died and when his wife did not appear to make her rounds, I knew with a certainty that there would be no more gifts of food from her.

HYSSOP FOR COUGH. Rosemary for fever. A sprig of mint to cleanse ill humors from the mouth. Slippery elm for the midwife. Horse chestnut for stiffness of limb. Golden bough for palsy. But what is the cure for rage? Chamomile can calm. Perhaps with enough of that and a strong physic of black powder and salts it can be purged from the body. What of a restless mind that will not sleep at its appointed hour? A pillow of lavender or a sleeping draught made of equal parts of rum and water with sweet balm will suffice.

And what finally of the tortures of a guilty soul? What concoction is there that can be chewed and swallowed and downed in the belly to force the poison of self-recrimination back through the pores in the skin? In what organ of the body does it reside? A seeping wound can be bound. Salve can be dabbed to a burn or a swelling bubo. Poison can be drawn with a leech, or a lance. But guilt is a ghost that takes the shape of the body it inhabits and consumes all that is tender within its shell: brain, bowels, and heart. I cannot pluck it out like a splinter of glass or treat it with herbal brews.

I hear a keening sound start up close by. The old woman with the rotted tooth does not, cannot, stop moaning. The doctor has come, entreating her to let him pull it out. Her sisters in captivity have pleaded and begged and hounded her to tie to it some bit of string so that its rotten stump can be yanked from her swollen jaw. But she will not. She clamps her hand over her mouth and moans and moans and moans until I think I shall start screaming and never stop.

It is full-on night. I watch her rocking back and forth, her bare feet stuck out in front of her, the toes curling and uncurling in pain. There is something about the way in which her thin white legs are revealed from the bottom of her shift that is poignant and awful in their nakedness. Something uncoils from my memory and suddenly I see a bare leg come rising up out of a shallow grave. I try to push the thought away, for I know it is not a real memory. Only one that has been conjured into my mind from overhearing the other women in the cell. They have been talking and passing stories from one to the other. Stories that have come from their families. About the hangings. And the burials afterward. The dead. They are cut down and dragged by the remnants of their ragged clothes or by the ends of the hangman's ropes to shallow graves close by. Into which they are rolled. Thin dirt shoveled over them. So thin that parts of the bodies show through. George Burroughs, his shirt and breeches pulled as loot from his body, laid in some rocky place. Covered over but for his chin and one of his hands, which uncurls from the soil as if beckoning. Lying next to him is Goodman Willard. And, hush, hush, quietly now, the girl is near to hearing, listen to what has come of Goody Carrier. She lies next to him. With one leg propped out of the rocks. As though waiting to step out of her grave.

The moaning woman has reached her fingers into her mouth and I pray as I have never prayed before that we could exchange our torments. That I could have the agony of her festering jaw if she could carry the agony of what I have done. She starts to work her hand frantically and I begin to see a thin trickle of blood running down the back of her hand through her fingers. She brings her other hand to her lip to pull it out of the way as she works and works at her tooth. She wrenches the tooth as she claws with her nails the flesh around it until she has torn it out of her mouth. She gazes stunned for a few moments at the black kernel in her hand and then a look of complete and swooning relief comes over her face as she holds out to me her demon, her lips bloody and smiling. I lie down in the straw, facing away from her, as close to Tom as I can get, my demon still writhing within me.

WHEN DR. AMES came the next day, I would not sit up to greet him or even look at him. He asked Tom if I had been eating and placed his ear against my chest to hear the beating of my heart. When he was satisfied he sat back and, taking my hand, said, "Sarah, you must keep faith that your innocence will be shown to the court. There are even now petitions being sent to the governor from many important people. Ministers from Boston, and your own Reverend Dane, are appealing directly to the Reverend Increase Mather, Cotton Mather's father, to try to redirect some reason into these trials."

He lowered his head closer to mine to better catch my eye and continued, "Many of us are taking up a collection to offer bail for your release. And the release of the other children."

I thought of returning to the ruined shell that had been my home. The rooms cluttered from lack of care. The cooking hearth cindered and tarred from no brush to the flue. The fields overgrown and untamed from the attentions of only one man. Five separate souls circling about the empty place in each room. Looking but finding no grave in which to put an end to their despairing.

"Sarah, I know you mourn for your mother, but she is in that place in which we all hope to be."

"She is in a shallow pit," I said, my voice hollow and flat.

He looked narrowly at the women around him, shaking his head and furrowing his brow as though he would shame them all with his eyes, and said softly so that only Tom and I could hear him, "Your father did not leave her in that terrible place. He has buried her properly, that I can promise you. He and a good many of the other families have returned under the cover of night and have taken their loved ones away to secret places."

I thought of Father returning to Gallows Hill to lift Mother's stiffening body from its narrow trench and I shuddered. Dr. Ames pulled my shawl tighter around my shoulders and sat with me silently for a while, clasping and unclasping his fingers in mine. I felt my eyes grow heavy against the touch of his fingers and I longed for sleep. A sleep that would go on and on, undisturbed and peaceful. When Mother used to wake Father on a Sabbath, his deep voice would rumble from beneath the blankets in Welsh, "I am asleep and don't waken me." But the sleep he summoned was from a fairy tale and meant a deeper sleep, an enchanted sleep. A misted, reveried decline that would outlast time. I felt my mind floating free with my drowsiness but I heard the doctor begin to speak, and there was an edge to his voice that made my ears twitch to listen.

"I do not know how much you know about your father, Sarah. About his past, before coming here from England. It may be that you know very little of him, and it is not for me to tell you of past deeds that would be . . . ," he said, and he paused, carefully selecting his words. "Your father was a soldier and fought long and hard for Cromwell. Many men here fought proudly for Cromwell and his Parliament but it is a pride quietly kept. But before your father fought for Parliament he was a soldier for the Crown and supported the King as did all his kinsmen. Over time he came to believe, as did many great men of that time, that the suffering of the people came mainly from that King. The tyranny of the King's unfair laws of taxation and religious intolerance ..."

I had opened my eyes, and he paused and smiled at the look of childish incomprehension on my face.

He squeezed my hand and said, "You don't know what I'm speaking of, do you?" I shook my head and he continued. "Then I will only say that your father is the bravest of men. He carries on his shoulders the terrible weight of his convictions and his losses. Losses that would have planted a lesser man into the ground. Do you think he would have let a group of deluded girls keep him from doing his duty to his wife?"

I said softly, "I cannot say what he will do. He did not save my mother."

He bowed his head for a moment and said, "It is easier to kill a tyrant with a sword than disassemble whole counties in the grip of superstitious dread. He could not save her, Sarah, without putting you and your brothers at terrible risk."

When I did not answer him he started gathering up his tools and vials into his bag and said as he rose to go, "He will not rest until he can carry you from here to home."

With dismay I remembered the message I was to give Father and I grabbed for the sleeve of his black coat and said, "I have forgotten to give him your message."

He patted my grasping hand and uncurled it from his sleeve, saying, "Then you will tell him when next you see him. It is important for him to know he has our fellowship. Sleep now and I will visit again soon." He parted with Tom, asking him to

watch over me, making certain that I ate my share of the bread
he had left us.

I slept deeply for the remainder of the day, and when I woke
at dusk, I felt a tightening and a rawness like the tickling of a
moth in my throat. I slept again for several hours and woke with
flames in my head and bone-shaking chills. A first dry cough
was quickly followed by a rattling one that came from somewhere deep in my chest. Tom put his hand to my neck and then
quickly pulled it away as though the palm had been scorched.
He beckoned for Goody Faulkner to come closer, but when she
saw I was not well, she pulled back, saying only, "You must keep
her well wrapped. And ask your father to bring soup or soak her
bread for she must not eat anything solid. Keep her head bathed.
There is nothing more that can be done." She pulled her daughters closer to her and three pairs of eyes regarded me with more
fear than sympathy.

FOR THE SECOND time in Salem jail Tom sat sick watch, covering me with his coat through the cold nights, trading his own
bread and meat for any bit of mash or soup or small beer that
could be passed down my burning throat. And within a few
days I entered into that fevered state where awakenings are indistinct and fragmented and dreams are etched clear and bright
upon the memory. It is a realm close to madness where what is
heard and seen during the fever can never be trusted to be sub-
stantial once the sickness has been burned free.

Once, I saw the cell door open wide of its own accord and a
dark man, long of limb and impossibly lean, swung back and

forth on it like a walking stick on a swaying branch. He had sharp-angled features and he placed a finger to his pursed and smiling lips as though we shared a wicked secret. When I looked to Tom to show him the man and looked back again, he had disappeared. The prison door was closed fast and not another person had raised their head to give any sign they had seen the taunting man. I heard the disembodied voice of Father or Dr. Ames calling me and telling me to get up and begin breakfast or to sit up and start the treadle on the spinner. When I answered them, my voice sounded deafening and petulant in my own ears.

At times I felt hands turning me over onto my back, though I struggled to stay buried in the straw, shielding my eyes from the blinding pinpricks of light that were held close to my eyes. Damp cloths were pressed onto my forehead, but I brushed them off as quickly as they were applied, for they felt like the hands of the dead being laid across my skin. I wanted only to sleep and yet in the depths of night when the cold shuddering of my limbs would start and the racking coughs threatened to crack all my ribs, the time between midnight and dawn seemed to last forever.

I could hear the rustling of vermin close by and once I saw two rats regarding me with a keen and somewhat sympathetic intelligence in their red eyes. They sat upright on their haunches and began to speak together, their voices high and wavering like the voices of old women. One said to the other, "It seems that they have hung a dog in Salem a few days past." And the other responded, "Aye, and I hear another is to be hanged in Andover at this very hour." They laughed confidingly together over this as would old friends over a good jest, but when they looked back at me their teeth were pointed sharp and yellow. I heard the sound of a small cat meowing, pitiful and puny, as though from the inside of a drowning sack. The rats shook their heads sorrowfully at me and the biggest one said, "It is very small and not like to live. And there is so much blood . . ." They fell back down into the furtive crouching attitude that all rats have taken since the days of Adam and soon vanished within the dark and crawling rushes on the floor.

Once I woke from a dream and found I was speaking with someone sitting next to me. There was a slight, but not unpleasant, ringing in my ears, and my sight was so clear that it seemed as if black lines had been drawn around every object, putting each thing in sharp contrast to everything else. A tight band was clenched around my chest and the passage for breath had been squeezed into one slender cord. I heard myself say, "But why must I stay?"

I felt some pressure on my fingers and when I turned my head I saw Tom sitting next to me, holding my hand. His face was glistening and wet and when I looked into his eyes, I saw that he had been crying. I tried to comfort him but my tongue felt swollen and lazy, and so I could only lie very still and listen to the low and broken sound of his voice. He said, "Do you remember last June, Sarah, after they had taken Mother and it was just us and Father in the fields?"

I lowered my chin slightly to nod, even though movement seemed beyond my abilities, and he continued, "We were plowing the fields for planting. And something happened. I . . . I looked behind me down the rows that had been furrowed the day before and the day before that and then I looked ahead of me and all I saw were stones and stumps to be taken out. For the rest of my life and for always, there would be a strap round my shoulders and rough earth waiting to be cleared. I couldn't see for the blackness of it. And so I shrugged off the harness and went to my bed.

"Later Father came and sat with me. He didn't say anything at first. He just sat until it came full-on dark. And then he started to talk. He told me I was his namesake because I was most like him. It started me up, Sarah, for I had always thought Richard most alike to Father. He said that some people can live from birth to death and have no more thoughts in their heads about the reasons for living than a beetle. But that we were different, he and I. We needed more than a clod of dirt to make our rising up and lying down worth something.

"I told him I would rather die than wind my days out only plowing and dusting clay off my shoes. Then he said if I were to die, a piece of him would die, too. He said I had to find one thing living that was greater than myself to cleave to, and in that would be my strength for walking upright like a man. A long time ago he was in despair and had sunk so low as to die from it. But he found Mother, and it was her that brought a quickening back to his living. I thought long on what he had said. And d'ye know what I told him, Sarah?"

He squeezed my hand painfully in his and paused, his voice choking into silence. He struggled for several moments to speak again and I waited for him to pour out his grief for Mother. But when he spoke, he said, "I told him it was you. It's you who are my strength. You mustn't die, Sarah, and leave me in this dark place."

A drowsiness had come over me and my eyes started to close. I could hear Tom's voice and I wanted to answer him, to reassure him that I would not leave but I could not find the breath to form the words. It seemed such a simple thing to sink beneath the weight within my chest, and in that moment I thought of Miles Corey beneath his blanket of stones. Breathing a little less and a little less each time until each rib was still and fixed. I pressed Tom's fingers in mine and slept.

I LAY SOMETIMES in flames, the straw glowing and then catching fire. The fire driving legions of rats and armies of lice before it across the floor to disappear like smoke under the door. Other times I lay locked in the cold-cellar, turning to ice, turning to stone, turning to bone and frozen ash. And always were the churning wet sounds of the bellows within my ribs struggling to work against a slow drowning. Once I opened my eyes and saw Margaret sitting next to me, her long black hair loose and wild about her shoulders. I shook my head, squeezing my eyes shut to drive this apparition away, but when I opened my eyes again, she was there. I felt a pressure on my arm and she said, "They have taken my poppet, Sarah. The one you gave me."

Like an ancient crone I croaked out, "They have taken mine as well." I looked for Tom to place me back into the hard world again but I could not see him.

She leaned in closer and whispered, "You mustn't blame

Father. He means well and he loves us all. He is but a little distracted these few days past. But look, see what I have found for you." She reached into her sleeve and pulled out a short length of thread.

"You see, I have a bit of ribbon for you. I have learned how to do it from Father. But once it has appeared, I cannot make it disappear again as Father would do." She placed it gently on my chest. She smiled sweetly, her eyes drifting into the unfocused and slanting gaze of one who would follow the footsteps of fairies off a canted cliff. She lay down beside me, wrapping her arms around my shoulders, and kissed me. Her lips were cold and smooth as riverbed stones but her breath was warm and she sang to me, "We shall always be sisters." I fell back into sleep and dreamt of swimming in a great dark ocean.

THERE WAS NEVER a time that Tom or Margaret would leave my side for very long. I do not know what Aunt made of Margaret's attentions to me, for she never again spoke to me, but she also never called for Margaret to return to the far side of the cell. I gave to Margaret the ancient piece of pottery that I had carried in the bodice of my dress for so many weeks and told her that if I should die, she would have something from me to keep with her always. The hard clay had for so long pressed against my breastbone that its absence felt as though I had given her a part of my rib. She delighted in it, looking at it, turning it over and over in her palm. When I showed her the cross-stitch piece that I had worn close to my heart, she wept and, drying her tears with it, tucked it back into its place.

When I had the strength to ask questions, Tom revealed to me what I had only imagined in my sickness and what had truly taken place. Some of the women in the cell had indeed taken turns caring for me, although most of them had given me up after a few days of raging fever. The only one who continued to watch vigil while Tom and Margaret slept was Lydia Dustin, the old woman with the sharp tongue. Two dogs had been hanged, one in Salem and one in Andover, for being familiars to the Devil. One of the prisoners, a young woman seven months into the family way, gave birth in silent agony to her first child. With a sudden understanding I knew that the meowing of the cat I had heard must have been the cries of the infant. The babe had quickly died and there would be no more for the girl, who all but poured her own life's blood into the straw.

In dismay I reminded Tom of the message I was to give Father from Dr. Ames but had lost again in my ravings. But Tom assured me he had passed it along word for word as it was given to me. When I asked Tom what it meant he said Father had told him that Dr. Ames and his fellows were New Levellers. When Tom asked Father what it meant, he responded only that they were men who believed that all men were to be protected equally under the common law. And that each man was to be free to follow his own conscience in practices of religion. I remembered the Quaker man in Uncle's barn, the man Margaret had called a heretic for believing such, and wondered if Dr. Ames was secretly a Quaker.

My fever rose again even as the cold of autumn dug in, and we all pressed together tighter for warmth. In a few weeks the groundwater would start to freeze and the first snows would drift through the high westward portals, dusting white our hair and lacing and stiffening our thin shawls to parchment. Margaret would lie next to me by the hour, rambling in her speech about the trial or her home in Billerica. At times she defended herself to invisible judges, which left her melancholy and spiritless, as though she had caught my fever and was jaded because of it. But she was always tender to me. Washing my face or urging me to drink broth when it could be had, or using the sordid light to pick from my scalp the lice that tormented me so.

It is often at sunset that the vital protective channels of the body are at their lowest. A fever will rise, a woman with child will ready herself for labor, the spirit will darken with the shadows and weaken. It was at such a time that I felt overcome by my guilt and I poured out my confession to Margaret.

"I have killed my own mother," I cried miserably into my hands. She held my head and rocked me, smoothing my hair back from my face. She smiled and bent to whisper something in my ear.

She said, "Shall I tell you a secret?" I nodded, for I remembered well the secrets we shared together when I lived with her family, and I expected her to tell me something pleasantly distracting.

"Hush, now. Don't cry. I have seen her only yesterday and she is well." She nodded and looked off to a far corner of the cell.

The well of my mouth dried to dust and I whispered, "Who?"

She seemed not to hear me and continued on as she deftly plaited strands of my hair. "If I gather your hair so, it will not pull and we will not have to fever-cut it to the scalp. But you have knots that will never come out. That's the thing about knots. They are easier tied than untied."

I grabbed her hand and asked again, "Margaret, who did you see yesterday?"

"Why, I saw Aunt Martha. She came into the cell while you were sleeping. She was quite sorry you have been ill and will be all the more sad if you do not mend. I asked her to stay but she would not. D'ye know what she told me to tell you?"

I shook my head, my eyes huge and staring, my bowels turning to water. She cocked her head and her gaze became suddenly clear and reflective.

"She said, 'Hold fast the stone . . .' "

I shut my eyes and remembered the touch of my mother's hand as she closed my fingers around the stone I had carried from Preston's farm. How Margaret could have known about it I cannot say. I could have, in the tossing of my fevered brain, spoken of it to her. Or perhaps the thread of knowingness had been passed to her as well and her tangled mind had caught some bit of message from the shaded world like a moth caught in a net. Margaret had resumed plaiting my hair and she sang a little song I had heard Aunt sing as she moved about the hearth. It was one that my own mother had hummed when she was unguarded and thought herself to be alone, and I wept again, not from the press of my guilt but from the easing of it. And from that moment on I began to get better.

ON A DAY close to the end of September, the door was opened by the sheriff and a tall, stately man in a flowing cape and large-brimmed hat walked into the cells and stood looking over us. He entered with a prim disdain, bringing the edge of his cloak up to cover his mouth and nose from the stench. He resisted the movement of his legs backwards and planted his feet as though enduring gale winds. The play of emotions upon his face, though, was remarkable and would stay with me through all my life. It was as though he held up to us the mirrored image of our slide from decent modesty, grace, and dignity to the degeneracy of fear and self-recrimination and sickness. His features, which were large, quivered and melted like wax held too close to the heat. His eyes, at first narrowed in righteous condemnation to view so many accused witches, widened and brimmed over with tears, which he dashed away as though they scalded his skin. His lips, pressed tightly together, a cage against speaking idly of profane things, opened to a sharp intake of breath. He put his fist up and covered the quivering mouth that muttered over and over again "My God, my God, my God . . ." There were no entreaties or pleas of mercy from the women. There were no moans of distress or even tears. They sat or lay mute, letting their bodies be the book of revelation.

Increase Mather, famed clergyman, friend to the King and the Governor alike, would work from that moment to cast doubt upon the accusers, and though he would never find fault outright with the judges or his son, Cotton Mather, this doubt would be a mighty blow to the Court of Oyer and Terminer. He would return again to the prison on October 19th to take statements from women who said they had been pressed into giving false witness against themselves, but I would not be in Salem to see him.

On Saturday, the first day of October, Dr. Ames came into our cell and told us that our bail had been collected and that within a very short time many of the youngest prisoners would be released. Coins had been raised from the towns of Andover and Boston and even faraway Gloucester. It gave proof, he said, that people's minds were changing in their belief in the Salem Court. Early on the morning of the 6th of October, the sheriff opened the door to let in the blacksmith. He stood in the corridor while our chains were removed to give us time to say our farewells and to walk from our cell as best we could. I was released with my three brothers, along with fourteen other children. Abigail Dane Faulkner's two daughters were freed, along with Moses Tyler's nieces. Mary Lacey, Mercy Williams' friend, who had been one of the first to cry out against my mother, was so weak from her confinement that she had to be carried from her place in the straw. Mercy Wardwell, whose father, Samuel, had been hanged on September 22nd, had turned nineteen just three days before and so was no longer a child. She hid her face in her hands and would not say good-bye to us as we left her under the cold autumn drafts from the high western wall. Behind us we left sisters and mothers and grandmothers who had no promise or even hope of release.

Lydia Dustin pressed my face in her hands and blessed me, saying, "This be but a dark dream. Now you can waken and stay with the living." Both she and her granddaughter would spend the whole of the winter in chains. The court would find them not guilty on the 1st day of February, but because they could not pay the prison fees, they would be returned to prison. On March 2nd Elizabeth Colson would be released and returned to Reading. On March 10th, 1693, Lydia Dustin would die, one of the few remaining women left in the "good" cell of Salem prison.

I rejoiced at our freedom until it was made known to me that only the children of Andover were to be released. The children of Salem and Beverly and Billerica were to remain. Margaret was returned to her mother's side, and as Richard carried me from the cell, she stretched her arm out to me, her fingers grasping the little piece of pottery I had given her. She held it out to me like a talisman against loss or as a promise that there would always be a connection between us that would hold tight beyond the crossing of dark and dangerous days. And as I was carried up the stairs I heard her voice calling to me, distant and metaled, as though calling from the bottom of a covered well, "Sarah, Sarah, Sarah..." I could hear her calling to me even after the door to the stairwell had been bolted fast again.

THE LEAVES OF autumn that October of 1692 were gold and red like the blood of martyrs and so suffused with color that it assaulted our prison-blind eyes like a fiery rod. We stood blinking and cringing at the outer door, not knowing whether to go forward or turn back, too weak at first to descend the few steps into the prison yard on our own. My brothers and I were the last to stand at the door and slowly, slowly, we could see, appearing through the sharp light, figures standing motionless in the prison yard.

A silent crowd had gathered around the steps, silent save for the few desperate greetings from families calling out to their children standing in front of us. One by one the children were reclaimed and dragged or carried away until we were the last four to stand wavering in the lifting wind. I was held upright between Richard and Tom and it was Andrew who walked first down the steps, still holding his injured arm close to his chest. The crowd had pressed in closer around us and I could see more clearly now what was in their faces. Pity and perhaps some portion of compassion, but withal, under every play of emotion was fear. Fear that perhaps the children of a woman hanged for a witch might yet still carry the seeds of devilry within them. It was Andrew, simple, tortured Andrew, who with the back of his knuckled fist gently pushed back the crowds, saying, "Go to home, then. Go to home."

When he had pushed them back far enough, we saw Father moving his way to us, his head rising above the tallest of them, his face shadowed from the brim of his hat. He placed himself in front of the townspeople and waited for us to come down the steps. He did not come to our aid or rise to greet us but waited for us to make our way down by ourselves. And when we at last descended the final step, he turned, and the rustling crowd parted raggedly, like crested waves before the prow of a ship, making a space for us to walk. I understood at that moment fully and suddenly why he would not carry me, and why he had not come to my defense in times past when I was battling for my place in the world. It was not because he failed to love me, but because he loved me so well. He had brought us food and clothing and kind words when we were imprisoned; he did not abandon us. But he would never seek to weaken me so that I could not withstand the burdens and cruelties or harsh judgments of the world. An infant must learn to walk only by cutting his lip on the harsh ground. Only by tasting blood is the toddler discouraged from falling.

I took a step. And then another. And so it went as we followed Father, who had come to take us forever away from Salem. And with every step I thought of my mother's courage as she faced her judges. With every step I thought of her cleaving to the truth even as she fell the short distance of the rope. With every step I thought of her pride, her strength, her love.

And with every step I thought, I am my mother's daughter, I am my mother's daughter . . .

SOON AFTER FATHER had brought us home, he took us to the place where he had buried Mother. It was south of Ladle Meadow on Gibbet Plain, where she used to go as a girl with her sister. The meadow she had taken me to last spring, close to the lone elm, where the red book was buried. He could not have known about the book. It was the only place where she felt alone from her cares. We set late sprigs of rosemary around the cairn of rocks he had used to mark her grave. The morning was quiet with little wind, the leaves gently falling, their use spent except to blanket the ground for the coming cold. There were no birds calling, no streamers of pigeons or wild geese overhead, for they had already flown away south. I knelt down and placed my ear over the cairn, listening to the settling of the stones.

I remembered wondering long ago what song my mother's bones would make. I had once imagined their singing would be as the crashing of waves, for I knew that even the fragile ocean shell carries within it the sound of hounding surf. But what I heard was a gentle rustling, an odd whistling. The sound the birdfoot violet makes as it grows through the early frosts of winter.

CHAPTER TEN

October 1692–May 1735

WE STAYED IN Andover for some time. We worked the farm, and always Father was there. His reserve never softened and yet he was gentle with us, attending every wound, every searing distemper, every horrific dream, until we were part whole again. We were left unmolested by our neighbors, and indeed the suspicion and fear people still held for us worked to our advantage. We were always given the best at barter, and in the early days of our release, there were even gifts of food or odd bits of clothing left at our doorstep. We would never know for certain who it was that brought us these gifts, as they were left in the dead of night and, as the lurcher had died, we had no warning of these visitations.

Dr. Ames traveled from Haverhill once to call on us, and

though Father thanked him warmly, I believe the good doctor was disappointed in the brief discourse. There were no illuminating ideas exchanged between them, no passionate debate of the righting of wrongs, only simple expressions offered on the unsteady courses of seasons and the increase or diminishment of our livestock. And after a long pause, Father saluted his visitor and left the doctor with us in the yard to attend to his fields. After the death of his father, Dr. Nathaniel Ames moved with his wife and children to his family home in Boston and spent the rest of his life petitioning the Crown and the courts of Massachusetts for the reform of the royal prisons in the colonies.

My aunt and cousin were not set free from prison until February of 1693. A trial by jury had found them not guilty in January, but Allen could pay their prison release only by first selling his father's horse, Bucephalus. Margaret and Aunt were carried home to Billerica in a cart but, as they took the more northerly Ipswich Road, did not pass by our door. Allen would inherit his father's farm and would by all accounts manage his family's homestead with a tight fist and a shrewd eye. And although Father petitioned him to allow me to be reunited with Margaret, he was unrelenting in his stony and embittered refusals.

By May all of the fifty-six remaining prisoners of the witch trials were found not guilty and freed. After months and years had passed, the wounds of our captivity were to be scabbed over by the weak-headed nods of civility from the townspeople. But these wounds were too wide and too deep to heal without a thorough scouring. Within five years of the witch trials, one Salem judge and twelve jurors made formal apologies for their part in the killing of innocents. In 1706, Ann Putnam Jr., the only one of the Salem accusers to do so, stood in front of the village meetinghouse and made a full and public renouncement of what she had done. She said, however, that her actions were not of her own doing, but rather from delusions brought on by the Devil himself. She would die at five-and-thirty years, unmarried and alone, haunted by dreams of the Salem dead.

In the same year as Ann Putnam's confession, Mercy Williams, the girl who had been indentured to us and who had given false testimony against me, died. On a cold December day, she had fallen or, some whispered, been pushed from the Haverhill ferry as it crossed the Merrimack River. She was found at dusk, floating among the clots of ice, her red underskirt ballooning up from the gray water acting as a beacon to the searchers on the riverbank. The news brought no satisfaction, only a bitter, lingering sadness over such a wasted and tawdry life.

Visitors to our farm were few, and even the Dane family, who kept Hannah as their own, paid us very little mind. Hannah remained a fearful and timid soul even to her womanhood, and though she would marry and have her own children, her eyes would forever hold the look of the lost. She had strange fits of melancholy and was plagued her whole life with night terrors. The Danes thought it best we not upset her with visits, and so she had turned nearly twelve before I saw her again. When I was finally admitted to the Dane house, I was taken to the common room, where my sister sat, head bowed, at her spinning. Gone were the soft and dimpled curves of infancy and in their place sat the angled and rigid form of austerity. She shook my hand wanly and raised her eyes for a moment, but I knew she had mostly forgotten me. We spoke of village things and hearth things, but she never asked after Father or our brothers and I left the past alone. When I said good-bye, she nodded once and began again to work the treadle of the spinner. I cried for her on the long walk home, hiding my tears from Father, telling him she sent home with me her fidelity and her love.

As we did not return to the meetinghouse, we did not witness the resurrection of Reverend Dane back to his place at the pulpit. It seems his adversary, the Reverend Barnard, had kenned the changing and lofty tides of opinion from stern judgment and harsh consignment to solemn and doubtful consideration of spectral evidence. He had jumped with Reverend Dane into the petitions for the prisoners' acquittal like a man caught fire.

Robert Russell stayed our friend and, with his wife, often came at times of harvest or sowing or sickness. Robert was to have his wish for sons and had five of them in startling succession with the former Widow Frye. Not two years after our release from prison, Richard married Robert's pale, shy niece, Elizabeth Sessions.

At the end of that year, smallpox danced its way from old England to the new, claiming many for its own. We were spared, but in December, Queen Mary, sovereign of England and all her colonies, died of it.

In 1695, in the early part of August, Margaret was taken away by the Indians. A small party of Wabanaki on horseback had approached the settlement in long coats and hats and so were mistaken for neighboring townspeople. Aunt was hacked down and killed, as were ten or twelve others living in that part of Billerica. They laid a headstone for my cousin next to her mother's because it was believed that even though her body was not found, her soul must have taken flight at the moment of capture. I was told it was a pleasant place where the headstones were set, although I would never travel there to see it. For many years after, I had dreams of Margaret, and in every one of them she was alive.

By 1701, Father, at the age of seventy-five, began to travel for great stretches of time to Colchester in Connecticut. Sometimes leaving with Richard, and sometimes with Tom, he carved out a great homestead for his children and grandchildren. In time following, Tom and even Andrew would marry, and altogether my three brothers would have twenty-nine children. Tom had five girls before his first son was born and he named one of his daughters after me. His fourth daughter he named Martha. He was the only one of us to name a child so. I think none of us could bear the thought of losing her again if the child did not survive.

When I was twenty-three, I went with Father and my brothers and their wives to Connecticut, carrying with me Mother's red book. I had dug it up from the ground early one evening a few years before, unwrapping the soiled layers of oilskin to find the book, for the most, dry and whole. I quickly opened its pages and saw my mother's writing, slender-veined and feathered, but shut it fast again, unable and unwilling yet to read the words inside.

We built two houses in Colchester, and soon after, I met and married my husband. I was made Sarah Carrier Chapman in September of 1707 and within a few months I made ready to read the book. I believed that I had come to the place of womanhood that could bear the weight of her words. But as I held it in my lap, I felt a cautioning dread building inside of me and I sat with it closed in my hands for hours. I feared some passage within would change the felicity that I had knit together with my father or somehow change the memory I held of my mother. And as I was with child, I harkened to the midwife's warning that too much fearful discovery would mar the unborn. I hid it in Father's old oaken chest in the cellar, and though it was never far from my thoughts, there was always another birth or death or laying-out that kept the book hidden.

In 1711 the General Court of the Massachusetts Bay Colony passed an act to reverse the attainders of the wrongly accused. In recompense for Mother's death, Father would receive from the court a little over seven pounds English money, the amount for her food and shackles. He was only ever granted what he had spent in her care. The reverse of attainder meant that Mother's sentence of guilt had been made null and void. Nine of the condemned women were not recompensed by the Crown. The best of their valuable houses and land had been seized, never to be returned. In the spring of 1712 we returned to collect our recompense and to carry back with us in two wagons what was left in the Andover house and barn. For the last time we visited Mother's grave on the great meadow, the stones over-grown to a grassy point, and planted rosemary for the fragrance it would bring in the summer and the remembrance it would bring in the winter.

Father died at age one hundred and nine in the tender middle part of May 1735. Still living at his passing were five children, thirty-nine grandchildren, and thirty-eight great-grandchildren.

He had taken to lapsing more and more into the Welsh tongue, as older men of his time and place of birth were wont to do. His hair had not much grayed and he stood always straight and sure-footed. He often walked the six miles to our nearest neighbor, an ailing widower, with a bag of grain on his back. The day of his death found him restless and searching and he rubbed at the joints in his hands as though they pained him. He did not complain or make petulant faces but said to me softly in Welsh, *"Henaint ni thow ay heenan."* Old age comes not on its own.

No, I thought, death follows age like the eager bridegroom the bride. I held his huge knotted hand in both of my own and reflected that my father had done more in the last quarter of his life than many men had done in the first. He closed his eyes and slipped without struggle into his lasting sleep. Two pine coffins had to be opened and refitted to receive his body but his shoulders were so broad that he was laid slanted sideways and he looked, before the coffin was closed over, as though he would rest forever with one ear pressed to the earth.

Soon after, I walked some distance through our wakening fields and sat on the ragged stone fence that marked its far edges. I opened the red book and read my mother's words and the words my father had given her, and all of my questioning and wondering and the gossiping of others were resolved into time and place and purpose. I laid the book aside, for suddenly the weight of it could not be supported by my hands, and I looked around me, amazed that the world had not changed beneath my feet. The sun had shifted across the sky as I read, turning morning to afternoon, but the trees were still in the trembling green of spring, the air was misted and freshening, the shoots of wheat still up-lifting through the fields. How could it be that all around me had remained the same when behind my eyes I still carried the images of the life of the two I had called Mother and Father? I understood then why my mother had demanded of me to wait before opening the book, to wait until I had been tested and hardened by the passing of ages.

I had in my fifty-odd years experienced cruelty and death, losses of the heart, despair, and redemption from that despair. But these things had little prepared me for the thundering shift of ideas, inscribed with ink faded to the rusted color of blood, which said that a land and its people could be governed without the smothering, grasping hand of a monarch. But that men being what they are will supplant that monarch with another so-called protector of the people, who will suppress and fight and betray his way back into tyranny. I looked through the branches of trees and saw great armies advancing upon each other, son against father, brother against his like, and heard through the cawing of crows the crying of children and women and old men as they were cut down and trammeled underfoot. I saw through the swaying of diaphanous shadows agents of the church plotting savagely against their fellow men at altar, and laymen and women preaching in fiery tongues to growing multitudes in the running, ruinous streets of London. Words like "treason" and "trickery" forced their way in whispered explosions from my mouth like metal bores being fired from a flintlock.

And finally, with the shifting light fingering its way up the garden stones, I witnessed the progression of a king from prison to scaffold to beheading. And beside this king stood a man, masked and hooded, who first with a kind hand gently pulled aside the straying locks of hair at the bent and ready neck that would mar the true progress of the blade, and then with a steady, practiced grip, arc the long shaft of the axe up and back and finally down, bringing the sharp, reflecting mirror of history through the air, cleaving at once and forever, past from future, darkness from illumination, servitude from liberty.

Long into dark I sat on the wall, Mother and Father alive to me then, and felt the blood of them both thrumming through my veins. In full darkness I returned the diary to Father's great chest and, in the years to follow, layered it over with the stuff of the living. Quilts packed away in summer's heat, linen outgrown by children, coarse cloth used for sacking and for shrouds. And always it was there, like a step-stone in a swift-moving river.

ACKNOWLEDGMENTS

First and foremost, I want to thank my wonderful agent, Julie Barer, who took an unknown writer out of the slush pile and, with her own special magic, helped turn her into a published author. Next, I'd like to thank my editor, Reagan Arthur, who, with patience and gentle direction, worked with me to shape a rough manuscript into a finished novel. My heartfelt thanks also go to the following people at Little, Brown and Company: Michael Pietsch, Sophie Cotrell, Sabrina Ravipinto, Heather Fain, Heather Rizzo, Mario Pulice, and Oliver Haslegrave, for their energy, enthusiasm, and commitment; and to Pamela Marshall, who worked so hard to give the manuscript its final polish.

Where would I be without the encouragement of my beloved family, who were also my first readers: Audrey, John, and Kevin Hickman; Kim, Katie, and Kelly Morrison; Rhoda, Seymour, and Janice Orlowsky; and Ilene, Kevin, and Alyssa Muething. Love to my girls, Patty, Bette, Elaine, and Rose; and, of course, to my "first" first reader, Mitchell. My love and gratitude to all of the "Friends of the Book," too numerous to list on this little page (but you know who you are). A big thank-you to Juliet Mofford, of the Andover Historical Society, for pointing me to the historical Carrier sites in Andover, Massachusetts, and to Violet Schwarzmann, for personally taking me to the Carrier family homestead in Marlborough, Connecticut. I'd also like to thank my mentor, Abigail Brenner, for her generosity and sage advice. And finally, thank you, Cary, for always listening.

To the descendants of Thomas and Martha Carrier, may you live long and prosper.

KATHLEEN KENT lives in Dallas
with her husband and son. *The Heretic's
Daughter* is her first novel.

corruption

Congress and, **2006:**4–6, 13–15,
188–89, 204–6, 226–28,
458–60, 478, **2007:**3, 16–17,
60–61, 305

election of 2006 and, **2006:**5–6,
22, 25–26, 28, 227, 266–68,
322, 426–28, 450–51, 478

as most important issue,
2001:121, **2002:**233, 360,
2003:25, 62, 86, 122, 155, 203,
284, 401, 442–43,
2006:138–39, 237, 288, 338,
384–86, 435, 479

political affiliation and, **2006:**4–6,
13–15, 139, 188–89, 193–94,
205–6, 227–28, 267–68, 412,
426–27, 435, 478

president and, **2007:**3, 16–17,
60–61, 305

as priority, **2007:**3, 16–17, 60–61,
148–49, 305

See also corporations, corruption in

"The Cosby Show," 1998:61–62

Costner, Kevin, 2000:99, **2001:**76

cost of living, 2004:37–38, 156,
174–77, 207

as biggest challenge you face
today, **2000:**192

Bush, George W., and, **2005:**155

Congress and, **2007:**3

families and, **2007:**266, 349

income and, **2006:**483

as most important issue, **1998:**60,
1999:194–95, **2001:**58, 121,
255, **2002:**9, 70, 116, 233, 359,
2003:25, 86, 122, 155, 203,
284, 401, 442, **2005:**45, 93–95,
99, 113, 153, 174, 213, 304,
347, 366, 409, **2007:**54, 349,
410–12, 442–43, 532

as most important issue facing
nation 25 years from now,
2002:117

president and, **2007:**3

race and, **2006:**459–60, 484

as worst problem facing your
community, **2000:**190

See also inflation; standard of
living

Coulter, Ann, 2003:405

**Council of Economic Advisors,
2004:**79

courts

as most important issue, **2002:**10,
71, 116, 233, 360, **2003:**25, 62,
86, 155, 203, 285, 443

as most important issue facing
nation 25 years from now,
2002:117

See also judicial system

CoverTheInsured.org, 2004:481

cover-ups, 2004:135, 146

Craig, Larry, 2005:420

Cranston, Alan, 2004:42

creationism, 2000:245, **2001:**52–53,
2004:462–64

and evolution, in public schools,
1999:207, **2000:**200, 245

credit cards, 2004:157–58, 174–76,
203–4, 207, **2006:**167, 207, 216,
222, 407–8

amount you pay on, **2001:**114,
2002:151

as most important issue, **2005:**45,
113, 152, 198, 366, 421

number of, **2002:**151

worry about, **2001:**113, **2005:**
159

See also debt

**Creedence Clearwater Revival,
2000:**265

crime, 2003:385–86

age and, **2004:**478–79,
2005:413–14, 438, **2006:**490,
2007:47

area near your home where you
would be afraid to walk alone

at night, **2000:**296, **2001:**234,
2002:325–26, **2003:**378
blacks and, **2007:**304, 316
Bush, George W., and, **1999:**67,
81, **2000:**24, 86, 143, **2001:**22
in Canada, **2004:**80–81
car owned by you stolen,
2000:329, **2002:**361
Catholicism and, **2007:**217
church attendance and, **2007:**217
cities you consider safe to live in
or visit [list], **2001:**235
Clinton, Bill, and, **1999:**44,
2000:262, **2005:**73, **2007:**38
community and, **2004:**478–79
concern for, **2004:**120, 126–27,
139, 159, 445–47, **2005:**136,
162–64, 170–72, 391, **2007:**126
confidence in police and,
1998:146, **1999:**163–64,
2001:234, **2002:**326
Conservative Party and, **2004:**81
conservatives and, **2007:**217
Democratic Party and, **1998:**224,
2004:38, 127, 156,
2007:16–17, 217
deterring, **2004:**50–51
economy and, **2004:**50, 80
education and, **2004:**201, 377
gender and, **2004:**478,
2005:170–72, 437
Gore and, **1999:**80, **2000:**23, 86,
143, 262
in Great Britain, **2004:**80–81
handled by Bush, **2000:**24, 86,
143
Hispanics and, **2007:**304, 316
home, car, or property owned by
you vandalized, **2000:**330,
2002:361
immigrants and, **2001:**171,
2002:227, **2004:**296
income and, **2004:**478–79,
2005:171–72, 413–14, 438

independents and, **2004:**38, 156,
2007:16–17, 217
Internet and, **2004:**477–78
Labour Party and, **2004:**81
law enforcement and, **2004:**50,
80
liberals and, **2007:**217
marijuana as, **2004:**55
McCain, John, and, **2007:**50
media and, **1998:**229
moderates and, **2007:**217
money or property stolen from
you, **2000:**329, **2002:**361
money or property taken from you
by force, **2000:**330, **2002:**361
as most important issue, **1998:**60,
1999:194–95, **2000:**191,
2001:58, 121, 255, **2002:**10,
71, 116, 233, 323, 360,
2003:25, 62, 86, 122, 155, 203,
284, 401, 443, **2004:**37–38,
156, 414, **2005:**99, 174, 213,
2006:138–39, 237, 279, 288,
338, 479, **2007:**37–38, 54,
123–24, 315–16, 410–12,
442–43, 501
as most important issue facing
nation 25 years from now,
2002:117
mugged or assaulted, **2000:**330,
2002:361
own gun for protection against,
2000:328
percentage of all crime not
reported to police, **2001:**245,
2002:361
percentage of households experi-
encing any crime, **2001:**245,
2002:361
percentage of households experi-
encing violent crime,
2001:245, **2002:**361
policies concerning, **2004:**80–81,
130

crime *(continued)*
political affiliation and,
2006:125–26, 139,
2007:16–17, 217
political ideology and, 2007:217
in predictions for 2007, 2007:1–2
against pregnant women, 2001:108
as priority, 1998:159, 225, 235,
2000:428, 2002:130
property, 2004:446, 478
Protestantism and, 2007:217
race and, 2004:478–79, 2007:217,
304, 316
rates of, 1998:228–29,
2000:296–97, 2001:234,
2002:325, 2003:377–78,
2004:50–51, 80–81, 445–46,
477–79, 2005:412–14, 437
1999 as year of rising rates,
1998:252
better in year 2025 than today,
1998:219
religion and, 2007:217
reporting of, 2006:491
Republican Party and, 1998:224,
2004:38, 127, 156,
2007:16–17, 217
by residence, place of, 2006:490
satisfaction with, 2001:29
as serious problem, 2000:296, 316
sexual assault, 2000:330,
2002:361
social problems and, 2004:50–51,
80
State of the Union address and,
2005:73, 2007:38
teenagers and, 2004:414
violent, 2004:50, 445–46, 478
as voting issue, 1999:68, 2000:19,
72, 192
which, if any, of these incidents
have happened to you or your
household in past twelve
months [list], 2001:245
which of these things you do
because of concern over crime
[list], 2001:235
which of these things you do to
prevent crime [list], 2002:326
whites and, 2007:304
worry about, 1998:145–46, 2001:
59, 66, 234–35, 2002:118,
2003:127–28, 378, 380
as worst problem facing your
community, 2000:190, 192
your house or apartment broken
into, 2000:329, 2002:361
criminal justice system,
2004:50–51, 80–81, 225, 306
confidence in, 1998:182,
2002:185, 2003:205–6
crocheting
as favorite way of spending
evening, 1998:237
Crocker, Ryan, 2007:406
Crosby, Bing, 2001:77
crossword puzzles
hobby you are particularly interested in, 2002:7
Crouching Tiger, Hidden Dragon,
2001:73
Crow, Mariesa, 2004:122
crowds
fear of, 1998:238, 2001:70
Crowe, Russell, 2001:77, 2002:79
Cruise, Tom, 2000:99, 2001:76
Crystal, Billy, 2000:98
C-Span
how often do you get your news
from, 1998:192
trust accuracy of news from,
1998:97
Cuba, 2004:73, 2005:71, 78–79, 128
and assassination of President
Kennedy, 2003:413
Baltimore Orioles and, 1999:254
diplomatic relations with,
2000:132, 147, 2002:317

know name (Castro) of leader of, **2000:**176
opinion of, **1999:**193, **2000:**174, **2001:**44, 84, **2002:**45, 52, **2003:**56
trade relations with, **1999:**194, **2000:**147, **2002:**317
See also González, Elían
Cunningham, Randy "Duke," **2006:**4, 226
Cuomo, Mario, 2007:101, 269
curricula, 2004:242, 376–77, 512–13
cycling, 2004:367
Czech Republic, 1998:171

D

Dalai Lama, 2002:400, **2003:**454, **2005:**482, **2006:**536
Dallas, 2000:298–99, **2001:**235, **2004:**448
Dalleck, Robert, 2004:403
Damon, Matt, 2006:507
dancing
favorite way of spending an evening, **2002:**6
as favorite way of spending evening, **1998:**237
dark
fear of, **1998:**238, **2001:**70
Darwin, Charles, 2004:462–64
Daschle, Tom, 2001:192, **2006:**235–36, 477, 531, **2007:**21, 67, 75
likely to support, **2002:**90, 355, 395
opinion of, **2002:**295
"Dateline NBC"
how often do you get your news from, **1998:**193
trust accuracy of news from, **1998:**98

dating
all right for girl to telephone boy for date, **2000:**5
Davis, Bette, 2001:77
Davis, Gray, 2003:278, 343, **2004:**164
Davis, Jamie, 2004:386
day care providers, 2004:483–84
honesty and ethical standards of, **1999:**148
D-Day, 2004:227–28
Dean, Dizzy, 2001:83
Dean, Howard, 2005:67, 206, **2006:**236, **2007:**354
admiration of, **2003:**454
age and, **2004:**30
Democratic Party and, **2004:**34
economy and, **2004:**31, 33
election of 2004 and, **2004:**5–8, 11–12, 27–28, 30–34, 40–41, 48–49, 60–61, 76
familiarity with, **2004:**48–49
gender and, **2004:**5–6
healthcare and, **2004:**31, 33
image of, **2004:**6, 43, 48–49
independents and, **2004:**34
Internet and, **2004:**21–22
Iraq war and, **2004:**20, 31–33, 115, 117
likely to support, **2002:**90, 355, 395, **2003:**16, 135, 190, 215–16, 277, 323, 335–36, 364, 374–75, 382, 390, 417, 432–33, 446–47
opinion of, **2003:**306
personal qualities of, **2004:**32–34, 41
as second choice for nomination, **2003:**335
Dean, John, 2005:392
death, 2005:117, 136
death penalty
accuracy of, **2005:**186
age and, **2004:**454, 495, **2005:**186

death penalty *(continued)*
applied fairly, **2000:**202,
2002:147, **2003:**166
Bush, George W., and, **2000:**202
church and, **2004:**454–55, 495,
2005:186
education and, **2005:**186
gender and, **2004:**453–54,
495–96, **2005:**185–86
God and, **2004:**496–97
Gore and, **2000:**202–3
for Hussein, Saddam, **2004:**209–10
ideology and, **2004:**250, 453, 495,
2005:186
imposed too often, **1999:**155,
2000:66, **2002:**147, **2003:**166
versus imprisonment, **1998:**158,
1999:155, **2000:**66, **2001:**51,
2002:147, **2003:**166,
2004:495–96
income and, **2005:**186
and innocent person, **2000:**66,
202, **2003:**166
for juveniles, **2002:**147, **2004:**496
for mentally ill, **2002:**147,
2004:496
for mentally retarded, **2002:**147
morality of, **2002:**149, **2003:**159,
178, 218, **2004:**226, 249–50
moratorium on, **2001:**94
for murder, **1999:**155,
2000:65–66, 201, **2001:**51,
2002:147, **2003:**165–66
political affiliation and, **2004:**453,
495
Protestantism and, **2005:**151
race and, **2004:**453–54, 495,
2005:186
religion and, **2004:**454–55,
495–97, **2005:**131–32, 150
September 11, 2001, terrorist
attacks and, **2004:**227
support for, **2004:**226–27,
453–55, 495–97

with reservations, **2000:**201
for women, **2002:**147
Death Penalty Information Center,
2004:495
debt, 2004:157–58, 174–76, 185–87,
203–4, 207
age and, **2005:**209
income and, **2006:**483
as most important issue, **2005:**40,
45, 93–95, 113, 153, 223, 366
race and, **2006:**484
taxes and, **2005:**138–39
See also national debt
Declaration of Independence
if signers were alive, would they
agree with way Constitution is
followed today, **1999:**206
think signers of would be pleased
by way U.S. has turned out,
2001:155
would signers be pleased by way
U.S. has turned out, **1999:**206
defense, 2007:87
age and, **2007:**391
approval ratings, **2002:**91
branches of, **1999:**153,
2004:220–21
Bush, George W., and, **2000:**242,
248, 258, 275, 293, **2002:**27,
91, **2004:**269–70, 352, 355,
358, 383–84, 395, **2007:**96
confidence in, **2002:**27,
2004:167–68, 224–25, 251,
306, **2007:**269–71, 393
Democratic Party and, **2001:**210,
2007:96–97, 256
Democrats in Congress and,
2002:27, 171
election of 2004 and, **2004:**352,
358, 383–84, 395
gender and, **2007:**391
Gore and, **2000:**242, 248, 258,
275, 293
homosexuality and, **2004:**505

Democratic Party *(continued)*
374–75, 421, 515–16, 527–28,
530, **2007:**14, 39, 53, 66–67,
100, 118–19, 152–53,
200–202, 210–12, 224–25,
249, 267, 297–99, 322–23,
364–67, 380, 400, 408, 417,
440–42, 484–85, 502
Ashcroft, John, and, **2004:**481
atheism and, **2004:**511
attentiveness of, **2004:**143, 313
Benedict XVI and, **2005:**483
Bible and, **2006:**210
Biden, Joe, and, **2006:**502
bin Laden, Osama, and, **2004:**363
blacks and, **2000:**280, 282, **2004:**
318, 368, **2007:**277–78, 281
bridges and, **2007:**340
Brownback, Sam, and, **2006:**532
Bush, George H. W., and,
2004:211–12, 229–30, 238,
2005:52, **2006:**190, 246
Bush, George W., and, **2004:**68,
77, 84, 92, 104, 112, 134–35,
145–46, 184–85, 211–12,
229–30, 238, 282, 319–20, 324,
337–38, 360, 375, 395, 401–2,
409, 422, 442, 450, 479, 504,
514, **2006:**41–42, 45–47, 54,
96, 105, 121, 155–56, 183,
189–90, 197, 214–15, 241, 244,
262–63, 303, 316, 318, 330,
348, 374–75, 390–91, 401–2,
421, 448–50, 515–16, 530
Bush, Laura, and, **2006:**53
business and, **2006:**139, **2007:**8
Cabinet and, **2004:**479
Canada and, **2005:**128, **2006:**130
Carter, Jimmy, and, **2004:**211–12,
229, 238, 514, **2005:**483,
2006:190, 246, 537
Catholicism and, **2005:**133
Cheney, Dick, and, **2004:**287–88,
353–54, **2005:**433, **2006:**95

children and, **2004:**38
China and, **2005:**128, **2006:**130
Christmas and, **2005:**478
church and, **2004:**93, 391–92,
512, **2005:**182–84, 268,
2006:109–10, 124, 231–32,
253, 355–56, 368, 378,
424–26, 472
citizenship and, **2006:**145
civil liberties and, **2006:**16
Clark, Wesley, and, **2004:**34
Clarke, Richard, and, **2004:**145
Clinton, Bill, and, **2004:**104,
211–12, 229–30, 237–38, 319,
514, **2005:**51–52, 398, 483,
2006:41–42, 172, 190, 246,
305, 401–2, 537, **2007:**71–72,
88–89, 135
Clinton, Hillary, and, **2004:**514,
2005:80–82, 206, 289–90,
300–301, 309, 483, **2006:**5,
34–35, 274–75, 300–301, 305,
330, 332, 456, 474, 532, 537
confidence in, **2004:**386–87,
2006:39, **2007:**204–5, 393
Congress and, **2004:**68–69, 205,
435–36, 451, **2005:**98, 144,
169–70, 172–73, 202, 214,
330, 360, 396–98, 411–12,
429–31, 453, **2007:**16–17,
39, 53–55, 66–67, 118–19,
153, 210–11, 267, 322–23,
364–65, 408, 441–42, 494–95,
502
conventions of, **2000:**224–25,
269–70, 273, **2004:**278–80,
297, 301, 311–14, 320–24,
326–28, 351, 357, 366,
371–73, 498–99
corruption and, **2006:**4–6, 13–15,
139, 188–89, 193–94, 205–6,
227–28, 267–68, 412, 426–27,
435
cost of living and, **2004:**38, 156

crime and, **2004:**38, 127, 156,
    2006:125–26, 139,
    2007:16–17, 217
Cuba and, **2005:**128, **2006:**130, 524
Dean, Howard, and, **2004:**34
death penalty and, **2004:**453, 495,
    2005:186, 192–93, 457,
    2006:212–13, 225, **2007:**449
defense and, **2004:**167–68, 269
DeLay, Tom, and, **2005:**453
Dole, Bob, and, **2004:**319
drugs and, **2004:**38, 127, 156,
    2005:408, **2006:**125–26, 139
Dubai ports sale and, **2006:**91
economy and, **2004:**15–16,
    23–25, 37–38, 70, 103, 107,
    113, 124, 127, 156, 269,
    301–2, 375, 387, 431–32,
    2006:54, 107, 125–26, 139,
    155–56, 159–60, 239–40,
    267–68, 293, 303, 318, 371,
    379–80, 383–86, 389–91, 418,
    426–27, 435, 455, 457–61,
    485, 500–501, 528
education and, **2004:**15, 38, 156,
    318, 347–48, 431–32, **2007:**61,
    123, 192, 256, 348, 367, 411
Edwards, John, and, **2004:**34,
    273, 354, **2006:**332, 502, 532
Egypt and, **2005:**128, **2006:**130
Eisenhower, Dwight D., and,
    2004:229
election of 2000 and, **1998:**65–66,
    227–28
election of 2004 and, **2001:**192,
    2002:396, **2004:**5–8, 11–12,
    15–16, 25, 27–28, 30–34, 38,
    40–43, 48–50, 59–60, 75–77,
    116–17, 124, 143, 278–80,
    287–88, 299, 301–2, 311–14,
    327–28, 337–38, 360, 372,
    375, 383–84, 394, 423–24,
    431–34, 442, 494–95, 498–99,
    2005:43, 68

election of 2008 and,
    2004:456–57, **2006:**34–35,
    66–67, 234–36, 300–301, 321,
    331–33, 456, 474, 477–78,
    502, 532, **2007:**84–86, 102–3,
    107–9, 127, 141–43, 222–23,
    253–54, 257–58, 346, 348,
    401–2, 423–24, 464, 476–79,
    546
employment and, **2004:**37–38,
    113, 127, 156, 345,
    2006:125–26, 139, 177, 318,
    383–84, 435, 485, **2007:**27,
    62–63, 301–2, 411
energy and, **2004:**121, 127, 156,
    235, **2007:**16–17, 61, 238
enthusiasm of, **2004:**143, 299,
    358, 412–13
environment and, **2000:**121, **2004:**
    15–16, 38, 121, 127, 142, 156,
    159–60, 431–32, **2007:**54–55,
    61, 111–12, 127, 175, 192
euthanasia and, **2005:**179–80
evolution and, **2004:**464,
    2007:250, 252
families and, **2004:**156, **2007:**411
family values and, **2007:**546
federal budget and, **2004:**15–16,
    38, 156, **2007:**16–17, 192
finances and, **2004:**38, 156,
    2007:486
Foley scandal and, **2006:**420, 426
Ford, Gerald, and, **2004:**211–12,
    229, 238, **2006:**246
foreign affairs and, **2004:**15, 38,
    65, 92, 102, 156, **2005:**1–4,
    356–57, 362, **2006:**54, 77,
    130–32, 139, 303, 418,
    2007:14, 81, 256, 367
foreign aid and, **2004:**38, 156,
    2006:139
foreign trade and, **2004:**156
France and, **2004:**73–74,
    2005:128, **2006:**130–31

240, **2000:**344, 386,
2002:17–18, 273, 307, 319
residential area and, **2006:**253,
378, 472
respect and, **2004:**38, 156
Rice, Condoleezza, and, **2004:**
145, 480, **2005:**116, 483,
2006:34–35, 502, 532, 537
Romney, Mitt, and, **2006:**502,
532, **2007:**346
Roosevelt, Franklin D., and,
2004:238
Rove, Karl, and, **2005:**277,
2006:351–52, 492, **2007:**139
Rumsfeld, Donald, and, **2004:**480,
503–4, **2006:**51–52, 401
Russia and, **2005:**128, **2006:**130
satisfaction of, **2004:**37–38, 69,
113, 156, 239, **2005:**214,
2006:81, 113, 236, 238, 337,
376, 528, **2007:**28–29, 54, 153,
410, 442, 553
Saudi Arabia and, **2005:**128,
2006:130
Schiavo, Terri, and, **2005:**105,
109–10, 122
September 11, 2001, terrorist
attacks and, **2004:**145–46,
325–26, 401, **2005:**334
smoking and, **2005:**269
social problems and, **2004:**103
Social Security and, **2004:**38,
109–10, 156, 431–32,
2007:16–17, 61, 192
State of the Union address and,
2004:29, **2006:**41–42, 45
stem cell research and, **2005:**
192–93, 195, **2006:**212–13,
298, **2007:**262–63
stress and, **2004:**182
Supreme Court and, **2005:**42, 202,
228, 244–47, 259–60, 283–84,
328–29, 344–45, 370–71, 400,
405, 473

swing states and, **2004:**375
Syria and, **2005:**128
Taiwan and, **2006:**130
taxes and, **2004:**15–16, 38, 154,
156, **2005:**3–4, 6–7, 39, 66,
2006:139, 267–68, 383–84,
448–50, 454–55, 460–61, 478
teenagers and, **2004:**391–92
terrorism and, **2004:**15–16,
20, 37–38, 113, 115, 127,
134–35, 156, 167–68, 302,
363, 375, 431–32, **2006:**8–9,
16, 54, 101–2, 107, 125–26,
138–39, 155–56, 243, 245,
267–68, 303, 349, 371–74,
379–80, 385, 387–91,
393–94, 401–2, 413–14,
426–27, 435, 448–50, 455,
459–61, 500–501, 528
Thatcher, Margaret, and,
2005:483
Thompson, Fred, and, **2007:**346
on threats, most critical,
2004:100–101, **2007:**8
torture and, **2005:**441
trade deficit and, **2006:**139
Truman, Harry, and, **2004:**229
trust and, **2005:**360, **2006:**398–99,
514
Ukraine and, **2005:**128
U.N. and, **2004:**102
values of, **2004:**328, 366–67,
2005:412
veterans and, **2004:**418
violence and, **2004:**38, 127, 156,
2006:125–26, 139
voter interest in, **2006:**18–19,
157–58, 171–72, 176, 184–85,
265–66, 377, 422, 467–69
voters for
are prejudiced against blacks,
2002:393
pleased with selection of
candidates running for

Democratic Party *(continued)*
    Democratic nomination for
      president, **2002**:395
    voter turnout for, **2005**:42–43,
      2006:157–58, 266, 286, 339,
      377, 422, 441–42, 465,
      467–69
    voting systems and, **2004**:315–16
    wages and, **2007**:11
    welfare and, **2004**:38
    whites and, **2007**:277–78, 281
    Winfrey, Oprah, and, **2004**:514,
      2005:483, **2006**:537
    World War II and, **2005**:292
Democrats in Congress
    approval ratings, **1999**:7, 91,
      2000:272, **2001**:141, 187,
      2002:102, 213–14, **2003**:388
    blacks and, **2002**:393
    and Bush, George W., **2000**:420,
      427–28, **2001**:37, 141,
      2002:18, 68, 355
    and Clinton, **1998**:223, 248
    confidence in, **2001**:144, **2002**:27,
      2003:123
    and corporations, **2002**:190
    and corruption, **2002**:101–2
    Enron and, **2002**:31–32, 38
    and finances, **2001**:206, **2002**:22,
      101–2, 213, 332, **2003**:5, 258,
      272
    and healthcare, **2002**:101–2
    and impeachment, **1998**:247, 249
    and Iraq, **2002**:246, 279
    and Medicare, **1999**:218,
      2003:229–30
    opinion of, **1998**:158, 231–32,
      2000:427, **2001**:210,
      2002:190, 214, 354–55
    Republicans and
      compared, **2001**:187, 229,
      2002:18, 190, 291, 343,
      354, **2003**:4–5, 258, 272
      relations with, **1998**:232

and September 11, 2001, **2002**:155
and Social Security, **2002**:101, 103
and tax cuts, **1999**:218, **2001**:195
and terrorism, **2002**:355
Dench, Judi, 2002:79
de Niro, Robert, 2000:99, **2001**:76,
    2006:507
dentist(s), 2006:519
    honesty and ethical standards of,
      1999:148, **2000**:388, **2001**:265,
      2003:422
    recommend as career for young
      man, **1998**:238
Depp, Johnny, 2001:76
depression, 2004:216–17
Depression, Great
    as most important event in twenti-
      eth century, **2002**:175
Detroit, 2000:298–99, **2001**:235,
    2004:448–49
Detroit Tigers, 2001:81
DeWine, Mike, 2006:364
diabetes
    worried you will experience this
      illness, **2003**:424
Diana, Princess of Wales, 1998:2,
    186, 205, **2004**:514, **2005**:8, 483
Diaz-Munoz, Javier, 2005:268
Dickens, Charles, 1999:267
diesel oil prices
    recent increases cause you finan-
      cial hardship, **2000**:55, 320
diet, 2003:253–54, **2004**:149, 191,
    294–95, 331–32, 385, **2005**:296,
    306, 440
    See also food
dietitian
    recommend as career for young
      woman, **1998**:239, **2001**:109
diMaggio, Joe, 1999:256, **2000**:1,
    2001:83
dining out
    favorite way of spending evening,
      1998:237, **1999**:252, **2002**:6

hobby you are particularly interested in, **2002:**7
how many times ate dinner out last week, **2003:**150–51
would seek out good food and restaurants on perfect vacation, **1999:**270
disaster aid
amount federal government spends on, **1999:**258
discrimination
education and, **2004:**199–201, 377
in employment, **2004:**290
in entertainment, **2004:**290–91
frequency of, **2004:**19
gender and, **2003:**360–62
in healthcare, **2004:**290–91
income and, **2004:**291
in law enforcement, **2004:**288–90
as most important issue, **2000:**282, **2004:**414
smoking and, **2004:**307, 330–431
teenagers and, **2004:**414
disease, 2005:99, 302, 431–32
as most important issue, **2001:**121, **2003:**203, 443
See also health
dishonesty
as most important issue, **2002:**10, 70, 116, 233, 360, **2003:**25, 62, 122, 155, 203, 284, 401, 443
diving
as favorite Summer Olympic event, **2000:**307
divorce, 2004:131–32, 249–50, **2006:**212–13, 217–18
as morally acceptable, **2001:**127, **2002:**149–50, **2003:**159, 178, 218
DNA evidence, 2000:168–69, **2005:**72
Dobson, James, 2007:217
Dockery, Trudy, 2004:317

doctor(s), 2004:485, **2006:**519
can be trusted, **2002:**199
fear of going to, **1998:**238, **2001:**70
health or medical information from, **2002:**293
homosexuals should be hired as, **1999:**169
honesty and ethical standards of, **1999:**148, **2000:**388, **2001:**265, **2002:**373, **2003:**422
recommend as career for young man, **1998:**238
recommend as career for young woman, **1998:**238, **2001:**109
satisfaction with, **2000:**312
vote for making marijuana legally available for them to prescribe, **1999:**170
wrong diagnosis or treatment by, **2000:**102
doctor-assisted suicide, 2002:149, **2003:**159, 179
Kevorkian and, **1999:**162
when person has incurable disease, **1999:**161
when person is in severe pain, **1998:**180
will be commonplace in year 2025, **1998:**221
will be legal in year 2025, **1998:**221
See also euthanasia
Dodd, Christopher, 2006:477, 531, **2007:**370
dogs
fear of, **1998:**238, **2001:**70
ownership of, **2001:**55
Dole, Bob, 1998:1, 205, **2004:**319, 342
conventions and, **2004:**279, 312–13, 356–57
Democratic Party and, **2004:**319
election of 1996 and, **2004:**8, 41, 125, 337–38

Dole, Bob *(continued)*
  familiarity with, **2004:**84
  gender and, **2004:**96
  Republican Party and, **2004:**319
  swing voters and, **2004:**283
  as vice presidential candidate,
    2004:126
Dole, Elizabeth, 2004:514,
  2005:483, **2006:**536
  admiration of, **1998:**2, 154,
    1999:242, **2000:**431,
    2001:278, **2002:**400, **2003:**455
  Gallup analysis of her candidacy,
    1999:94
  likely to support, **1998:**65,
    180–81, 227, **1999:**71, 84, 99
  opinion of, **1998:**64, **1999:**45
dollar coin (Sacagawea), 2000:136,
  233–34
domestic issues, 2004:7, **2005:**368
  confidence in government han-
    dling of, **1998:**253, **1999:**49
  as most important issue in decid-
    ing your vote for president in
    2004, **2003:**416
  as priority for Congress, **1998:**236
Domino, Fats, 2000:265
The Doors, 2000:265
Douglas, Michael, 2001:76–77
Dowd, Matthew, 2004:211, 278
Dow Jones Industrial Average
  below 10,000 mark, as significant
    economic milestone, **2001:**65
  when will it hit 11,000 mark
    again, **2002:**221
  See also stock market; economic
    conditions
draft, military, 1998:182–83,
  2004:182–83, **2005:**230
  homosexuals in, **1998:**183
dreams, 2004:499–501
dressmaker
  recommend as career for young
    woman, **1998:**239

"The Drew Carey Show,"
  1998:61–62
drivers and driving
  cut back your driving if price of
    gasoline went up to $1.50 per
    gallon, **1999:**255
  See also traffic problems
drought, 1999:217, **2000:**191,
  2002:76
druggists
  honesty and ethical standards of,
    1999:148, **2000:**388, **2002:**
    373
drugs
  age and, **2005:**407
  in baseball, **2004:**144, 487–88
  Bush, George W., and, **2001:**8–9
  in Canada, **2004:**55–56
  as cause of trouble in your family,
    2000:414, **2003:**372
  cheating and, **2004:**192
  church and, **2005:**408
  community and, **2004:**55,
    2005:163–64
  for depression, **2004:**217
  education and, **2000:**241,
    2004:201, 377, **2005:**408
  families and, **2004:**55
  gender and, **2005:**170–72, 407,
    2007:457–58
  geographic region and, **2005:**163,
    408
  in Great Britain, **2004:**55–56
  ideology and, **2005:**408
  important for a president to have
    never used illegal drugs,
    1999:106
  income and, **2007:**457–58
  marijuana, **1999:**170, **2000:**414,
    2004:47–48, 55, 270–71
  as most important issue, **1998:**60,
    1999:195, **2000:**191, **2001:**58,
    121, 255, **2002:**10, 71, 116,
    233, 360, **2003:**25, 62, 86, 122,

155, 203, 284, 401, 443,
2004:37–38, 156, 182–83,
2005:99, 174, 213, 431,
2006:138–39, 237, 288, 338,
479
in community, **2000:**190, 192
as most important issue facing
nation 25 years from now,
2002:117
need to know if presidential candidate had used drugs,
1998:37–38
perceptions of, **2004:**55–56
political affiliation and, **2004:**38,
127, 156, **2005:**408,
2006:125–26, 139
predictions on, **1998:**221
as priority, **2001:**8–9
progress coping with, **2003:**372
progress made in coping with
problem of illegal drugs,
2000:414
religion and, **2005:**408
in school, **1999:**221, **2004:**426
seriousness of, **2000:**414,
2003:371–72
teenagers and, **2004:**26, 47–48,
182–83, 270–71
unfair for candidate to bring up
opponent's use of illegal drugs,
2000:218
worry about, **2001:**59, 66,
2002:118, **2003:**127–28,
2004:126–27, 139, 159,
2007:126
See also alcohol; prescription
drugs
Dukakis, Michael, 2004:28, 42–43,
279–80, 283, 313, 356–57,
2007:269, 355
gender and, **2004:**96
Gallup analysis of gender gap,
versus Bush, **2000:**159
Duke University, 2003:299

DVD watching
favorite way of spending an
evening, **2002:**6
Dylan, Bob, 2000:265

E

The Eagles, 2000:265
Earle, Ronnie, 2005:453
Earnhardt, Dale, 2000:289
Earth
survival of, as most important
issue facing nation 25 years
from now, **2002:**117
Easter, 2005:114
Easterbrook, Gregg, 2004:292
Eastern Europe, 1999:231,
2000:186
East Timor, 1999:224–25
Eastwood, Clint, 2000:98, **2001:**76
economic conditions, 1998:45–46,
1999:48, **2000:**13–14, 73, 163,
185, 347, 377–78, 407, **2001:**93,
198, 268, **2002:**12, 71, 107, 128,
174, 233–34, 298, 315, **2003:**
22–23, 63, 88, 123, 157–58, 242,
370, 398, 442, **2004:**244–45,
2007:87
age and, **2004:**205, **2005:**66, 108,
470, **2007:**47
approval ratings, **2001:**55, 166,
228, **2002:**27, 57, 91, 332, 351,
357, **2004:**6–7, 49, 58, 64, 139,
187–88, 191, 230–31, 236,
257–59, 389, 450, 452, **2006:**
54, 92, 116–17, 154–56, 187,
200–201, 243–44, 303, 348, 422
Asia and, **1998:**157–58
blacks and, **2007:**304, 316
Bush, George H. W., and,
2004:85, 258, **2005:**33
Bush, George W., and, **1999:**63,
80, 116, **2000:**24, 85, 143, 196,

economic conditions *(continued)*
206, 242, 248, 258, 262, 267,
275, 309, 357, **2001:**22, 38,
2004:6–7, 12, 14–15, 20, 29,
49, 58, 64–65, 85, 107,
111–12, 139, 171–72, 187–88,
191, 196, 236, 255, 257–59,
301–2, 321–22, 334, 347,
351–52, 355, 358, 374–75,
381–84, 389, 394, 397–99,
402, 409–10, 418–21, 432,
444, 450, 452, 469, 497–99
Carter, Jimmy, and, **2004:**85
China and, **1998:**83, **2000:**154,
2004:394
Clark, Wesley, and, **2004:**31, 33
Clinton and, **1998:**73, 202, 245,
1999:44, **2000:**170–71, 206,
261–62, 335, **2004:**258,
2005:33
community and, **2005:**108
competition for, **2004:**100–101
computer industry and, **2000:**206
confidence in, **2001:**229, **2002:**27,
2004:9–13, 20, 23–25, 35–36,
69–70, 78, 107–8, 125,
150–51, 189–91, 235–37,
246–47, 254–55, 285–86,
333–35, 359, 379–81, 451–53,
491–92, 507–9
confident the economy currently
strong, **2001:**49
Congress and, **2000:**206,
2001:275, **2002:**8, **2005:**3–4,
65–67, 130, 172–73, 412
conservatives and, **2007:**295
consumers and, **2004:**64, 107–8,
150–51, 285–86, 451–53,
491–92, 507–9
corporations and, **2000:**42,
2007:10
crime and, **2004:**50–51, 80
Dean, Howard, and, **2004:**31,
33

Democratic Party and, **1998:**224,
2001:275, **2002:**8, 17–18, 171,
291, 312, 332, 336, **2003:**5,
2004:15–16, 23–25, 70, 103,
107, 113, 124, 127, 156, 269,
301–2, 375, 387, 431–32
Dow Jones and, **2001:**65,
2002:221
economic stimulus bill, **2002:**8,
2003:6
education and, **2004:**201, 377,
2005:108, **2007:**10–11
Edwards, John, and, **2004:**31, 33
election of 1992 and,
2004:125–26
election of 2004 and, **2004:**31, 33,
41, 64–65, 84–85, 111–12,
115–16, 124–26, 170–72, 196,
257–59, 299–302, 321–22,
333–35, 347, 351–52, 355,
358, 374–75, 381–84, 389,
397–99, 402, 409–10, 418–21,
431–32, 444, 447, 451–52,
469, 497–99
election of 2006 and, **2006:**22,
25–26, 28, 266–68, 318, 322,
389–91, 426–28, 455, 460–61,
467
election of 2008 and, **2007:**46–48,
50, 255–56, 287–89, 295,
329–31, 336–37, 432–33,
479–80, 527–28, 543
elections (historic) and, **2006:**467
employment and, **2004:**34–35,
39–40, 70, 100–101, 150–53,
189–90, 235–36, 243, 260,
2005:108, **2006:**216–17,
221–22, 407–8, 485
energy and, **2004:**131, **2007:**10
environment and, **1998:**177,
1999:171, **2001:**27, **2002:**119,
2004:159, **2006:**161
European Union and,
2004:244–45

factors affecting [list], **2002:**223
families and, **2007:**266, 349
federal budget and, **2004:**150,
2007:10
Federal Reserve and, **2000:**206
finances and, **2007:**266, 349
foreign affairs and, **2004:**84–85,
2007:10
foreign aid and, **2007:**10
foreign trade and, **2000:**206,
2007:10
gasoline and, **2004:**343,
2006:216, 222, 429
gender and, **2004:**69
geographic region and,
2004:23–25, 35–36, **2005:**108,
156–57, 470, **2007:**11, 160,
296
globalization and, **2004:**40, 131,
508–9
Gore and, **1999:**57, 80, **2000:**23,
85, 143, 195, 206, 242, 248,
258, 262, 275, 309, 357
government and, **2001:**275,
2007:10
healthcare and, **2007:**10
Hispanics and, **2007:**304, 316
Hurricane Katrina and,
2005:347–49, 365
ideology and, **2004:**102–3, 269,
2005:108
immigrants and, **1999:**160,
2000:314, **2001:**171,
2002:226, **2004:**14–15, 296,
2005:248–49, 451
improvement in, timing of,
2001:93
income and, **2004:**69–70, 190–91,
237, 254–55, 379–81, 452–53
2004:507, 508, **2006:**239–40,
293
independents and, **2004:**70, 103,
156, 269, 302, 352, 375,
431–32

interest rates and, **2004:**235,
2007:10, 297
investors and, **2004:**35–36, 39, 78,
260–61, 359
Iraq war and, **2007:**10–11
Kerry, John, and, **2004:**31, 33,
41, 58, 111–12, 171–72, 196,
257–58, 301–2, 321–22, 334,
347, 351–52, 355, 358,
374–75, 381–84, 389,
397–99, 402, 409–10,
418–21, 432, 444, 469,
497–99
law enforcement and, **2004:**51
liberals and, **2007:**295
Lieberman, Joe, and, **2004:**33
in local community, **2002:**12
Microsoft and, **2000:**140, 149,
2001:157
moderates and, **2007:**295
as most important issue, **1998:**60,
1999:194–95, **2001:**58, 255,
2002:323, 359, **2003:**204,
285, **2004:**20, 35, 37–38,
84–85, 112–13, 116, 125–26,
155–56, 159, 183, 239–40,
246–47, 334, 381–82, 386–87,
414, 466–67, **2006:**2–3,
68–69, 129–30, 138–39, 162,
167, 197, 202, 216–17,
222–23, 237, 250, 288, 293,
336, 338, 383–86, 430,
434–35, 467, 479, 482–83,
528, **2007:**37–38, 54–55,
123–26, 219, 255–56, 265,
271–73, 315–16, 319–20,
349, 410–12, 442–43,
479–80, 500–501, 527–28,
532, 543
as most important issue facing
nation 25 years from now,
2002:116
oil and, **2004:**424, **2007:**10
opportunities in, **2004:**276–78

economic conditions *(continued)*

outlook for, **2004:**10, 20, 23–25, 39, 107, 150, 189–91, 236, 254–55, 260, 285–86, 333–35, 379–81, 451–53, 491–92, 507–9

outsourcing and, **2004:**35, 79, 107, 131, 153

political affiliation and, **2006:**54, 107, 125–26, 139, 155–56, 159–60, 223, 239–40, 267–68, 293, 303, 318, 370–71, 379–80, 383–86, 389–91, 418–19, 426–27, 435, 455, 457–61, 485, 500–501, 528

political ideology and, **2007:**295

population and, **2006:**292

predictions for, **1998:**220, 251, **2000:**185, **2001:**32, 65, 222, 268, 274, **2002:**142–43, 201, 221, 332, **2003:**23–24, 158, 242–44, 286, 370

predictions for—over next six months unemployment will go up a lot, **2001:**268, **2002:**143

president and, **1999:**105, **2004:**58, 64, 269–70, **2007:**2, 10, 16–17, 60–61, 90, 191–92, 237–38, 305

as priority, **1998:**235, **2000:**212, 428, **2001:**229, **2002:**17, 130, 171, **2003:**4, **2007:**2, 16–17, 60–61, 90, 148–49, 191–92, 237–38, 305

proposals for, **2003:**7

race and, **2004:**69, 276–78, 317, **2007:**304, 316

rated today, **1998:**44–45, 116, 141, 188, **1999:**48, 129–30, **2000:**13, 72–73, 163, 184–85, 347, 377, 407, **2001:**14, 32, 58, 93, 120, 143–44, 182, 197, 217, 222, 268, 274, **2002:**71, 107, 128, 141, 173–74, 233, 297–98, 314, 331–32, **2003:**22,

62–63, 78, 88, 122, 157, 242, 370, 398, 442

Reagan, Ronald, and, **2004:**230–31, **2005:**33

recession, **2001:**32–33, 58, 93, 120, 218, 222, 275, **2002:**70, 143, 315, **2004:**10

Republican Party and, **1998:**224, **2001:**275, **2002:**8, 17–18, 171, 291, 312, 332, 336, 376, **2003:**5, **2004:**15, 23–25, 37–38, 70, 103, 113, 127, 156, 269, 302, 375, 431–32

satisfaction with, **2000:**13, 204, **2001:**28, **2002:**232, **2004:**205, 296, 317

September 11 terrorist attacks and, **2001:**275

space program and, **2004:**82

spending and, **2004:**107–8, 150–51, 185–86, 452–53, **2007:**297

State of the Union address and, **2005:**72, **2006:**45

states and, **2004:**23–25, 333–35, 374–75

stock market and, **1998:**116–17, **2004:**10, **2006:**216, 221–22, 429, **2007:**297

stress and, **2004:**182

tax cuts and, **2001:**61, 124

taxes and, **2004:**343, 355

teenagers and, **2004:**183, 414

as threat, most critical, **2007:**508

unemployment and, **2005:**108

veterans and, **2004:**418–19

as voting issue, **1998:**159, 225, **1999:**68, **2000:**19, 27, 35–36, 47, 49, 72, 193, 242, 280, **2002:**291, 312, **2003:**338–39, 416, 453

whites and, **2007:**304, 316

worry about, **2001:**59, 67, **2002:**118, **2003:**127, **2004:**10,

58, 64, 120, 126–27, 159,
2007:126
as worst problem facing your
community, 2000:190
Y2K computer problem and,
1999:246
young voters on, 2003:390
See also financial situation, personal; stock market
**education, 2001:201, 2002:240,
2003:289**
access to, as most important issue,
2002:360, 2003:25, 62, 86,
122, 155, 203, 284, 401, 443
affirmative action and, 2005:338
age and, 2005:66, 156
agnosticism and, 2004:511
animal testing and, 2004:215
approval ratings, 2001:166,
2002:91, 2004:7, 184–85,
2005:15–16, 19, 27, 144,
2006:215
atheism and, 2004:511
Bible and, 2006:210, 2007:230
Brown, Jerry, and, 2007:355
budget surplus and, 2000:318
Bush, George W., and, 1999:66,
81, 116, 2000:24, 85, 143, 242,
248, 258, 275, 309, 357,
2001:105–6, 2004:7, 112,
184–85, 301–2, 317–18, 348,
352, 376, 383–84, 409–10,
420, 427, 442–43, 469,
498–99, 2005:3–4, 15–16, 19,
27, 29, 31–32, 37, 39, 48,
65–67, 156–57
children and, 2004:199–201,
276–77
Christmas and, 2005:478
Clark, Wesley, and, 2007:354
Clinton, Bill, and, 2000:262,
2007:355
Clinton and, 1999:44
community and, 2004:377, 455

confidence in, 1998:56–57,
2002:27, 2004:276–77
Congress and, 2004:164, 2005:
3–4, 65–67, 144, 2007:2,
60–61, 90, 191–92, 237–38, 305
cost of, 2004:183, 200–201,
376–77
creationism and, 2004:463,
2005:191, 355, 379
crime and, 2004:201, 377
curricula for, 2004:376–77,
512–13
Dean, Howard, and, 2007:354
death penalty and, 2005:186
Democratic Party and, 1998:224,
2001:211, 2002:17, 171, 291,
312, 336, 2003:5, 2004:15, 38,
156, 318, 347–48, 431–32,
2007:61, 123, 192, 256, 348,
367, 411
discrimination and,
2004:199–201, 377
drugs and, 2004:201, 377,
2005:408
Dukakis, Michael, and, 2007:355
economy and, 2004:201, 377,
2005:108, 2006:216, 222,
2007:10–11
election of 1988 and, 2007:355
election of 1992 and, 2007:355
election of 2004 and, 2004:22, 41,
112, 115–16, 170, 301,
317–18, 352, 376, 383–84,
408–10, 420, 423–24, 431–32,
442–43, 469, 498–99,
2007:354
emphasis in, 2005:333
employment and, 2004:67–68,
345, 2005:340, 2006:264,
323–24, 340
European Union, knowledge of,
and, 2004:245
evolution and, 2004:463–64,
2005:191, 355, 379

education *(continued)*
  families and, **2004:**200–201, 377,
    2007:266, 349
  finances and, **2007:**266, 349
  funding for, **2004:**200–201,
    376–77
  gambling and, **2004:**123
  gasoline and, **2006:**185
  gender and, **2005:**67
  geographic region and, **2005:**157,
    332
  Gephardt, Dick, and,
    2007:354–55
  getting through school as biggest
    challenge you face today,
    2000:192
  Gingrich, Newt, and, **2007:**187
  Gore and, **1999:**58, 80, 116,
    2000:23, 85, 143, 242, 248,
    258, 262, 275, 309, 357
  government and, **2000:**241,
    2004:164
  guns and, **2006:**439
  Harkin, Tom, and, **2007:**355
  Hart, Gary, and, **2007:**355
  health and, **2004:**475
  healthcare and, **2007:**308
  Hispanics and, **2007:**286–87, 316
  homosexuality and, **2005:**142,
    2007:78
  ideology and, **2006:**357
  image of, **2005:**311, 422
  improvement of, **2004:**200–201,
    375–77
  independents and, **2004:**38, 156,
    352, 431–32, **2007:**192, 256,
    348, 367, 411
  influence of, **2000:**294
  inheritances and, **2007:**374
  Internet and, **2004:**22
  Iraq war and, **2004:**400,
    2005:244, **2006:**278, **2007:**11
  Jackson, Jesse, and, **2007:**355
  judicial system and, **2004:**164

Kerrey, Bob, and, **2007:**355
Kerry, John, and, **2004:**82, 112,
  301–2, 318, 348, 352, 376,
  383–84, 409–10, 420, 427,
  442–43, 469, 498–99, **2007:**354
labor unions and, **2005:**323
law enforcement and, **2005:**420
legislation passed this year will
  make difference for you and
  your family, **2001:**187
Lieberman, Joe, and, **2007:**354
marriage and, **2004:**86–87, 223,
  2005:142, **2007:**78
media and, **2004:**163–64, 388
Middle East and, **2006:**123
morality and, **2004:**215
as most important issue, **1998:**60,
  1999:195, **2000:**191, **2001:**58,
  121, **2002:**10, 70, 116, 233, 323,
  360, **2003:**25, 62, 86, 122, 155,
  203, 284, 401, 443, **2004:**20,
  37–38, 113, 155–56, 182–83,
  246, 467, **2005:**18, 45, 99, 113,
  152, 174, 198, 213, 332, 348,
  366, 421, **2006:**138–39, 162,
  237, 279, 288, 338, 385–86,
  479, **2007:**37–38, 54, 123–24,
  271–73, 315–16, 349, 410–12,
  442–43, 501
  in community, **2000:**190, 192
as most important issue facing
  nation 25 years from now,
  2002:116
news and, **2006:**59
opportunities for, **2004:**199–201,
  276–77, 317–18, 377
parents and, **2004:**376–77, 455–56
Patriot Act and, **2004:**94
political affiliation and, **2007:**61,
  192, 256, 348, 367, 411
politicians and, **2004:**164
poor, as most important issue,
  2003:25, 62, 86, 122, 155, 203,
  284, 401, 443

poverty and, **2004:**201, 377

president and, **2004:**164, **2007:**2, 60–61, 78, 90, 191–92, 237–38, 305

as priority, **1998:**235, **2000:**212, 428, **2001:**8–9, 22, 38, 141, 229, **2002:**17, 130, 171, **2003:**4, **2007:**2, 60–61, 90, 148–49, 191–92, 237–38, 305

public, private, or parochial school, **2000:**294

public opinion and, **2005:**378

race and, **2004:**18–19, 199–201, 223, 276–77, 317–18, 377, 455–56

reading and, **2005:**203

religion and, **2004:**120, 511–12, **2005:**132, 234, 447, **2007:**78, 230

Republican Party and, **1998:**224, **2001:**211, **2002:**17, 171, 291, 312, 336, 376, **2003:**5, **2004:**15, 38, 156, 318, 347–48, 431–32, **2007:**61, 123, 192, 256, 348, 367, 411

retirement and, **2006:**264

Richardson, Bill, and, **2007:**420

satisfaction with, **1998:**137, **1999:**221, **2000:**204, 294, **2001:**29, **2003:**360, **2004:**18–19, 199, 376

Simon, Paul, and, **2007:**355

Social Security and, **1999:**125

spending on, **1998:**237

stem cell research and, **2006:**298

teaching and, **2004:**376–77

teenagers and, **2004:**182–83

testing and, **2004:**376–77

threats, most critical, and, **2004:**101

Tsongas, Paul, and, **2007:**355

types of, **2004:**386

U.S., satisfaction with, by, **2006:**81, 238

as voting issue, **1998:**225, **2000:**18, 72, 242, 281, 356, **2002:**291, 312, **2003:**338–39, 416, 453

Wilder, Doug, and, **2007:**355

See also school(s)

Education Commission of the States, 2004:455

Education Trust, 2004:426–27

Edwards, Elizabeth, 2007:127

Edwards, John, 2001:192, **2005:**80, 300, 468

age and, **2007:**47, 124, 227–29, 419

conventions and, **2004:**313–14

Democratic Party and, **2004:**34, 273, 354

economy and, **2004:**31, 33

election of 2004 and, **2004:**5–6, 11, 27–28, 30–34, 40–41, 48–49, 59–61, 75–76, 272–74, 283–85, 287, 308, 311, 313–14, 323–24, 353–54, **2007:**354

election of 2008 and, **2004:**456–57

familiarity with, **2004:**48–49, **2007:**225–26, 367–69, 388–89, 550

gender and, **2007:**21, 47–48, 124, 127, 227–29, 419

healthcare and, **2004:**31

image of, **2004:**6, 43, 48–49, 272, 284–85, 323–24, 353–54, 406, **2006:**532

income and, **2007:**227–29, 419

Iraq war and, **2004:**31–32

Kerry, John, and, **2004:**272–74

likely to support, **2002:**90, 355, 395, **2003:**16, 135, 190, 215–16, 277, 323, 335, 374–75, 382, 390, 417, 432–33, 446–47

opinion of, **2003:**306

320–23, 325–26, 351–52, 355,
374–76, 381–84, 389, 395,
397–402, 409–10, 418–21,
428, 431–33, 437–38, 447,
469–72, 497–99
Kerry, John, and, **2004:**5–6, 11,
27–28, 30–34, 40–43, 48–50,
59–61, 75–77, 82–84, 111–12,
124, 132–34, 140–41, 156–57,
161–63, 171–72, 188–89,
196–97, 256–60, 267–70,
283–85, 297–302, 308–9,
311–14, 318–24, 326, 332–35,
337–40, 345–47, 351–52,
354–58, 371–75, 378–79,
381–84, 388–90, 395–402,
405–7, 409–14, 418–24,
428–34, 436–38, 442–45,
469–72, 497–99
Kerry, John, in, **2007:**253–54, 354
Kucinich, Dennis, and, **2004:**11,
27–28, 30, 33, 76
leadership and, **2004:**381–82, 389,
399, 444, 498–99
Libertarian Party in, **2004:**349,
378–79
Lieberman, Joe, and, **2004:**5–6,
11, 27–28, 30–34, 40–41,
48–49, 272–73, **2007:**354
marriage and, **2004:**112, 170,
431–32, 442–43, 469
media and, **2004:**433–34
Medicaid and, **2004:**116
Medicare and, **2004:**41, 109–10,
116, 352, 420, 431–32, 469
morality and, **2004:**383–84,
431–32, 447, 469–72, 497–99
most important issues in,
2003:415–16, **2004:**37–38,
84–85, 246–47, 420, 467
Nader, Ralph, and, **2004:**87–88,
132, 162, 188–89, 257, 284,
299–300, 311–12, 346,
348–50, 355–56, 364, 378–79,

388, 396–98, 405, 410, 413,
418, 421, 423–24, 429–30,
436–37, 442
National Guard service and,
2004:76–77
national security and,
2004:382–84, 497–99
negativity in, **2004:**314, 357,
360–61, 433–34
Peroutka, Michael, and,
2004:378–79
political affiliation and,
2004:102–3, 494–95
poverty, **2004:**111–12
primaries for, **2004:**5–6, 11–12,
27–28, 30–34, 40–43, 48–50,
60–61, 75–76, 92, 96, 104,
107, 113, 124, 132–33,
142–43, 166, 197, 323, 356,
366, 389, 398
privacy and, **2004:**112
projections for, **2004:**6–8, 11–12,
15–16, 25, 29, 48, 60, 75–76,
111–12, 132–34, 156–57,
161–63, 188–89, 193, 196,
257–60, 265–66, 278–80,
283–85, 297–300, 311–13,
328, 332–35, 337–40, 345–47,
354–58, 364–65, 371, 374–75,
378–79, 388–90, 396–98,
405–7, 410, 412, 429–31,
436–38
red states in, **2004:**162, 184, 189,
299–300, 333–36, 338–40,
354, 430
religion and, **2004:**92–93, 256–57,
328–29, 383–84, 428–29,
442–43, 497–99
Republican Party and, **2004:**25,
38, 59–60, 75, 77, 116–17,
143, 278–80, 287–88, 299,
301–2, 313–14, 337–38, 354,
360, 372, 375, 423–24,
431–34, 442, 494–95, 498–99

terrorism and, **2007:**46–48, 50,
255, 329–31, 336–37, 432–33,
479–80, 527–28, 543
Vilsack, Tom, and, **2005:**468
Warner, Mark, and, **2005:**300, 468
electoral vote, 2004:437
electric and gas utilities
are to blame for country's energy
problems, **2001:**131
confidence in, **2001:**149
confidence in (by political party),
2001:149
overall view of, **2001:**201,
2002:240, **2003:**289
electricians
honesty rating, **1999:**148
electricity
price caps on, important to deal
with this issue next year,
2001:141
used to heat your home, **2000:**56
Elizabeth II, queen of England,
1998:2, 154–55, **1999:**242,
2000:431, **2002:**163, 400,
2003:455, **2004:**514, **2005:**483,
2006:536
Elizabeth **(movie), 1999:**254
e-mail, 2001:150–51, 175–78,
2003:168
See also Internet
emissions standards, 2002:73
emotions, 2004:104, 117, 270, 466,
475–77, **2005:**382–84, 477
emphysema
worried you will experience this
illness, **2003:**424
employment
affirmative action and,
2005:287–88, 338
age and, **2004:**345, **2005:**135,
287, 290–92, 308,
2006:177–78, **2007:**378
assessment of, **2005:**17, 198–99,
220, 256, 290–92, 304, 460,

2006:3, 50, 68, 176–78,
221–22, 232, 293, 407–8, 430,
485, **2007:**27, 51–52, 62–63,
116–17, 180–81, 219, 319, 500
blacks and, **2007:**287, 293–94,
304
Bush, George W., and,
2004:14–15, 58, 111–12,
382–84, 469
Clinton, Hillary, and, **2007:**301
competition for, **2004:**100–101
concern for, **2004:**10, 58, 64,
126–27, 159, 271–72, 340–41,
343
confidence in, **2004:**35, 39, 107,
110, 152–53, 235–36, 242–43,
276–77, 286, 340–41, 451–52,
508
Congress and, **2007:**3, 60–61,
191–92, 237–38, 305, 385
consumers and, **2004:**110–11,
286, 508
Democratic Party and,
2004:37–38, 113, 127, 156,
345, **2007:**27, 62–63, 301–2,
411
discrimination in, **2004:**290
economy and, **2004:**34–35,
39–40, 70, 100–101, 150–53,
189–90, 235–36, 243, 260,
2005:108, **2006:**216–17,
221–22, 407–8, 485
education and, **2004:**67–68, 345,
2005:340, **2006:**264, 323–24,
340
election of 2004 and,
2004:110–12, 116, 382–84,
469
election of 2006 and, **2006:**318,
455, 467
employed full time, part time,
retired, or unemployed,
2000:5, 43
gasoline and, **2004:**343

116–17, 154–56, 169–71,
186–87, 243–44, 348
Bush, George H. W., and,
2006:170
Bush, George W., and, **2004:**121,
139, 235, **2007:**52–53, 122
concern for, **2004:**120–22,
126–27, 129–31, 139, 159,
271–72
Congress and, **2007:**16–17,
60–61, 237–38, 305
cost of, **2004:**130–31, 260–61,
342–44, 453, **2007:**538
Democratic Party and,
2007:16–17, 61, 238
economy and, **2004:**131, **2007:**10
election of 2004 and, **2004:**121,
130
election of 2006 and, **2006:**467
environment and, **2004:**121–22,
131, **2006:**128, 161
foreign affairs and, **2005:**73
geographic region and,
2005:156–57, 470
Giuliani, Rudy, and, **2007:**50
image of, **2005:**422
income and, **2004:**453, **2005:**102,
2006:483
independents and, **2007:**16–17,
238
industry, image of, **2004:**361,
407
investors and, **2004:**131, 260–61,
271–72, 342–44
Iraq war and, **2004:**131
Kerry, John, and, **2004:**121
McCain, John, and, **2007:**50
as most important issue,
2004:155–56, **2005:**45, 93–95,
99, 113, 148, 153, 174, 198,
213, 220, 286, 304, 321,
347–48, 365–66, 409–10, 421
nuclear energy plants, **2004:**129,
2005:161

outlook for, **2005:**102, **2006:**116
political affiliation and, **2004:**121,
127, 156, 235, **2007:**16–17, 61,
238
president and, **2007:**16–17,
60–61, 237–38, 305
as priority, **2007:**16–17, 60–61,
121–22, 237–38, 305
race and, **2005:**286, **2006:**459–60,
484
Republican Party and,
2007:16–17, 61, 238
State of the Union address and,
2006:45
See also fuel oil; gasoline; oil
Energy Department, 2004:129, 381
energy policies, 2001:67–68,
118–19, 130–31, 141, 156, 258,
2002:73–74, **2003:**338–39
Bush, George W., and, **2001:**68,
102, 156, 187, **2002:**27, 73, 92,
351
Democratic Party and, **2001:**210,
2002:18, 171
energy crisis
as most important issue,
2002:10, 71, 116, **2003:**25,
62, 86, 203, 443
seriousness of, **2001:**68, 114,
156, **2002:**73–74, **2003:**93,
126–27
energy sources
as most important issue,
2001:59, 121, 255,
2002:10, 71, 116, 360,
2003:25, 62, 86, 203, 443
as most important issue facing
nation 25 years from now,
2002:117
environment and, **2002:**73, 120,
2003:92, 126
predictions for, **2003:**93, 127
price increases caused financial
hardship, **2001:**47, 115

energy policies *(continued)*
as priority, **2001:**27, **2002:**17,
130, 171
production versus conservation,
2003:93
Republican Party and, **2001:**210,
2002:18, 171
satisfaction with, **2001:**27, 29,
2005:20, 22, 40
worry about, **2001:**59, 66,
2002:118, **2003:**127–28
engineering, engineers, 2006:519
honesty and ethical standards of,
1999:148, **2000:**388,
2001:265, **2003:**422–23
recommend as career for young
man, **1998:**238
recommend as career for young
woman, **1998:**239, **2001:**109
England
know name (Blair) of prime minister of, **2000:**176
English language
teach non-English-speaking students using immersion or bilin-
gual education, **1998:**70–71
Enron, 2002:13, 31–32, 37–39, 129
as crisis for U.S., **2002:**190
executives did something illegal,
2002:13, 31, 38, 197
members of Bush administration
did something illegal, **2002:**13,
31, 38
entertaining/visiting friends
favorite way of spending an
evening, **2002:**6
entertainment, 2007:293
reading and, **2005:**203–4
spending on, **2005:**86–87, 222,
367, 411
See also recreation; sports
entertainment industry
executives, honesty rating,
1999:148

and Littleton shootings, **1999:**
192
"Entertainment Tonight"
how often do you get your news
from, **1998:**193
trust accuracy of news from,
1998:98
environment, 2000:119–22,
2001:67, 89–90, 99–100, 102,
2002:119, **2004:**139
age and, **2004:**121, 160, **2007:**47,
127
approval ratings, **2001:**166,
2002:92, **2004:**139,
2005:15–16, 19, 27
Bush, George W., and, **1999:**81,
2000:24, 85, 196, 242, 248,
2001:22, 68, 102, 105–6,
2002:27, **2004:**138–40, 469,
2005:3–4, 15–16, 19, 27, 29,
37, 39, 156
business and, **1999:**171
Clinton and, **1999:**44
concern for, **2004:**126–27, 131,
138–42, 158–61
condition of, **2004:**158–59
Congress and, **2007:**3, 60–61, 90,
191–92, 237–38, 305
consider yourself an environmen-
talist, **1999:**172
Democratic Party and, **1998:**224,
2002:27, 171, 291, **2003:**5,
2004:15–16, 38, 121, 127, 142,
156, 159–60, 431–32,
2007:54–55, 61, 111–12, 127,
175, 192
economy and, **1998:**177,
1999:171, **2001:**27, **2002:**119,
2003:126, **2004:**159, **2006:**161
election of 2004 and, **2004:**140,
170, 431–32, 469
energy and, **2002:**73, 120,
2003:92, **2004:**121–22, 131,
2006:128, 161

European Union and, **2004:**244–45
Exxon Valdez oil spill, **1999:**166
favor specific environmental proposals [list], **2002:**73
gender and, **2007:**47–48, 127
Giuliani, Rudy, and, **2007:**50
Gore and, **1999:**58–59, 80,
　2000:23, 85, 196, 242, 248
government and, **1999:**171
income and, **2004:**142
independents and, **2004:**38, 156,
　159–60, 431–32, **2007:**54–55,
　127, 175, 192
Kerry, John, and, **2004:**140, 469
McCain, John, and, **2007:**50
media and, **2006:**142
as most important issue,
　1998:60–61, **1999:**195,
　2001:59, 121, 255, **2002:**10,
　71, 116, 233, 360, **2003:**25, 62,
　86, 122, 155, 203, 285, 443,
　2004:37–38, 156, 159,
　2005:3–4, 38, 99, 147–48, 174,
　213, 348, **2006:**138–39, 237,
　288, 338, 479, **2007:**37–38,
　54–55, 125–26, 410–12,
　442–43, 501
as most important issue facing
　nation 25 years from now,
　2002:116
name nuclear power plant in
　Pennsylvania [Three Mile
　Island] with breakdown,
　1999:166
outlook for, **2005:**147
political affiliation and,
　2007:54–55, 61, 111–12, 127,
　175, 192
predictions for, **1998:**219–20,
　223, **2002:**112
president and, **2007:**3, 60–61, 90,
　191–92, 237–38, 305
as priority, **2000:**428, **2001:**8–9,
　2002:130, 171, **2003:**4, **2007:**3,

　60–61, 90, 121–22, 148–49,
　191–92, 237–38, 305
production versus conservation,
　2003:127
progress in dealing with,
　2002:112
progress made in dealing with,
　1999:171
quality of, **2001:**99, **2002:**112,
　2003:126
regulation and, **2001:**131,
　2006:128
regulation of, **2003:**93
Republican Party and, **1998:**224,
　2002:171, 291, 376, **2003:**5,
　2004:15–16, 38, 121, 127, 142,
　156, 159–60, 431–32,
　2007:54–55, 61, 111–12, 127,
　175, 192
satisfaction with, **1999:**171,
　2001:29
as serious problem for country,
　2000:316
should take immediate, drastic
　actions concerning the environment, **2002:**119–20, **2003:**126
spending on, **1998:**4
Three Mile Island nuclear plant
　breakdown is likely to happen
　again, **1999:**166
as voting issue, **1998:**225,
　2000:19, 72, 193, 243,
　2002:291, **2003:**338–39, 416
worry about, **1999:**165–66, 171,
　2000:316, **2001:**59, 67, 90,
　2002:76–77, 81, 112–14, 118,
　2003:127–28
as worst problem facing your
　community, **2000:**191
See also global warming
**EPA (Environmental Protection
Agency)**
　trust it to protect environment,
　2000:120

Erin Brockovich, **2001:**73, 136
Estonia, 1998:171
ethics
    Bush, George W., and,
        2005:276–77, 398–99, 402
    Clinton and, **2005:**399
    as most important issue, **1998:**60,
        1999:194–95, **2000:**191,
        2001:58, 121, 255, **2002:**10,
        70, 116, 233, 323, 359, **2003:**
        25, 62, 86, 122, 155, 203,
        284–85, 401, 443
    as most important issue facing
        nation 25 years from now,
        2002:117
    as priority, **1998:**236
    rate honesty and ethical standards
        of people in different fields
        [list], **2002:**49–50
    Reagan and, **2005:**399
    See also honesty; morality
Europe. *See* Western Europe
euthanasia, 2004:249–50, 280–81,
    2005:178–80
    See also doctor-assisted suicide
evangelical Christianity, 2004:119
    See also born again Christianity;
        Christianity; church
Evans, Kurt, 2002:340
evolution, 2000:245, **2001:**52–53,
    2004:462–64
    and creationism, in public schools,
        1999:207, **2000:**200, 245
exercise, 2004:149, 191, 482–83,
    2006:489
    favorite way of spending evening,
        2002:6
    health ratings, by categories on
        exercise scale, **2002:**5–6
    participation in, **2003:**10
    total exercise index, **2002:**4
existentialism, 2004:47–48, 270–71
extinction, 2004:141, 160
    worry about, **2001:**90

extramarital affairs
    Kennedy and, **1998:**36
    presidents and, **1998:**35, 38–39
extraterrestrials. *See* aliens

F

fairness, 2004:50–51
faith-based organizations
    government support for, approval
        ratings for Bush's handling of,
        2001:166
familiarity, 2004:8–9, 48–49, 94,
    2005:211–12, 265–66, 354, 414,
    2007:225–26, 367–69, 388–89,
    550
    See also image; understanding
family(ies), 2006:334–36, 345,
    349–51
    afraid that your family will
        become victim of terrorist
        attack, **1998:**201
    alcohol and, **2004:**123, **2005:**271
    all right to lie to family member,
        1998:238
    balancing work and family as
        biggest challenge you face
        today, **2000:**192
    in Canada, **2004:**26
    care of family as biggest chal-
        lenge you face today, **2000:**
        192
    Clinton and, **1998:**202
    Congress and, **2007:**3
    decline of
        blamed for Littleton shootings,
            1999:192
        as most important issue,
            1998:60, **1999:**194–95,
            2001:121, 255, **2002:**10,
            70, 116, 233, 323, 359,
            2003:25, 62, 86, 122, 155,
            203, 284, 401, 443,

2004:37–38, 156, 467,
2005:99, 174, 348
as most important issue facing
nation 25 years from now,
2002:117
Democratic Party and, **2004:**156,
2007:411
drug use and, **2004:**55
economy and, **2007:**266, 349
education and, **2004:**200–201, 377
ensuring that next generation can
live better than parents, handled by Bush, **2000:**86
ensuring that next generation can
live better than parents, handled by Gore, **2000:**86
gambling and, **2004:**123
geographic region and, **2007:**59
in Great Britain, **2004:**26
immigration and, **2007:**179
importance in your life, **2003:**1
independents and, **2004:**156,
2007:411
more families where both parents
are employed by year 2025,
1998:220
news from
how often do you get your
news from family, **1998:**193
trust accuracy of news from
family, **1998:**98
political affiliation and, **2007:**411
president and, **2007:**3
as priority for Congress, **1998:**236
race and, **2004:**18–19
Republican Party and, **2004:**156,
2007:411
satisfaction with, **1998:**137,
2003:360, **2004:**18–19,
99–100
single-parent, **2004:**25
common by year 2025,
1998:220
size of, **2004:**127–28

spending time with
entertaining relatives, as
favorite way of spending
evening, **1998:**237
as favorite way of spending
evening, **1998:**237,
1999:252, **2002:**6
hobby you are particularly
interested in, **2002:**7
mealtime together,
2004:25–26, **2005:**481
on perfect vacation, **1999:**270
visiting relatives, as favorite
way of spending evening,
1998:237
support enough to parents from
extended family, **1998:**190
support from extended family as
essential to parents in raising
children, **1998:**190
See also children; parents
"Family Matters," 1998:61–62
family values. *See* morality; values
farms, farming
hobby you are particularly interested in, **2002:**7
overall view of, **2001:**200,
2002:240, **2003:**289
prefer to live in city, suburban
area, small town, or on farm,
1998:238
Farrakhan, Louis, 2003:252
fashion
recommend as career for young
woman, **1998:**239
fast food restaurants, 2004:26
approve of holding industry
legally responsible for diet-
related health problems,
2003:254
food served in very good for you,
2003:253
frequency of fast food dining,
2003:253–54

fast food restaurants *(continued)*
  if offered healthier menu options
    very likely to choose,
    2003:254
  responsible for health problems of
    obese people, **2003:**254
fat, 2004:294–95
father
  had greater influence on you (than
    mother), **2000:**150
  had positive or negative influence
    on you, **2000:**151
  have shown enough appreciation
    to, **2000:**187
  your family appreciates you
    enough (asked of fathers),
    2000:187
  your relationship today with, as
    positive or negative, **2000:**151
Favre, Brett, 2000:289, **2004:**367
fear
  feelings of
    as most important issue, **2003:**
      122, 155, 203, 284, 401, 442
  of war, **1999:**195
    as most important issue,
      2001:59, 121, 255, **2002:**9,
      70, 116, 233, 323, 359,
      2003:25, 62, 86, 122, 155,
      203, 284–85, 401, 442
    as most important issue facing
      nation 25 years from now,
      2002:116
**Federal Bureau of Investigation
  (FBI), 2005:**391
**Federal Cigarette Labeling and
  Advertising Act, 2004:**417
**Federal Communications Commis-
  sion (FCC), 2004:**61–62, 471
**Federal Emergency Management
  Agency (FEMA), 2005:**336–37,
  341–44, 346, 383–84, 389
federal government, 2002:266,
  2003:290

alternative fuels and, **2006:**114
approval ratings, **2001:**145
big government as biggest threat
  to country, **1998:**240,
  2000:360
bipartisanship in, **2002:**130
Christianity and, **2006:**256
church attendance and, **2006:**256
and Clinton, **1998:**245
Clinton and, **1998:**197
confidence in, **1998:**253, **1999:**
  49–50, 158, 226, **2000:**215–16,
  2001:56, 230, **2002:**168, 265,
  271, 281–82, **2003:**355–56,
  388, 390, **2006:**76
Democratic Party and, **1998:**232
and disaster aid, **1999:**258
dissatisfaction with
  as most important issue,
    1998:60, **1999:**195,
    2000:191, **2001:**58, 121,
    2002:10, 71, 116, 233, 323,
    360, **2003:**25, 62, 86, 122,
    155, 203, 284, 401, 443
  as most important issue facing
    nation 25 years from now,
    2002:117
and education, **2000:**241
and environment, **1999:**171,
  2001:100
and finances, **2002:**22
and healthcare, **2000:**321
ideology and, **2006:**256
immigrants and, **2001:**171,
  2002:226
individual influence on, **2001:**231
and Medicare, **2000:**321
as most important issue, **2000:**191
and NASA, **1999:**243
and nuclear defense, **2001:**181
opinion of, **1998:**229–30,
  2000:125, 216, 279,
  2001:230–31, **2003:**347–48
and parents, **1998:**190

Gore and, **1999:**57–58, 80, 116,
2000:23, 85, 143, 242, 248,
275
harmed while Senate conducts
trial of Clinton, **1998:**245
human rights and, **2005:**73
ideology and, **2004:**102
important for a president to have
experience in, **1999:**106
as important issue influencing
your vote for Congress,
2002:291
as important issue influencing
your vote for president,
2003:338–39
important president and Congress
deal with next year, **2002:**17,
171, **2003:**4
independents and, **2007:**14, 256,
367
Iraq war and, **2004:**91–92, 101–2
as issue to be addressed by next
president, **2000:**212
Kerry and, **2004:**101–2, 111–12,
383–84, 389
McCain and, **2007:**50
Middle East and, **2001:**34–35, 219
military and, **2005:**73
most critical threats and,
2004:100–101
as most important issue,
1998:60–61, **1999:**195,
2000:191, **2004:**37–38, 84–85,
156, 183, 414, **2005:**3–4, 38,
45, 99, 113, 152, 174, 198,
213, 348, 366, 421, **2006:**
138–39, 237, 288, 338,
385–86, 479
as most important issue facing
nation 25 years from now,
2002:117
as most important issue in deciding your vote for president in
2004, **2003:**416

national security and, **2005:**73
nuclear weapons and, **2005:**73
political affiliation and, **2004:**15,
38, 65, 92, 156, **2005:**1–4,
356–57, 362, **2007:**14, 81, 256,
367
president and, **2007:**3, 60–61, 90,
237–38, 305
as presidential election issue,
2000:193, 243
as priority, **1998:**225, **2000:**428,
2002:130, **2007:**3, 60–61, 90,
148–49, 237–38, 305
Reagan and, **2005:**34
Republican Party and, **1998:**224,
2002:17, **2003:**5, **2007:**14, 81,
256, 367
Republicans in Congress and,
2002:171, 291, 336
satisfaction with, **2004:**130
standard of living and, **2005:**73
teenagers and, **2004:**183, 414
terrorism and, **2005:**73
time spent on, **2004:**7
U.N. and, **2004:**101–2
weapons of mass destruction and,
2005:73
foreign aid, 2004:37–38, 155–56, 467
assessment of, **2006:**408
Bush, George W., and, **2005:**156
Congress and, **2007:**3, 60–61,
237–38, 305
economy and, **2006:**216, 222,
2007:10
as most important issue,
1998:60–61, **1999:**195,
2001:58–59, 121, 255,
2002:10, 71, 116, 233, 360,
2003:25, 62, 86, 122, 155, 203,
284–85, 401, 443, **2005:**45, 99,
113, 152, 174, 198, 213, 348,
366, 421, **2006:**138–39, 237,
288, 338, 385–86, 479,
2007:54, 442–43, 501

foreign aid, 2004 *(continued)*
  political affiliation and, **2006:**139
  president and, **2007:**3, 60–61,
    237–38, 305
  as priority, **2007:**3, 60–61,
    148–49, 237–38, 305
  spending on, **2001:**56
foreign countries, **2002:**43, **2004:**73–75
  country you consider to be Amer-
    ica's greatest enemy today
    [list], **2001:**84
  leaders of other countries have
    respect for George W. Bush,
    2002:42
  opinion of [list], **2001:**84,
    2002:52, 134–35, **2003:**56
  possession of nuclear weapons by
    as threat to U.S., **1998:**77, 180,
      2000:89, 92, 101
    as threat to world peace, **1998:**
      78–79, **2000:**89, 92, 101
  satisfaction with position of U.S.
    in the world today, **2002:**42–43
foreign trade, **2004:**58, 156
  Bush, George W., and, **2000:**242,
    248, **2005:**155
  with China, **1998:**83, 87
  free trade good or bad for U.S.,
    2000:124
  Gore and, **2000:**242, 248
  increase U.S. economic aid to
    Israel, **1999:**215
  as most important issue, **1998:**60,
    1999:194–95, **2002:**9, **2003:**
    442, **2005:**45, 99, 113, 152,
    174, 198, 213, 347, 366, 421
  positive state of economy credited
    to increase in, **2000:**206
  as presidential election issue,
    2000:19, 72, 243
  someone in your household works
    in job that depends on,
    2000:124
  See also trade deficit

Foreman, Matt, **2005:**142
Fourth of July
  think signers of Declaration of
    Independence would be
    pleased by way U.S. has turned
    out, **2001:**155
  from what country did America
    gain its independence follow-
    ing Revolutionary War [list],
    2001:155
  what event is celebrated on,
    1999:206, **2001:**155
  will attend a fireworks display,
    2001:155
  will display American flag,
    2001:155, **2002:**188
  will do something in remem-
    brance of September 11,
    2002:188
  will fire off your own fireworks,
    2001:155
  will get together with family
    members, **2001:**154, **2002:**188
  will give or attend barbecue, pic-
    nic, or cookout, **2001:**154,
    2002:188
  will watch parade, **2001:**155
The Fourth Turning, **2005:**47
Fox, Michael J., **2006:**463
Fox News Channel
  how often do you get your news
    from, **1998:**192
  trust accuracy of news from,
    1998:97
France, **2004:**73–74, **2005:**70–72,
    78–79, 128, **2006:**77, 79–80, 90,
    130–31
  as ally/enemy, **2000:**174, **2003:**99,
    340
  important U.S. restores good rela-
    tions with, **2003:**118
  and Iraq War
    main reason France opposed,
      2003:340–41

right or wrong to have opposed, **2003:**340

taking more reasonable approach than U.S., **2003:**40

U.S. can count on to support possible invasion, **2003:**39

not willing to do fair share in war on terrorism, **2003:**39

opinion of, **2001:**35, 43, 84, **2002:**52, **2003:**56, 99

think calling French foods "freedom fries" or "freedom toast" silly or expression of patriotism, **2003:**100

Franken, Al, 2003:405

"Frasier," 1998:61–63

freedoms, personal

losing because of war, as most important issue, **2001:**256, **2002:**10, 116

more or less, in year 2025, **1998:**220

See also civil liberties

Freeman, Morgan, 2001:76–77

free trade

good or bad for U.S., **2000:**124

friends, 2004:98–100, 282

all right to lie to, **1998:**238

entertaining, as favorite way of spending evening, **1998:**237, **1999:**252

importance in your life, **2003:**1

news from

accuracy of, **1998:**98

frequency of, **1998:**193

support from, to parents, **1998:**190

visiting, as favorite way of spending evening, **1998:**237, **1999:**252

"Friends," 1998:61–62

Frist, Bill, 2004:457, **2005:**37, 206, 300, 306, 310, 468, **2006:**66–67, 235–36, 477, 501–2, 531, **2007:**22, 68

Froman, Sandra S., 2005:140

fuel oil

approve of release of oil from Strategic Petroleum Reserve, **2000:**56, 107, 334

prices

Bush and, **2000:**86, 309, 320

cause you financial hardship, **2000:**55, 320

Gore and, **2000:**86, 309, 320

lower tax on in your state to deal with, **2000:**56, 106

as most important issue, **2001:** 58, 121, 255, **2002:**9, 70, 116, 233, 359, **2003:**25, 62, 86, 122, 155, 203, 401, 442

as most important issue facing nation 25 years from now, **2002:**117

what is responsible [list] for, **2000:**334

used to heat your home, **2000:**56

The Full Monty **(movie), 1998:**175

funeral directors

honesty and ethical standards of, **1999:**148, **2000:**388, **2002:**373

fur, 2002:149, **2003:**159, 178, 218, **2004:**215, 250

G

Gable, Clark, 2001:76

Gaddafi, Muammar, 2004:74

gambling, 1999:263–64, **2002:**89, **2004:**44, 122–23, 249–50

as morally acceptable, **2003:**159, 178, 218

gambling *(continued)*
need to know if presidential candidate has gambling problem,
1998:37
games
as favorite way of spending
evening, **1998:**237, **2002:**6
hobby you are particularly interested in, **2002:**7
Gandhi, Indira, 2000:141, 155,
2002:401, **2004:**514, **2005:**483
Gandhi, Mahatma, 2000:264
gangs
as worst problem facing your
community, **2000:**190
gap changes, 2004:364–65
Garamendi, John, 2003:278–79
Garcia, Jerry, 2000:265
gardening
hobby you are particularly interested in, **2002:**7
gasoline
age and, **2004:**234, **2005:**196, 470
approval ratings, **2004:**222,
2005:169, 325, 346
Bush, George H. W., and, **2006:**170
Bush, George W., and, **2004:**222,
2005:130, 155, 168–69, 325,
346, 422
business and, **2004:**222, **2006:**170
Congress and, **2005:**130, 325,
412, 422, **2007:**2, 60–61, 90,
191–92, 237–38, 305
consumers and, **2004:**148, 286
Democratic Party and, **2006:**170,
267–68, 371, 383–84, 396, 459
economy and, **2004:**343,
2006:216, 222, 429
election of 2006 and, **2006:**22,
25–26, 28, 266–68, 322,
396–97, 426–28, 455, 467
employment and, **2004:**343
finances and, **2004:**147–48,
150–51, 221–22, 233–34,

236–37, 286, 343, 359–60,
381, **2005:**195–97, 325
gender and, **2005:**196
geographic region and, **2004:**
233–34, **2005:**168, 196, 470,
2006:396, **2007:**234, 296
Hurricane Katrina and,
2005:331–32, 422
image of, **2005:**311–12, 422
income and, **2004:**148, 221, 234,
236–37, 381, 424–25, 508,
2005:126, 196, **2006:**396, 483,
2007:234
investors and, **2004:**260–61,
271–72, 343, 359–60
Iraq war and, **2004:**222
as most important issue,
2004:147–48, 246, 271–72,
424–25, **2005:**45, 93–95, 99,
113, 152, 174, 198, 213, 220,
286, 304, 321, 347, 365–66,
409–10, 421, **2007:**37–38, 54,
123–24, 216, 265, 271–73,
348–49, 410–12, 442–43,
532
OPEC and, **2004:**222
outsourcing and, **2004:**343
political affiliation and, **2004:**148,
156, 234
predictions for, **1999:**255,
2004:360, 424–25, **2007:**1
president and, **2007:**2, 60–61, 90,
191–92, 237–38, 305
prices, **2000:**56, 80–81, 86,
106–7, 189, 309, 320, 334,
2001:114–15, **2004:**130,
147–48, 150–51, 221–22,
233–37, 239–40, 260–61, 286,
343, 359–60, 381, 424–25,
492, 508, **2007:**1, 38, 51–52,
216, 233–35, 265, 296–97,
525–26, 538
country is in state of crisis
because of, **2001:**130

and driving habits, **1999:**255,
2000:168, 190
increases cause you financial
hardship, **2000:**55, 80, 106,
167, 190, 320
as issue to be addressed by
next president, **2000:**212
rise in, represents temporary
fluctuation or permanent
change, **2000:**80, 106, 167,
189
as priority, **2007:**2, 60–61, 90,
148–49, 191–92, 237–38, 305
race and, **2005:**196, 286,
2006:279, 459–60, 484
Saudi Arabia and, **2004:**222
spending and, **2004:**148, 233,
235–37, 286, 492, 508
Y2K problems and, **1999:**246
See also energy; oil
Gates, Bill, 2000:34, **2004:**513,
2005:482–83, **2006:**536
admiration of, **1998:**1, 154,
1999:242, **2000:**431,
2002:400, **2003:**454
opinion of, **1998:**53, 155, 233,
1999:46–47, 128, **2000:**148
Gates Foundation, 2004:109
gay marriage, 2006:208–9, 219–21,
266–68, 448–50
See also homosexuals and
homosexuality
Geffen, David, 2007:94
Gehrig, Lou, 1999:256, **2001:**83
gender
abortion and, **2004:**170,
2005:175, 245–46, 443
affirmative action and, **2005:**288
agnosticism and, **2004:**511
Albright, Madeleine, and, **2006:**537
animal testing and, **2004:**215
approval ratings, **2004:**184–85,
2005:145, **2006:**53, 215, 316,
348, 530

atheism and, **2004:**511
Biden, Joe, and, **2007:**124
blogs and, **2005:**98
Bush, George W., and, **2006:**215,
316, 348, 530, **2007:**253
Bush, Laura, and, **2006:**53, 537
business and, **2005:**415
CBS News National Guard story
and, **2004:**394
cheating and, **2004:**192
Christmas and, **2004:**461,
2005:436
church and, **2004:**303–4, 332–33,
512, **2005:**114, **2007:**150
Clark, Wesley, and, **2004:**5–6,
2007:124
Clinton, Hillary, and, **2005:**80–82,
2006:274–75, 301, 304–5, 537,
2007:21, 47–48, 124–25,
141–43, 227–29, 253, 398–99,
419, 423–24, 471–72, 547
clothing and, **2007:**434
Congress and, **2005:**145, **2007:**91
creationism and, **2004:**463,
2006:231
crime and, **2004:**478,
2005:170–72, 437
Dean, Howard, and, **2004:**5–6
death penalty and, **2004:**453–54,
495–96, **2005:**185–86, 457,
2006:225
Democratic Party and, **2004:**5–6,
130
and discrimination, **2003:**360–62
domestic problems and, **2005:**368
driving age and, **2005:**106
drugs and, **2005:**170–72, 407,
2007:457–58
economy and, **2004:**69
education and, **2005:**67
Edwards, John, and, **2007:**21,
47–48, 124, 127, 227–29, 419
election(s) and, **2004:**95–97
election of 2000 and, **2007:**253

gender *(continued)*
    election of 2004 and, **2007:**253
    election of 2006 and, **2006:**73–74,
      253, 378, 471–72
    election of 2008 and, **2006:**301,
      2007:21, 47–48, 77–78, 106–9,
      124–25, 127, 141–43, 187,
      227–29, 253, 321–22, 398–99,
      419, 423–24, 462–63, 471–72,
      546–47
    electronics and, **2005:**480
    employment and, **2004:**25, 182,
      345, **2005:**135, 153–55,
      287–88, 307–8, 336, 340
    entrepreneurship and, **2005:**135
    environment and, **2007:**47–48, 127
    euthanasia and, **2005:**179–80
    evolution and, **2004:**464, **2006:**231
    family values and, **2007:**546
    finances and, **2005:**95
    find negative gender stereotypes
      in movies offensive, **2001:**126
    friendship and, **2004:**99
    gambling and, **2004:**123
    gasoline and, **2005:**196
    Gingrich, Newt, and, **2007:**187
    global warming and, **2007:**106
    Gonzales, Alberto, and, **2005:**246
    Gore, Al, and, **2006:**321,
      2007:124, 227–29, 253
    guns and, **2004:**472, **2005:**140,
      438–39, **2006:**439
    happiness and, **2004:**1
    health and, **2004:**468
    healthcare and, **2004:**51, **2005:**46,
      67, 170–71, 442, 454,
      2007:47–48, 61, 91
    health insurance and, **2005:**14
    homosexuality and, **2004:**505,
      2005:142, **2007:**232
    ideology and, **2004:**103
    image by, **2006:**499–500, 537,
      2007:141–43, 423–24, 462–63,
      465, 545

    income and, **2004:**103, **2006:**326
    independents and, **2004:**130
    Internet and, **2004:**22, 109
    investment and, **2004:**78, 315
    Iraq war and, **2004:**198–99, 400,
      2006:403, **2007:**47–48,
      185–86, 206–7, 352
    Jolie, Angelina, and, **2006:**537
    junk food and, **2004:**191
    Kerry, John, and, **2007:**124, 253
    labor unions and, **2005:**323
    law enforcement and, **2005:**420
    lawsuits and, **2005:**67
    mad cow disease and, **2004:**9
    manufactured goods and,
      2007:456
    marriage amendment and,
      2004:86–87
    marriage and, **2005:**67, 142
    McCain, John, and, **2007:**187
    Medicaid and, **2005:**14
    Medicare and, **2004:**38–39, 110,
      2005:14
    Middle East and, **2006:**123
    military and, **2006:**403
    money and, **2005:**162, **2006:**513
    morality and, **2004:**215, 250,
      2007:47–48, 239
    movies and, **2006:**535
    Nader, Ralph, and, **2007:**253
    national defense and, **2007:**391
    national security and, **2005:**368
    news and, **2005:**369
    New Year and, **2006:**537
    nuclear energy plants and,
      2005:161
    nuclear weapons and, **2005:**292
    Obama, Barack, and, **2007:**21,
      47–48, 124, 227–29, 321–22,
      398–99, 419, 462–63, 547
    Patriot Act and, **2004:**94
    patriotism and, **2005:**62, 267
    Pelosi, Nancy, and, **2006:**499
    personal lives and, **2006:**143

political affiliation and, **2004:**5–6, **2006:**73–74, 253, 378, 471–72
president and, **2007:**77–78, 91
priorities by, **2007:**61, 91
reading and, **2005:**203
Reid, Harry, and, **2006:**500
religion and, **2004:**70, 120, 506, 511–12, **2005:**132, 234, 447, 463, **2006:**260, 493, **2007:**260
Republican Party and, **2004:**130
Rice, Condoleezza, and, **2005:**116, **2006:**537
Richardson, Bill, and, **2007:**124
Romney, Mitt, and, **2007:**187
September 11, 2001, terrorist attacks and, **2007:**395
sex offender registries and, **2005:**212
smoking and, **2004:**79, 307, **2006:**302
Social Security and, **2004:**110
society and, **2007:**353
spending and, **2004:**461, **2005:**86–87, 436
stem cell research and, **2006:**298
stress and, **2004:**182
suicide and, **2004:**216, 281, **2005:**179–80
Supreme Court and, **2005:**244–46, 259, 363, 370–71, 400–401, 405
taxes and, **2005:**67
teenagers and, **2004:**183, 191–92, 216, 242, 369, 490, **2006:**70
terrorism and, **2006:**8
Thatcher, Margaret, and, **2006:**537
tolerance and, **2004:**70
U.S., satisfaction with, **2006:**81–82, 238
veterans and, **2004:**418
weight and, **2004:**148–49, 331–32, 486–87, **2005:**296, 305–6, 440, **2006:**103–4, 488

Winfrey, Oprah, and, **2006:**537
women's position and, **2004:**130
World War II and, **2005:**292
See also gender gap
See also women
gender gap
Bush, George W., and, **2004:**95
cheating and, **2004:**192
church and, **2004:**304, 506
elections and, **2004:**95–97
gay marriage and, **2004:**369
junk food and, **2004:**191
morality and, **2004:**506
and most important issues, **2004:**183
politics and, **2004:**506
religion and, **2004:**506
school and, **2004:**242
sex, premarital, and, **2004:**490
suicide and, **2004:**216
women, position of, and, **2004:**130
General Motors Corp.
favor company or union in United Auto Workers strike, **1998:**194
genetic information, 2001:162
Geneva Conventions, 2006:393
geographic region
abortion and, **2006:**307
agnosticism and, **2004:**511
approval ratings by, **2006:**215, 316, 530
atheism and, **2004:**511
automobile ownership and, **2004:**441
Bible and, **2006:**210, **2007:**230–31
Brownback, Sam, and, **2007:**344
Bush, George W., and, **2006:**215, 316, 530
church and, **2004:**512, **2005:**114
creationism and, **2004:**463
drugs and, **2005:**163, 408

Gere, Richard, 2000:99,
2001:76–77
Germany, 2004:73–74, 228
better off since fall of Berlin Wall,
1999:231, 2000:4
and Iraq, 2003:39–40
opinion of, 2000:174, 380,
2001:35, 43, 84, 2002:52,
2003:39, 56, 99, 118
ghosts
believe in, 2000:359
Giambi, Jason, 2004:144, 487
Gibson, Mel, 2000:98, 2001:76,
2006:507–8, 536
Gillespie, Ed, 2004:210, 358
Gilmore, Jim, 2007:222, 326
Gingrich, Newt, 2007:187, 222, 239,
247
approval ratings, 1998:175
church attendance and,
2007:113–14, 187–88, 326
election of 2008 and, 2007:22,
68, 101, 103–4, 113–14,
117–18, 129–31, 154–55,
172–74, 186–88, 198, 214,
222, 239, 242–44, 246–48,
263–64, 308–10, 313–14,
326
likely to support, 1998:65, 177,
227
opinion of, 1998:28–29, 64, 155,
232, 252
religion and, 2007:113–14,
187–88, 326
Ginsburg, William, 1998:181
Girl Scouts, 1998:190
Giuliani, Rudy, 2003:454,
2004:354, 456–57, 2006:66–67,
234–36, 477, 501–2, 531–32, 536,
2007:50
admiration of, 2001:278,
2002:400
chances of winning nomination,
2007:238

church attendance and,
2007:113–14, 187–88, 253–54,
326, 548
conservatives and, 2007:186–87,
253–54, 294–96, 548
Democratic Party and, 2007:215,
253–54, 346
in election match-ups,
2007:68–69, 130, 136, 155,
198, 213, 244, 253–54,
267–69, 275–76, 285–86, 302,
310, 320–22, 397, 487–88,
505–6, 536, 538–40
familiarity with, 2007:225–26,
367–69, 388–89, 550
image of, 2007:22–23, 49–50,
55–56, 71–72, 84–86, 103–4,
118, 130–31, 136–38, 155,
162–63, 214–15, 223–24, 226,
247, 256–58, 281–83, 345–46,
362, 397–98, 424–26, 452,
462, 541, 551
independents and, 2007:215,
253–54, 346
liberals and, 2007:186–87,
253–54, 294–96, 548
moderates and, 2007:186–87,
253–54, 294–96, 548
political affiliation and, 2007:215,
253–54, 346
political ideology and,
2007:117–18, 186–87, 253–54,
294–96, 548
religion and, 2007:113–14, 187–88,
253–54, 326, 424–26, 548
Republican Party and, 2007:215,
253–54, 294–96, 346
Gladiator, 2001:73
Glass, Fred, 2005:414–15
Glass, Stephen, 1998:194
Glenn, John, 1998:155, 2004:42
admiration of, 1998:154,
1999:242
return to space, 1998:158, 230

globalization, **2004:**40, 79, 131, 508–9

global warming, 2004:141, 160–61, **2006:**140–42, 161–62, 164, 166
gender and, **2007:**106
government and, **2007:**146–48, 177
opinion of, **2001:**90, **2002:**81–82
political affiliation and, **2007:**175
worry about, **1999:**166, **2000:**316, **2001:**90, **2002:**77, 81, 113

God, 2004:462–63, 496–97, **2005:**463

The Godfather **(movie), 1998:**187

gold, **2004:**314–15

Goldberg, Whoopi, 2000:98, **2001:**76

Goldman, Ronald, 2004:54

Goldwater, Barry, 2004:95–96, 279–80, 356–57
Gallup analysis of gender gap, Johnson vs., **2000:**159

golf, 2004:44, 367, 489, **2006:**135, **2007:**24
as favorite sport to watch, **1998:**237, **2000:**136
how often do you play, **2000:**108
professional
approve of decision to invite Annika Sorenstam to compete in PGA golf tournament this weekend, **2003:**174
fan of, **2000:**108, **2001:**41, 81, **2003:**174
greatest player today [list], **2000:**108
like to see more women compete with men in golf tournaments, **2003:**174
top, know name of, **2000:**34
which course [list] would you choose to play on, **2000:**108

Gone With the Wind **(movie), 1998:**187

Gonzales, Alberto, 2005:211, 246

Gonzales v. Carhart, **2007:**248

González, Elían, 1999:244, **2000:**11, 31–32, 103–4, 113, 128–32, 137–38

Good Will Hunting **(movie), 1998:**175

Gordon, Jeff, 2001:142

Gore, Al, 2000:57, **2005:**183
and abortion, **2000:**242, 248, 258, 275
admiration of, **2000:**431, **2002:**400, **2003:**455, **2006:**536
agrees with you on issues, **1999:**65, **2000:**83, 248, 257, 276, 332
approval ratings, **2000:**262, **2006:**95–96
and Bush, George W., **2002:**104
and campaign finance reform, **2000:**86
can name him as your party's nominee, **2000:**90
cares about needs of people like you, **1998:**203, **1999:**59, 65, 81, 102, 105, **2000:**21, 83, 142, 248, 257, 276, 332, 358
cares about needs of the poor, **1999:**105
characteristics of, **1998:**203, **1999:**82, 102, **2000:**22, 27, 37, 49, 57, 332, 358, 423, **2002:**90
and Clinton, Bill, **1998:**126, 131, 199, 247, 249, **1999:**58–60, **2000:**261, 352
and Clinton, Hillary, **2006:**332–33
as conservative or liberal, **2000:**248, 277
conventions and, **2004:**279–80, 312, 356–57
and crime, **1999:**80, **2000:**23, 86, 143, 262
and death penalty, **2000:**202–3
and debates, **2000:**326, 332, 336, 345

and defense, **2000:**248, 258, 275, 293

Democratic convention acceptance speech rated, **2000:**269

Democratic Party and, **2007:**346, 348

and economy, **1999:**116, **2000:**23, 85, 143, 242, 248, 258, 274–75

and education, **1999:**58, 80, 116, **2000:**23, 85, 143, 242, 248, 258, 262, 275, 309, 357

as effective manager, as important for a president, **1999:**105

election of 1988 and, **2004:**43, **2007:**355

election of 2000 and, **1999:**101, **2000:**78, 182, 250, **2004:**6, 41, 87–88, 315–16, 337–38, **2007:** 101, 253, 269, 354–55, 459

election of 2004 and, **2001:**192, **2002:**104, 396, **2004:**5

now that he has dropped out, Democrats have better chance of winning the presidency in 2004, **2002:**396

election of 2008 and, **2004:**456–57, **2007:**93

and Elían González situation, **2000:**129, 131

and employment, **2000:**242, 248

ensuring that next generation can live better than parents, **2000:**86

ensuring that poor person can get ahead, **2000:**86

and environment, **1999:**58, 80, **2000:**23, 85, 196, 242, 248, **2006:**141

expectations of, **2000:**195–96, **2001:**247, **2002:**104

familiarity, **1999:**63, **2000:**34, 90, **2004:**83–84

and finances, **1999:**57, 80, 116, **2000:**24, 27, 36, 49, 242, 248, 258, 262, 275, 309, 357

and foreign affairs, **1999:**57–58, 80, 116, **2000:**23, 85, 143, 242, 248, 275

Gallup analysis of closeness of popular vote, **2000:**367

and gasoline and fuel oil prices, **2000:**86, 309, 320

gender and, **2000:**197, **2004:**96, **2007:**124, 227–29, 253

Gallup analysis of gender gap, versus Bush, **2000:**159, 166

as good husband and father, **1999:**59–60

and government surveillance, **2006:**33

and guns, **1999:**80, **2000:**23, 85, 143, 242, 248, 258, 275

has best chance of beating Republican candidate, **2000:**27, 36, 49

has new ideas, **1999:**102, **2000:**22, 49

has vision for country's future, **1999:**102, 105, **2000:**22, 27, 36, 83, 143, 248, 257, 276, 332

and healthcare, **1999:**80, 102, **2000:**23, 85, 143, 242, 248, 258, 275, 309

and homelessness, **2000:**24

as honest and trustworthy, **1998:**202, **1999:**59–60, 82, **2000:**83, 248, 257, 276, 332, 354, 358

image of, **2004:**6, 323, **2006:**320–21, 504–7, 532

important that he is elected president, **2000:**223

independents and, **2007:**346, 348

interested in hearing a live speech by, **2001:**80

investigations of, **1998:**167, 204, **1999:**58–59, **2000:**198

lacks vision, **1999:**58–59

and Lieberman, **2000:**253–54, **2004:**273

Gore, Al *(continued)*
likely to support, **1998:**66, 177,
180, 227–28, 228, **1999:**57,
60, 72, 84, 88–89, 99, 101,
118–19, **2000:**9–10, 17, 26,
29, 33, 49, 53–54, 62, 68–69,
75, 77–78, 82–83, 105,
114–15, 138–39, 161, 181,
197–98, 223, 231–32, 235–36,
269–70, 352, 423, **2001:**193,
2002:90, 355
and Medicare, **1999:**80, **2000:**24,
85, 143, 242, 248, 258, 275,
309, 357
and Middle East, **2000:**343
and morality, **2000:**85, 262
most like to have dinner with,
2000:57
and nuclear defense system,
2000:228
opinion of, **1998:**27, 65, 155, 203,
252, **1999:**45, 58–59, 65, 81,
96, 101–2, 105, 113,
2000:21–22, 27, 36, 49, 83,
142–43, 169, 206, 248, 257,
276, 332, 354, 357–58
political affiliation and, **2006:**332,
502, 532, **2007:**346, 348
and poverty, **2000:**24
and prescription drugs, **2000:**309
and privacy, **2000:**86
and problems of raising children,
1999:80, **2000:**24, 85, 309
puts country's interests ahead of
his own, **2000:**143, 277
qualifications of, **1998:**159, 203,
250, **1999:**59, 65, 102, 105–6,
116, **2000:**21, 49, 83, 115, 237,
247, 256, 303, 353
and race relations, **2000:**258
as reformer, **2000:**49
Republican Party and, **2007:**346,
348
satisfaction with, **2000:**9, 15

shares your values, **1998:**202, **1999:**
81, **2000:**21, 83, 142, 248, 256,
276, 281, 332, 358
and Social Security, **1999:**80,
2000:24, 85, 143, 242, 248,
258, 275, 309, 357
and stock market, **2000:**355
swing voters and, **2004:**283
and taxes, **1999:**58, 80, **2000:**23,
85, 143, 242, 248, 258, 275,
288, 309, 357
in touch with average voter,
2000:357
and town meeting, **1999:**101
understands complex issues, **2000:**
22, 143, 248, 257, 277, 332, 357
use Internet to visit his Web site,
2000:397
and USS *Cole* situation, **2000:**343
as vice presidential candidate,
2004:273, 314
voted for, **2000:**78, 397
who really won the election, Bush
or Gore, **2001:**20
and women, **2000:**85
Gore, Tipper, 2000:431, **2002:**400,
2003:455
Gosford Park (movie), **2002:**79
Goss, Porter, 2005:441
government
age and, **2004:**278
blacks and, **2007:**179–80, 316
Bush, George W., and, **2005:**156,
374–75, 425
business and, **2005:**415–16, 421
church and, **2004:**447, 505–7
civil liberties and, **2005:**374
confidence in, **2004:**163–64,
2005:378
Congress and, **2005:**412
conservatives and, **2007:**8
economy and, **2007:**10
education and, **2004:**164
food and, **2007:**333

global warming and, **2007:**
146–48, 177
healthcare and, **2004:**459, **2006:**487
Hispanics and, **2007:**179–80, 316
housing and, **2007:**537
ideology and, **2004:**269, 447
image of, **2005:**311–12, 422
independents and, **2007:**8, 16–17,
54–55, 410–11
and Iraq, **2004:**117, 166, 173,
177–79, 210, 218–19, 261–63,
337, 510, **2005:**11–13, 234–35,
278–79, 327, 388, 445–46,
466–67, 471, **2006:**21, 47, 413,
2007:56–57, 393–94, 405
liberals and, **2007:**8
minorities and, **2004:**278
moderates and, **2007:**8
morality and, **2004:**469–72
as most important issue, **2004:**20,
37–38, 113, 147, 155–56, 467,
2005:18, 45, 99, 113, 152, 174,
198, 213, 220, 348, 366, 421,
2006:138–39, 162, 237, 279,
288, 338, 384–86, 435, 479,
528, **2007:**54–55, 123–24, 216,
271–73, 315–16, 349, 410–12,
442–444
officials, can be trusted, **2002:**199
political affiliation and, **2004:**56,
156, 269, 278, **2005:**356–57,
360, 374–75, 412, **2006:**139,
398–99, 435, 446, 528
political ideology and, **2007:**8
power of, **2004:**56
president and, **2004:**269–70,
2007:3, 16–17, 60–61, 191–92,
305
as priority, **2007:**3, 16–17, 60–61,
148–49, 191–92, 305
race and, **2005:**341–44, 394,
2007:316
recommend as career for young
man, **1998:**238

recommend as career for young
woman, **2001:**109
religion and, **2004:**177–78, 447,
505–7, **2005:**412
role of, **2005:**356–57, 374–75,
2006:446
satisfaction with, **2004:**20, 56,
155
sex and, **2004:**491
size of, **2004:**56
social problems and, **2004:**470–71
values and, **2004:**469–72
whites and, **2007:**316
See also federal government; local
government; state government
government surveillance
attentiveness to, **2006:**15–16,
33–34, 65, 198
election of 2006 and, **2006:**22,
25–26, 28
as most important issue, **2006:**22,
25–26, 28
news and, **2006:**199
wiretapping, **2006:**16, 33–34,
65–66, 82–84, 393
See also intelligence system
governors, state, 2006:519
honesty and ethical standards of,
1999:148, **2000:**388,
2003:422–23
as presidential preparation,
2003:375
**Graduated Driver Licensing
(GDL) laws, 2005:**106
The Graduate **(movie), 1998:**187
Graham, Billy, 2004:230, 233,
513–14, **2005:**230–32, 482–83
admiration of, **1998:**1, 154,
1999:242, **2000:**264, 431,
2001:278, **2002:**399–400,
2003:454
Graham, Bob
likely to support, **2003:**16, 135,
190, 215–16, 277, 323, 335,

Graham, Bob *(continued)*
374–75, 382, 417, 432–33,
446–47
opinion of, **2003:**306
as second choice for nomination,
2003:335
Grammy Awards, 2004:62
Grant, Cary, 2001:76
Grant, Ulysses S., 2000:59, 410
Grantski, Ron, 2004:496
The Grateful Dead, 2000:265
Gravel, Mike, 2007:370
Great Britain. *See* United Kingdom
Great Depression
as most important event in twentieth century, **2002:**175
The Great Gatsby **(Fitzgerald),**
1999:267
Greece, 2000:174
Greek Orthodox, 2004:118
greenhouse effect. *See* global
warming
greenhouse gases
favor imposing mandatory controls on, **2003:**93
The Green Mile **(movie), 2000:**98
Green Party, 2004:87, 349,
378–79
Greenspan, Alan, 2005:172–73,
2007:204–5
confidence in, **2002:**108, **2003:**123
on employment, **2004:**65, 79, 110,
152
on globalization, **2004:**40
on interest rates, **2004:**235
nomination of, **2004:**255
on oil, **2004:**424–25
opinion of, **1998:**155, 253,
1999:47, **2000:**206, 262
on spending, **2004:**379
on stock market bubble, **2004:**110
Gregory, Winton D., 2004:13
Grenada, invasion of, 2004:231
Gretzky, Wayne, 2000:1

Griffey, Ken, Jr., 1998:226,
2000:289, **2001:**83
Griffin, Michael, 2005:298–99
Grisham, John, 1999:267
grocery industry
overall view of, **2001:**200,
2002:240, **2003:**289
Guantanamo Bay captives
treatment of, **2002:**34–35
Gulf War. *See* Persian Gulf War
gun(s), 2004:15, 130, 170, 442–43,
464–65, 472–73, **2006:**63–65,
438–40, 480
age and, **2005:**140, 438–39
on airplanes, **2005:**140
anyone close to you ever been
shot, **1999:**168
anywhere else on your property,
2002:328
arming occupations with, **2005:**
140
availability of
and Littleton shootings,
1999:179
as most important issue,
2000:192
and school shootings and violence, **2001:**87
causes of violence with, **2000:**157
in entertainment, **2001:**87
ever fired, **1999:**168
gender and, **2005:**140, 438–39
geographic region and, **2005:**140,
438
have in house, **1999:**167,
2000:156–57, 327–28,
2001:235, **2002:**328
ideology and, **2005:**141
in judicial system, **2005:**140
law enforcement and, **2000:**20,
2005:420
and Littleton shootings, **1999:**192
as most important issue, **2001:**59,
121, 256, **2005:**99, 175, 213

ownership of, **2000:**157, 328,
2005:140–41, 438
political affiliation and, **2005:**141,
438–39
race and, **2005:**438
salesmen, honesty rating, **1999:**148
satisfaction with, **2005:**20, 22, 39,
2007:30–32, 167
in schools, **2005:**140
violent groups at school and,
1999:189
gun control
allow local governments to sue
gun manufacturers to recover
costs of gun violence,
1999:208
background checks for buyers at
gun shows, **1999:**196
ban importing of high-capacity
ammunition clips, **1999:**201, 208
ban possession of handguns
except by police and author-
ized persons, **2002:**327–28
better gun control could prevent
another incident like Littleton
shootings, **1999:**192
Bush, George W., and, **1999:**66,
81, **2000:**24, 85, 143, 242, 248,
258, 275
Congress and, **2002:**171, 291, 336
Democratic Party and, **1999:**196
Gore and, **1999:**80, **2000:**23, 85,
143, 242, 248, 258, 275
hold parents legally responsible if
children commit crimes with
parents' guns, **1999:**201,
2000:127
impose lifetime ban on gun ownership for juveniles convicted
of felony, **1999:**201
laws covering sale of firearms
should be more strict,
1999:196, 216, **2000:**20, 127,
157, **2002:**327

mandatory prison sentences for
felons who commit crimes
with guns, **1999:**200
as most important issue,
1998:60–61, **1999:**195,
2002:10, 71, 116, 360,
2003:25, 62, 87, 443
in community, **2000:**190
as most important issue facing
nation 25 years from now,
2002:117
movement
agree with goals of, **2000:**119
impact of, **2000:**119
no restrictions on owning guns,
1998:178, **1999:**177
as priority, **1998:**236, **2000:**212,
2002:171
raise minimum age for handgun
possession to 21 years,
1999:201
registration of all firearms,
1999:201
registration of all handguns,
2000:20
Republican Party and, **1999:**196
safety locks required with
new handgun purchases,
1999:201
satisfaction with, **2001:**29
stricter gun law enforcement,
2000:20
for teenagers, **1999:**173
as voting issue, **1999:**132, 196,
2000:19, 72, 157, 193, 242,
281, **2002:**291
Gwynn, Tony, 1998:226,
2006:529
gymnastics, 2004:44, 489,
2007:24
as favorite sport to watch,
1998:237, **2000:**136
as favorite Summer Olympic
event, **2000:**307

H

Hadley, Stephen, **2007:**37
Hagel, Chuck, **2004:**440, 504,
    2005:300, 310, 315, **2006:**477,
    531, **2007:**222, 326, 344
  church attendance and, **2007:**326
Hagelin, John, **2000:**397
Halloween, **2000:**358–59, **2001:**244
Hamilton, Lee, **2006:**513–16
Hamm, Mia, **2004:**368
ham radio
  hobby you are particularly inter-
    ested in, **2002:**7
Hanks, Tom, **2000:**98, **2001:**76,
  2006:507
Hanson, Bill, **2004:**370
happiness, **2004:**1–2
  how happy would you say you
    are, **2000:**339
  outlook for U.S. for next twenty
    years as optimistic, **2000:**339
  See also satisfaction
"Hard Copy"
  how often do you get your news
    from, **1998:**193
  trust accuracy of news from,
    1998:98
Harding, Warren
  as worst president, **2000:**59
Harken Energy Corporation
  Bush and, **2002:**197
Harkin, Tom, **2007:**355
Harris, Fred, **2004:**42
Harris, Katherine, **2000:**390,
  2004:315
Harry, Prince, **2002:**163
Harry Potter books, **2000:**214
Hart, Gary, **2003:**16, **2007:**101, 269,
  355, 459
Harvard University, **1999:**219,
  2003:299
  School of Public Health,
    2004:361

Hastert, Dennis, **1999:**46, **2000:**34,
  2001:186, **2002:**296
Hatch, Orrin
  likely to support, **1999:**71, 99,
    117–19, **2000:**7–8, 26, 28
hate crimes, **1999:**66, 154
Hawaii, **2002:**160
Hayworth, J. D., **2005:**429,
  2007:178
health
  age and, **2004:**468, 476–77
  alcohol and, **2004:**476, 483,
    2006:311
  alcoholic beverages and,
    2007:328
  community and, **2004:**476
  current
    mental/emotional, **2001:**260
    physical, **2001:**259, **2002:**4
    satisfaction with, **1998:**137
    you have been sick with short-
      term illness in past thirty
      days, **2001:**260
    you have long-term medical
      condition, illness, or dis-
      ease, **2001:**260
    you have physical disability
      that limits your activity,
      2001:260
  Democratic Party and,
    2007:518–20, 522
  diet and, **2004:**191
  drink alcoholic beverages, how
    often, **2002:**5
  education and, **2004:**475
  emergence of deadly new
    disease by year 2025,
    1998:220
  exercise and, **2004:**191, 482–83,
    2005:450, **2006:**489
  gender and, **2004:**468
  geographic region and, **2004:**476,
    2007:506
  healthcare and, **2005:**442

Hurricane Katrina and, **2006:**345, 354

importance of, **2003:**1

income and, **2004:**475

independents and, **2007:**518–20, 522

of Kennedy, John F., **2004:**403

of Kerry, John, **2004:**404

mental/emotional, **2004:**216–17, 468, 475–77

current, **2001:**260

how many days during past month did poor mental or emotional health keep you from your usual activities, **2001:**260

how many days during past month was your mental or emotional health not good, **2001:**260

as most important issue, **2005:**175, 213

most urgent health problem facing country at this time [list], **2003:**402

physical

current, **2001:**259, **2002:**4

how many days during past month did poor physical health keep you from your usual activities, **2001:**259

how many days during past month was your physical health not good, **2001:**259

more or less health and physical well-being in year 2025, **1998:**220

political affiliation and, **2004:**476, **2007:**518–20, 522

race and, **2004:**18–19, 291

of Reagan, Ronald, **2004:**232, 404

Republican Party and, **2007:**518–20, 522

satisfaction with, **2003:**360, **2004:**18–19, 100

current, **1998:**137

smoked cigarettes in past week, **2002:**4–5

smoking and, **2004:**417, 468, 476, 483, **2005:**302

staying healthy as biggest challenge you face today, **2000:**192

surveys of, **2004:**467–68, 475–77, 482–83

teenagers and, **2004:**149

total exercise index, **2002:**4

vaccinations and, **2004:**425–26

whites and, **2007:**506

See also disease; healthcare; weight

Health Affairs, 2004:51

Health and Human Services, Department of, 2004:417

healthcare

age and, **2004:**177, 477, **2005:**66, 156, 442, 454, 470, **2007:**47, 91, 182–83, 533

approval ratings, **2002:**92, **2004:**7, 49–50, 450, **2005:**15–16, 19, 27, 325

assessment of, **2007:**181–83, 516

availability of, **2004:**458–59

blacks and, **2007:**307–8, 316

Bradley and, **1999:**102

Bush, George W., and, **1999:**81, **2000:**24, 85, 143, 242, 248, 258, 275, 309, **2001:**8–9, 22, 105–6, **2002:**27, **2004:**7, 21, 29, 49–50, 104, 109–12, 301–2, 321–22, 374–75, 381–84, 389, 398–99, 409–10, 419–21, 432, 445, 450, 469, 498–99, **2005:**3–4, 15–16, 19, 27, 29, 31–32, 37, 39, 52, 65–67, 130, 156–57, 325

in Canada, **2004:**26–27

Clark, Wesley, and, **2004:**31

healthcare *(continued)*

Clinton, Bill, and, **2005:**73, **2007:**38, 514

Clinton, Hillary, and, **2007:**46–48, 287–89, 329–31, 432–33, 469–71, 514

Clinton and, **1999:**44

companies in lawsuit to recover federal health costs, **1999:**277

confidence in, **1998:**182, **1999:**209, **2000:**209, **2001:**149, **2002:**184, **2003:**205–6, **2004:**225, **2005:**201, **2006:**233

Congress and, **2002:**27, 291, 312, 336, **2005:**3–4, 65–67, 130, 412

costs, **2003:**4–5, **2004:**10, 21, 27, 51–52, 174–75, 177, 207, 304–5, 458–59, 467, 481–82, **2006:**201–2, 249, 481–84, 486

as most important issue, **2001:**121, **2002:**10, 70, 116, 233, 359, **2003:**25, 62, 86, 122, 155, 203, 284, 401, 443

coverage, rated, **2003:**403

Dean, Howard, and, **2004:**31, 33

Democratic Party and, **1998:**224, **2001:**211, **2003:**5

Democrats in Congress and, **2002:**27, 291, 312, 336

discrimination in, **2004:**290–91

economy and, **2006:**216, 222, **2007:**10

education and, **2007:**308

Edwards, John, and, **2004:**31

election of 2004 and, **2004:**31, 33, 41, 109–12, 115–16, 170, 299–302, 321–22, 374–75, 381–84, 389, 398–99, 407, 409–10, 419–21, 431–32, 445, 469, 498–99

election of 2008 and, **2007:**46–48, 50, 255–56, 287–89, 329–31,

432–33, 466–67, 469–71, 479–80, 527–28, 543

gender and, **2004:**51, **2005:**46, 67, 170–71, 442, 454, **2007:**47–48, 61, 91

geographic region and, **2005:**157, 470

Gore and, **1999:**80, 102, **2000:**23, 85, 143, 242, 248, 258, 275, 309

government and, **1998:**236, **2000:**318, 321, **2002:**378–79, **2003:**403, **2004:**27, 459, **2006:**487

in Great Britain, **2004:**26–27

Hispanics and, **2007:**307–8, 316

image of, **2005:**311, 422

income and, **2004:**51, 305, **2005:**454, **2006:**483, 486, **2007:**308, 533

as issue to be addressed by next president, **2000:**212

Kerry, John, and, **2004:**31, 33, 41, 109–12, 301–2, 321–22, 374–75, 381–84, 389, 398–99, 409–10, 419–21, 432, 445, 469, 498–99

Lieberman, Joe, and, **2004:**33

medical mistakes happened to you recently, **2000:**102

as most important issue, **1998:**60–61, **1999:**195, **2000:**191, **2001:**58, 255, **2002:**323, **2004:**246, 381–82, 387, 414, 467, **2005:**18, 43, 45–46, 93–95, 98–99, 113, 148, 152, 174, 198, 213, 220, 223, 348, 365–66, 409–10, 421, 431, **2006:**2–3, 36, 129–30, 138–39, 162, 167, 201–2, 222, 237, 250, 279, 288, 293, 337–38, 383–86, 435, 479, 481–84, 528, **2007:**37–38, 54–55, 123–26,

216, 255–56, 271–73, 315–16,
348–49, 410–12, 442–43,
479–80, 501, 521–22, 527–28,
532, 543
in community, **2000:**190, 192
as most important issue facing
nation 25 years from now,
2002:116
news reports on, **2002:**293
parents and, **2007:**533
plans for, **2007:**514
political affiliation and,
2004:15–16, 38, 51, 127, 156,
301–2, 375, 387, 407, 431–32,
459, **2006:**54, 125–26, 139,
155–56, 267–68, 370–71,
383–84, 389–91, 426–27, 435,
455, 459–61, 486–87,
500–501, 528
poor
as most important issue, **2001:**
121, **2002:**10, 70, 116, 233,
359, **2003:**25, 62, 86, 122,
155, 203, 284, 401, 443
as serious problem for country,
2000:316
predictions on, **1998:**219–20
president and, **2007:**2, 16–17,
60–61, 90–92, 191–92,
237–38, 305
as priority, **1998:**235, **2000:**428,
2001:8–9, **2002:**130, **2007:**2,
16–17, 60–61, 90–92, 148–49,
191–92, 237–38, 305
quality of, rated, **2002:**378,
2003:403
race and, **2004:**290–91, 304–5,
2005:136, **2006:**279, 459–61,
484, **2007:**307–8, 316
reform of, **1999:**102, **2000:**321
versus maintenance of current
system, **2003:**403
Republican Party and, **1998:**224,
2001:211, **2002:**376, **2003:**5

Republicans in Congress and,
2002:291, 312, 336
retirement and, **2004:**466
satisfaction with, **1999:**137,
2000:204, 312, **2001:**29–30,
2002:378, **2003:**403, **2004:**21,
26–27, 109–10, 130, 458–59
smoking and, **2005:**442
in state of crisis, **2002:**378,
2003:403
State of the Union address and,
2005:73, **2006:**45, **2007:**38
teenagers and, **2004:**414
and voting
Congressional, **1998:**217, 225,
1999:131, **2002:**291, 312
presidential, **1999:**69, **2000:**18,
72, 192, 242, 281,
2003:338–39, 416
swing states and,
2004:374–75
weight and, **2005:**442
whites and, **2007:**307–8, 316
worry about, **2001:**59, 66, 113,
2002:118, 219–20, **2003:**127,
2004:10, 26–27, 64, 120,
126–27, 147, 159, 174–75,
177, 207, 458–59
Y2K problem and, **1999:**158, 247
healthcare industry
honesty in, **2004:**485
image of, **2004:**361, 407
overall view of, **2001:**201,
2002:240, **2003:**290
health insurance, 1999:137,
2000:312, 321, **2004:**40, 304–5,
344, 471, 481–82, **2005:**13–15,
45, 152, 431, 442–43, 455
coverage, **1998:**68, **2002:**379
as presidential election issue,
2000:18, 72, **2003:**416
type you currently have,
2003:234–35
See also Medicaid; Medicare

health maintenance organizations
(HMOs), **2004:**225, 306,
2005:201, **2006:**232–33, 520
confidence in, **1999:**210,
2000:210, **2001:**149,
2002:185, **2003:**205–6
Democrats versus Republicans on,
1999:211
managers of
can be trusted, **2002:**199
honesty and ethical standards
of, **1999:**148, **2003:**422–23
need to be completely overhauled,
1999:211
as voting issue, **1999:**131,
2000:19, 72
hearing loss
worried you will experience this
illness, **2003:**424
heart disease/heart attack,
2005:431, **2006:**481–82
think that cigarette smoking is
cause of, **1999:**276
worried you will experience this
illness, **2003:**424
Heath, Rollie, 2002:340
height(s)
current, **2003:**419
fear of, **1998:**238, **2001:**70
Heisman Trophy, 2004:487, 489
Hemingway, Ernest, 1999:267
Hendrix, Jimi, 2000:265
Hepburn, Katharine, 2001:77
Herrera, Carolina, 2004:215
Heston, Charlton, 1999:178,
2001:76, **2003:**80
heterosexuals
find portrayal of sexual activity in
movies offensive, **2001:**126
high blood pressure
worried you will experience this
illness, **2003:**424
high school, 2006:356–357
See also education; school(s)

highway construction
increase spending on, as priority
for using budget surplus,
1998:163
Hinckley, Gordon, 2002:400,
2003:454, **2005:**483
Hinckley, John, Jr., 2004:231
**Hiroshima, dropping bomb on,
1945**
as most important event in twentieth century, **2002:**175
Hispanics
approval ratings, **2001:**145
Bush, George W., and, **2004:**329,
2006:276
Catholicism and, **2004:**329
Clinton and, **1999:**224
clothing and, **2005:**274
community and, **2004:**18, 282
crime and, **2007:**304, 316
Democratic Party and, **2000:**282,
2007:277–78, 281
demographics of, **1998:**222,
2001:135
discrimination and, **2001:**147,
2004:290–91
economy and, **2004:**276–78,
2007:304, 316
education and, **2004:**18, 276–77,
455–56, **2007:**286–87, 316
elections and, **2004:**329,
2006:297–98, 378
employment and, **2004:**18, 276,
290, 350–51, **2007:**304
energy and, **2005:**286
experiences of, **2003:**221
families and, **2004:**18
finances and, **2004:**18, 291–92
food and, **2005:**274, **2007:**304
friendship and, **2004:**282
gasoline and, **2005:**286
government and, **2004:**278,
2007:179–80, 316
health and, **2004:**18

healthcare and, **2007**:307–8, 316
homelessness and, **2005**:286,
  2007:316
housing and, **2004**:18, 277
hunger and, **2005**:286, **2007**:316
independents and, **2007**:281
Iraq war and, **2007**:316
Kerry, John, and, **2004**:329
law enforcement and,
  2004:288–90
marriage and, **2004**:223–24,
  2006:290
morality and, **2007**:304, 316
most important issues for,
  2006:279, 281, **2007**:316
national security and, **2007**:316
oil and, **2005**:286
opportunities and, **2001**:147, 152,
  2004:18, 276–78, **2005**:287
party identification and, **2007**:281
political affiliation and,
  2005:264–65, 268, **2006**:276,
  297–98, 378, **2007**:281
poverty and, **2004**:291–92,
  2005:133, 286, **2007**:316
race relations and, **2004**:67,
  274–76, 350–51
racial profiling and, **2004**:288–90
religion and, **2006**:494
Republican Party and, **2000**:282,
  2007:281
safety and, **2004**:18
satisfaction of, **2001**:146–47, 158,
  2003:360, **2004**:18–19,
  316–17, **2007**:289–90, 294
school and, **2004**:455–56
Supreme Court and, **2005**:259
taxes and, **2007**:304
terrorism and, **2007**:316
think few black people dislike
  whites, **2003**:220
unemployment and, **2005**:286
violent groups at school,
  1999:189

Hitler, Adolf
  identified with what nation,
    2000:141, 155
HIV, 2006:521
hobbies/recreational activities
  importance in your life, **2003**:1
hockey, 2004:43–45, 489–90,
  2006:135, **2007**:24
  as favorite sport to watch,
    1998:237, **2000**:136
  as favorite Winter Olympic event,
    2002:36
  most like to get a ticket to Stanley
    Cup finals, **2001**:25
  professional
    fan of, **2001**:81
Hoffman, Dustin, 2001:76
Hollings, Ernest, 2004:42
Holocaust (World War II)
  as most important event in twenti-
    eth century, **2002**:175
home economics
  recommend as career for young
    woman, **1998**:239, **2001**:109
home equity loans, 2004:185–87
"Home Improvement," 1998:61–62
**Homeland Security, Department
  of, 2002**:168, 351
homelessness, 2004:37–38, 126–27,
  155–56, 159, 414
  Bush, George W., and, **2000**:25
  church and, **2005**:134
  Clinton and, **1999**:44
  concern for, **2007**:126
  Congress and, **2007**:3, 60–61,
    237–38, 305
  Gore and, **2000**:24
  Hispanics and, **2007**:316
  ideology and, **2005**:134
  as issue to be addressed by next
    president, **2000**:212
  as most important issue, **1998**:60,
    1999:195, **2001**:58, 255,
    2002:10, 116, 233, 360,

homelessness *(continued)*
  2003:25, 62, 86, 122, 155, 203,
    284–85, 401, 443, **2005:**3–4,
    18, 38, 45, 99, 113, 152, 174,
    198, 213, 286, 348, 366, 421
  in community, **2000:**190
  as most important issue facing
    nation 25 years from now,
    2002:117
  policies concerning, satisfaction
    with, **2005:**20, 22, 40
  political affiliation and, **2007:**411
  president and, **2007:**3, 60–61,
    237–38, 305
  as presidential election issue,
    2000:19, 72
  as priority, **1998:**236, **2007:**3,
    60–61, 148–49, 237–38, 305
  as priority for, **2000:**428
  race and, **2005:**133, 286, **2007:**316
  religion and, **2005:**134
  satisfaction with, **2000:**204,
    2001:29
  as serious problem for country,
    2000:316
  worry about, **2001:**59, 67,
    2002:118, **2003:**127
homemaker
  recommend as career for young
    woman, **1998:**239, **2001:**109
home ownership, 2004:185–87
  geographic region and, **2006:**475
  housing market and, **2006:**179
  Hurricane Katrina and, **2006:**344
  income and, **2006:**483
  race and, **2006:**484
home schooling, 2004:386
home values, 2002:371–72
**homosexuals and homosexuality,
  1999:**54
  abortion and, **2004:**202–3
  acceptability of, **1999:**169,
    2001:133, **2002:**149,
    2003:159, 161, 179, 218, 264

  satisfaction with, **2001:**29,
    2005:11, 20–22, 40
  age and, **2004:**62, 405, **2005:**142,
    2007:232
  born with, or due to other factors,
    1998:90–91, 187–88,
    2001:134, **2003:**160–61
  Bush, George W., and, **2004:**85,
    104–6, 111–12, 329, 369, 469,
    471, **2005:**188
  Canada and, **2004:**404–5
  church and, **2004:**202–3,
    2005:142, **2007:**233
  civil unions and, **2001:**134,
    2002:244, **2003:**161, 264,
    2004:105–7, 201–2, 404–5,
    2005:143
    should have same rights and
      benefits of traditional mar-
      riages, **2002:**244
  Congress and, **2004:**369
  Constitution and, **2005:**142–43,
    188, **2006:**208
  couples should have same legal
    rights regarding health care
    benefits and Social Security,
    2003:161
  Democratic Party and, **2007:**233
  education and, **2005:**142, **2007:**78
  employment and, **2004:**213,
    2006:219–20
  entertainment and, **2004:**62
  find portrayal in movies offensive,
    2001:126
  gay marriage
    should be recognized by law as
      valid, **2002:**244,
      2003:391–92
    will be commonplace in year
      2025, **1998:**221
    will be legal in year 2025,
      1998:221
  gender and, **2004:**505, **2005:**142,
    2007:232

geographic region and, **2005:**142

Great Britain and, **2004:**404–5

hate crime law should cover, **1999:**154

ideology and, **2004:**250, 505

independents and, **2007:**233

Kerry, John, and, **2004:**111–12, 329, 469, 471

marriage and, **2004:**85–87, 104–7, 132, 170, 201–3, 329, 369–71, 404–5, 431–32, 469, 471, **2005:**3–4, 38, 65–67, 72, 142–43, 188

morality and, **2004:**249–50

morality of, **1998:**89–90, **2002:**149

as most important issue, **2004:**156, 467, **2005:**99, 174, 213, **2006:**288, 338, 479

need to know if presidential candidate were a homosexual, **1998:**38

opinions on, **2004:**212–13

opportunities and, **2004:**213

origin of, **2007:**233

political affiliation and, **2004:**156, 202, 431–32, **2007:**233

religion and, **2004:**369–71, 405

Republican Party and, **2007:**233

rights movement
agree with goals of, **2000:**120
impact of, **2000:**119

roles of, **1998:**183, **1999:**169, **2000:**199, **2001:**133, **2004:**505

sex and, **2005:**188

should be legal between consenting adults, **2001:**133, **2003:**160, 217–18, 264

women, in own home, **2003:**217

should have equal rights, **2003:**160

in job opportunities, **1999:**169, **2001:**133

television and, **2004:**62

violent groups at school and, **1999:**189

vote for homosexual presidential nominee, **1999:**54

as voting issue, **2000:**19, 72, **2003:**338–39, 454, **2004:**112, 170, 431–32, 469

honesty
in banking, **2004:**485

of Bush, George W., **2004:**82–84, 104, 138, 145, 172, 308–9, 320–23, 351–52, 371–73, 383–84, 399, 497–99, **2005:**32–33, 35, 276–77, 280, 300, 402, 425, **2006:**43, 97, 187

cheating and, **2004:**192

of Clinton, Bill, **2005:**300

of Clinton, Hillary, **2005:**300

in Congress, **2004:**484–85, **2006:**520

decline in, as most important issue, **2001:**255, **2004:**467, **2005:**174, 213, 348

election of 2004 and, **2004:**383–84, 399, 497–99

of Kerry, John, **2004:**82–83, 172, 308–9, 320–23, 351–52, 371–73, 383–84, 399, 497–99

of occupations, **2004:**483–85 [list], **1999:**148, **2001:**265

of political advertisements, **2006:**440

political affiliation and, **2006:**423, 445, 520

of politicians, **2004:**483–84

in professions, **2004:**483–85

See also ethics; trust

Hoover, Herbert, 2004:413–14, 514, **2005:**482

Hope, Bob, 2000:98

Hopkins, Anthony, 2001:76–77

hormone replacement therapy, 2002:247–348

horse racing
as favorite sport to watch,
1998:237, **2000:**136
horse riding
hobby you are particularly interested in, **2002:**6
hospitals
emergency room, use of,
2003:234
as most important issue,
2001:121, 255, **2002:**10, 70,
116, 233, **2003:**62, 86, 122,
155, 203, 284, 401
wrong treatment or operation
while at hospital, **2000:**102
See also healthcare
household chores
as favorite way of spending
evening, **1998:**237, **2002:**6
households, **2005:**86–87, 222,
307–8, 366–67, 410–11
See also family(ies); housing
House of Representatives
confidence in, **1999:**50
most members deserve to be
reelected, **2003:**374
as preparation for presidency,
2003:375
representative in your district
deserves to be reelected,
2003:374
See also Congress
housing, **2004:**18–19, 99–100,
174–76, 185–87, 207, 277
blacks and, **2007:**287
concern for, **2005:**159
costs, **2006:**249
as most important issue,
2005:40, 93–95, 113, 153,
223, 366
economy and, **2006:**216, 222
for elderly, **2006:**497
geographic region and, **2006:**475,
2007:296, 392

government and, **2007:**537
Hurricane Katrina and, **2005:**381,
2006:344–46, 354
income and, **2006:**483,
2007:296–97, 392
opportunities for, **2007:**287
political affiliation and,
2007:525–27, 537
race and, **2006:**484, **2007:**287
satisfaction with, **1998:**137,
2003:360
whites and, **2007:**287
See also home ownership
Houston, **2000:**298–99, **2001:**235,
2004:448
Houston Astros, **2001:**82
Howe, Neil, **2005:**47
Hubbell, Carl, **2001:**83
Huckabee, Mike, **2002:**340,
2006:235–36, 477, 531,
2007:222, 326, 548
in election match-ups, **2007:**536,
538–40
evolution and, **2007:**250
familiarity with, **2007:**388–89,
550
image of, **2007:**362, 541, 551
Huffington, Arianna, **2003:**278–79,
343–44
humanity
as most important issue facing
nation 25 years from now,
2002:117
human rights, **2005:**73
China and, **1998:**81–83, 86,
1999:197, **2000:**154
military action and, **1999:**38, 40
See also civil liberties
Humphrey, Hubert, **2004:**42–43,
48, 95–96, 279, 356–57
Gallup analysis of gender gap,
versus Nixon, **2000:**159
Hungary
allow it to join NATO, **1998:**171

hunger, **2004:**37–38, 126–27, 156, 159
blacks and, **2007:**316
church and, **2005:**134
Congress and, **2007:**3, 60–61, 237–38, 305
Democratic Party and, **2007:**411
in Eastern Europe, **1999:**231
government and, **1998:**236
Hispanics and, **2007:**316
ideology and, **2005:**134
independents and, **2007:**411
as most important issue, **2001:**58, 255, **2002:**10, 116, 233, 360, **2003:**25, 62, 86, 122, 155, 203, 284, 401, 443, **2005:**18, 45, 99, 113, 152, 174, 198, 213, 286, 348, 366, 421
political affiliation and, **2007:**411
president and, **2007:**3, 60–61, 237–38, 305
as priority, **1998:**236, **2007:**3, 60–61, 148–49, 237–38, 305
race and, **2005:**133, 286, **2007:**316
religion and, **2005:**134
Republican Party and, **2007:**411
as serious problem for country, **2000:**316
whites and, **2007:**316
worry about, **2001:**59, 67, **2002:**118, **2003:**127, **2007:**126
Hunter, Duncan, 2006:477, 531, **2007:**118, 222, 326, 344
hunting
hobby you are particularly interested in, **2002:**6
support banning all types of hunting, **2003:**170
hurricane
ever personally been in, **1999:**258
Hurricane Katrina
approval ratings and, **2005:**351
attentiveness to, **2005:**336

Congress and, **2005:**353
economy and, **2005:**347–49, 365
employment and, **2005:**381
evacuation for, **2005:**331, 381
federal budget and, **2005:**352, 354
FEMA and, **2005:**336–37, 341–44, 383–84, 389
gasoline and, **2005:**331–32, 422
housing and, **2005:**381
investigation of, **2005:**353
media and, **2005:**337
race and, **2005:**341–44, 395–96, 406–7
taxes and, **2005:**352, 354
Hurricane (movie), **2000:**34
Hussein, Qusay, 2003:262–63, **2004:**394, **2006:**240
Hussein, Saddam, 2005:26, 441, **2006:**110, 240
backed down to resolve confrontation, **1998:**170
Bush, George W., and, **2002:**258, **2004:**135
capture of, **2004:**6–7, 12, 17–18, 20, 49, 52, 59, 68, 92, 104, 114, 187, 198, 211, 241, 400, 509
confidence in, **2003:**223, 262, 440
Clinton and, **1998:**232
defeat of, **2004:**114, 116, 124, 172–73
image of, **2004:**210
and Iraqi civilians, **1998:**166
is alive or dead, **2003:**102, 137, 333
as most important issue, **1999:**195
opinion of, **1998:**155
political affiliation and, **2004:**54, 401
removal from power, **1998:**166, 170
air strikes and, **1998:**168
versus attack on Iraq, **1998:**169

Hussein, Saddam *(continued)*
    versus complying with UN
      inspections, **1998:**233
    versus disarming Iraq, **2002:**385
    favor invading with U.S.
      ground troops for, **2001:**47,
      2002:180, 230, 285, 364
    importance of, **2002:**44,
      86–87, 180, 231
    versus peace in Middle East,
      2002:231
    reasons for, **2002:**258
    versus reducing weapons
      capacity, **1998:**31–32
    and September 11, 2001, terrorist
      attacks, **2002:**245–46,
      2003:333, 449, **2004:**399–401
    and terrorist groups, **2002:**245
    as threat, **1998:**165–66,
      2002:285–86, 302
    trial of, **2004:**53–54, 209–10
    and UN resolutions, **1998:**33–34,
      166, 170, **2002:**349
    and weapons of mass destruction,
      2002:246, 286, 349, 365,
      384–85
    See also under Iraq
Hussein, Uday, 2003:262–63,
    2004:394, **2006:**240
Hutchinson, Tim, 2002:339–40
Hyde, Henry, 1998:155, 245, 247,
    252, **1999:**46

I

ice hockey. *See* hockey
ice skating, 2007:24
    as favorite sport to watch,
      1998:237, **2000:**136
Idaho, 2002:160
ideology
    abortion and, **2004:**250, 473–74,
      2005:245–46, 260, 405–6,
      443–44, **2007:**295

agnosticism and, **2004:**511
approval ratings and,
    2004:184–85, **2005:**144–45,
    417
atheism and, **2004:**511
automobile ownership and,
    2004:441
blogs and, **2005:**98
Bush, George W., and,
    2004:102–3, 133, 318–20,
    441–42, **2005:**309–10, 417
business and, **2007:**8
church and, **2004:**103
Clinton, Hillary, and, **2005:**207,
    309, **2007:**21, 33–34, 141–43,
    227–29, 253–54, 423–24,
    471–72, 547
creationism and, **2004:**463,
    2005:191
crime and, **2007:**217
death penalty and, **2004:**250, 453,
    495, **2005:**186, 457
defense and, **2004:**269
Democratic Party and, **2007:**493
drugs and, **2005:**408
economy and, **2004:**102–3, 269,
    2005:108, **2007:**295
education and, **2006:**357
election of 2004 and, **2004:**102–3,
    318–20, 424, 441–42, 473–74
election of 2006 and, **2006:**253,
    378, 455, 460–61, 470
election of 2008 and, **2005:**310,
    2007:21, 33–34, 77–78, 107–9,
    117–18, 141–43, 186–87,
    227–29, 253–54, 294–96,
    423–24, 462–63, 471–72,
    546–48
employment and, **2004:**345
euthanasia and, **2005:**179–80
evolution and, **2004:**463–64,
    2005:191
family values and, **2007:**546
federal government and, **2006:**256
foreign affairs and, **2004:**102

gasoline and, **2006:**186
gender and, **2004:**103
geographic region and, **2004:**103
ghosts and, **2005:**253
Ginsburg, Ruth Bader, and,
    2005:329
Giuliani, Rudy, and,
    2007:117–18, 186–87, 253–54,
    294–96, 548
Gonzales, Alberto, and, **2005:**246
government and, **2004:**269, 447,
    2007:8
government surveillance and,
    2006:66
guns and, **2004:**472, **2005:**141,
    2006:439
homelessness and, **2005:**134
homosexuality and, **2004:**250,
    505
Huckabee, Mike, and, **2007:**548
hunger and, **2005:**134
Hunter, Duncan, and, **2007:**118
identification with, **2004:**102–3
immigration and, **2007:**113
income and, **2004:**103
Iraq war and, **2004:**400, **2005:**
    244
John Paul II and, **2005:**85, 131
Kerry, John, and, **2004:**102–3,
    133, 318–20, 441–42
labor unions and, **2007:**8
law enforcement and, **2005:**420
marriage and, **2004:**103
McCain, John, and, **2007:**117–18,
    186–87, 548
media and, **2004:**388
morality and, **2004:**250,
    2006:214, 219–20, 256,
    2007:239
Mormonism and, **2007:**94
music and, **2004:**441
national pride and, **2005:**62
Obama, Barack, and, **2007:**21,
    227–29, 462–63, 547
Pelosi, Nancy, and, **2006:**499

political affiliation and, **2004:**103,
    354, **2006:**253, 378, 418–19,
    446, 455, 460–61, 470,
    2007:493
poverty and, **2005:**134
presidency and, **2004:**269
race and, **2004:**103
Reid, Harry, and, **2006:**500
religion and, **2004:**120, 511,
    2005:124–25, 133, 151, 234,
    448, **2007:**77–78, 94
Republican Party and, **2004:**103,
    354, **2007:**294–96, 493
of Roberts, John, **2005:**329
Romney, Mitt, and, **2007:**117–18,
    186–87, 548
Schiavo, Terri, and, **2005:**105
September 11, 2001, terrorist
    attacks and, **2007:**395
suicide and, **2005:**179–80
Supreme Court and, **2005:**40,
    238–39, 246, 259, 363, 401
swing voters and, **2004:**421
Tancredo, Tom, and, **2007:**118
taxes and, **2006:**153
Thomas, Clarence, and, **2005:**329
Thompson, Fred, and,
    2007:186–87, 548
threats, most critical, by, **2007:**8
traditional values and, **2004:**57,
    447
United Nations and, **2004:**102
U.S., satisfaction with, by,
    2006:81, 238
See also political affiliation
illegal drugs. *See* drugs
illegal immigration. *See* immigrants,
    illegal
Illinois, 2002:160
image
of accounting, **2005:**311
of advertising, **2005:**311
of Afghanistan, **2005:**79, 128–29
of agriculture, **2005:**311–12
of airplanes, **2005:**311

image *(continued)*

of Albright, Madeleine, **2005:**116

of Ashcroft, John, **2004:**480–81

of automobile industry, **2005:**311

of banking industry, **2004:**361, 407

of banks, **2005:**311

blacks and, **2007:**281–83, 423–24, 462–63, 465

of Blair, Tony, **2004:**210

of Bloomberg, Michael, **2007:**302

of Bremer, Paul, **2004:**210

of Brown, Michael, **2005:**343

of Brownback, Sam, **2006:**532, **2007:**362

of Bush, Barbara, **2006:**53

of Bush, George H. W., **2004:**233, 237–38, 249

of Bush, George W., **2004:**49, 91–92, 133, 162–63, 210, 233, 237–38, 249, 259–60, 272, 284–85, 288, 298, 318–24, 351–52, 354, 358, 371–73, 402, 406, 411–12, 445, 479–80, **2006:**75–76, 186–87, 190–91, 330, 422

of Bush, Laura, **2004:**354, **2006:**53

of business, **2005:**310–13, 422

of Canada, **2005:**79, 128

of Carter, Jimmy, **2004:**233, 237–38, 249

of Cheney, Dick, **2004:**272, 284–85, 288, 353–54, 358, 406, 479–80

of China, **2005:**79, 128

of Clinton, Bill, **2005:**49, 76, 206

of Clinton, Hillary, **2005:**79–82, 204–7, 288–89, 300–301, 309, **2006:**34–35, 273–75, 300–301, 304–5, 330, 504–7, 532

of computers, **2005:**311

of Cuba, **2005:**79, 128, **2006:**79–80, 130, 524

of Dean, Howard, **2005:**206

of DeLay, Tom, **2005:**170, 452, **2006:**5

of Democratic Party, **2004:**59–60, 324, 327–28, **2007:**141–43, 215, 247, 346, 406–7, 423–24, 465, 545

of Earle, Ronnie, **2005:**453

of education, **2005:**311

of Edwards, John, **2004:**6, 43, 48–49, 272, 284–85, 323–24, 353–54, 406, **2006:**532

of Egypt, **2005:**79, 128

of Eisenhower, Dwight D., **2004:**233, **2007:**545

of energy industry, **2004:**361, 407

of entertainment industry, **2004:**361–62

of food, **2005:**311, 422

of Ford, Gerald, **2004:**233, 237–38, 249

of foreign nations, **2004:**73–75

of France, **2005:**70–72, 79, 128

of Frist, Bill, **2005:**206

gender and, **2006:**499–500, 537, **2007:**141–43, 423–24, 462–63, 465, 545

of Gephardt, Dick, **2004:**6

of Gingrich, Newt, **2006:**532

of Giuliani, Rudy, **2004:**354, **2006:**532, **2007:**22–23, 49–50, 55–56, 71–72, 84–86, 103–4, 118, 130–31, 136–38, 155, 162–63, 214–15, 223–24, 226, 247, 256–58, 281–83, 345–46, 362, 397–98, 424–26, 452, 462, 541, 551

of Gonzales, Alberto, **2005:**246

of Gore, Al, **2004:**6, 323, **2006:**320–21, 504–7, 532

of government, **2005:**311–12

of Great Britain, **2004:**177, **2005:**79, 128

of healthcare, **2004:**361, 407, **2005:**311

image *(continued)*
 of restaurants, **2005:**311
 of retail industry, **2005:**311
 of Rice, Condoleezza, **2004:**145,
  168, 480, **2005:**116,
  2006:34–35, 532
 of Romney, Mitt, **2006:**532,
  2007:22–23, 103–4, 118,
  130–31, 155, 162–63, 223–24,
  226–27, 247, 256–58, 281–83,
  345–46, 362, 397–98, 424–26,
  452, 462, 541, 551
 of Roosevelt, Franklin D.,
  2004:232–33, 237–38, 249
 of Roosevelt, Theodore, **2004:**233
 of Rove, Karl, **2005:**402,
  2007:139
 of Rumsfeld, Donald, **2004:**480,
  2006:52, 190–91, 401
 of Russia, **2005:**79, 128
 of Saudi Arabia, **2005:**79, 128
 of Schwarzenegger, Arnold,
  2004:354
 of sports, **2005:**311–12
 of Syria, **2005:**79, 128, **2006:**295
 of telephone industry, **2005:**311
 of television, **2004:**361–62, 407,
  2005:311
 of Thompson, Fred, **2007:**144–45,
  155, 223–24, 226–27, 247,
  256–58, 281–83, 345–46, 362,
  397–98, 424–26, 452, 462,
  541, 551
 of travel industry, **2005:**311
 of Truman, Harry, **2004:**233
 of Ukraine, **2005:**79, 128
 of United Nations, **2005:**83–84
 of U.S., **2004:**91–92, 173–74, **2006:**
  75, 117–19, 244–45, 295, 517
 of utilities, **2005:**311
 of Washington, George, **2004:**233
 of Woods, Tiger, **2004:**480
immigrants, immigration, 2003:238
 age and, **2005:**156, 470

 amnesty and, **2001:**211
 approval ratings and, **2005:**15–16,
  19, 425, 451
 art and, **2004:**296
 assimilation and, **2001:**170,
  2003:237
 Bush, George W., and,
  2004:14–15, 21, 420,
  2005:3–4, 15–16, 19, 72,
  156–57, 425, 451
 citizenship and, **2001:**211, **2006:**
  136–38, 145–46, 203–4, 282
 concern for, **2004:**21, 126–27,
  159, **2007:**126
 conservatives and, **2007:**113
 crime and, **2004:**296
 Democratic Party and, **2002:**18
 demographics of, **1999:**160,
  2001:161–62, **2003:**237–38
 economy and, **1999:**160,
  2000:314, **2004:**14–15, 296,
  2005:248–49, 451, **2006:**216,
  222
 election of 2004 and, **2004:**170,
  420
 election of 2006 and, **2006:**22,
  25–26, 28, 266–68, 318, 322,
  389–91, 426–28, 455
 election of 2008 and,
  2007:255–56, 432–33, 479–80,
  527–28, 543
 employment and, **1999:**160,
  2000:314, **2004:**14–15, 21,
  296, **2005:**248–49,
  2006:136–38, 145, 148, 281,
  2007:179
 English and, **2001:**89
 families and, **2007:**179
 food and, **2004:**296
 geographic region and,
  2005:156–57, 470
 as good thing for country today,
  2001:170, **2002:**226, 266,
  2003:236–37

as good thing for U.S. in the past,
2001:170, **2002:**226, **2003:**237
illegal
as most important issue,
1998:60–61, **1999:**195,
2001:121, **2002:**10, 71,
116, 233, 360, **2003:**25, 62,
86, 122, 155, 203, 285, 401,
443
as most important issue facing
nation 25 years from now,
2002:117
as serious problem for country,
2000:316
worry about this problem,
2001:59, 67, **2002:**118,
2003:127
as worst problem facing your
community, **2000:**191
impact of, **2001:**170–72,
2002:226–27, **2004:**296,
2006:281, 283
income and, **2007:**113
independents and, **2007:**2, 16–17,
54–56, 112, 192, 238, 244–45,
411
Kerry, John, and, **2004:**420
language and, **2001:**89
levels of, **1999:**159, **2000:**314,
2001:170, **2002:**225–26, 266,
2003:236
liberals and, **2007:**113
moderates and, **2007:**113
morality and, **2004:**296
as most important issue,
1998:60–61, **1999:**195,
2001:59, 121, **2002:**10, 71,
116, 360, **2003:**25, 62, 86, 122,
155, 203, 285, 401, 443,
2004:37–38, 155–56, **2005:**45,
99, 113, 152, 174, 198, 213,
348, 366, 421, **2006:**138–39,
162, 197, 237, 279, 281, 283,
288–89, 338, 384–86, 435,

479, 528, **2007:**37–38, 54–55,
123–24, 216, 255–56, 271–73,
304–5, 315–16, 349, 410–12,
442–43, 479–80, 501, 527–28,
532, 543
as most important issue facing
nation 25 years from now,
2002:117
policies concerning, **2004:**14–15,
21
political affiliation and, **2004:**15,
38, 127, 156, **2006:**125–26,
139, 145, 155–56, 162,
267–68, 318, 370–71, 389–91,
426–27, 435, 455, 459–61,
500–501, 528
political ideology and, **2007:**113
president and, **2007:**2, 16–17,
60–61, 90, 191–92, 237–38,
305
as priority, **2002:**17, **2007:**2,
16–17, 60–61, 90, 148–49,
191–92, 237–38, 305–6
as productive citizens,
1999:159–60, **2000:**314
Republican Party and, **2002:**18
satisfaction with, **2001:**29, 158,
2003:360, **2005:**20–22, 40
September 11, 2001, terrorist
attacks and, **2004:**14–15,
295–96
sources for, **2006:**284
State of the Union address and,
2005:72
support for, **2004:**295–97
taxes and, **2004:**296,
2005:248–49, 451
as threat, most critical,
2004:100–101, **2007:**508
impeachment. *See* Clinton impeachment controversy
imprisonment, 2004:226–27,
495–96, **2005:**456, **2006:**225
See also prisoners

Imus, Don, 2005:429, **2007:**169

income

age and, **2005:**209

approval ratings and, **2005:**144

Bush, George W., and,
2004:184–85, **2006:**215

charitable giving by, **2006:**60

child abuse and, **2005:**164

Christmas and, **2004:**460–61

church and, **2004:**512

college and, **2006:**483

Congress and, **2005:**144

cost of living and, **2006:**483

creationism and, **2004:**463

crime and, **2004:**478–79,
2005:171–72, 413–14, 438

death penalty and, **2005:**186

debt and, **2004:**185–86, **2006:**483

dining and, **2005:**481

discrimination and, **2004:**291

drugs and, **2007:**457–58

economy and, **2004:**69–70,
190–91, 237, 254–55, 379–81,
452–53, 507–8, **2006:**239–40,
293

Edwards, John, and,
2007:227–29, 419

election of 2004 and, **2004:**22–23,
408, 423–24

employment and, **2004:**190,
242–43, 344–45, 381, 508,
2007:11

energy and, **2004:**453, **2005:**102,
2006:483

environment and, **2004:**142

finances and, **2004:**176, 221, 234,
2005:94–95, 222, 322

friendship and, **2004:**99

gambling and, **2004:**123

gasoline and, **2004:**148, 221, 234,
236–37, 381, 424–25, 508,
2005:126, 196, **2006:**185, 396,
483, **2007:**234

gender and, **2004:**103, **2006:**326

geographic region and, **2007:**59

Greenspan, Alan, and, **2006:**39

happiness and, **2004:**1–2, **2007:**4,
553

health and, **2004:**475

healthcare and, **2004:**51, 305,
2005:454, **2006:**483, 486,
2007:308, 533

health insurance and, **2004:**481,
2005:14

home ownership and, **2004:**185–86

housing and, **2006:**179, 211, 483,
2007:296–97, 392

Hurricane Katrina and,
2006:86–87

ideology and, **2004:**103

immigration and, **2007:**113

Internet and, **2004:**22–23

Iraq war and, **2004:**400

labor unions and, **2005:**323,
2006:361

law enforcement and, **2005:**420

life and, **2004:**2, 72, **2005:**2

manufactured goods and,
2007:456

marriage amendment and,
2004:86

means, living within, **2005:**181

media and, **2004:**388

Medicaid and, **2005:**14

Medicare and, **2005:**14, 372

money and, **2006:**483, 513

mortgages and, **2007:**392

as most important issue, **2005:**45,
93–95, 99, 113, 152, 174, 198,
213, 304, 321, 347, 365–66,
409, 421

movies and, **2004:**88–89,
2005:60, **2006:**535

outlook for, **2004:**243, 373,
379–81

pay raises and, **1999:**135

personal lives and, **2006:**143

pets and, **2007:**518

political affiliation and, **2004:**373

prices and, **1999:**134–35

race and, **2004:**291, **2006:**280

religion and, **2004:**512, **2005:**133, 234, 447, **2006:**259–60, 494

restaurants and, **2005:**481

retirement, **2001:**122–23, **2002:**122–23, **2003:**124, **2005:**159–60, 182, **2006:**180, 261–63, 483, **2007:**207–8, 436

in rural areas, **2007:**59

satisfaction and, **2007:**4, 553

satisfaction with, **1999:**137, **2004:**344

school and, **2004:**391, 426–27

school safety and, **2005:**350, **2006:**358

sex offender registries and, **2005:**212

spending and, **2004:**236, 254–55, 460–61, 508

sports and, **2004:**44

spousal, **2003:**171

standard of living and, **2006:**168

Stewart, Martha, and, **2005:**101

stock market and, **2004:**453

stress and, **2004:**182

in suburban areas, **2007:**59

taxes and, **2004:**153–55, **2005:**6–7, 38, 137, **2006:**153, **2007:**11, 157–58, 163–65

threats, most critical, and, **2004:**101

time and, **2007:**449

in urban areas, **2007:**59

U.S., satisfaction with, by, **2006:**81, 238

vacation and, **2005:**474–75

wages and, **2006:**3–4, 483

See also financial situation, personal; money; wages

income tax

adjust plan in favor of lower-income taxpayers, **2001:**60

approve of reducing additional taxes for working couples, **2003:**7

approve of reducing payroll taxes for Social Security and Medicare (asked of representatives), **2001:**120

audits, **2002:**106

Bush, George W., and, **2001:**38, 119, **2002:**21, 27

cheating on, **2003:**120

Clinton and, **1999:**132

consider which tax least fair, **2003:**121

credits

approve of expanding tax credits for families with children, **2003:**7

expanding child tax credits will help the economy, **2003:**6

for fuel-efficient vehicles, **2000:**107

Democratic Party and, **2002:**21

Democrats in Congress and, **2002:**27

on dividends

elimination of, **2003:**18

reduction of, **2003:**6–7

evaluation of, **1998:**176, **1999:**123, **2000:**117, **2001:**96, **2002:**105, **2003:**120

filing, mail versus electronic, **1999:**124, **2001:**96, **2002:**105–6, **2003:**120–21

if you receive a tax rebate, what will you do with it, **2001:**179

lower-income people pay their fair share, **1999:**123, **2003:**120

middle-income people pay their fair share, **2003:**120

preparation of

have main responsibility for filing taxes in your household, **2002:**105

income tax *(continued)*

income tax *(continued)*
> have you, or will you, use a computer program to prepare your taxes, **2001:**96
> how do you feel about doing your income taxes, **2001:**96
> how do you prepare your taxes, **2002:**105
> pay for help of tax specialist, **1999:**124
> as priority, **2001:**38, 119, **2003:**152–53
> reducing additional taxes for married couples will help the economy, **2003:**6
> Republican Party and, **2002:**21
> Republicans in Congress and, **1999:**132
> satisfaction with, **2001:**30
> Senate and, **2001:**60
> upper-income people pay their fair share, **1999:**124, **2003:**120
> as voting issue
>> presidential, **1999:**69, **2000:** 18–19, 72, 192, 242, 280
> *See also* tax cuts; taxes

independence, U.S.
> declared in what year, **2000:**141

Independence Day. *See Fourth of July*

independents
> abortion and, **2004:**141, **2005:**175, 245–46, 405, 444, **2006:**134, 139, 307
> admiration by, **2005:**483
> age and, **2005:**265
> agnosticism and, **2004:**511
> American people and, **2005:**360
> approval ratings, **2004:**184–85, 211–12, 229–30, 235, 422, 450, 504, **2005:**141–42, 144, 169, 214, 320, 330, 346, 391–92, 398, 417, 461, **2006:**24–25, 46, 51–54, 95–96, 104–5, 121, 154–56, 183,

189–90, 197, 214–15, 241, 244, 246, 262–63, 303, 316, 348, 374–75, 421, 515–16, 527–28, 530, **2007:**14, 39, 53, 66–67, 100, 118–19, 152–53, 200, 202, 210–12, 224–25, 249, 267, 297–99, 322–23, 364–67, 380, 400, 408, 417, 440–42, 484–85, 502
> Ashcroft, John, and, **2004:**481
> atheism and, **2004:**511
> attentiveness of, **2004:**143, 313
> Benedict XVI and, **2005:**483
> Bible and, **2006:**210
> Biden, Joe, and, **2006:**502
> bin Laden, Osama, and, **2004:**363
> blacks and, **2004:**368, **2007:**281
> bridges and, **2007:**340
> Brownback, Sam, and, **2006:**532
> Bush, George H. W., and, **2004:**211–12, 229–30, 238, **2006:**190, 246
> Bush, George W., and, **2004:**68, 112, 134–35, 145–46, 184–85, 211–12, 229–30, 238, 337–38, 352, 360, 375, 395, 402, 409, 422, 442, 450, 479, 504, **2006:**41–42, 46–47, 54, 96, 105, 121, 155–56, 183, 189–90, 197, 214–15, 241, 244, 262–63, 303, 316, 330, 348, 374–75, 401–2, 421, 515–16, 530, 537, and
> Bush, Laura, and, **2005:**483, **2006:**53, 537
> business and, **2006:**139, **2007:**8
> Cabinet and, **2004:**479
> campaign finance and, **2007:**375
> Carter, Jimmy, and, **2004:**211–12, 229, 238, **2005:**483, **2006:**190, 246, 537
> Cheney, Dick, and, **2004:**287–88, 353, **2006:**95
> children and, **2004:**38, **2006:**139

independents *(continued)*

prosperity and, **2005:**1

public officials and, **2005:**360

public opinion and, **2005:**378

race and, **2004:**38, 278, 368, **2005:**264–65, 268, **2006:**125, 139, 276, **2007:**281

Reagan, Ronald, and, **2004:**211–12, 229, 238, **2006:**190, 246

Reid, Harry, and, **2006:**500

religion and, **2004:**92–93, 120, 217–18, 391–92, 506, 511, **2005:**133, 234, 447

Republican Party and, **2004:**217–18, **2006:**194, 285–86, 423, 470

respect and, **2004:**38, 156

Rice, Condoleezza, and, **2004:**145, 480, **2005:**116, 483, **2006:**34–35, 502, 532, 537

Romney, Mitt, and, **2006:**502, 532, **2007:**346

Roosevelt, Franklin D. and, **2004:**238

Rove, Karl, and, **2005:**277, **2006:**351–52, 492, **2007:**139

Rumsfeld, Donald, and, **2006:**51–52, 401

satisfaction of, **2004:**156, 239, **2007:**28–29, 54, 153, 410, 442, 553

Schiavo, Terri, and, **2005:**105

September 11, 2001, terrorist attacks and, **2004:**145–46, 325–26, **2005:**334

smoking and, **2005:**269

social problems and, **2004:**103

Social Security and, **2004:**38, 110, 156, 431–32, **2005:**6, 64, 88, 119–20, 130, 165, 239, **2007:**16–17, 192

State of the Union address and, **2004:**29

states and, **2007:**29

stem cell research and, **2005:**195, **2006:**298, **2007:**262–63

suicide and, **2005:**179

Supreme Court and, **2005:**42, 202, 244–46, 259–60, 283–84, 328–29, 344–345, **2006:**9–10, 404

swing states and, **2004:**375

taxes and, **2004:**38, 156, 352, **2005:**39, **2006:**139, 383–84, 478, **2007:**11, 165–66, 256

teenagers and, **2004:**391–92

terrorism and, **2004:**113, 115, 134–35, 156, 167–68, 302, 352, 363, 375, 431–32, **2005:**272–73, 295, **2006:**8–9, 16, 54, 101–2, 125, 138–39, 155–56, 243, 245, 303, 349, 371–74, 393–94, 401–2, 435, 500–501, 528, **2007:**14, 16–17, 54–55, 192, 367, 411

Thatcher, Margaret, and, **2005:**483, **2006:**537

Thompson, Fred, and, **2007:**346

on threats, most critical, **2004:**101, **2007:**8

trade deficit and, **2006:**139

Truman, Harry, and, **2004:**229

trust and, **2005:**360

tsunami relief and, **2005:**9

United Nations and, **2007:**59

U.S. and, **2004:**37–38, 69, 113, 156, **2005:**214, **2006:**81, 113, 236, 238, 337, 376, 528, **2007:**28

veterans and, **2004:**418

violence and, **2004:**38, 156, **2006:**125, 139

voter turnout by, **2006:**465

welfare and, **2004:**38

whites and, **2007:**281

Winfrey, Oprah, and, **2005:**483, **2006:**537

World War II and, **2005:**292

India, **2004:**73, 100–101, **2005:**79,
128, **2006:**78–79, 130
and nuclear weapons, **1998:**78,
180, **2000:**89
opinion of, **2000:**89–90, 173–74,
2001:44, 84, **2002:**52
Indiana University, 2003:299
Indonesia, 2005:79, 128
opinion of, **2002:**55, 134–35
industry. *See* business and industry
inflation
Bush, George W., and, **2005:**155
concern for, **2004:**58
Congress and, **2007:**3
economy and, **2006:**216, 222
election of 2006 and, **2006:**467
families and, **2007:**266, 349
income and, **2006:**483
interest rates and, **2004:**261
investors and, **2004:**260–61
as most important issue, **1998:**60,
1999:194–95, **2001:**58, 121,
255, **2002:**9, 233, 359, **2003:**25,
61, 86, 122, 155, 284, 401, 442,
2004:37–38, 156, 414, **2005:**45,
93–95, 99, 113, 152–53, 198,
213, 223, 304, 347, 366, 409,
421, **2007:**37–38, 54, 349,
410–12, 442–43, 532
as most important issue facing
nation 25 years from now,
2002:117
outlook for, **2004:**189, **2005:**348,
436
political affiliation and, **2004:**38,
156
predictions for, **2001:**268,
2002:201, **2003:**23, 158, 243,
286, 370
president and, **2007:**3
as priority for Congress, **1998:**236
race and, **2006:**459–60, 484
teenagers and, **2004:**414
See also cost of living

influenza, 2004:425–26,
2006:481–82
vaccination for, **2002:**30, 299
worried you will experience this
illness, **2003:**424
infrastructure
poor, as worst problem facing
your community, **2000:**190
insects
fear of, **1998:**238, **2001:**70
The Insider **(movie), 2000:**98
**Institute for International Social
Research, 2004:**71
Institute of Medicine, 2004:290–91
insurance, 2006:87, 520
companies, should have access to
genetic information, **2001:**162
salesmen, honesty and ethical
standards of, **1999:**148,
2000:389, **2001:**265,
2003:422–23
**Insurance Institute for Highway
Safety, 2005:**106
integrity
decline in, as most important
issue, **2001:**121, 255, **2002:**10,
70, 116, 233, **2003:**25, 62, 122,
155, 203, 284, 401, 443
intelligence system, 2004:52–53,
94–95, 134–35, 144–47, 167–68,
2006:144, 413–14
See also government surveillance
interest rates
certificates of deposit and,
2004:315
concern for, **2004:**58
debt and, **2004:**185–87
economy and, **2004:**235,
2006:216, 222, **2007:**10, 297
effects of, **2000:**80, 185
employment and, **2004:**152–53
families and, **2007:**266, 349
Federal Open Market Committee
(FOMC) and, **2004:**379, 381

interest rates *(continued)*
Federal Reserve Board and,
2004:39
homeowners and, **2004:**185–87
inflation and, **2004:**261
investors and, **2004:**39, 260–61
as most important issue, **2005:**22,
45, 93–95, 113, 152–53, 198,
366, 409, 421, **2007:**349
predictions for, **2002:**201, **2003:**
23–24, 158, 243, 286, 370,
2004:39, 189–90, **2005:**436
real estate and, **2004:**315
spending and, **2004:**150
**Interfaith Hospitality Network
(IHN), 2005:**134
international issues
government and, **1998:**253,
1999:49
as most important issue, **1998:**
60–61, **1999:**195, **2000:**191,
2001:59, 121, 255, **2002:**10,
71, 116, 233, 323, 360,
2003:25, 62, 86, 122, 155,
284, 401, 443
as most important issue facing
nation 25 years from now,
2002:117
as priority, **2002:**130
as voting issue, **2003:**416
See also foreign affairs/policy
international law, 2006:393
Internet, 2001:201
age and, **2004:**22, 108–9, 503
annoyances on, **2001:**176
bias in, **1998:**171
business surveillance and, **2001:**150
children and, **1998:**189–90
comfort with data over, **2000:**44,
63, 385, **2001:**150–51
companies
collapse of, most important
reason for state of economy,
2002:223

investment in, **1999:**126–27
confidence in news on, **1999:**210
Dean, Howard, and, **2004:**21–22
economy and, **2000:**206
education and, **2004:**22
effects of, **2000:**63, 67, **2001:**175
election of 2004 and, **2004:**21–23
e-mail, **2001:**150–51, 175–78
as favorite way of spending
evening, **1998:**237
and Florida election controversy,
2000:396–97, 409
gender and, **2004:**22
government surveillance and,
2000:385–86
hackers and, **2000:**44, 63
health/medical information from,
2002:293
honesty rating of journalists who
publish only on, **1999:**148
importance of, **2001:**176–77
income and, **2004:**22–23
industry
image of, **2004:**361
overall view of, **2002:**240,
2003:289
instant messaging, **2001:**178,
2004:108–9
and Littleton shootings, **1999:**179,
192
as news source, **1998:**98, 193,
2000:225, **2003:**2, **2004:**501–3
politics and, **2000:**225,
2004:21–23
predictions for, **1998:**222
presidential campaigns and,
2000:67, 396–97
privacy and, **2000:**385–86,
2001:150–51
service provider surveillance and,
2001:150
shopping patterns, **1999:**126, 150,
2000:63, 388, **2001:**189,
2004:492

Iraq War *(continued)*

election of 2008 and, **2007:**46–48,
50, 191, 255–56, 274–76,
287–89, 329–31, 336–37,
432–33, 479–80, 496–97,
527–28, 543

energy and, **2004:**131

feelings on, **2002:**306, **2003:**98,
101–2, 109

first strike in, **2002:**307–8

foreign affairs and, **2004:**91–92,
101–2

gasoline and, **2004:**222

gender and, **2004:**198–99, 400,
2006:403, **2007:**47–48,
185–86, 206–7, 352

geographic region and, **2004:**400,
2005:156–57, 470

goals of, **2002:**86–87, **2005:**387

Hadley, Stephen, and, **2007:**37

Hagel, Chuck, and, **2005:**315

Hispanics and, **2007:**316

homefront activities during,
2006:112

Hussein, Saddam, and, **2005:**441

ideology and, **2004:**400, **2005:**244

impact of, **2004:**113–17, 172–74,
178–79, 218–19, 510

importance of, **2003:**116

income and, **2004:**400

Iraqi people and, **2006:**517

Iraq Study Group on,
2006:513–16

justification of, **1998:**169,
2002:230, 258, 365, **2003:**11,
33, 45, 49, 95, 115, 129,
141–42, 183, 222–23, 261,
301, 320, 332–33, 383, 397,
408, 439–40, 449, **2004:**228

Kerry, John, and, **2004:**31–33, 41,
111–12, 115–17, 165, 171–72,
196–97, 257–58, 267–68,
301–2, 308, 321–22, 335–37,
355, 358, 374–74, 381–84,

389, 395, 397–402, 418–21,
432, 437–38, 444, 469,
497–99

Kucinich, Dennis, and, **2004:**117

Lieberman, Joe, and, **2004:**33

McCain, John, and, **2006:**514

Middle East and, **2006:**244–45, 517

military and, **2006:**244–45, 295,
514, 517

as mistake, **2003:**240–41, 397,
2004:20, 166–67, 195,
240–42, 257–58, 335–36, 355,
368, 399–400, 421, 509,
2005:12–13, 23–24, 41, 59,
89–90, 110–11, 166, 235,
243–44, 278–79, 281, 296–97,
315–16, 326, 353, 418,
426–28, 463–64, 471, **2006:**21,
46, 72, 93–94, 106, 108–10,
151, 240–41, 250–51, 269,
309–10, 320, 322–23, 391,
427–28, 444, 465, 471, 517,
2007:4, 14–16, 20, 65, 83,
98–100, 134, 183, 205–7, 299,
349–51, 394, 405–6, 455, 489,
523

as most important issue,
2003:122, 155, 284–85, 401,
442, **2004:**20, 35, 37–38, 64,
112–13, 116, 147, 155–56,
159, 239–40, 246–47, 271,
381–82, 387, 414, 466–67,
2005:18, 45–46, 72, 89,
98–99, 113, 152, 174, 198,
213, 220, 317, 321, 332, 348,
354, 365–66, 421, **2006:**2–3,
138–39, 162, 197, 206, 237,
279, 283, 288–89, 320,
338–39, 384–86, 434–35, 467,
479, 528, **2007:**37–38, 54–55,
123–24, 183, 216, 219,
255–56, 265, 271–73, 315–16,
349, 410–12, 442–43, 479–80,
500–501, 527–28, 532, 543

national security and,
2004:113–15
North Korea and, **2003:**9
occupation of, **2003:**116, 118,
183, 223, 261–62, 301, 321,
396–97, 409
opinion of, **2002:**52, 230, **2003:**
105, 116, 129, 137–38, 142
other nations and, **2003:**32,
39–40, 95–96, 118,
2004:73–74, 493, **2007:**88
plans for, **2005:**31–32, 41, 236,
242, 445–46, 464, 471
policies concerning, **2007:**201–2,
394
political affiliation and, **2004:**15,
37–38, 114–17, 156, 165, 167,
198–99, 218–19, 301–2, 336,
375, 387, 400–401, 431–32,
509–10, **2006:**46–47, 54,
72–73, 94, 107–10, 112,
138–39, 151–52, 155–56, 162,
193, 241, 245, 252, 267–69,
277–78, 303, 310–11, 317–20,
370–71, 385, 389–92, 394–95,
402–4, 415, 418–19, 426–29,
435, 444, 448–50, 453–55,
459–61, 471, 478, 500–501,
514, 528
Powell, Colin, and, **2005:**23
predictions for, **2001:**272,
2002:246, 286, **2003:**12, 49,
98, 129, **2007:**1–2, 14–16,
19–20, 57, 199–200, 394, 404,
489–90, 496–97, 523
president and, **2007:**2–3, 16–17,
60–61, 90–92, 191–92,
237–38, 305
as priority, **2007:**2–3, 16–17,
60–61, 90–92, 148–49, 183,
191–92, 237–38, 305, 349
prisoners of, **2004:**187–88,
193–95, 198, 218, 220, 241,
267, 394

race and, **2004:**368–69, **2007:**83,
316
red states and, **2004:**336
Republican Party and, **2002:**246,
291, 307, 312, 336
Rumsfeld, Donald, and, **2004:**194,
503–4, 509, **2005:**234
Snow, Tony, and, **2007:**4–6, 37,
88
spending on, **2005:**352,
2007:98–100, 185
State of the Union address and,
2005:72, **2006:**45, **2007:**38
as success, **2003:**101, 105, 130,
2006:47
support for, **2004:**20, 52–53,
113–17, 165–67, 172–74, 193,
195, 218–19, 240–42, 258,
262–63, 335–37, 355, 368–69,
509–10, **2007:**35–37, 82–84,
134
swing voters and, **2004:**336
taxes and, **2006:**153
teenagers and, **2004:**414
terrorism and, **2003:**98, 118, 147,
384, 408, 450, **2006:**110,
240–41, 244–45, 295, 388–89,
517, **2007:**184, 199–200, 274,
350, 394
as threat, **2002:**302
timeframe of, **2002:**286, 365,
2003:32, 58–59
training Iraqi opposition forces,
2002:86
troops in, **2003:**262, **2006:**151,
402–4, 414–15, 444, 448–50,
478, 515, 517
UN and, **2002:**277, 384–85,
2003:48, 58, **2004:**101–2
understanding of, **1998:**168,
2002:230
UN inspections and, **2002:**286,
349, 384
UN resolution and, **2002:**365

Iraq War *(continued)*
UN Security Council and,
2003:95
U.S., satisfaction with, and,
2004:187
veterans and, **2004:**198, 400,
418–19
versus Vietnam War,
2004:166–67, 240–42, 258
as voting issue, **2002:**257–58,
291, 306, 312, **2003:**416
war on terrorism and, **2002:**286,
302, **2003:**141, 302
weapons of mass destruction and,
2002:44, 246, 365, 384–85,
2003:46, 138, **2004:**52–53,
102, 104, 335, 394
whites and, **2007:**316
withdrawal from, **2004:**174,
198–99, 262–63, 336–37,
2005:215–16, 235, 241,
243–44, 297, 326, 353–54,
387–88, 428–29, 445, 465, 467,
472, **2006:**21–22, 26–27, 47,
93–94, 111, 151, 241, 251–52,
268–69, 277–78, 300–301,
310–11, 317–20, 392, 414–15,
444, 448–50, 478, 515, 517
worry about, **2003:**12
IRS (Internal Revenue Service)
does good job collecting nation's
taxes, **2000:**118
given right amount of power to do
its job, **1998:**176
opinion of, **2000:**118
uses its powers responsibly,
1998:176
Islam, 2004:100–101, 177–78,
2007:430–32, 508
Islamic people
opinion of, **2001:**233
Israel, 2004:73, 100, 261, 389, 394,
2005:69–71, 78–79, 107–8, 128
aid to, **1999:**215, **2001:**219

Bush, George W., and, **2007:**110
elections and, **1999:**184
image of, **2007:**78–80, 97, 508
in Iraq Study Group report,
2006:515
opinion of, **1999:**185, **2000:**57,
173–74, **2001:**35, 43, 84,
2002:47, 52, **2003:**56, 69
prime minister of, **1999:**184,
2000:34
as threat, **1998:**79, 180, **2007:**542
Israeli-Palestinian conflict,
2006:413
Arafat and, **2002:**94
attentiveness to, **2003:**201
blame and, **2002:**86
Bush, George W., and, **2002:**94,
133, 169, 182, **2003:**182
goals in, **1999:**214, **2000:**57, 211,
2001:34, **2002:**48, 85, **2003:**201
Iraq and, **2002:**231
Israeli policy in, **2002:**93–94
justification of, **2002:**10
opinion of, **2002:**10
Palestinian policy in, **2002:**94
Palestinian state and, **1999:**185,
2000:211, **2002:**162, 182
predictions for, **1998:**240,
1999:215, **2000:**57, 341,
2002:48, **2003:**182, 201
pressure in, **1998:**178, **1999:**214,
2002:86, **2003:**118
sympathies in, **1998:**240,
2000:57, 211, 341, **2001:**34,
219, **2002:**48, 75, 99, 109,
126–27, 161–62, 181–82,
2003:69
UN and, **2002:**134
U.S. policy on, **1998:**178, 240,
2000:57, 211, **2001:**35, 219,
2002:93–94, 99, 133, 169,
2003:181, 201
war on terrorism and, **2002:**93
See also Middle East

jobs *(continued)*

likely you would find a job just as good as one you now have, **2001**:104

more trade between U.S. and China would increase jobs for American workers, **1999**:151

as most important issue, **1999**:194–95, **2001**:58, 121, 255, **2002**:9, 232, 359, **2003**:24, 61, 86, 122, 154, 203, 284–85, 401, 442

as most important issue facing nation 25 years from now, **2002**:117

outside home, preference for, **2001**:152

presidential candidate's position on job availability as priority in voting for, **1999**:69

as priority for Congress, **2002**:130

protecting

as important issue influencing your vote for president, **2003**:338–39

satisfaction with, **1999**:136, **2001**:207, 212, **2002**:252, **2003**:287, 360

satisfaction with amount earned, **1999**:137, **2001**:213, **2002**:252

satisfaction with amount of on-the-job stress, **1999**:137, **2001**:213, **2002**:253

satisfaction with amount of work required, **1999**:136, **2001**:213, **2002**:252

satisfaction with chances for promotion, **1999**:137

satisfaction with coworker relations, **1999**:136, **2001**:212, **2002**:252

satisfaction with employer, **1999**:136, **2002**:252

contribution to society, **2001**:212, **2002**:252

respect for your opinions, **2001**:213, **2002**:252

satisfaction with family and medical leave benefits, **1999**:137

satisfaction with flexibility of hours, **1999**:136, **2001**:212, **2002**:252

satisfaction with health insurance, **1999**:137, **2001**:213, **2002**:252

satisfaction with job security, **1999**:136, **2001**:212, **2002**:252

satisfaction with opportunity to do what you do best, **2001**:212, **2002**:252

satisfaction with opportunity to grow, **1999**:136, **2001**:213, **2002**:252

satisfaction with promotion chances, **2001**:213, **2002**:252

satisfaction with recognition you receive, **1999**:137, **2001**:213, **2002**:252

satisfaction with retirement plan, **1999**:137, **2001**:213, **2002**:252

satisfaction with safety of workplace, **1999**:136, **2001**:212, **2002**:252

satisfaction with vacation time, **1999**:136, **2001**:212, **2002**:252

women have equal job opportunities with men, **2001**:152

worry benefits will be reduced, **2003**:288

worry company will move jobs overseas, **2003**:288

worry hours of work will be cut back, **2003**:288

worry you will be laid off, **2003**:288

would be happier in a different job, **2001**:207

yourself as high achiever, workaholic, or underachiever, **1999**:137

Jones, Paula *(continued)*
considered sexual harassment, **1998**:50
her description as true, **1998**:174
probably did occur, **1998**:50
Lewinsky's testimony on, **1999**:3–4, 9
opinion of, **1998**:155, 253
resolve her lawsuit against Clinton in court or in out-of-court settlement, **1998**:228
Jones, Tommy Lee, 2000:99, **2001**:76
Jordan, 2005:79, 128
as ally or enemy of U.S., **2000**:175
favor U.S. military action against Iraq if it would turn Jordan against U.S., **1998**:32
opinion of, **2002**:54, 134
Jordan, Michael, 2004:367
admiration for, **1998**:1, 154, **1999**:242, **2001**:278, **2002**:400, **2003**:455
as greatest athlete, **2000**:1, 289, **2001**:142
Jordan, Vernon, 1999:6
journalism
recommend as career for young woman, **1998**:239, **2001**:109
journalists, 2004:484–85, **2005**:201–2, 448
can be trusted, **2002**:199
honesty and ethical standards of, **1999**:148, **2000**:389, **2001**:265, **2002**:373, **2003**:422–23
See also media; news
Journal of the American Medical Association, 2004:191
Joyner, Florence Griffith, 2000:1
Joyner-Kersee, Jackie, 2000:1
Judaism, 2004:118, 217–18, 251–53, 256–57, 358–59
See also Jews

judges, 2004:484
federal
decisions by, better or worse with Republicans in control, **2002**:376
good or bad thing that judges nominated by Bush will be approved by a mostly Republican Senate, **2002**:351
honesty rating, **1999**:148, **2000**:388
judicial branch
confidence in, **1998**:253, **1999**:50, **2002**:282
judicial system, 2004:37–38, 156, 163–64, 467
Bush, George W., and, **2005**:72, 130, 156
confidence in, **2005**:201–2, **2006**:233, 398
Congress and, **2005**:130, **2007**:3, 60–61, 305
guns in, **2005**:140
as most important issue, **2001**:59, 121, 255, **2002**:10, 71, 116, 233, 360, **2003**:25, 62, 86, 155, 203, 285, 443, **2005**:99, 130, 174, 213, 348, **2006**:138–39, 237, 288, 338, 479
as most important issue facing nation 25 years from now, **2002**:117
as most important issue in deciding your vote for president in 2004, **2003**:416
political affiliation and, **2005**:202, 360
president and, **2007**:3, 60–61, 305
as priority, **2007**:3, 60–61, 148–49, 305
State of the Union address and, **2005**:72

Kennedy, John F., Jr. *(continued)*
too much news coverage given to
his death, **1999:**268
your reaction to his death,
1999:268
Kennedy, Mark, 2006:364
Kennedy Onassis, Jacqueline,
2004:514, **2005:**483, **2006:**536
Kenya embassy bombing, 1998:198
Kerrey, Bob, 2007:355
likely to support, **1998:**66,
227–28, **1999:**72
opinion of, **1998:**65
Kerry, John, 2005:68, 80, 182,
288–90, 300, 468
abortion and, **2004:**140–41, 329,
383–84, 428, 471, 473–74
admiration of, **2004:**320–22,
351–52, 513–14
blue states and, **2004:**189
character ratings of, **2004:**82–84,
308–9, 320–23, 351–52,
371–73, 398–99
versus Clinton, Hillary,
2006:332–33
community and, **2004:**442–43
conventions and, **2004:**278–80,
297, 301, 311–14, 320–24,
326, 351–52, 356–58, 361,
371–73, 444, 498–99
debate by, **2004:**395–96, 398,
400–403, 406, 409–11, 416,
444, 498–99
defeat of, desire for, **2004:**497–99
defense and, **2004:**269–70, 352,
355, 358, 383–84, 395
as Democratic choice for presidential nominee in 2004,
2001:192
Democratic Party and, **2004:**34,
77, 112, 319–20, 337–38, 360,
375, 395, 401–2, 409, 442, 514
economy and, **2004:**31, 33, 41,
111–12, 171–72, 196, 257–58,

301–2, 321–22, 334, 347,
351–52, 355, 358, 374–75,
381–84, 389, 397–99, 402,
409–10, 418–21, 432, 444,
469, 497–99
education and, **2004:**82, 112,
301–2, 318, 348, 352, 376,
383–84, 409–10, 420, 427,
442–43, 469, 498–99
Edwards, John, and, **2004:**272–74
elderly and, **2004:**383–84
election of, desire for, **2004:**497–99
election of 2004 and, **2004:**5–6,
11, 18–424, 428–34, 436–38,
442–45, 469–72, 497–99,
2007:253–54, 354
election of 2008 and,
2004:456–57
employment and, **2004:**58,
111–12, 382–84, 469
energy and, **2004:**121
environment and, **2004:**140, 469
familiarity with, **2004:**48–49,
82–84
federal budget and, **2004:**111–12,
420
foreign affairs and, **2004:**101–2,
111–12, 383–84, 389
healthcare and, **2004:**31, 33, 41,
109–12, 301–2, 321–22,
374–75, 381–84, 389, 398–99,
409–10, 419–21, 432, 445,
469, 498–99
health of, **2004:**404
homosexuality and, **2004:**111–12,
329, 469, 471
honesty of, **2004:**82–83, 172,
308–9, 320–23, 351–52,
371–73, 383–84, 399, 497–99
ideology and, **2004:**102–3, 133,
318–20, 441–42
image of, **2004:**6, 43, 48–49, 112,
133, 162–63, 259–60, 272,
284–85, 298, 318–24, 351–52,

358, 371–73, 402, 406,
411–12, 445, **2006:**504–7, 532
immigration and, **2004:**420
independents and, **2004:**34, 112,
337–38, 352, 360, 375, 395,
402, 409, 442
investors and, **2004:**347
Iraq war and, **2004:**31–33, 41,
111–12, 115–17, 165, 171–72,
196–97, 257–58, 267–68,
301–2, 308, 321–22, 335–37,
355, 358, 374–75, 381–84,
389, 395, 397–402, 418–21,
432, 437–38, 444, 469, 497–99
Israeli/Palestinian conflict and,
2004:389
leadership of, **2004:**82–83, 112,
308–9, 320–23, 351–52, 355,
358, 371–73, 381–82, 389,
397, 399, 444, 498–99
likely to support, **1998:**66,
227–28, **1999:**72, **2002:**90,
355, 395, **2003:**16, 135, 190,
215–16, 277, 323, 335–36,
364, 374–75, 382, 390, 417,
432–33, 446–47
marriage and, **2004:**111–12, 329,
442–43, 469
media and, **2004:**433–34
Medicare and, **2004:**109, 351–52,
420, 469
morality and, **2004:**82–83,
383–84, 469–72, 497–99
national security and,
2004:382–84, 497–99
opinion of, **1998:**66, **1999:**46,
2003:306
personal qualities of, **2004:**32–34,
41, 82–84, 112, 308–9, 320–23,
351–52, 358, 371–73, 383–84,
398–99, 402–3, 409, 497–99
political affiliation and, **2006:**332,
502, 532
poverty and, **2004:**111–12

privacy and, **2004:**112
race and, **2004:**333, 441–43
red states and, **2004:**189
religion and, **2004:**255–57,
328–29, 383–84, 428–29,
442–43, 497–99
Republican Party and, **2004:**77,
84, 112, 319–20, 324, 337–38,
360, 375, 395, 401–2, 409, 442
as second choice for nomination,
2003:335
September 11, 2001, terrorist
attacks and, **2004:**325
Social Security and, **2004:**111–12,
420, 469
space program and, **2004:**82
special interest groups and,
2004:82–83
stem cell research and, **2004:**329
swing states and, **2004:**189,
374–75, 430, 442
swing voters and, **2004:**282–83,
436
taxes and, **2004:**112, 301–2,
321–22, 352, 355, 383–84,
409–10, 420, 469, 498–99
terrorism and, **2004:**111–12,
171–72, 197, 258–59, 267–68,
301–2, 321–22, 325–26, 352,
358, 374–75, 381–84, 389,
397–99, 402, 418–21, 432,
437–38, 444, 469, 497–99
understanding of, **2004:**171–72
United Nations and, **2004:**101–2
values and, **2004:**82–83, 308–9,
320–22, 351–52, 371–73,
383–84, 399, 469–72, 497–99
Vietnam War and, **2004:**76–77,
82–84, 345–47, 351, 444
weapons of mass destruction and,
2004:335
Kevorkian, Jack, 1998:155,
1999:162, **2004:**280, **2007:**240
followed news about, **1999:**162

Keyes, Alan
can get things done in Washington, **2000:**35
did best job in South Carolina debate, **2000:**61
has best chance of beating Democratic candidate, **2000:**35
has best plan for cutting taxes, **2000:**36
has vision for the country's future, **2000:**35
likely to support, **1999:**99, 117, **2000:**7–8, 26, 28, 44, 50, 59
as someone you can trust, **2000:**36
in touch with average American, **2000:**36
will keep economy strong, **2000:**35
would improve moral standards, **2000:**36
Kidd, Jason, 2004:367
Kidman, Nicole, 2002:79
"Kids Say the Darndest Things," **1998:**61–62
Kilmer, Val, 2001:76
King, Martin Luther, Jr., 2000:264
King, Stephen, 1999:267
Kissinger, Henry, 2002:400–401, **2003:**455, **2004:**514, **2005:**482
Kitten, Brian, 2004:307
Klobuchar, Amy, 2006:364
Knight, Bob, 2000:150
knitting
as favorite way of spending evening, **1998:**237
knowledge, 2006:118
Knowledge Networks, 2004:48
Koontz, Dean, 1999:267
Koppel, Ted, 2002:63
Korean War, 2004:228, **2006:**72, 479, **2007:**349
as mistake, **2000:**194, **2003:**241
as most important event in twentieth century, **2002:**175

U.S. won or lost, **2000:**194
Kosovo situation
approve of call-up of U.S. reservists to NATO air war on Yugoslavia, **1999:**26
approve of ending all military action, **1999:**32
approve of helping U.S. rebuild area that refugees will return to, **1999:**34
Serbian areas bombed by U.S. in Yugoslavia, **1999:**34
approve of sending U.S. ground troops, **1999:**25–27, 32, 35
if peace agreement is worked out, **1999:**27
approve of suspending air strikes to negotiate, **1999:**32
approve of U.S. being part of NATO attacks against Serbs in Yugoslavia, **1999:**31
Clinton and, **1999:**25, 28, 31, 34, 36
confident that U.S. will accomplish its goals with few casualties, **1999:**22
Congress and, **1999:**27
continue action against Yugoslavia until Milosevic complies with terms acceptable to NATO, **1999:**29
have followed closely, **1998:**225–26
likely that new Cold War will break out as result of disagreements between NATO countries and Russia on NATO action in Yugoslavia, **1999:**183
military action in Yugoslavia will prevent other governments from committing human rights atrocities, **1999:**38
as mistake, **1999:**33
as most important issue, **1999:**195

NATO military action in
Yugoslavia
as making situation better,
1999:23
as success, **1999**:26
open your home to ethnic Albanian refugees, **1999**:30
peace process in
approve of committing U.S.
troops to peacekeeping
force, **1999**:19
approve of presence of U.S.
ground troops in peacekeeping force, **1999**:37
approve of terms of peace
agreement, **1999**:37
likely that Milosevic will comply with peace agreement,
1999:34
peace agreement probably will
work, **1999**:35
peaceful solution to, as U.S.
foreign policy goal,
1999:214
peace possible in Yugoslavia
only if Milosevic is
removed, **1999**:38
U.S. and NATO or Serbs in
Yugoslavia have won more
in peace settlement,
1999:33
U.S. has moral obligation
to help keep peace,
1999:20
presidential candidate's position
on, as priority in voting for
him, **1999**:68
Republicans and, **1999**:28
support decision to bring ethnic
Albanian refugees to U.S.,
1999:30
U.S. air strikes in Yugoslavia
justified by Serbian attacks on
civilians, **1999**:24

justified by threat to U.S.
strategic interests, **1999**:24
U.S. and its allies should strike
against Serbian forces,
1998:226
U.S. and NATO doing everything
to minimize civilian casualties,
1999:32
U.S. and NATO should continue
military action in Yugoslavia
until Milosevic is removed,
1999:33
U.S. needs to be in Kosovo to protect its own interests, **1999**:20
Kournikova, Anna, 2004:368
Kucinich, Dennis, 2004:11, 27–28,
30, 33, 76, 117, **2006:**531
likely to support, **2003:**135, 190,
215–16, 277, 323, 335,
374–75, 382, 390, 417,
432–33, 446–47
opinion of, **2003:**306
as second choice for nomination,
2003:335
veterans and, **2007:**370
Kuwait, 2002:54, 134, **2003:**56
Kwan, Michelle, 2004:368
Kyoto Protocol, 2001:102,
2004:161, **2006:**141

L

L.A. Confidential **(movie), 1998:**175
labor (organized; unions),
2004:225, 306, **2005:**201–2,
313–14, 322–23, 448
approval ratings, **1999:**273,
2002:254, **2003:**303
as biggest threat to country,
1998:240, **2000:**360
confidence in, **1998:**181, **1999:**
209, **2000:**209, **2001:**149,
2002:185, **2003:**205–6

labor (organized; unions) *(continued)*
leaders of, honesty and ethical
standards of, **1999:**148,
2000:389, **2001:**265, **2002:**
373
membership in, self or household,
2002:254, **2003:**303
opinions on
like to see have more influence, **2002:**254
mostly help companies where
workers are unionized,
2003:304
mostly help U.S. economy in
general, **2003:**303
mostly help workers who are
members, **2003:**303
mostly help workers who are
not members, **2003:**303–4
will become stronger than they
are today, **2002:**254
sympathies with unions or companies, **1999:**273, **2002:**254–55
in airlines strike, **2001:**85
in General Motors strike,
1998:194
Labour Party, 2004:57, 81
LaDuke, Winona, 2000:232
LaFollette, Robert, 2004:88
lakes
pollution of, worry about,
2002:81, 112
Lamont, Ned, 2006:321, 364
l'Amour, Louis, 1999:267
Lampson, Nick, 2005:452
Land, Richard, 2007:113
LaPierre, Wayne, 2005:140
**"Late Show" with David Letter-
man, 2002:**63
Latvia, 1998:171
Law, Bernard, cardinal, 2002:132,
391
law enforcement. *See* police and
police officers

Lawrence of Arabia **(movie),
1998:**187
Lawrence v. Texas, **2004:**505
laws
as most important issue, **2002:**10,
71, 116, 233, 360, **2003:**25, 62,
86, 155, 203, 285, 443
as most important issue facing
nation 25 years from now,
2002:117
lawsuits, 2005:3–4, 38, 65–67
See also judicial system
lawyer(s), 2004:485, **2005:**311, 422,
448, **2007:**179–80, 385–87,
528–29
can be trusted, **2002:**199
honesty and ethical standards of,
1999:148, **2000:**389, **2001:**265,
2002:373, **2003:**422–23
recommend as career for young
man, **1998:**238
recommend as career for young
woman, **1998:**239, **2001:**109
Lazio, Rick, 2004:457
leadership
assessment of, **2006:**50
of Bush, George W., **2002:**137,
2004:82–84, 112, 308–9,
320–23, 351–52, 355, 358,
371–73, 381–82, 389, 397,
399, 444, 498–99
of Clinton, Hillary, **2005:**300
Congress and, **2007:**3, 60–61, 305
corrupt, as most important issue,
by partisan identification,
2003:285
in Democratic Party, **2006:**
193–94, 272–73, 418, 445
dissatisfaction with, as most
important issue, **2001:**121,
2002:10, 71, 116, 233, 323
election of 2004 and,
2004:381–82, 389, 399, 444,
498–99

independents and, **2004:**156
of John Paul II, **2005:**85
of Kerry, John, **2004:**82–83, 112,
     308–9, 320–23, 351–52, 355,
     358, 371–73, 381–82, 389,
     397, 399, 444, 498–99
as most important issue,
     2004:37–38, 156, 467,
     2005:18, 174, 213, 348,
     2007:54–55, 123–24, 410–12,
     442–43, 501
political affiliation and, **2004:**156,
     372
poor, as most important issue,
     2002:360, **2003:**25, 62, 86,
     122, 155, 203, 284–85, 443
president and, **2007:**3, 60–61, 305
as priority, **2007:**3, 60–61,
     148–49, 305
in Republican Party,
     2006:193–94, 272–73, 419–20,
     445
League of Conservation Voters,
     2004:138
Leahy, Patrick, 2004:287
Lebanon, 2002:55, 134, **2004:**231
Led Zeppelin, 2000:265
Lee, Robert E., 2000:410
legal field
overall view of, **2001:**201,
     2002:240, **2003:**290
legislative branch
confidence in, **1998:**253
Leinart, Matt, 2004:489
leisure time
favorite way of spending evening
     [list], **1998:**237, **1999:**252,
     2002:6
hobby you are particularly inter-
     ested in [list], **2002:**6–7
importance of, **2003:**1
satisfaction with amount of,
     1998:138
Lennon, John, 2000:265

Leno, Jay, 2000:409, **2001:**80,
     2002:63, 146
Leslie, Lisa, 2004:368
Letterman, David, 2000:98, 409,
     2002:63, 146
Levin, Carl, 2007:19
Levy, Chandra, 2001:165, 188,
     202
Lewinsky, Monica, 2004:54, 230,
     247–49, **2005:**49, **2007:**544
charge that Clinton influenced
     her testimony in Paula Jones
     lawsuit
as serious enough for removal,
     1999:4
as true, **1999:**3, 9
controversy over
charges against Clinton more
     serious than against Nixon
     in Watergate, **1999:**76
Gore went too far in defending
     Clinton during, **1999:**58
less likely to vote for Gore
     because he went too far in
     defending Clinton during,
     1999:59
as most important issue,
     1999:195
interested in reading her book
     when it comes out, **1998:**
     235
interested in watching Barbara
     Walters's television interview
     of, **1998:**235
nature of her relationship with
     Clinton described, **1998:**172
opinion of, **1998:**18, 28, 155,
     252, **1999:**46
believe her or Clinton if she
     said she had affair,
     1998:195
believe her or Clinton if she
     says he advised her to lie
     under oath, **1998:**195

Lewinsky, Monica *(continued)*
    believe her or Clinton now that
      statements conflict, **1998**:208
    feel sympathetic toward,
      1998:160–61
    likely that she will tell truth
      when she testifies before
      grand jury, **1998**:195–96
    as most admired woman,
      1998:154, **1999**:242
    took first steps to establish
      relationship, **1998**:164
  as part of right-wing conspiracy to
    damage Clinton, **1998**:18, 164
  Starr/Senate and
    appropriate for Starr to call her
      mother as witness, **1998**:167
    approve of Senate calling her
      as witness in impeachment
      trial, **1999**:6
    favor her immunity agreement
      with Starr, **1998**:94
    Senate censure acceptable
      which condemns Clinton's
      behavior, **1999**:10
    Senate censure acceptable
      which states that Clinton
      committed crimes, **1999**:10
    Tripp's tapes of her conversa-
      tions about Clinton might
      be important evidence,
      1998:231
  what does her voice sound like,
    1998:233–34
  See also Clinton impeachment
  controversy
Lewis, Carl, 2000:1
Libby, I. Lewis "Scooter,"
2005:399, 401–3, 418
Liberal Democratic Party, 2004:57
liberals
  abortion and, **2004**:250, 473–74,
    2005:245–46, 260, 405–6,
    443–44, **2007**:295

age and, **2004**:103
agnosticism and, **2004**:511
animals and, **2004**:250
approval ratings and, **2004**:
    184–85, **2005**:144–45, 417
atheism and, **2004**:511
automobile ownership and,
    2004:441
blacks and, **2004**:103
blogs and, **2005**:98
Bush, George W., and, **2004**:133,
    184–85, 441–42, **2005**:309–10,
    417
Bush as conservative or liberal,
    2000:248
business and, **2007**:8
CBS News National Guard story
    and, **2004**:394
Christmas and, **2005**:478
church and, **2004**:103
Clinton, Hillary, and, **2005**:309,
    2007:21, 33–34, 141–43,
    227–29, 253–54, 423–24,
    471–72, 547
Clinton as conservative or liberal,
    1998:158
cloning and, **2004**:250
cohabitation and, **2004**:103
creationism and, **2004**:463,
    2005:191
crime and, **2007**:217
death penalty and, **2004**:250, 453,
    495, **2005**:186, 457, **2007**:449
defense and, **2004**:97–98, 269
Democratic leaders in Congress as
    conservative or liberal,
    1998:158
Democratic party as conservative
    or liberal in its views, **1998**:231
divorce and, **2004**:250
drugs and, **2005**:408
economy and, **2004**:102–3, 269,
    2005:108, **2007**:295
education and, **2006**:357

liberals *(continued)*
    sex and, **2004:**250
    social problems and, **2004:**102–3
    suicide and, **2004:**250,
        2005:179–80
    Tancredo, Tom, and, **2007:**118
    taxes and, **2006:**153
    Thompson, Fred, and,
        2007:186–87, 548
    traditional values and, **2004:**57, 447
    United Nations and, **2004:**102
Liberia, 2003:240, **2004:**394
Libertarian Party, 2004:349, 378–79
librarian
    recommend as career for young
        woman, **1998:**239, **2001:**109
libraries, 2004:109
Library Program, 2004:109
Libya, 2001:44, 84, **2002:**52, **2003:**
    56, **2004:**73–74, **2006:**79, 130
Lieberman, Joe, 2006:321–23, 364,
    2007:354
    as Democratic choice for presi-
        dential nominee in 2004,
        2001:192
        if Al Gore doesn't run,
            2001:192
    Democratic Party and, **2004:**34
    economy and, **2004:**33
    election of 2004 and, **2004:**5–6,
        11, 27–28, 30–34, 40–41,
        48–49, 272–73
    Gore's choice of, **2004:**273, 314
        approval ratings, **2000:**253
        excited by, **2000:**254
        reflects favorably on his ability
            to make decisions,
            2000:253
    healthcare and, **2004:**33
    Iraq war and, **2004:**33
    Jewishness of
        makes people in your area
            more in favor of him,
            2000:253

    makes you more in favor of
        him, **2000:**253
    will help Gore's chances,
        2000:253
    likely to support, **2002:**90, 355,
        395, **2003:**15, 135, 190,
        215–16, 277, 323, 335–36,
        364, 374–75, 382, 390, 417,
        432–33, 446–48
    opinion of, **2000:**252, 311, 406,
        2003:306
    personal qualities of, **2004:**32–34
    presidential qualifications of,
        2000:253, **2004:**273
    as second choice for nomination,
        2003:335
Liesveld, Roseanne, 2004:513
life, 2005:1–2, 20–22, 333–34
    age and, **2004:**72
    finances and, **2004:**204
    income and, **2004:**2, 72
    in Iraq, **2004:**178–79
    opportunities in, **2004:**199
    race and, **2004:**18–19, 199
    satisfaction with, **1998:**256,
        2004:1–2, 18–19, 71–73,
        99–100, 129–30, 199, 271
    September 11, 2001, terrorist
        attacks and, **2004:**71, 362
    striving scale and, **2004:**71–72
    teenagers and, **2004:**271
    thought about basic meaning of
        your life, **1998:**239
    thought about living worthwhile
        life, **1998:**239
    See also quality of life
Life Is Beautiful **(movie), 1999:**254
lifestyle
    do anything daily to keep fit,
        2000:5
    lack of time as biggest challenge
        you face today, **2000:**192
    living alone as biggest challenge
        you face today, **2000:**192

what time do you get up on Saturdays, **2000**:5
lightning
fear of, **1998**:238, **2001**:70
Limbaugh, Rush, 2003:405
Lincoln, Abraham, 2004:233, 237–38
as greatest president, **2000**:58, **2001**:44–45, **2003**:163–64, 412
as worst president, **2000**:59
would he or Washington be best president today, **2001**:45
Lindbergh's transatlantic flight, 1927
as most important event in twentieth century, **2002**:175
Lindsay, John, 2004:43
liquor, 2005:260–262
See also alcohol
Lithuania, 1998:171
Littleton, Colorado, school shootings, 1999:172–73, 176, 192, **2000**:126, **2004**:48, 472
any of your children expressed worry about feeling unsafe since, **1999**:176, 220
blame for [factors], **1999**:179–80
See also students (age 13 to 17), asked of
Livingston, Robert, 1998:251
living wills, 2005:123, 208
lobbying, 2005:170, 260, **2006**:188
See also corruption
local government, 2004:163–64, 485
allow to sue gun manufacturers to recover costs of gun violence, **1999**:208
confidence in, **1998**:254, **1999**:51, 158, **2003**:354
influence larger in year 2025 than today, **1998**:219
and regulation of violent entertainment, **1999**:203
state government and, **2003**:354

local proximity bias, 2004:55
Lopez, Jennifer, 2002:400, **2003**:455
Lord of the Rings (movie), **2002**:79
Los Alamos nuclear secrets controversy, 2000:207–8
Los Angeles, 2000:298–99, **2001**:235, **2004**:448–49
Los Angeles Dodgers, 2001:81
Lott, Trent, 2002:392–93, **2004**:504
opinion of, **1998**:155, 252, **1999**:46
lotteries, 1999:263, **2004**:122–23
Louie, Michael, 2004:317
Louis, Joe, 2000:1
Louisiana State University (LSU), 2003:299
love, 2004:62–63, 100
believe in love at first sight, **2000**:49
ever fallen in love at first sight, **2000**:49
lower class
you belong in, **2000**:288
Luce, Clare Boothe, 2002:400, **2004**:514, **2005**:483
luge
as favorite Winter Olympic event, **2002**:36
lung cancer
heard or read that cigarette smoking is cause of, **1999**:275
think that cigarette smoking is cause of, **1999**:275
Lunsford, Jessica, 2005:211
lying
all right to lie to family member or friend, **1998**:238
all right to lie to someone not close to you, **1998**:238
Lyme disease
worried you will experience this illness, **2003**:424
Lyne, Susan, 2005:100
Lynyrd Skynyrd, 2000:265

M

MacArthur, Douglas, **2000:**410,
2002:400, **2004:**233, 514,
2005:482
"Mad About You," **1998:**61–63
mad cow disease, **2001:**74,
2004:8–9, 147
Maddux, Greg, **1998:**226
Madonna, **2001:**278, **2002:**400,
2003:455
mafia
and assassination of President
Kennedy, **2003:**413
magazines, **1998:**98, 171, 193,
2002:293, **2004:**502–3
Maine, **2002:**160
malaria, **2006:**521
management, **2006:**97, 187, 353,
362–63
Mandela, Nelson, **1998:**1, 154,
1999:242, **2000:**264, 431, **2001:**
278, **2002:**400, **2003:**252, 454,
2004:513–14, **2005:**482–83
Mann, Horace, **2005:**47
Mantle, Mickey, **1999:**256, **2001:**83,
2007:261
Marburger, John, III, **2004:**139
Mardi Gras, **2006:**84
marijuana, **1999:**170, **2000:**414,
2004:47–48, 55, 270–71
Marines, **2002:**152, **2004:**220–21
Maris, Roger, **2007:**261
marital status
which describes your marital status, **2001:**26
marriage
abortion and, **2004:**202–3,
2006:307
age and, **2004:**86–87, 131–32,
223, 405, **2005:**66, 142
agnosticism and, **2004:**511
atheism and, **2004:**511
Bush, George W., and, **2004:**85,
104–6, 111–12, 329, 369,

442–43, 469, 471, **2005:**3–4,
65–67, 72, 188
in Canada, **2004:**404–5
children and, **2004:**132
children outside of, **2003:**159,
177–78, 218, **2005:**177–78,
2006:212–13, 218, **2007:**232
Christmas and, **2005:**477
church and, **2004:**202–3,
2005:142
Congress and, **2004:**369, **2007:**3
constitutional amendment on,
2004:85–87, 105–6, 201–3,
369, 371, 471
Constitution and, **2005:**142–43,
188, **2006:**208
couples who live together before
marriage more or less likely to
get divorced, **2002:**238
did you and your [husband/wife]
live together before marriage
[currently married], **2002:**
238
divorce and, **2004:**131–32
education and, **2004:**223,
2005:142, **2007:**78
election of 2004 and, **2004:**112,
170, 431–32, 442–43, 469
election of 2006 and,
2006:266–68, 322, 448–50,
472
gender and, **2005:**67, 142
geographic region and,
2004:86–87, 223, **2005:**142
grade you would give your marriage today, **2002:**238
in Great Britain, **2004:**404–5
happiness and, **2004:**2
homosexuality and, **2004:**85–87,
104–7, 132, 170, 201–3, 329,
369–71, 404–5, 431–32, 469,
471, **2005:**3–4, 38, 65–67, 72,
142–43, 188
Hurricane Katrina and, **2006:**345
ideology and, **2004:**103

Kerry, John, and, **2004:**111–12, 329, 442–43, 469
law enforcement and, **2005:**420
love and, **2004:**63
morality and, **2001:**127, 159, **2006:**218
as most important issue, **2006:**322
outlook for, **2006:**218
pets and, **2006:**533, **2007:**518
political affiliation and, **2004:**86, 202, 431–32, **2005:**3–4, 66, 142, **2006:**208–9, 212–13, 219–20, 267–68, 448–50, 472
as priority, **2007:**3
race and, **2004:**223–24
rates of, **2006:**217
religion and, **2004:**369–71, 405, 511
retirement and, **2004:**466, **2006:**181
sex and, **2004:**490–91
State of the Union address and, **2005:**72
teenagers and, **2004:**369–71, 490–91
urban areas and, **2004:**223
vacation and, **2005:**474
See also civil unions; parents
Mars, 2004:82, **2005:**250–51, 299
Maryland, 2006:415–17
Massachusetts, 2002:160
Massachusetts Institute of Technology (MIT), 1999:219, **2003:**299
mass transit, 2005:273
See also transportation
Mathewson, Christy, 2001:83
Mays, Willie, 1999:256, **2001:**83, **2007:**261
Mazur, Diane H., 2004:505
McCain, John, 2000:26, 35–36, 46–47, 57, 60–61, 70, **2004:**354, 457, 488, 504, **2005:**207, 288–90, 299–300, 308–10, 467–68, 482, **2007:**50

admiration of, **1999:**242, **2000:**60
chances of winning nomination, **2007:**238
church attendance and, **2007:**113–14, 187–88, 326–27, 548
conservatives and, **2007:**186–87, 548
Democratic Party and, **2007:**215, 346
familiarity with, **2007:**225–26, 367–69, 388–89, 550
gender and, **2007:**187
image of, **2006:**329–31, 532, **2007:**22–23, 49–50, 55–56, 71–73, 84–86, 103–4, 118, 130–31, 137–38, 155, 162–63, 215, 223–24, 226, 247, 256–58, 281–83, 308–9, 345–46, 362, 397–98, 424–26, 452, 462, 541, 551
independents and, **2007:**215, 346
Iraq war and, **2006:**514
liberals and, **2007:**186–87, 548
likely to support, **1998:**65, **1999:**71, 84, 99, 117–18, 120, **2000:**7–8, 10, 26, 28, 44, 50, 54, 57, 62, 69, 75, 232
likely to vote for Bush if he named McCain as running mate, **2000:**139
moderates and, **2007:**186–87, 548
opinion of, **1998:**65, **1999:**45, **2000:**44, 146, 231
personal qualities of, **2007:**49–50, 72–73, 137–38
political affiliation and, **2006:**330–31, 502, 532, 537, **2007:**215, 346
political ideology and, **2007:**117–18, 186–87, 548
religion and, **2007:**113–14, 187–88, 326–27, 424–26, 548
Republican Party and, **2007:**215, 346

Medicare *(continued)*

Republican Party and, **1998:**55, **1999:**204, **2002:**17, 312, 376, **2003:**5, 229–30

satisfaction with, **2001:**29, **2004:**109–10, **2005:**20, 22, 40

State of the Union address and, **2007:**38

support for, **2004:**38–39, 137–38

versus tax cuts, **1999:**133

Viagra and, **1998:**68

as voting issue

Congressional, **1998:**159, **1999:**132, **2002:**312

presidential, **1999:**68, **2000:**18, 72, 243, 280, **2003:**338–39, 416, 454

medications. *See* drugs

Mehlman, Ken, 2005:263, 265

memorial at the site of the Twin Towers

what should be built there in addition to the memorial, **2002:**262

Memorial Day

[list of reasons] why we celebrate, **2000:**165

ways of celebrating, **2000:**165–66

men

abortion and, **2004:**170, **2005:**175, 245–46, 443

admiration of, **2004:**230, 233, 513–14

affirmative action and, **2005:**287–88

agnosticism and, **2004:**511

animal testing and, **2004:**215

approval ratings, **2001:**145, **2004:**184–85, **2005:**145

atheism and, **2004:**511

business and, **2005:**415

CBS News National Guard story and, **2004:**394

Christmas and, **2004:**461, **2005:**436

church and, **2004:**303–4, 332–33, 512, **2005:**114

Clark, Wesley, and, **2004:**5–6

Clinton, Hillary, and, **2005:**80–82

Congress and, **2005:**145

creationism and, **2004:**463

crime and, **2004:**478, **2005:**170–72, 437

criminal justice system and, **2004:**50

Dean, Howard, and, **2004:**5–6

death penalty and, **2004:**453–54, 495, **2005:**185–86, 457

Democratic Party and, **2004:**5–6

driving age and, **2005:**106

drugs and, **2005:**170–72, 407

economy and, **2004:**69

education and, **2005:**67

election of 2004 and, **2004:**5–6, 22, 96–97, 332–33, 384, 424, 442–43

electronics and, **2005:**480

employment and, **2001:**10, **2002:**138–39, **2004:**345, **2005:**135, 153–55, 287–88, 307–8, 336, 340

entrepreneurship and, **2005:**135

euthanasia and, **2005:**179–80

evolution and, **2004:**464

fears of [list], **2001:**70

finances and, **2005:**95

friendship and, **2004:**99

gambling and, **2004:**123

gasoline and, **2005:**196

gender and, **2001:**10, **2002:**138–39, **2004:**95–97, 130

find gender stereotypes offensive in movies, **1999:**271

Gallup analysis of gender gap on issues [list], **2000:**362

Gonzales, Alberto, and, **2005:**246

guns and, **2004:**472, **2005:**140, 438–39

happiness and, **2004:**1
health and, **2004:**468
healthcare and, **2004:**51, **2005:**46,
   67, 170–71, 454
health insurance and, **2005:**14
homosexuality and, **2004:**505,
   2005:142
ideology and, **2004:**103
income and, **2004:**103
Internet and, **2004:**22, 109
investment and, **2004:**78, 315
Iraq war and, **2004:**198–99
labor unions and, **2005:**323
law enforcement and, **2005:**420
lawsuits and, **2005:**67
love and, **2004:**62–63
mad cow disease and, **2004:**9
marriage and, **2000:**373, **2005:**67,
   142
   marriage amendment and,
     2004:86–87
Medicaid and, **2005:**14
Medicare and, **2004:**38–39, 110,
   2005:14
money and, **2005:**162
morality and, **2004:**215, 250
most admired man [list], **1998:**1,
   154, **1999:**242, **2000:**431
news and, **2005:**369
nuclear energy plants and,
   2005:161
nuclear weapons and, **2005:**292
parenting and, **2004:**182
Patriot Act and, **2004:**94
patriotism and, **2005:**62, 267
Peterson, Scott, and, **2004:**54
presidency and, **2004:**95–97
reading and, **2005:**203
religion and, **2004:**70, 120, 506,
   511, **2005:**132, 234, 447, 463
Rice, Condoleezza, and, **2005:**116
satisfaction of, **2001:**146–47
sex offender registries and,
   2005:212

smoking and, **2004:**79, 307
Social Security and, **2004:**110
spending and, **2004:**461,
   2005:86–87, 436
sports and, **2005:**54
Stewart, Martha, and, **2005:**101
stress and, **2004:**182
suicide and, **2004:**281,
   2005:179–80
taxes and, **2005:**67
think few black people dislike
   whites, **2003:**220
tolerance and, **2004:**70
as veterans, **2004:**418
weight and, **2004:**331–32,
   486–87, **2005:**296, 305–6, 440
were any of your grandparents
   born in the U.S. or another
   country, **2001:**162
World War II and, **2005:**292
Menendez, Bob, 2006:417, 462
mental health, 2004:216–17, 468,
   475–77, 496
mental retardation, 2004:496
Metallica, 2000:266
Mexico, 2000:175, **2004:**73,
   2005:79, 128, **2006:**70–71,
   78–80, 130, 282
   opinion of, **2001:**35, 43, 84,
     2002:52, **2003:**56
Mfume, Kweisi, 2003:251, 297
Miami, 2000:298–99, **2001:**235,
   2004:448–49
mice
   fear of, **1998:**238, **2001:**70
Michelman, Kate, 2004:169
Michener, James, 1999:267
Michigan, 2002:160
**Michigan State University,
2003:**299
Microsoft Corporation, 1998:52,
   185–86, **1999:**145, **2000:**140,
   149, 178, **2001:**157
   investigations of, **1998:**51–52

Microsoft Corporation *(continued)*
  Justice Department and, **1998:**52,
    186, 233, **1999:**128, 145,
    2000:148, **2001:**157
  know name of chairman of,
    2000:34
  as monopoly, **1999:**129, **2000:**148
  opinion of, **1998:**52, 233,
    1999:128, 145, **2000:**148,
    2001:157, **2002:**129
  opinion of Bill Gates, **1998:**53,
    155, 233, **1999:**46–47, 128
middle class, 1998:219, **2000:**288
  political parties and, **1998:**232
  tax cuts and, **1999:**134
  you belong in, **2000:**288
Middle East
  as America's greatest enemy
    today, **2001:**84
  approval ratings, **2002:**92, 133,
    2006:303, 348
  Bush, George W., and, **2000:**343,
    2002:94, 133
  Clinton and, **1998:**228
  concerned that recent events will
    lead to war between Israel and
    Palestinian Arabs, **2000:**341
  Congress and, **1998:**235, **2002:**
    130, **2007:**3, 237–38, 305
  Democratic Party and, **2002:**291
  diplomatic solutions in, **2001:**194
  goals in, **1999:**214, **2000:**57, 211,
    2001:34
  Gore and, **2000:**343
  importance of, **2000:**186
  Iraq war and, **2006:**244–45, 517
  as most important issue,
    2006:338, 479
  political affiliation and, **2007:**531
  predictions on, **1998:**221, **1999:**
    215, **2000:**57, **2001:**34–35,
    194
  president and, **2007:**3, 237–38,
    305
  as priority, **2002:**130, **2007:**3,
    148–49, 237–38, 305
  Republican Party and, **2002:**291
  U.S. military action in, **1998:**32
  as voting issue, **2000:**356,
    2002:291
  See also Israeli-Palestinian conflict
military
  in Afghanistan, **1998:**201–2, 204
  age and, **2005:**218, **2006:**403
  approval ratings, **2002:**67–68, 91
  branches of, **1998:**236, **1999:**153,
    2002:152
  Bush, George W., and, **2001:**22,
    38, **2005:**32, 37, 39, 209
  confidence in, **1998:**181,
    2000:208, **2001:**3, 149,
    2002:184, **2003:**205–6,
    2005:201, 229, **2006:**232–33,
    411, 514
  Congress and, **2002:**171,
    2005:209
  downsizing as most important
    issue, **1998:**60–61
  in East Timor, **1999:**225
  foreign affairs and, **2005:**73
  gender and, **2006:**403
  general, as presidential prepara-
    tion, **2003:**375
  goals for, **2001:**57, **2002:**44
  homosexuals in, **1998:**183,
    1999:169
  honesty and ethical standards of,
    2001:265
  important for a president to have
    served in, **1999:**106
  in Iraq, **2003:**241
  Iraq war and, **2006:**244–45, 295,
    514, 517
  in Israel, **1999:**215
  in Kosovo, **1998:**226
  in Liberia, **2003:**240
  as most important issue,
    2000:192, **2005:**348, **2006:**480

officers, **2004:**483–84

can be trusted, **2002:**199

honesty and ethical standards of, **2002:**373

peacekeeping forces, **1999:**40

political affiliation and, **2006:**245, 402–4, 413

preparation of, **2000:**286

as presidential election issue, **2000:**19, 72

as priority, **2000:**428, **2001:**8–9, 229, **2002:**17, 171

recommend as career for young man, **1998:**238

satisfaction with, **2001:**29, **2002:**68

should use military force against another country if some allies support action, **2002:**183

spending on, **1998:**236, **1999:**153, **2000:**286

strength of, **2003:**67

in Sudan, **1998:**201–2, 204

in Taiwan, **1998:**185

taxes and, **1998:**236

terrorism and, **2006:**393, 413

and terrorist organizations, **2001:**216

tribunals, **2006:**393

U.S. made mistake in sending troops to following countries [list], **2003:**240–41

uses of, **1999:**40

millennium, 1999:284–85

See also New Year's Eve; Y2K computer problem

Miller, Dennis, 2000:291, **2003:**405

Miller, Zell, 2004:357, 360

Million Man March, 2004:276

Milosevic, Slobodan, 1999:29–30, 33–34, 38, 195, **2000:**333–34

Milwaukee Brewers, 2001:82

minimum wage, 2006:3–4, 448–50

See also wages

ministers, sexual abuse by

widespread problem in the U.S., **2002:**125

Minneapolis, 2000:299, **2001:**235, **2004:**448

Minnesota, 2006:364

Minnesota Twins, 2001:81

minorities, racial, 2004:278, 304–5, 316–17, 391

Bush, George W., and, **2000:**428, **2001:**8–9, 22

Democratic Party and, **2000:**282

hate crime law should cover, **1999:**154

opportunities and, **2001:**147, 152

Republican Party and, **2000:**282

satisfaction with position of, **2001:**29

should blend into the American culture, **2003:**392

violent groups at school and, **1999:**189

See also Asians; blacks; Hispanics; nonwhites; race

Miramax Films

heard or read about Tina Brown resigning from *New Yorker* for, **1998:**194

Miss America pageant, 2000:338

missile defense system, 2000:172, 227–28, 293, **2001:**141

Mississippi, 2002:160

Missouri, 2002:340, **2004:**299–300, 374–75, **2006:**364, 415–17, 461–63

Mitchell, George, 2007:531

Mitchell, Susan, 2004:390–91

Mitchum, Robert, 2001:77

model aviation

hobby you are particularly interested in, **2002:**7

modeling

recommend as career for young woman, **1998:**239, **2001:**109

moderates
abortion and, **2004:**473–74,
2005:245–46, 260, 405–6, 444,
2007:295
approval ratings and,
2005:144–45, 417
blogs and, **2005:**98
Bush, George W., and,
2004:184–85, 442,
2005:309–10, 417
business and, **2007:**8
CBS News National Guard story
and, **2004:**394
Christmas and, **2005:**478
Clinton, Bill, and, **2004:**318
Clinton, Hillary, and, **2005:**309,
2007:21, 33–34, 141–43,
227–29, 253–54, 423–24,
471–72, 547
creationism and, **2005:**191
crime and, **2007:**217
death penalty and, **2004:**453, 495,
2005:186, 457, **2007:**449
defense and, **2004:**98, 269
drugs and, **2005:**408
economy and, **2004:**102–3, 269,
2005:108, **2007:**295
education and, **2006:**357
election of 2004 and, **2004:**102–3,
424, 442
election of 2006 and, **2006:**253,
378, 470
election of 2008 and, **2005:**310,
2007:21, 33–34, 77–78, 107–9,
117–18, 141–43, 186–87,
227–29, 253–54, 294–96,
423–24, 462–63, 471–72,
546–48
euthanasia and, **2005:**179–80
evolution and, **2004:**464,
2005:191
family values and, **2007:**546
federal government and, **2006:**256
gambling and, **2004:**123

gasoline and, **2006:**186
ghosts and, **2005:**253
Giuliani, Rudy, and,
2007:117–18, 186–87, 253–54,
294–96, 548
Gonzales, Alberto, and, **2005:**246
government and, **2004:**269, 447,
2007:8
guns and, **2004:**472, **2005:**141
homelessness and, **2005:**134
homosexuality and, **2004:**505
Huckabee, Mike, and, **2007:**548
hunger and, **2005:**134
Hunter, Duncan, and, **2007:**118
identification with, **2004:**102–3
immigration and, **2007:**113
Iraq war and, **2004:**400, **2005:**244
Kerry, John, and, **2004:**442
labor unions and, **2007:**8
law enforcement and, **2005:**420
marriage amendment and,
2004:86
McCain, John, and, **2007:**117–18,
186–87, 548
media and, **2004:**388
Middle East and, **2006:**122–23
morality and, **2006:**214, 219–20,
256
Mormonism and, **2007:**94
Nader, Ralph, and, **2004:**87
national pride and, **2005:**62
Obama, Barack, and, **2007:**21,
227–29, 462–63, 547
Pelosi, Nancy, and, **2006:**499
political affiliation and, **2004:**103,
354, **2006:**253, 378, 470
poverty and, **2005:**134
president and, **2004:**269
Reid, Harry, and, **2006:**500
religion and, **2004:**120, **2005:**133,
151, 234, 448, **2007:**77–78, 94
Romney, Mitt, and, **2007:**117–18,
186–87, 548
Schiavo, Terri, and, **2005:**105

social problems and, **2004:**102–3
suicide and, **2005:**179–80
swing voters and, **2004:**421
Tancredo, Tom, and, **2007:**118
taxes and, **2006:**153
Thompson, Fred, and,
   2007:186–87, 548
on threats, most critical, **2007:**8
traditional values and, **2004:**57,
   447
U.S., satisfaction with, **2006:**81,
   238
Mondale, Walter, 2004:28, 42, 231,
   341, **2007:**101, 459
conventions and, **2004:**279–80,
   313, 356–57
gender and, **2004:**96
   Gallup analysis of gender gap,
     versus Reagan, **2000:**159
**"Monday Night Football" (televi-
sion show), 2000:**291
money, 2005:162
age and, **2005:**162
concern for, **2005:**159
economy and, **2006:**216, 222
gender and, **2005:**162, **2006:**513
importance of, **2003:**1
income and, **2006:**483, 513
lack of, as most important issue,
   2001:121, 255, **2002:**359,
   2003:25, 86, 122, 155, 203,
   284, 401, 442
as most important issue, **2005:**45,
   93–95, 99, 113, 152–53, 174,
   198, 213, 223, 304, 347,
   365–66, 409–10, 421
race and, **2006:**459–60, 484
See also financial issues; financial
   situation, personal; income;
   wages
Monroe, Marilyn, 2001:77
Montana, 2002:160, **2006:**364,
   461–63
Montana, Joe, 2000:1

months, 2005:224
Montreal Expos, 2001:82
moon, 2005:299
landing, as most important event
   in twentieth century, **2002:**175
Moore, Michael, 2004:445
morality, 2004:214
abortion and, **2004:**249–50
acceptability of various issues
   [list], **2003:**159
of adultery, **2006:**218
age and, **2004:**214–16, 250,
   2005:92, **2007:**47, 239
alcohol and, **2005:**270
animals and, **2004:**215–16,
   249–50
blacks and, **2007:**239, 304, 316
Bush, George W., and, **2000:**85,
   196, **2001:**22, 105–6,
   2004:82–84, 383–84, 447–48,
   469–72, 497–99, **2005:**27, 29,
   37, 39, 130, 156
church and, **2004:**13, 506–7,
   2005:132, **2007:**239
of clergy, **2004:**13
Clinton and, **1998:**174, 197,
   2000:262
cloning and, **2004:**249–50
Congress and, **1998:**236,
   2002:171, **2005:**130, **2007:**3
conservatives and, **2007:**239
death penalty and, **2004:**226,
   249–50
decline in
   as most important issue,
     1998:60, **1999:**194–95,
     2001:121
   as worst problem facing your
     community, **2000:**190, 192
Democratic Party and, **1998:**225
divorce and, **2004:**249–50,
   2006:218
education and, **2004:**215
elderly and, **2007:**239

morality *(continued)*

election of 2004 and,
2004:383–84, 431–32, 447,
469–72, 497–99

euthanasia and, **2004:**280–81

of extramarital children,
2006:212–13, 218, **2007:**232

gambling and, **2004:**249–50

gender and, **2004:**215, 250,
2007:47–48, 239

Giuliani, Rudy, and, **2007:**50

Gore and, **2000:**85, 196, 262

government and, **2004:**469–72

Hispanics and, **2007:**304, 316

homosexuality and, **2004:**249–50

ideology and, **2004:**250,
2006:214, 219–20, 256

immigrants and, **2001:**172,
2004:296

independents and, **2007:**411

Kerry, John, and, **2004:**82–83,
383–84, 469–72, 497–99

and Littleton shootings, **1999:**192

marriage and, **2006:**218

McCain, John, and, **2007:**50

as most important issue,
2000:191, **2001:**255, **2002:**10,
70, 233, 323, 359, **2003:**25, 62,
86, 122, 155, 203, 284–85,
401, 443, **2004:**246, 467,
2005:18, 99, 130, 174, 213,
220, 348, **2006:**138–39, 162,
237, 288, 338, 385–86, 435,
479, 528, **2007:**37–38, 54,
123–24, 271–73, 315–16,
410–12, 442–43, 501, 532

as most important issue facing
nation 25 years from now,
2002:117

opinion of, **1998:**173,
2002:148–49

political affiliation and,
2004:37–38, 156, 213, 431–32,
2006:139, 212–13, 219–20,

256, 318, 418–19, 426–27,
455, 460–61, 528

political ideology and, **2007:**239

of polygamy, **2006:**218

predictions on, **1998:**219,
2004:214, **2006:**214

president and, **1998:**163, 165,
213, **1999:**105, **2007:**3

as priority, **1998:**236, **2002:**171

Protestantism and, **2007:**239

race and, **2007:**239, 304, 316

religion and, **2004:**13, 506–7,
2007:239

Republican Party and, **1998:**225,
1999:87

satisfaction with, **2000:**204,
2001:28, **2004:**214

sex and, **2004:**249–50, **2006:**218

stem cell research and,
2004:249–50, 415–16,
2005:177, 192–93, 195

suicide and, **2004:**216–17,
249–50

survey of, **2004:**213–15, 249–50,
2007:232

teenagers and, **2004:**183

as voting issue, **1998:**218,
2000:18, 36, 72

weight and, **2004:**331–32

whites and, **2007:**304, 316

women and, **2007:**239

See also ethics; values

Mormonism, 2004:251–53, 358–59

vote for Mormon presidential
nominee, **1999:**54

morning, 2005:225

Morocco, 2002:54, 134

mortality, 2004:79, 270, 280–81,
291, **2005:**117, 136

mortgages, 2004:185–87

mother, 2000:150–51

recommend as career for young
woman, **2001:**109

Mother's Day, 2000:151, **2001:**116

Mother Teresa, **1998**:2, **1999**:249, **2000**:264, **2002**:400, **2004**:514, **2005**:483, **2006**:536
motorcross, **2004**:44, 489
Moulin Rouge (movie), **2002**:79
movies, **2004**:88–89, 361–62
  age and, **2005**:60
  attended theater in past twelve months, **2000**:98, **2001**:75
  best movie ever made [list], **1998**:187
  as favorite way of spending evening, **1998**:237, **1999**:252, **2002**:6
  getting better or worse, **2001**:125
  hobby you are particularly interested in, **2002**:7
  household has DVD or VCR, **2001**:75
  how many movies do you view per month on VCR or DVD, **2001**:75
  how many movies have you attended in last 12 months, **2002**:79
  image of, **2005**:311–12, 422
  income and, **2005**:60
  industry, overall view of, **2001**:201, **2002**:240, **2003**:289
  movie stars you'd make a special effort to see, **2000**:98, **2001**:76
  offensive material in, **1999**:271, **2001**:126
  prefer watching movies in theater or at home on VCR or DVD, **2001**:75
  reading and, **2005**:203–4
  responsibility of, **1998**:189, **1999**:179, 192, **2000**:157
  satisfaction with, **2001**:125
  violence in, **1999**:173, 179, 202
  See also Academy Awards
Muhammad Ali, **2000**:1
Murphy, Eddie, **2001**:76

Murtha, John, **2007**:19, 390, 522
Musial, Stan, **2001**:83
music
  as favorite way of spending evening, **1998**:237, **1999**:252, **2002**:6
  greatest rock and roll singer or band member [list], **2000**:265
  hobby you are particularly interested in, **2002**:7
  immigrants and, **2002**:226
  popular
    and children, **1998**:190
    responsibility of, **1999**:179, 192
    violence in, **1999**:179, 202–3
  recommend as career for young woman, **1998**:239, **2001**:109
Muskie, Edmund, **2004**:42–43, 48
Muslim nations, **2002**:54–55, 58–60, 62, **2003**:409

N

Nader, Ralph
  blue states and, **2004**:189
  election of 2000 and, **2004**:349, 443
  election of 2004 and, **2004**:87–88, 132, 162, 188–89, 257, 284, 299–300, 311–12, 346, 348–50, 355–56, 364, 378–79, 388, 396–98, 405, 410, 413, 418, 421, 423–24, 429–30, 436–37, 442
  likely to support, **2000**:139, 161, 181, 197–98, 223, 232, 236
  opinion of, **2000**:182
  political affiliation and, **2004**:88
  red states and, **2004**:189
  religion and, **2004**:257
  swing states and, **2004**:189
  used Internet to visit his Web site, **2000**:397

election of 2004 and, **2004:**
382–84, 497–99
election of 2006 and, **2006:**455,
460–61, 467, 478
foreign affairs and, **2005:**73
gender and, **2005:**368
Hispanics and, **2007:**316
independents and, **2007:**192
investors and, **2004:**40
Iraq and, **2004:**113–15, 219,
2005:40–41, 445–46, 471
Kerry, John, and, **2004:**382–84,
497–99
as most important issue, **2001:**59,
121, 255, **2002:**10, 70, 116, 233,
323, 359, **2003:**25, 62, 86, 122,
155, 203, 284, 401, 443, **2004:**
387, 467, **2005:**99, 174, 213,
348, 366, 421, **2006:**138–39,
237, 288, 338, 384–86, 467, 479
as most important issue facing
nation 25 years from now,
2002:117
political affiliation and, **2004:**38,
113, 115, 156, 167–68,
2005:295, **2007:**61, 192
president and, **2007:**2, 60–61, 90,
191–92, 237–38, 305
as priority, **1998:**236, **2007:**2,
60–61, 90, 148–49, 191–92,
237–38, 305
race and, **2007:**316
racial profiling and, **2005:**294
reform of, **2004:**167–68
satisfaction with, **2004:**129–30,
2005:11, 20, 22, 39
surveillance and, **2001:**241
terrorism and, **2004:**167–68,
2005:334
as voting issue, presidential,
2003:416
whites and, **2007:**316
See also homeland security;
defense

**NATO (North Atlantic Treaty
Organization)**
alliance makes U.S.-Russia
relations better, **1998:**
171–72
approve of American troops in
peacekeeping forces under
NATO command, **1999:**40
expansion of, by country,
1998:171
See also Kosovo situation
natural disasters, 2005:337,
343, 352–53, 356–57, 386–87,
421
assessment of, **2006:**50
Democratic Party and,
2007:16–17, 106, 210, 473
independents and, **2007:**16–17,
106, 210, 473
as most important issue,
2006:138–39, 385–86, 479
political affiliation and,
2007:16–17, 106, 210, 473
in predictions for 2007, **2007:**1
Republican Party and,
2007:16–17, 106, 210, 473
See also Hurricane Katrina;
tsunami disaster
natural gas
used to heat your home, **2000:**56
nature, 2004:161
Navy, 2002:152, **2004:**220–21
Nebraska, 2002:160
needlepoint
as favorite way of spending
evening, **1998:**237, **2002:**6
hobby you are particularly interested in, **2002:**7
needles, getting shots
fear of, **2001:**70
negative campaigning
better if candidates ran equally
negative and positive advertisements, **2000:**220

how much about impeachment
hearings have you read,
1998:244

how much information about
health or medicine you get
from, **2002:**293

how often do you get your news
from, **1998:**191

how often you get your news from
local newspapers, **2003:**2

how often you get your news from
national newspapers, **2003:**2

local

  how often do you get your
news from, **1998:**191

  as important source of news
about Florida election controversy, **2000:**408

  news reported with liberal or
conservative bias, **1998:**171

  trust accuracy of news from,
1998:96

national

  how often do you get your
news from, **1998:**191

  as important source of news
about Florida election controversy, **2000:**408

  news reported with liberal or
conservative bias, **1998:**171

  trust accuracy of news from,
1998:96

recycled, **2000:**122

reporters

  honesty rating, **1999:**148,
2000:389

Newton, Christopher, 2007:240

New Year's Eve

expect to have good or bad time,
1999:285

likely to feel annoyed by hype,
1999:285

likely to feel apprehensive,
1999:285

likely to feel bored, **1999:**285

likely to feel excited, **1999:**285

likely to feel joyous, **1999:**285

likely to feel reflective, **1999:**
285

See also Y2K computer problem

New York (state), 2002:160

New York City, 2000:298–99,
2001:235

New Yorker **Magazine, 1998:**194

New York Giants, 2001:25

New York Mets, 2001:81

New York Times

how often do you get your news
from, **1998:**191

as important source of news about
Florida election controversy,
2000:408

news reported with liberal or conservative bias, **1998:**171

trust accuracy of news from,
1998:96

New York University, 2003:299

New York Yankees, 2001:81

Nichols, Terry, 2004:226

agree with jury's verdict in trial
of, **1998:**5

responsibility for Oklahoma City
bombing, **1998:**5, **2000:**125

sentenced to death or life in
prison, **1998:**5

Nicholson, Jack, 2000:99, **2001:**76

Nicklaus, Jack, 2000:108–9,
2001:143

**"Nightline" with Ted Koppel,
2002:**63

nighttime, 2005:225

1999

as year free of international dis-
putes, **1998:**251

as year of economic prosperity,
1998:251

as year of full employment,
1998:251

law enforcement and, **2005:**420
music and, **2004:**441
national pride and, **2005:**62
patriotism and, **2005:**267
political affiliation and, **2004:**391
position in society and,
 2004:66–67
poverty and, **2005:**133
race relations and, **2004:**66–67
Rice, Condoleezza, and, **2005:**
 116
school and, **2004:**67, 391
Simpson, O.J., and, **2005:**218
Social Security and, **2005:**46
sports and, **2005:**54
time of day and, **2005:**225
unemployment and, **2005:**46
See also Asians; blacks; Hispanics; minorities, racial
Norris, Chuck, 2001:76–77
North Dakota, 2002:160
Northern Ireland situation
new agreement will lead to lasting
 peace, **1998:**89
peaceful solution to, as U.S. foreign policy goal, **1999:**214
remain in United Kingdom or
 unite with Republic of Ireland,
 1998:88
your sympathies more with Irish
 Catholics or Irish Protestants,
 1998:87–88
North Korea, 2004:73, 100–101,
 147, 394, 493–94, **2005:**71,
 78–79, 128–29, **2007:**3, 78–81,
 199–200, 508, 542
as ally/enemy, **2000:**175, **2001:**84,
 2003:99, 340, **2006:**63, 76–78,
 287
approaches to
 favor using military action
 against if economic and
 diplomatic efforts fail,
 2003:9

important to prevent development of weapons of mass
 destruction, **2003:**8
situation in can or cannot be
 resolved using only economic and diplomatic
 efforts, **2003:**8
U.S. cannot fight two wars at
 same time against North
 Korea and Iraq and win
 both wars, **2003:**9
U.S. should go to war with,
 2003:119
has weapons of mass destruction,
 2002:44
has weapons that threaten U.S.,
 2002:45
have closely followed news about
 programs to develop weapons
 of mass destruction, **2003:**8
military and weapons capability is
 crisis for U.S., **2003:**9
as most important issue,
 2006:287–88, 338, 479
nuclear weapons and, **2006:**287
opinion of, **2000:**380, **2001:**44,
 84, **2002:**44–45, 52, **2003:**9,
 56, 99
political affiliation and, **2006:**77,
 130, 459
Notre Dame University, 2003:299
**NRA (National Rifle Association),
 1999:**178, **2000:**157
nuclear agreement, U.S.-Russia
approve or disapprove agreement
 to reduce number of nuclear
 weapons in each of these countries, **2002:**156
major accomplishment if U.S. and
 Russia sign the treaty, **2002:**156
nuclear attack/war
confident in ability of U.S. government to respond to,
 2001:237

nuclear attack/war *(continued)*
U.S. will get into, within ten
years, **2000:**176
nuclear defense system
government should spend money
to build, **2001:**181
nuclear power
aware of whether Senate voted to
approve, **1999:**230
favor expanding use of, **2002:**73,
2003:92
followed arguments closely,
1999:230
heard about, **1999:**230
likely that systems could fail as
result of Y2K problem,
1999:158, 247
plants, **2004:**129, **2005:**161
name plant in Pennsylvania
[Three Mile Island] with
breakdown, **1999:**166
safety of, **1999:**166
Three Mile Island plant breakdown is likely to happen
again, **1999:**166
Senate should have voted to ratify,
1999:230
or withdrawn treaty, **1999:**230
worry about threat of accidents,
1999:166
nuclear weapons, 2005:73, 292–93,
2006:38, 62–63, 287,
2007:482–84, 542
Bush and, approval ratings on,
2002:92
foreign possession of, by country
as threat to U.S., **1998:**77, 180,
2000:89, 92, 101
as threat to world peace, **1998:**
78–79, **2000:**89, 92, 101
good that atomic bomb was developed, **1998:**77
predictions on, **1998:**79, 220,
222–23, **2000:**176

See also weapons of mass destruction
nudity
find it offensive in movies,
1999:271
nurses, 2004:485
health and medicine information
received from, **2002:**293
honesty and ethical standards of,
1999:148, **2000:**388,
2001:265, **2002:**50, 373,
2003:422
recommend as career for young
woman, **1998:**238, **2001:**109
satisfaction with, **2000:**312
nursing homes, 2004:485

O

Oakland Athletics, 2001:81
Obama, Barack, 2004:456–57
Afghanistan and, **2007:**341
age and, **2007:**47, 124, 227–29,
419, 462–63, 547
al Qaeda and, **2007:**341
conservatives and, **2007:**21,
227–29, 462–63, 547
familiarity with, **2007:**225–26,
367–69, 388–89, 550
gender and, **2007:**21, 47–48, 124,
227–29, 321–22, 398–99, 419,
462–63, 547
image of, **2006:**504–7, 532
liberals and, **2007:**21, 227–29,
462–63, 547
moderates and, **2007:**21, 227–29,
462–63, 547
Pakistan and, **2007:**341
political affiliation and, **2006:**502,
532, 537
political ideology and, **2007:**21,
227–29, 462–63, 547
in predictions for 2007, **2007:**1

Petraeus, David, **2007**:393
pets
  have cat or dog, **2000**:5
Pettitte, Andy, 2007:531
pharmaceutical industry
  overall view of, **2001**:201,
    2002:240, **2003**:290
pharmacists, 2004:483–84,
  2006:519–520
  honesty and ethical standards of,
    1999:148, **2000**:388, **2001**:
    265, **2002**:373, **2003**:422–23
  wrong prescription or dosage by
    pharmacy, **2000**:102
  See also prescription drugs
Philadelphia, 2000:298–99,
  2001:235, **2004**:448–49
Philadelphia Phillies, 2001:81
Philbin, Regis, 2000:65, **2001**:80
Philippines, 2002:24, **2006**:78–79,
  130
  opinion of, **2001**:35, 44, 84,
    2002:52
Phillips, Howard, 2000:161, 397
photography
  hobby you are particularly inter-
    ested in, **2002**:7
physical fitness
  do anything daily to keep fit, **2000**:5
physicians. *See* doctor(s)
Pingree, Chellie, 2006:189
Pink Floyd, 2000:265
Pitt, Brad, 2001:76
Pittsburgh Pirates, 2001:81
Pius XII, 2004:514, **2005**:482
planet
  survival of, as most important
    issue facing nation 25 years
    from now, **2002**:117
Planned Parenthood, 2004:169
Plant, Robert, 2000:265
planting
  hobby you are particularly inter-
    ested in, **2002**:7

plant species
  worry about extinction of,
    2002:77, 81, 114
plumbers
  honesty rating, **1999**:148
Poitier, Sidney, 2001:76
Poland, 1998:171, **2005**:79, 128
police and police officers
  any of your children had run-ins
    with [asked of parents],
    1999:241
  approval ratings, **1999**:164
  brutality by, **1999**:164, **2000**:301,
    2005:420
  called for help, **2000**:301
  confidence in, **1998**:146, 182,
    1999:163, 209, **2001**:149, 234,
    2002:184, **2003**:205–6,
    2004:81, 224–25, 251, 306
  crime and, **2004**:50, 80
  have been arrested, **2000**:301
  have been detained, **2000**:301
  have received speeding ticket,
    2000:301
  honesty and ethical standards of,
    1999:148, **2000**:388,
    2001:265, **2002**:50, 373,
    2003:422–23, **2004**:485,
    2005:448–49
  inform person when arrested of
    his constitutional rights,
    2000:200
  in Iraq, **2005**:445–46, 471
  Patriot Act and, **2004**:94–95
  political affiliation and, **2005**:
    295
  prosecution of, **1999**:164
  racial profiling by, **2004**:
    288–90
  recommend as career for
    young man, **1998**:238
  respect for, in your area,
    1999:163, **2000**:301
  unfair treatment by, **1999**:164

political affiliation
   abortion and, **2005:**3–4, 175,
      192–93, 245–46, 405, 443–44,
      2007:221
   admiration by, **2005:**483
   Afghanistan and, **2005:**128–29,
      2006:130–31, **2007:**341
   age and, **2005:**265
   Albright, Madeleine and,
      2006:537
   American people and, **2005:**360
   Angelou, Maya, and, **2005:**483
   approval ratings, **2005:**43, 69,
      120, 141–42, 144, 168–69,
      214, 320, 330, 346, 391–92,
      397–98, 412, 417, 426, 430,
      461–62, **2006:**5, 24–25, 46,
      51–54, 94–96, 104–5, 120–21,
      154–56, 172, 183, 189–90,
      193, 214–15, 241, 244, 246,
      262–63, 272–73, 303, 316,
      348, 374–75, 421, 515–16,
      527–28, 530, **2007:**14, 39, 53,
      66–67, 100, 118–19, 152–53,
      200–202, 210–12, 224–25,
      249, 267, 297–99, 322–23,
      364–67, 380, 400, 408, 417,
      440–42, 484–85, 502
   Benedict XVI and, **2005:**483
   Bible and, **2006:**210
   Biden, Joe, and, **2006:**502
   blacks and, **2007:**281
   blogs and, **2005:**98
   bridges and, **2007:**340
   Brownback, Sam, and, **2006:**532
   Bush, Barbara, and, **2006:**537
   Bush, George H. W., and,
      2005:52, **2006:**190, 246, 537
   Bush, George W., and,
      2006:41–42, 45–47, 54, 96,
      105, 121, 155–56, 172, 183,
      189–90, 197, 214–15, 241,
      244, 262–63, 303, 316, 318,
      330, 348, 374–75, 390–91,

   401–2, 421, 448–50, 515–16,
      530, 537
   Bush, Laura, and, **2005:**483,
      2006:53, 537
   business and, **2006:**139, 419
   campaign finance and,
      2007:375–76
   Canada and, **2005:**128, **2006:**130
   Carter, Jimmy, and, **2005:**483,
      2006:190, 246, 537
   Cheney, Dick, and, **2005:**433
   children, concern for, and,
      2004:38
   China and, **2005:**128, **2006:**130
   Christmas and, **2005:**478
   church and, **2004:**391–92,
      2005:182–84, 268,
      2006:109–10, 124, 231–32,
      253, 355–56, 368, 378,
      424–26, 472
   citizenship and, **2006:**145
   civil liberties and, **2006:**16, 455
   Clinton, Bill, and, **2005:**51–52,
      398, 483, **2006:**41–42, 172,
      190, 246, 305, 401–2, 537,
      2007:71–72, 88–89, 135
   Clinton, Hillary, and, **2005:**80–82,
      289–90, 300–301, 309, 483,
      2006:5, 34–35, 274–75,
      300–301, 305, 330, 332, 456,
      474, 532, 537
   Congress and, **2005:**98, 144,
      169–70, 172–73, 202, 214,
      330, 360, 396–98, 411–12,
      429–31, 453, **2007:**16–17, 39,
      53–55, 66–67, 118–19, 153,
      210–11, 267, 322–23, 364–65,
      408, 441–42, 502
   corruption and, **2006:**4–6, 13–15,
      139, 188–89, 193–94, 205–6,
      227–28, 267–68, 412, 426–27,
      435, 478
   crime and, **2006:**125–26, 139,
      2007:16–17, 217

political affiliation *(continued)*
 Gonzales, Alberto, and, **2005:**246
 Gore, Al, and, **2006:**320–21, 332,
  502, 532, **2007:**346, 348
 government and, **2004:**56, 156, 269,
  278, **2005:**356–57, 360, 374–75,
  412, **2006:**139, 256, 373–74,
  381–83, 398–99, 435, 446, 528
 Graham, Billy, and, **2005:**483,
  2006:537
 Great Britain and, **2005:**128,
  2006:130
 Greenspan, Alan, and, **2006:**39
 Guantanamo Naval Base detention
  facility and, **2005:**226
 guns and, **2005:**141, 438–39,
  2006:63–64, 439
 happiness and, **2004:**2, **2007:**553
 health and, **2007:**518–20, 522
 healthcare and, **2004:**15–16, 38,
  51, 127, 156, 301–2, 375, 387,
  407, 431–32, 459, **2006:**54,
  125–26, 139, 155–56, 267–68,
  370–71, 383–84, 389–91,
  426–27, 435, 455, 459–61,
  486–87, 500–501, 528
 Hinckley, Gordon B., and,
  2005:483
 Hispanics and, **2007:**281
 homeland security and, **2007:**256
 homelessness and, **2007:**411
 homosexuality and, **2004:**156,
  202, 431–32, **2007:**233
 honesty and, **2006:**423, 445, 520,
  2007:256
 housing and, **2007:**525–27, 537
 hunger and, **2007:**411
 Hurricane Katrina and, **2005:**331,
  346
 Hussein, Saddam, and, **2004:**54,
  401, **2005:**441
 identification by, **2004:**2–5,
  23–25, 59–60, 133, 217–18,
  368, 494–95

 ideology and, **2004:**103, 354,
  2006:253, 378, 418–19, 446,
  455, 460–61, 470
 image by, **2006:**52, 130–32,
  192–94, 379–80, 411–13,
  418–19, 422–23, 445–46,
  475–76, 499–500, 532, 537,
  2007:141–43, 215, 247, 346,
  406–7, 423–24, 465, 495–96,
  545
 immigration and, **2004:**15, 38,
  127, 156, **2006:**125–26, 139,
  145, 155–56, 162, 267–68,
  318, 370–71, 389–91, 426–27,
  435, 455, 459–61, 500–501,
  528
 income and, **2004:**373
 India and, **2005:**128, **2006:**130
 Indonesia and, **2005:**128
 inflation and, **2004:**38, 156
 intelligence system and,
  2006:144, 413
 Internet and, **2006:**56
 Iran and, **2005:**128–29, **2006:**38,
  63, 77, 130–31
 Iraq and, **2004:**262, **2005:**40–41,
  128–29, **2006:**46–47, 77,
  130–31, 245, 413
 Iraq war and, **2004:**15, 37–38,
  114–17, 156, 165, 167,
  198–99, 218–19, 301–2, 336,
  375, 387, 400–401, 431–32,
  509–10, **2006:**46–47, 54,
  72–73, 94, 107–10, 112,
  138–39, 151–52, 155–56, 162,
  241, 245, 252, 267–69,
  277–78, 303, 310–11, 317–20,
  370–71, 385, 389–92, 394–95,
  402–4, 415, 418–19, 426–29,
  435, 444, 448–50, 453–55,
  459–61, 471, 478, 500–501,
  514, 528
 Israel and, **2005:**128
 Japan and, **2005:**128, **2006:**130

16, 54, 101–2, 107, 125–26,
138–39, 155–56, 243, 245,
267–68, 303, 349, 370–74,
379–80, 385, 387–91, 393–94,
401–2, 413–14, 419, 426–27,
435, 448–50, 455, 459–61,
500–501, 528
Thatcher, Margaret, and,
2005:483, **2006:**537
third party needed for, **2006:**382
Thompson, Fred, and, **2007:**346
threats, most critical, by, **2007:**8
torture and, **2005:**441
trade deficit and, **2006:**139
Truman, Harry, and, **2004:**229
trust and, **2005:**360
Ukraine and, **2005:**128
United Nations and, **2004:**102
values and, **2005:**412
violence and, **2004:**38, 127, 156,
2006:125–26, 139
voter interest by, **2006:**18–19,
157–58, 171–72, 176, 184–85,
265–66, 377, 422, 467–69
voter turnout by, **2005:**43,
2006:157–58, 266, 286, 339,
377, 422, 441–42, 465, 467–69
wages and, **2007:**11
whites and, **2007:**281
Winfrey, Oprah, and, **2005:**483,
2006:537
World War II and, **2005:**292
See also ideology; *specific party*
politicians
confidence in, **1998:**254,
2002:282, **2003:**355, **2004:**164
dissatisfaction with
as most important issue,
2001:121, **2002:**10, 71,
116, 233, 360, **2003:**25, 62,
86, 122, 155, 203, 284, 401,
443
as most important issue facing
nation 25 years from now,
2002:117

education and, **2004:**164
honesty of, **2004:**483–84
as most important issue,
2004:37–38, 156, 239, 467
political affiliation and, **2004:**156
politics, 2004:21–23, 439–40, 505–7
closely follow news about,
2002:265, **2003:**324, 390–91
hobby you are particularly interested in, **2002:**7
immigrants and, **2001:**171,
2002:226
as most important issue, **2000:**191
pollution, 1998:163, **2000:**191,
2001:69, 90, **2004:**141–42, 156,
160–61, **2007:**146–48
emissions standards and, **2003:**93
as most important issue, **2001:**59,
121, 255, **2002:**10, 71, 116,
233, 360, **2003:**25, 62, 86, 155,
203, 285, 443
worry about, **2002:**76–77, 81,
112–13
See also environment
polygamy, 2003:159, 179, 218,
2004:249–50
Pons, Michael, 2004:390–91
poor people, 1998:232, **1999:**263,
2000:86
Bush administration and,
2001:8–9, 22
gap between rich and poor, as
most important issue, **2001:**58,
121, 255, **2002:**359, **2003:**25,
62, 86, 122, 155, 203, 284, 442
oil prices and, **2000:**56
opportunities and, **2000:**204
president and, **1999:**105
quality of life better in year 2025
than today for, **1998:**219
Republican Party and, **1999:**87
and taxes, **1999:**123
See also poverty
popular culture
and children, **1998:**189–90

population, **2004:**127–28, 244–45, **2005:**99, 175, 213, **2006:**291–92, 479

growth of, **1999:**227–28

Postal Service

and War on Terrorism, **2001:**254

Potomac Associates, 2004:71

Potter, Harry, 2000:214

poverty

blacks and, **2007:**316

Bush, George W., and, **2000:**25, **2004:**111–12, **2005:**3–4, 156

church and, **2005:**134

Clinton and, **1999:**44

concern for, **2004:**139

confidence in, **2004:**224–25, 306

Congress and, **2007:**3, 60–61, 179–80, 237–38, 305

defense and, **2004:**269–70

Democratic Party and, **2007:**123, 411

in Eastern Europe, **1999:**231

economy and, **2004:**58, 64, 269–70, **2006:**216, 222

education and, **2004:**164, 201, 377

election of 2004 and, **2004:**111–12

election of 2006 and, **2006:**455

employment and, **2004:**58

European Union and, **2004:**244–45

gender gap and, **2004:**95–97

Gore and, **2000:**24

government and, **2004:**269–70

greatest, **2004:**233, 237–38

health insurance and, **2004:**481

Hispanics and, **2007:**316

ideology and, **2004:**269, **2005:**134

independents and, **2007:**411

Internet and, **2004:**109

Kerry, John, and, **2004:**111–12

as most important issue, **1998:**60, **1999:**195, **2000:**191, **2001:**58,

121, 255, **2002:**10, 71, 116, 233, 360, **2003:**25, 62, 86, 122, 155, 203, 284–85, 401, 443, **2004:**37–38, 155–56, 414, **2005:**3–4, 18, 38, 45, 99, 113, 152, 174, 198, 213, 286, 347–48, 366, 421, **2006:**138–39, 237, 288, 338, 385–86, 479, **2007:**37–38, 54, 123–24, 271–73, 315–16, 410–12, 442–43, 501

as most important issue facing nation 25 years from now, **2002:**117

political affiliation and, **2004:**37–38, 156, 269, **2005:**3–4, 356–57, 394, **2006:**125–26, 139, 455, **2007:**411

president and, **2007:**3, 60–61, 237–38, 305

as priority, **2000:**212, **2002:**130, **2004:**124–26, 151, 211–12, 229–30, 265–66, **2007:**3, 60–61, 148–49, 237–38, 305

race and, **2004:**291–92, **2005:**133, 286, 394, **2007:**316

rankings of, **2004:**232–33, 237–38, 249

rates of, **2004:**291–92

religion and, **2005:**134

Republican Party and, **2007:**123, 411

satisfaction with, **2000:**204, **2001:**29

spending on, **2005:**394

teenagers and, **2004:**414

as voting issue, **2000:**19, 72

whites and, **2007:**316

as worst problem facing your community, **2000:**190

See also poor people

Powell, Colin, 2001:79–80, **2003:**46, 51–52, **2004:**457, 480, 513–14,

2005:9, 23, 116, 482–83,
2007:545
admiration of, 1998:1, 154,
1999:242, 2000:410, 431,
2001:278, 2002:399,
2003:251, 454
approval ratings, 2001:254
opinion of, 2000:231, 421,
2002:296, 2003:252, 273
Powell, Michael, 2004:61
power, 2004:56, 156, 505–7,
2006:138–39, 237, 288, 338, 479
abuse of, as most important issue,
2003:122, 155
as most important issue, 2005:99,
175, 213
Patriot Act and, 2005:375
political affiliation and, 2005:2,
374–75
of U.S., 2005:1–2
power supply problems,
2003:308–9
prayer
Gallup analysis of habits of,
1999:257–58
in public schools, 1999:192, 207,
2000:200, 241, 2001:50
Pregler, Jerry, 2004:281
pregnancy, 2004:490
See also teen pregnancy
Prescott, Margaret, 2005:134
prescription drugs
budget surplus and, 2000:318
Bush versus Gore on, 2000:309
cost of, as priority, 2000:212
for elderly, 2003:229–30, 434–36
approval ratings, 2001:166
from Canada, 2003:305–6
Congress and, 2003:230, 305
Democrats versus Republicans
on, 2002:17, 171, 291,
336
Medicare and, 2000:321,
2003:435

as priority, 2001:141, 229,
2002:17, 171
as voting issue, 2002:291,
2003:416
president/presidency
age and, 2007:77–78, 91
Bush, George W., and, 2001:22,
105–6, 2005:27, 29, 37, 39
Clinton and, 1998:35–36
confidence in, 1998:181–82,
1999:209, 2000:209, 2001:3,
149, 2002:184, 2003:205–6,
2005:201–2
and Congress, 1998:175,
2002:273
corruption and, 2007:16–17,
60–61, 305
dynasty and, 2007:513
economy and, 2007:10, 16–17,
60–61, 90, 191–92, 237–38,
305
education and, 2007:60–61, 78,
90, 191–92, 237–38, 305
employment and, 2007:60–61,
191–92, 237–38, 305
energy and, 2007:16–17, 60–61,
237–38, 305
environment and, 2007:60–61, 90,
191–92, 237–38, 305
federal budget and, 2007:16–17,
60–61, 90, 191–92, 237–38, 305
foreign affairs and, 2007:60–61,
90, 237–38, 305
foreign aid and, 2007:60–61,
237–38, 305
gasoline and, 2007:60–61, 90,
191–92, 237–38, 305
gender and, 2007:77–78, 91
government and, 2007:16–17,
60–61, 191–92, 305
greatest presidents, 2000:58,
2001:44–45
Washington versus Lincoln,
2001:45

president/presidency *(continued)*
  healthcare and, **2007:**16–17,
    60–61, 90–92, 191–92,
    237–38, 305
  history of, **2006:**477
  homelessness and, **2007:**60–61,
    237–38, 305
  hunger and, **2007:**60–61, 237–38,
    305
  immigration and, **2007:**16–17,
    60–61, 90, 191–92, 237–38, 305
  Iraq war and, **2007:**3, 16–17,
    60–61, 90–92, 191–92,
    237–38, 305
  judicial system and, **2007:**60–61,
    305
  leadership and, **2007:**60–61, 305
  Medicare and, **2007:**16–17,
    60–61, 90, 237–38, 305
  Middle East and, **2007:**237–38,
    305
  morality and, **1998:**35, 163, 165,
    213
  national security and,
    2007:60–61, 90, 191–92,
    237–38, 305
  oil and, **2007:**60–61, 90, 191–92,
    237–38, 305
  poverty and, **2007:**60–61, 237–38,
    305
  predictions for, **1998:**225
  priorities for, **2007:**2–3, 16–17,
    60–61, 90–92, 148–49,
    191–92, 237–38, 305, 349
  role of, **2005:**48
  Social Security and, **2007:**16–17,
    60–61, 90, 191–92, 237–38,
    305
  taxes and, **2007:**60–61, 191–92,
    237–38, 305
  terrorism and, **2007:**16–17,
    60–61, 90, 191–92, 237–38,
    305
  trust in, **2005:**359, 378, **2006:**398

unemployment and, **2007:**60–61,
    191–92, 237–38, 305
presidential candidates
  any candidate running who would
    make a good president,
    2000:15
  atheist as, **1999:**53
  Baptist as, **1999:**54
  black as, **1999:**53, **2003:**192
  Catholic as, **1999:**53, **2003:**192
  Democratic candidate preference,
    2003:135–36
  in election of 2004, **2003:**134–35,
    214
  gender gap on twenty issues,
    2000:362
  and gun control, **2000:**157
  happened to vote for president on
    November 7, **2000:**397
  homosexual as, **1999:**54
  how much thought have you given
    to upcoming election,
    2000:350
  integrity of, **2003:**416
  Internet and, **2000:**67, 396
  issues [list] important to you when
    you vote, **2000:**18–19, 72
  issues [list] to be addressed by
    next president, **2000:**212
  Jew as, **1999:**53, **2003:**192
  made up your mind about whom
    you will vote for, **2000:**161
  makes a difference who is elected,
    2000:15
  more enthusiastic about voting
    than usual, **2000:**342
  Mormon as, **1999:**54
  as most important issue,
    2003:285, 443
  need to know background of,
    1998:36–39
  positions of, as voting issues,
    1999:68–69, **2000:**243, 355
  predictions for, **2003:**135–36

priorities *(continued)*
Iraq war as, **2007:**2–3, 16–17,
60–61, 90–92, 148–49, 183,
191–92, 237–38, 305, 349
judicial system as, **2007:**3, 60–61,
148–49, 305
leadership as, **2007:**3, 60–61,
148–49, 305
marriage as, **2007:**3
Medicare as, **2007:**3, 16–17,
60–61, 90, 148–49, 237–38, 305
Middle East as, **2007:**3, 148–49,
237–38, 305
national security as, **2007:**2,
60–61, 90, 148–49, 191–92,
237–38, 305
North Korea as, **2007:**3
oil as, **2007:**2, 60–61, 90, 148–49,
191–92, 237–38, 305
by political affiliation,
2007:16–17, 61, 91, 192, 238
poverty as, **2007:**3, 60–61,
148–49, 237–38, 305
for president, **2007:**2–3, 60–61,
90–92, 148–49, 191–92,
237–38, 305, 349
Republican Party and,
2007:16–17, 61, 91, 192, 238
respect as, **2007:**3
Social Security as, **2007:**2, 16–17,
60–61, 90, 148–49, 191–92,
237–38, 305
taxes as, **2007:**2, 60–61, 148–49,
191–92, 237–38, 305
terrorism as, **2007:**2, 16–17,
60–61, 90, 148–49, 191–92,
237–38, 305
unemployment as, **2007:**3, 60–61,
148–49, 191–92, 237–38, 305
See also issues, most important
prisoners, 2005:167, 225–26,
2006:393
See also imprisonment
prisons, 2000:301

privacy, 2004:112
invasions of, **2000:**86
more or less, in year 2025, **1998:**220
See also civil liberties
private school, 2004:386
See also school(s)
problems, most important
[list] **2001:**121, **2002:**9, 70,
115–16, 232–33, 359,
2003:24–25, 61–62, 86, 122,
154–55, 203, 284, 401, 442
profanity, 2004:61–62
find offensive in movies, **1999:**271
**Program for International Student
Assessment, 2004:**512
The Progress Paradox, 2004:292
prosperity, 2004:139, **2005:**1, 27,
29, 37, 362
Bush administration and, **2001:**8–9
Democratic versus Republican
Party and, **1998:**229
Protestants, Protestantism
abortion and, **2005:**151, **2006:**133
age and, **2004:**511
approval ratings and,
2004:217–18
Bible in, **2006:**209–10, **2007:**230
blacks and, **2007:**83
Catholicism and, **2005:**150–51,
2006:196
church and, **2004:**119, 225, 370,
512, **2005:**233, **2006:**149–50,
234, **2007:**150
confidence in, **2004:**225,
2007:270
creationism and, **2004:**463
crime and, **2007:**217
death penalty and, **2004:**454,
2005:151, 186
divorce and, **2005:**151
election of 2006 and, **2006:**253
euthanasia and, **2005:**179
evolution and, **2004:**464
friendship and, **2004:**99

Q

quality of life
  better in year 2025 than today
    for average Americans,
      1998:218
    for middle class, **1998:**219
    for the poor, **1998:**219
    for the rich, **1998:**219
  immigrants making the quality of
    life better or worse, **2001:**170,
    2002:226
Quayle, Dan, 2004:124, 126, 273,
    287–88, 314, **2006:**95–96
  likely to support, **1998:**65, 227,
    1999:71, 99
  opinion of, **1998:**65, **1999:**46

R

race
  affirmative action and,
    2005:314–15, 338
  age and, **2004:**19, 223
  alcohol and, **2005:**262
  approval ratings, **2004:**184–85,
    2005:145, 263–64, 342,
    2006:215, 276, 530
  Bush, George W., and, **2005:**3–4,
    263–64, 341–44, 346,
    2006:215, 276, 297, 410,
    458–60, 530
  children, **2004:**276–77
  church and, **2004:**303–4, 333, 512
  clothing and, **2005:**274
  college and, **2006:**484
  community and, **2004:**18–19, 223,
    282
  Congress and, **2005:**3–4, 145
  cost of living and, **2006:**459–60,
    484
  crime and, **2004:**478–79,
    2007:217, 304, 316

death penalty and, **2004:**453–54,
    495, **2005:**186, 457
debt and, **2006:**484
Democratic Party and,
    2007:277–78, 281
economy and, **2004:**69, 276–78,
    317, **2007:**304, 316
education and, **2004:**18–19,
    199–201, 223, 276–77,
    317–18, 377, 455–56
election of 2004 and, **2004:**257,
    329, 332–33, 423–24, 441–43
election of 2006 and, **2006:**253,
    297–98, 355–56, 378, 424–26,
    459–60, 465, 471–72
employment and, **2004:**18–19,
    276–77, 290, 350–51,
    2005:135, 286–87, 314,
    2007:287, 293–94, 304
energy and, **2005:**286,
    2006:459–60, 484
entertainment and, **2007:**293
entrepreneurship and, **2005:**135
families and, **2004:**18–19
finances and, **2004:**18–19,
    291–92, 317, **2005:**93–94, 274
food and, **2005:**274, **2007:**304
friendship and, **2004:**282
gambling and, **2004:**123
gasoline and, **2005:**196, 286,
    2006:279, 459–60, 484
geographic region and, **2004:**223
Gonzales, Alberto, and, **2005:**246
Gore, Al, and, **2006:**321
government and, **2004:**278,
    2005:341–44, 394, **2007:**316
guns and, **2004:**472, **2005:**438
happiness and, **2004:**1, **2007:**554
health and, **2004:**18–19, 291
healthcare and, **2004:**290–91,
    304–5, **2005:**136, **2006:**279,
    459–61, 484, **2007:**307–8,
    316
health insurance and, **2005:**14

race relations *(continued)*
　　Hispanics and, **2001:**158, **2003:**
　　　221, **2004:**67, 274–76, 350–51
　　immigrants and, **2001:**158
　　independents and, **2004:**38
　　as most important issue, **1998:**
　　　60–61, **1999:**195, **2000:**192,
　　　2001:59, 121, 255, **2002:**10,
　　　71, 116, 233, 360, **2003:**25, 62,
　　　86, 155, 203, 285, 443,
　　　2004:37–38, **2005:**99, 174,
　　　213, 348, **2006:**138–39, 479
　　as most important issue facing
　　　nation 25 years from now,
　　　2002:117
　　opinion of, **1998:**70, 183–84,
　　　2002:177–78, **2003:**220,
　　　295–97
　　outlook for, **1998:**219, 222,
　　　2004:275–76, 292–94
　　as presidential election issue,
　　　2000:19, 72, 281
　　as priority, **2001:**9
　　rated, **1998:**69, **2003:**220, 296
　　Republican Party and, **2004:**38,
　　　127
　　satisfaction with, **2001:**29, 158,
　　　2003:296, **2004:**19, 66–67,
　　　130, 223, 274–76, **2005:**20, 22,
　　　40
　　whites and, **2004:**274–76, 292–94,
　　　350–51
　　worry about, **2001:**59, 67,
　　　2002:118, **2003:**127–28,
　　　2004:126–27, 139, 159,
　　　2007:126
racism, 2000:145, 282, **2004:**201,
　　377, 414, **2005:**99, 174, 213, 348
　　as most important issue,
　　　1998:60–61, **1999:**195,
　　　2000:191, 316, **2001:**255,
　　　2002:10, 71, 116, 233, 360,
　　　2003:25, 62, 86, 155, 203, 285,
　　　443

as most important issue facing
　　nation 25 years from now,
　　2002:117
racial stereotypes offensive in
　　movies, **1999:**271
radio, 2001:201, **2002:**240,
　　2003:289, **2004:**361–62, 407,
　　427, 501–3
　　bias in, **1998:**171
　　confidence in, **1998:**97, 254,
　　　1999:51, **2002:**282
　　and Florida election controversy,
　　　2000:409
　　health/medical information from,
　　　2002:293
　　hobby you are particularly inter-
　　　ested in, **2002:**7
　　as news source, **1998:**192,
　　　2002:293, **2003:**2
　　talk shows, **2000:**409, **2003:**2
radioactivity
　　worry about contamination of soil
　　　and water by, **2001:**90
rain forests, 2004:141, **2006:**164–66
Ramsey family, 2000:88
Rangel, Charles, 2007:390
Rather, Dan, 2004:392–94,
　　2007:193
reading, 1999:267, **2004:**427
　　as favorite way of spending
　　　evening, **1998:**237, **1999:**252,
　　　2002:6
　　hobby you are particularly inter-
　　　ested in, **2002:**7
　　who is your favorite author [list],
　　　1999:267
　　would read book on perfect vaca-
　　　tion, **1999:**270
***Ready or Not: Creating a High
　　School Diploma That Counts,***
　　2004:67
Reagan, Nancy, 1998:2, **1999:**242,
　　2002:400, **2003:**455, **2004:**514,
　　2005:483, **2006:**52

Reagan, Ronald

admiration of, **1998:**1, 154,
1999:242, **2000:**264, 431,
2002:400, **2003:**454,
2004:230, 233, 514, **2005:**482,
2006:536

approval ratings, **1998:**25, **2002:**
96–97, **2004:**8, 17, 151, 211–12,
229–32, 247–48, 259, 265–66,
303, 413–14, 416, 444, 450,
2006:7, 23–24, 40–41, 92, 182,
190, 200–201, 245–46, 329,
375, 434, 466, 539, **2007:**
25–26, 166, 313, 484

after two years in office (Oct.
1982), **2002:**387

averages during seventh quarter as president, **2002:**322

in December of last year in
office, *Gallup analysis* of,
2000:422

volatility of, *Gallup analysis*
of, **1998:**22–23

assassination attempt on,
2004:231

conventions and, **2004:**279–80,
356–57

death of, **2004:**237

debate by, **2004:**411

defense spending and, **2004:**97

economy and, **2004:**230–31,
2005:33

elections and, **2004:**17, 85, 113,
125, 151, 231, 259, 265–66,
387, **2007:**101

ethics of, **2005:**399

foreign affairs and, **2005:**34

gender and, **2004:**96

Gallup analysis of gender gap,
versus Carter/Mondale,
2000:159

as greatest president, **2000:**58,
2001:44–45, **2003:**163–64,
413, **2004:**233, 237–38

Grenada invasion and, **2004:**231

health of, **2004:**232, 404

image of, **2004:**230–33, 237–38,
249

inauguration of, **2005:**24–25

Iran-Contra affair and, **1998:**19,
2004:230–31, 248

Lebanon and, **2004:**231

legacy of, **2006:**518

national defense and, **2007:**96

as outstanding president, **1999:**77

political affiliation and,
2004:211–12, 229–30, 238,
2006:190, 246

U.S., satisfaction with, and,
2004:239, 341

as worst president, **2000:**59

real estate, 2005:311, 422, 448

agents, honesty and ethical standards of, **1999:**148, **2000:**389

developers, honesty and ethical
standards of, **1999:**148

industry

honesty and ethical standards
in, **2002:**373

overall view of, **2001:**201,
2002:240, **2003:**289

recession, 2004:10, **2006:**237, 288

and budget deficit, **2002:**22

current, **2001:**58, 93, 120, 218,
222, **2002:**70, 143, 315,
2003:143

mild, moderate, or serious,
2003:143

as most important issue, **1998:**60,
2001:58, 121, 255, **2002:**9, 70,
116, 233, **2003:**25, 62, 86, 122,
155, 203, 284, 442

as most important issue facing
nation 25 years from now,
2002:117

recession in next year, **1998:**206,
2000:407, **2001:**58

tax cuts and, **2001:**39

recreation, **2004:**44, 100, 122–23,
249–50, 466, **2005:**86–87, 367,
411, 438–39, 478–81, **2006:**
489
See also entertainment; sports
Red Cross work
hobby you are particularly interested in, **2002:**7
Redford, Robert, 2001:76
red states
approval ratings in, **2004:**184
Bush, George W., and, **2004:**189
economy and, **2004:**333–35
election of 2004 and, **2004:**162,
184, 189, 299–300, 333–35,
338–40, 354, 430
Iraq war and, **2004:**336
Kerry, John, and, **2004:**189
Nader, Ralph, and, **2004:**189
political affiliation and, **2004:**3,
23, 25
Reeve, Christopher, 2004:415
Reeves, Keano, 2001:76
Reform party, 1999:89
refunds, tax, 2005:139
region. *See* geographic region
Rehnquist, William, 1999:47,
2005:329, **2007:**417, 427
Reid, Harry, 2005:206, **2006:**319,
499, **2007:**190–91, 473
reincarnation
believe in, **2001:**137
religion
abortion and, **2005:**125, 131–32,
150–51
age and, **2004:**120, 511–12,
2005:133, 234, 447, **2006:**196,
210, 259, 334, 493,
2007:230–31
approval ratings, **2004:**217–18
believe in God or higher power,
1999:281
Bible in, **2001:**98, **2004:**462–63

Brownback, Sam, and,
2007:113–14, 326
Bush, George W., and,
2004:217–18, 255–57, 328–29,
383–84, 428–29, 442–43,
497–99, 505
in Canada, **2004:**405, 415
can answer today's problems,
2001:98
Catholicism and, **2002:**125,
2005:233
Christianity and, **2005:**233
Christmas and, **2004:**510–11,
2005:477–78
church/synagogue attendance,
1998:186, 237, 242, **2000:**94,
2001:98, 276, **2002:**88,
390–91, 397–98, **2003:**427–28,
2005:463, **2007:**43–44, 94,
150
on Easter Sunday, **2002:**88
confidence in, **1998:**181,
1999:208, **2000:**208,
2001:149, **2002:**184,
2003:205–6, **2004:**13, 224–25,
251, 306, **2005:**201–2,
2006:232–34
conservatives and, **2007:**77–78,
94
creationism and, **2004:**462–64
crime and, **2007:**217
death penalty and, **2004:**454–55,
495–97, **2005:**131–32, 150,
457
decline in, as most important
issue, **2001:**255, **2002:**10, 70,
116, 233
describe self as "born-again" or
evangelical, **1998:**186, 242,
2000:97, **2001:**98, 276,
2002:398
displays of religious symbols,
2003:352–53

drugs and, **2005:**408

education and, **2004:**120, 511–12, **2005:**132, 234, 447, **2007:**78, 230

election of 2004 and, **2004:**92–93, 256–57, 328–29, 383–84, 428–29, 442–43, 497–99

election of 2006 and, **2006:**253, 355–56, 378, 424–26, 459–60, 465, 472

election of 2008 and, **2007:**77–78, 106–9, 113–15, 187–88, 227–29, 253–54, 326–27, 424–26, 479–80, 527–28, 548

entertainment and, **2004:**358–59

euthanasia and, **2005:**179–80

evangelical Christianity and, **2005:**233

friendship and, **2004:**99

gender and, **2002:**88, **2003:**205, **2004:**70, 120, 506, 511–12, **2005:**132, 234, 447, 463, **2006:**260, 493, **2007:**260

geographic region and, **2004:** 120, 251–53, 511–12, **2005:**132–33, 234, 447, 463, **2006:**210, 260, 494, **2007:**94–95, 230–31

Gilmore, Jim, and, **2007:**326

Gingrich, Newt, and, **2007:**113–14, 187–88, 326

Giuliani, Rudy, and, **2007:**113–14, 187–88, 253–54, 326, 424–26, 548

God and, **1999:**282, **2004:**462–63, **2005:**463

government and, **2003:**353, **2004:**177–78, 447, 505–7, **2005:**412

Graham, Billy, and, **2005:**231

in Great Britain, **2004:**405, 415

Hagel, Chuck, and, **2007:**326

happiness and, **2007:**554

hate crime law should cover religious and ethnic minorities, **1999:**154

homelessness and, **2005:**134

homosexuality and, **2004:**369–71, 405

Huckabee, Mike, and, **2007:**326, 548

hunger and, **2005:**134

Hunter, Duncan, and, **2007:**326

identification with, **2004:**118, 217, 251–53, 255–57, 358–59

ideology and, **2004:**120, 511–12, **2005:**124–25, 133, 151, 234, 448

importance of, **1998:**186, 242, **1999:**265, **2000:**93, **2001:**97, 276, **2002:**88, 265, 390, 397, **2003:**1, 427–28, **2004:**118–20, 255–56, 405, 415, 512

income and, **2004:**512, **2005:**133, 234, 447, **2006:**259–60, 494

increasing its influence, **1998:**186, **2001:**98, 276, **2002:**397, **2003:**428

index of, **2004:**13–14

law enforcement and, **2005:**420

liberals and, **2007:**77–78, 94

and Littleton shootings, **1999:**192

marriage and, **2004:**369–71, 405, 511

McCain, John, and, **2007:**113–14, 187–88, 326–27, 424–26, 548

moderates and, **2007:**77–78, 94

morality and, **2004:**13, 506–7, **2007:**239

as most important issue, **2002:**359, **2003:**25, 62, 86, 155, 203, 284, 401, 443, **2004:**414, 467, **2005:**18, 99, 174, 213, 348

Nader, Ralph and, **2004:**257

need to experience spiritual growth, **1998:**239

religion *(continued)*

opinion of, **1998:**239, **1999:**281–82

can answer all or most of today's problems, **2001:**276

can answer today's problems, **1998:**186–87, **2000:**95, **2002:**88, 398

likely that world will end on Judgment Day in next century, **1998:**223

postpone release of videotape of Clinton's testimony because of Rosh Hashanah, **1998:**214

spirituality as biggest challenge you face today, **2000:**192

your sympathies more with Irish Catholics or Irish Protestants, **1998:**87–88

paranormal and, **2005:**221

and parents, **1998:**190

party identification and, **2003:**84

Paul, Ron, and, **2007:**326

political affiliation and, **2004:**92–93, 120, 217–18, 391–92, 506, 511, **2005:**133, 151, 183–84, 234, 412, 447, **2006:**108–9, 210, 253, 260, 355–56, 367–69, 378, 413–14, 424–26, 446, 472

political ideology and, **2007:**77–78, 94

political power of, **2004:**505–7

poverty and, **2005:**134

predictions on, **1998:**219, 221

preference for, **2000:**96, **2003:**428, **2005:**114

president and, **1999:**106

Protestantism and, **2002:**125, **2005:**233

in public schools, **1999:**192, 207, **2000:**200, 241, **2001:**50

race and, **2004:**120, 329, 512, **2005:**133, 233, 267–68, 447, **2006:**108, 459–60, 494

received any religious training as child, **1998:**239

religious right, **2000:**70

Romney, Mitt, and, **2007:**113–14, 187–88, 326, 424–26, 548

satisfaction with, **2001:**28, **2004:**99–100, **2005:**11, 20–22, 46, **2007:**30–32, 43–45, 428–30, 554

sex and, **2004:**490–91

stem cell research and, **2004:**415, **2005:**125, 131–32, 150–51

suicide and, **2004:**281, **2005:**179–80

Supreme Court and, **2005:**283

surveys of, **2004:**13–14, 117–20

Tancredo, Tom, and, **2007:**326

teenagers and, **2004:**358–59, 369–71, 391–92, 414, 490–91

Thompson, Fred, and, **2007:** 187–88, 326, 424–26, 548

Thompson, Tommy, and, **2007:**113–14, 326

tolerance of, **2004:**70–71

traditional values and, **2004:**447

U.S., satisfaction with by, **2006:**81, 238

Reno, Janet, 1998:2, 154–55, 186, 204, 252, **1999:**242, **2000:**34, 129, 131

renting, 2006:179, 210–12

See also home ownership

Republican Party, 2004:15–17, 37–38, 69, 113, 127, 156, **2005:**360, **2007:**28

abortion and, **2004:**141, **2005:**3–4, 175, 192–93, 245–46, 405, 443–44, **2007:**221, 295

admiration by, **2004:**514, **2005:**483

Republican Party *(continued)*
    322–23, 364–65, 408, 441–42,
    502
    conventions of, **2000:**224–25,
        2004:278–80, 297, 312–14,
        351–54, 356–58, 361, 366,
        371–73, 378, 444, 498–99
    corruption and, **2006:**4–6, 13–15,
        139, 188–89, 193–94, 205–6,
        227–28, 267–68, 412, 426–27,
        435, 478
    cost of living and, **2004:**38, 156
    creationism and, **2004:**463
    crime and, **2004:**38, 127, 156,
        2006:125–26, 139,
        2007:16–17, 217
    Cuba and, **2005:**128, **2006:**130, 524
    death penalty and, **2004:**453, 495,
        2005:186, 192–93, 457,
        2006:212–13, 225
    defense and, **2004:**167–68, 269
    DeLay, Tom, and, **2005:**453
    versus Democratic Party,
        1998:194, 224–25, 229, 240,
        1999:211, **2000:**344, 386,
        2002:17–18, 273, 307, 319,
        2003:328
    Dole, Bob, and, **2004:**319
    drugs and, **2004:**38, 127, 156,
        2005:408, **2006:**125–26, 139
    Dubai ports sale and, **2006:**91
    economy and, **2004:**15, 23–25,
        37–38, 70, 103, 113, 127, 156,
        269, 302, 375, 431–32, **2006:**
        54, 107, 125–26, 139, 155–56,
        159–60, 223, 239–40, 267–68,
        293, 303, 318, 371, 379–80,
        383–86, 389–91, 419, 426–27,
        435, 455, 457–61, 485,
        500–501, 528
    education and, **2004:**15, 38, 156,
        318, 347–48, 431–32, **2007:**
        61, 123, 192, 256, 348, 367,
        411

Edwards, John, and, **2004:**
    272–74, 354, **2006:**332, 502,
    532
Egypt and, **2005:**128, **2006:**130
Eisenhower, Dwight D., and,
    2004:229
election of 2000 and, **1998:**64–65
    likely to support [list],
        1998:65, 227, **1999:**71, 99
election of 2004 and, **2004:**25, 38,
    59–60, 75, 77, 116–17, 143,
    278–80, 287–88, 299, 301–2,
    313–14, 327–28, 337–38, 354,
    360, 372, 375, 423–24,
    431–34, 442, 494–95, 498–99,
    2005:43
election of 2008 and,
    2004:456–57, **2006:**34–35,
    66–67, 234–36, 300–301, 332,
    456, 474, 477–78, 502, 532,
    2007:84–86, 102–3, 107–9,
    127, 141–43, 222, 253–54,
    257–58, 346, 348, 401–2,
    423–24, 464, 476–79, 546
employment and, **2004:**37–38,
    113, 127, 156, 345,
    2006:125–26, 139, 177, 318,
    383–84, 455, 485, **2007:**27,
    62–63, 301–2, 411
energy and, **2004:**121, 127, 156,
    235, **2007:**16–17, 61, 238
enthusiasm of, **2004:**143, 299,
    358, 412–13
environment and, **2004:**15–16, 38,
    121, 127, 142, 156, 159–60,
    431–32, **2007:**54–55, 61,
    111–12, 127, 175, 192
euthanasia and, **2005:**179–80
evolution and, **2004:**464,
    2007:250, 252
families and, **2004:**156, **2007:**411
family values and, **2007:**546
federal budget and, **2004:**15, 38,
    156, **2007:**16–17, 192

Republican Party *(continued)*
  image of, **2004:**59–60, 324,
    327–28, **2006:**52, 130–32,
    499–500, 532, 537,
    2007:141–43, 215, 247, 346,
    406–7, 423–24, 465, 545
    Gallup analysis of,
      1998:144–45
  immigration and, **2004:**15, 38,
    127, 156, **2006:**125–26, 139,
    145, 155–56, 162, 267–68,
    318, 371, 389–91, 426–27,
    435, 459–61, 500–501, 528
  income and, **2004:**373
  independents and, **2004:**217–18,
    2006:194, 285–86, 423, 470
  India and, **2005:**128, **2006:**130
  Indonesia and, **2005:**128
  inflation and, **2004:**38, 156
  intelligence system and, **2004:**
    145, 167–68, **2006:**144, 413
  Internet and, **2006:**56
  Iran and, **2004:**493, **2005:**128–29,
    2006:38, 63, 77, 130–31
  Iraq and, **2003:**184, **2004:**262,
    2005:40–41, 128–29,
    2006:46–47, 77, 130–31, 245,
    413
  Iraq war and, **2004:**15, 37–38,
    114–17, 156, 167, 198–99,
    218–19, 302, 336, 375, 401,
    431–32, 509–10, **2006:**46–47,
    54, 72–73, 94, 107–10, 112,
    138–39, 151–52, 155–56, 193,
    241, 245, 252, 267–68, 278,
    303, 310–11, 317–20, 371,
    385, 389–92, 394–95, 402–4,
    415, 419, 426–29, 435, 444,
    453–55, 459–61, 471, 478,
    500–501, 528
  Israel and, **2005:**128
  Japan and, **2005:**128, **2006:**130
  Johnson, Lyndon, and,
    2004:229–30, 238, **2006:**246

  Jordan and, **2005:**128
  Judaism and, **2004:**217–18
  judicial system and, **2004:**38, 156,
    2005:202, 360
  Kennedy, John F., and, **2004:**238,
    2006:246
  Kerry, John, and, **2004:**77, 84,
    112, 319–20, 324, 337–38,
    360, 375, 395, 401–2, 409,
    442, **2006:**332, 502, 532
  labor unions and, **2005:**202,
    313–14, 323, **2006:**361,
    2007:8, 380
  law enforcement and, **2005:**295,
    420
  lawsuits and, **2005:**3–4, 66
  leadership and, **2004:**156, 372,
    2006:193–94, 272–73, 419–20,
    445
  Libby, I. Lewis "Scooter," and,
    2007:115
  Libya and, **2006:**130
  lobbying and, **2007:**375–76
  love and, **2004:**63
  loyalty in, **2006:**285
  marriage and, **2004:**86, 202,
    431–32, **2005:**3–4, 66, 142,
    2006:208–9, 212–13, 219–20,
    267–68, 472
  math and science aptitudes and,
    2005:96
  McCain, John, and, **2005:**289–90,
    309, **2006:**330–31, 502, 532,
    537, **2007:**215, 346
  media and, **2000:**408, **2004:**156,
    164, 387–88, 393–94, 433,
    2005:360
  Medicare and, **2004:**38, 109–10,
    156, 431–32, **2006:**139
  Mexico and, **2005:**128, **2006:**
    130
  Middle East and, **2007:**531
  military and, **2006:**89–90, 245,
    402–4, 413

minimum wage and, **2007:**11
and minorities, **2000:**282
morality and, **2004:**37–38, 156,
213, 431–32, **2006:**139,
212–14, 219–20, 256, 318,
419, 426–27, 460–61, 528
Mormonism and, **2007:**94
most important issues for,
2003:155–56, **2004:**414,
2006:138–39, 162, 384, 435,
528, **2007:**54–55, 123, 256,
411
music and, **2004:**441
Nader, Ralph, and, **2004:**87–88
national security and, **2004:**38,
113, 115, 156, 167–68,
2005:295
natural disasters and, **2006:**139,
371, **2007:**16–17, 106, 210,
473
news and, **2005:**360, 369
Nixon, Richard, and,
2004:211–12, 229–30, 238,
2006:246
North Korea and, **2004:**493,
2005:128–29, **2006:**77,
130–32, 459
nuclear energy plants and,
2005:161
nuclear weapons and, **2005:**292,
2006:38
Obama, Barack, and, **2006:**502,
532
oil and, **2007:**61, 192, 238
opinion of, **1998:**175, 231–32,
250, **1999:**45, 81, 87, 114–15,
196, **2000:**12–13, 272, 378,
2001:128, **2002:**18, 265, 272,
344, 353–54, 376–77,
2003:327–28
Pakistan and, **2005:**128, **2006:**130
Palestinian Authority and,
2005:128, **2006:**130
parents and, **2006:**472

Patriot Act and, **2004:**94, **2006:**17
patriotism and, **2004:**366–67,
2005:61, 267
Pelosi, Nancy, and, **2006:**499
Philippines and, **2006:**130
Poland and, **2005:**128
political ideology and, **2007:**
294–96, 493
politicians and, **2004:**156
pollution and, **2004:**156
poverty and, **2004:**37–38, 156,
2005:3–4, 356–57, 394,
2006:125–26, 139, 455,
2007:123, 411
Powell, Colin, and, **2004:**480,
514, **2005:**483, **2006:**502, 537
power and, **2004:**156, **2005:**2,
374–75, **2006:**139
prescription drugs and, **2006:**478
presidency and, **2004:**269
primaries of, **2000:**69, **2003:**16
priorities for, **2007:**16–17, 61, 91,
192, 238
privacy and, **2005:**295
on professions, **2006:**520
prosperity and, **2005:**1, 362
public officials and, **2005:**360
public opinion and, **2005:**378
Quayle, Dan, and, **2004:**126
race and, **2004:**38, 127, 278, 318,
368, **2005:**3–4, 264–65, 268,
342, **2006:**125–26, 139, 253,
276, 297–98, 355–56, 378,
424–26, 471–72
Reagan, Ronald, and,
2004:211–12, 229–30, 238,
2006:190, 246
Reid, Harry, and, **2006:**500
religion and, **2004:**92–93, 120,
217–18, 391–92, 506, 512,
2005:133, 151, 234, 412, 447,
2006:108–9, 210, 253, 260,
355–56, 367–69, 378, 413–14,
424–26, 446, 472

voter interest in, **2006:**18–19,
157–58, 171–72, 176, 184–85,
265–66, 377, 422, 467–69
voters for
are prejudiced against blacks,
2002:393
voter turnout for, **2005:**42–43,
2006:157–58, 266, 286, 339,
377, 422, 441–42, 465, 467–69
voting systems and, **2004:**315–16
wages and, **2007:**11
welfare and, **2004:**38
Winfrey, Oprah, and, **2004:**514,
2005:483, **2006:**537
women and, **2004:**130
World War II and, **2005:**292
Republicans in Congress
approval ratings, **1999:**6, 91,
2000:272, **2001:**141, 186,
2002:102, 213–14, **2003:**258,
388
blacks and, **2002:**393
Bush, George W., and, **1999:**91
and Clinton, **1998:**223, 248
confidence in, **2002:**376
and corporations, **2002:**190
and corruption, **2002:**101–2
and Democrats
compared, **1998:**227,
2002:101–3, 213, 246, 291,
332, **2003:**4–5, 258, 272
relations with, **1998:**232,
2000:427, **2002:**101, 103,
190
dissatisfaction with, as most
important issue, **1998:**60,
1999:195
and education, **1998:**56–57
and Enron, **2002:**38
and finances, **1998:**2–3, 54–56,
157, 162, **1999:**92, **2002:**
21–22, **2003:**123, 258, 272
and healthcare system,
2002:101–2

and impeachment, **1998:**246,
248–51, **1999:**6
and Iraq, **2002:**246, **2003:**4, 258
and Medicare, **1998:**55, **1999:**204,
2003:229–30
opinion of, **1998:**158, 175, 215,
231–32, **1999:**91, **2001:**7–9,
187, 206, 210, 229, **2002:**18,
190, 214, 353, 355, 376
responsibility of, **1998:**160, 204–5,
215, 223, 250, **2001:**37, 141
and September 11, 2001, **2002:**155
and Social Security, **2002:**101,
103, **2003:**5
and tax cuts, **1999:**132, 218,
2001:195
and terrorism, **2003:**4, 258
and Yugoslavia, **1999:**28
reservoirs
worry about pollution of, **2002:**81,
112
residential areas
Bush, George W., and, **2006:**215
crime in, **2006:**490
election of 2006 and, **2006:**253,
378, 472
guns and, **2006:**439
New Year and, **2006:**537
political affiliation and, **2006:**253,
378, 472
population and, **2006:**291
See also geographic region
respect, 2004:37–38, 156, 183,
2005:99, 174, 213, 336, 348,
2006:458–61, 479
lack of
as most important issue,
2001:59, 121, 256,
2002:10, 71, 116, 233, 360,
2003:25, 62, 87, 122, 155,
203, 284, 443
as most important issue facing
nation 25 years from now,
2002:117

restaurants
ban cigarette smoking in,
1999:277, **2001:**182
industry, overall view of,
2001:200, **2002:**240, **2003:**289
would seek out on perfect vacation, **1999:**270
resting/relaxing
favorite way of spending an
evening, **2002:**6
retail industry, 2005:311, 422
overall view of, **2001:**200,
2002:240, **2003:**289
retirement, 2004:174–75, 206–9,
344, 465–66, **2005:**159
age of, **2002:**123, **2003:**124
assessment of, **2006:**408
economy and, **2006:**216, 222
education and, **2006:**264
employer pension plans, **2001:**123
satisfaction with, **1999:**137
employment and, **2007:**208–9, 378
families and, **2007:**266, 349
income, **2001:**122–23,
2002:122–23, **2003:**124,
2005:159–60, 182, **2006:**180,
261–63, 483, **2007:**207–8, 436
marriage and, **2006:**181
money for, as biggest challenge
you face today, **2000:**192
as most important issue, **2005:**22,
45, 93–95, 113, 152–53, 198,
366, 409, 421, **2007:**349
race and, **2006:**484
savings for, **2007:**436
See also Social Security
Revolutionary War
from what country did America
gain its independence following, **2001:**155
Rhode Island, 2006:415–17, 461–63
Rice, Condoleezza, 2003:251, 297,
2005:71, 115–16, 299–300, 310,
467–68, 483, **2006:**401

admiration of, **2001:**278,
2002:400, **2003:**455,
2004:513–14
election of 2008 and, **2004:**457
gender and, **2006:**537
image of, **2004:**145, 168, 480,
2006:34–35, 532
political affiliation and, **2004:**480,
514, **2006:**34–35, 502, 532,
537
Richardson, Bill, 2000:208,
2005:300, 468, **2006:**66, 477,
531, **2007:**124, 370, 420
rich people
paying their fair share in federal
taxes, **1999:**124
political parties and, **1998:**232
quality of life better in year 2025
than today for, **1998:**219
richest person in U.S., know name
of, **2000:**34
tax cuts and, **1999:**133–34
Ridge, Tom, 2001:255, 270,
2004:479
Riordan, Richard, 2003:2 **2003:**78,
279
Ripken, Cal, Jr., 1998:226,
2000:289, **2001:**83, 142,
2006:529
rivers
pollution of, worry about, **2002:**
81, 112
Roberts, John, 2007:417, 427
Roberts, Julia, 2000:98, **2001:**76,
278, **2002:**400, **2003:**455, **2006:**507
Roberts, Oral, 2004:251
Robert Wood Johnson Foundation,
2004:481
Robinson, Jackie, 2001:83
Robinson, Susan, 2004:386
Rock, Chris, 2001:76–77
rock and roll music
greatest singer or band member
[list], **2000:**265

Rockefeller, Nelson, **2004**:126
Roddick, Andy, **2004**:367
rodeo, **2004**:44, 489
Roe v. Wade, **2006**:29, 32,
    2007:211–13, 220, 248–49
    See also abortion
The Rolling Stones, **2000**:265
romance. *See* love
Romania, **1998**:171
Romney, Mitt, **2005**:300, 310, 468,
    2007:186–87, 346, 548
    church attendance and, **2007**:
        113–14, 187–88, 326, 548
    elections and, **2007**:239, 267–69,
        397, 505–6, 536, 538–40
    familiarity with, **2007**:225–26,
        367–69, 388–89, 550
    image of, **2007**:22–23, 103–4,
        118, 130–31, 155, 162–63,
        223–24, 226–27, 247, 256–58,
        281–83, 345–46, 362, 397–98,
        424–26, 452, 462, 541, 551
    political ideology and,
        2007:117–18, 186–87, 548
    religion and, **2007**:113–14,
        187–88, 326, 424–26, 548
Roosevelt, Eleanor, **2000**:264,
    2002:400, **2004**:514, **2005**:483,
    2006:52
Roosevelt, Franklin D., **2005**:74–75,
    135
    admiration of, **2000**:264
    approval ratings, **2004**:450
    as greatest president, **2000**:58,
        2001:44–45, **2003**:163–64,
        413, **2004**:233, 237–38
    health of, **2004**:404
    image of, **2004**:232–33, 237–38,
        249
    political affiliation and, **2004**:238
    vice presidents of, **2004**:126
    as worst president, **2000**:59
Roosevelt, Theodore, **2004**:233,
    2007:76

as greatest president, **2000**:58,
    2001:44, **2003**:163–64, 413
Roper, Elmo, **2007**:165
Roper Poll, **2007**:viii, 165
Rose, Pete, **1999**:256, 266, **2000**:1,
    2001:83
Rounds, Mike, **2002**:340–41
Rove, Karl, **2005**:276–77, 399, 402,
    2007:139, 357–59
Rumsfeld, Donald, **2002**:296,
    2003:115, **2004**:194, 480, 503–4,
    509, **2005**:234
    approval ratings, **2001**:254, 269,
        2003:114
rural and domestic arts
    hobby you are particularly inter-
        ested in, **2002**:7
rural areas
    drugs and, **2005**:163–64
    economy and, **2005**:108
    euthanasia and, **2005**:179
    gambling and, **2004**:123
    guns and, **2004**:472, **2005**:141
    health and, **2004**:476
    Internet and, **2004**:109
    law enforcement and, **2005**:420
    movies and, **2004**:89
    Patriot Act and, **2004**:94
    school, confidence in, **2004**:305
    sex offender registries and,
        2005:212
    stress and, **2004**:182
    suicide and, **2005**:179
Russia, **2004**:73, 100, **2005**:71,
    78–79, 128, **2006**:70–71, 77, 79,
    130, **2007**:78–81, 508, 542
    economic aid to, **1999**:183
    know name (Putin) of president
        of, **2000**:175
    NATO and, **1998**:171–72
    and nuclear weapons, **1998**:78,
        180, **2000**:101
    opinion of, **1999**:183, 231,
        2000:3–4, 101, 172–73, 175,

Russia *(continued)*
380, **2001:**44, 84, **2002:**45, 52,
2003:39, 56, 99
predictions for, **1998:**221, **1999:**183
Russian Orthodox Christianity,
2004:118
Ruth, Babe, 1999:256, **2000:**1,
2001:83, **2003:**198, **2007:**261
Ryan, George, 2007:329
Ryan, Meg, 2000:98, **2001:**76
Ryan, Nolan, 2001:83

S

safety, 1998:137, 184–85,
2004:18–19, 448–50
See also crime; national security
St. Anselm College, 2004:30
St. Louis Cardinals, 2001:81
salesperson, sales clerk, 2005:222
homosexuals should be hired as,
1999:169
honesty and ethical standards of,
1999:148
recommend as career for young
man, **1998:**238
recommend as career for young
woman, **1998:**238–39,
2001:109
Sampras, Pete, 2000:289
Samuels, Rose, 2004:317
Sanchez, Loretta, 2003:278–79
Sanchez, Ricardo, 2007:454
Sanders, Deion, 2000:289
San Diego Padres, 2001:82
Sandoval, Brian, 2004:129
San Francisco, 2000:298–99,
2001:235, **2004:**448–49
San Francisco Chronicle, **2004:**144
San Francisco Giants, 2001:81
Sanger, David, 2006:6
Santorum, Rick, 2006:364
Sarandon, Susan, 2003:80

Sarbanes-Oxley Act, 2004:271–72
Sarkar, Simon, 2004:55
SARS (Severe Acute Respiratory
Syndrome), 2003:131, 133, 425,
2004:394
Satanism
violent groups at school and,
1999:189
satisfaction
with abortion policies, **2004:**130,
140, **2005:**20–22, 40
with amount of leisure time,
1998:138
with availability of health care,
2000:204
with availability of transportation,
1998:137
better off than eight years ago,
2000:13
blacks and, **2005:**20, 22, 39,
2007:289–90, 292–94, 554
with campaign finance, **2005:**11,
20, 22, 40
with career, **2004:**100
church attendance and, **2007:**554
with community, **2004:**18–19,
2005:11
with corporations, **2005:**20–22,
2007:30–32
with crime policies, **2004:**130
with defense, **2004:**129–30
Democratic Party and, **2004:**69,
113, 156, 239, **2007:**28–29, 54,
153, 410, 442, 553
with economy, **2000:**13, 204,
2004:205, 296, 317
with education, **1998:**137,
2000:204, **2004:**18–19, 199,
376
elections and, **2004:**156–57,
433–34, 499
with families, **2004:**18–19,
99–100
with federal government, **2004:**56

satisfaction *(continued)*
  with women's position,
    2004:129–30, **2005:**20, 22, 39
  See also approval ratings
Saudi Arabia, 2004:73, 75, 222,
  2005:71, 78–79, 128, **2006:**77, 79,
  130, **2007:**79–81, 530–31, 542
  and Iraq, **1998:**32, **2003:**39
  opinion of, **2000:**175, **2001:**44,
    84, **2002:**52, 55, 59, 134,
    2003:56, 340
Saving Private Ryan, **1999:**254,
  2004:228
savings, 2003:370, **2005:**162, 181,
  208–9, 366, 386–87, 409,
  2007:266, 349, 436
  age and, **2006:**261
  assessment of, **2006:**249
Sawyer, Diane, 2004:30, **2005:**9
scandals, 2005:32
Scanlan, Suzanne, 2005:253
Schiavo, Michael, 2005:105,
  109–10, 117–18, 122
Schiavo, Terri, 2004:280–81,
  2005:105–6, 109–10, 112,
  116–18, 121–23, 131, 145, 208
Schieffer, Bob, 2007:193
Schindler's List **(movie), 1998:**187
school(s), 2006:358–59, 432–33,
  437–38, 479, **2007:**383–84
  Bush, George W., and, **2004:**471
  cheating in, **2004:**192
  class standing in, **2004:**47, 192
  community and, **2004:**305, 455
  confidence in, **2004:**225, 305–6,
    2005:201
  cost of, **2004:**386
  creationism versus evolution in,
    2005:190–92, 379
  curricula in, **2004:**242, 376–77,
    512–13
  drugs in, **2004:**426
  educational emphasis in,
    2005:333

  funding for, **2004:**376–77,
    390–91, 394, 426–27, 455–56
  geographic region and, **2004:**386
  guns in, **2005:**140
  income and, **2004:**391, 426–27
  junk food in, **2004:**385
  most important issues of,
    2004:426–27
  parents and, **2004:**376–77, 455–56
  performance in, **2004:**67–68, 512
  political affiliation and, **2004:**305
  private, **2004:**386
  race and, **2004:**317, 391, 455–56
  satisfaction with, **2004:**317
  subjects in, favorite, **2004:**242
  teaching in, **2004:**376–77, 426
  teenagers and, **2004:**26, 47,
    67–68, 242
  types of, **2004:**386
  vouchers for, **2004:**390–91, 394
  See also education; public schools
School Choice Wisconsin, 2004:390
school shootings and violence,
  1998:184–85, **1999:**172–73, 176,
  179, 220–21, **2001:**78, 87–88,
  2004:426
  as most important issue,
    1999:195, **2001:**59, 121, 256,
    2002:10, 71, 116, 360,
    2003:25, 62, 87
  as most important issue facing
    nation 25 years from now,
    2002:117
  See also Littleton, Colorado,
    school shootings; students (age
    13 to 17), asked of
Schroeder, Gerhard, 2002:296,
  2004:74
Schumer, Charles, 2006:352
Schwarzenegger, Arnold, 2000:98,
  2001:76, **2003:**279, 344, 454,
  2004:354, 457, **2006:**536
  did best job in gubernatorial
    debate, **2003:**344

likely to support, **2003:**278–79, 282–83, 343–44, 350

opinion of, **2003:**80, 279, 343

qualifications of, **2003:**279, 344, 350, 367

would vote for him if he were running for governor in your state, **2003:**367

Schwarzkopf, Norman, 1998:1, **2000:**410

Schweitzer, Albert, 2002:401, **2004:**514, **2005:**482

Seagal, Steven, 2000:99, **2001:**76

seasons, 2005:223

Seattle, 2000:298–99, **2001:**235, **2004:**448–49

Seattle Mariners, 2001:81

secondhand smoke, 2001:182

secretary

recommend as career for young woman, **1998:**239, **2001:**109

security. *See* national security

Seger, Bob, 2000:265

"Seinfeld," 1998:61–63

Seinfeld, Jerry, 1998:155

self-employment

recommend as career for young man, **1998:**238

recommend as career for young woman, **2001:**109

Selig, Bud, 2003:245, **2005:**115

Selleck, Tom, 2001:77

make special effort to see, **2001:**76

Senate, 2006:53, 364–65, 415–17, 461–64, 520

and Clinton, **1999:**2, 8–10, 13, 16

confidence in, **1999:**50

filibuster in, **2005:**189–90, 203–4, 239

honesty of, **2005:**448

and impeachment, **1999:**6–9

and Nuclear Test Ban Treaty, **1999:**230

See also Congress

senators

honesty and ethical standards of, **1999:**148, **2000:**388, **2001:**265, **2003:**422–23

September 11, 2001 terrorist attacks, 2005:8, 26–27, 333–36, **2007:**115, 395–96, 416

and American life, **2001:**216, **2002:**1, 64, 264, **2004:**71, 362

2002 anniversary of, **2002:**261

Bush, George W., and, **2001:**216, **2004:**104, 144–47, 211, 230, 267–68, 325–26

Clinton, Bill, and, **2004:**134–35, 145–46, 267–68

Congress and, **2002:**155, **2004:**205, 325–26

cover-up concerning, **2004:**135, 146

death penalty and, **2004:**227

Democrats in Congress and, **2002:**155

and economy, **2002:**223

effects of, **2001:**240, **2002:**64–65, 166, 264–65, 275, **2003:**110

election of 2004 and, **2004:**145

Hussein, Saddam, and, **2003:**333, **2004:**399–401

immigration and, **2004:**14–15, 295–96

investigation of, **2004:**134–35, 144–46, 325–26, 394

Kerry, John, and, **2004:**325

media and, **2002:**261

opinion of, **2001:**215–16, **2002:**64, 155, 262

versus Pearl Harbor

a hundred years from now, which event will historians say had a greater impact on the United States, 2001:266

political affiliation and, **2004:**145–46, 325–26, 401

September 11, 2001 terrorist
attacks *(continued)*
prevention of, **2004:**134–35,
145–46, 267–68
return to normality after, **2002:**65,
2003:313, 318
Saudi Arabia and, **2004:**75
should be national holiday, **2002:**65
things in country now back to nor-
mal, **2002:**65
U.S., satisfaction with, and,
2004:187
want to visit site of the World
Trade Center, **2002:**66
White House officials and,
2002:154–55
your view on why there have been
no additional attacks since
September 11, **2002:**262
See also terrorism; War on
Terrorism
Serbia, 1998:225–26
sewing
as favorite way of spending
evening, **1998:**237, **2002:**6
hobby you are particularly interested in, **2002:**7
sex, sexual activity, 2004:61–62,
183, 249–50, 490–91,
2006:69–70, 212–13, 218
affairs, as morally acceptable,
2002:149, **2003:**159, 179, 218
extramarital, **1998:**237
find offensive in movies, **1999:**271
premarital, **1998:**237
think two people have had, only if
they have had intercourse,
1998:216
between unmarried man/woman
as morally acceptable,
2002:149, **2003:**159, 178, 218
See also homosexuals and homosexuality; marriage
sexual harassment, 1998:174

sexually transmitted diseases,
2004:490
Shakespeare, William, 1999:267
Shakespeare in Love **(movie),**
1999:254
Sharapova, Maria, 2004:368
Sharon, Ariel, 2002:48, 161, 169–70,
2005:69, 79, 107, **2007:**97
Sharpton, Al, 2003:251, 297
Bush, George W., and, **2004:**360
election of 2004 and, **2004:**5, 11,
27–28, 30, 33, 76
likely to support, **2002:**90, 395,
2003:16, 135, 190, 215–16,
277, 323, 335, 374–75, 382,
390, 417, 432–33, 446–47
opinion of, **2003:**306
as second choice for nomination,
2003:335
Sheen, Martin, 2003:80
Sheldon, Sidney, 1999:267
Shepherd, Cybill, 1999:90
shopping
are you type of person who more
enjoys spending or saving
money, **2001:**189
by catalog, **2001:**189
as favorite way of spending
evening, **2002:**6
hobby you are particularly interested in, **2002:**7
at malls, department stores, or
other shopping areas, **2001:**189
most stores will be replaced by
shopping on Internet by year
2025, **1998:**222
online, **2001:**189
shots, needles
fear of, **2001:**70
Shriver, Sargent, 2004:42
Sierra Club, 2004:138
Sigelman, Lee, 2007:421
silver, 2004:314–15
Simon, Bill, 2003:278–79

Simon, Paul, 2004:43, 2007:355
Simpson, Nicole Brown, 2004:54
Simpson, O. J., 1999:199, 2004:54
"The Simpsons," 1998:61–62
Singin' in the Rain (movie),
  1998:187
The Sixth Sense (movie), 2000:98
"60 Minutes"
  happen to see interview with
    Kathleen Willey, 1998:41
  how often do you get your news
    from, 1998:193
  trust accuracy of news from,
    1998:98
skateboarding, 2004:359, 367
skating
  as favorite Summer Olympic
    event, 2000:307
  speed, as favorite Winter Olympic
    event, 2002:36
  See also figure skating
skiing, downhill
  as favorite Winter Olympic event,
    2002:36
ski jumping
  as favorite Winter Olympic event,
    2002:36
sleep, 2004:499–501
Slovakia
  allow it to join NATO, 1998:171
Slovenia
  allow it to join NATO, 1998:171
smallpox, 2001:237, 2005:432
  vaccination for, 2001:242,
    2002:375
  worried you will experience this
    illness, 2003:425
Smith, Bob
  likely to support, 1999:71
  opinion of, 1999:46
Smith, Margaret Chase, 2002:400,
  2004:514, 2005:483
Smith, Patricia, 1998:194
Smith, Tom, 2007:420

Smith, Will, 2002:79, 2006:507
smoking. *See* cigarette smoking and
  smokers
snakes
  fear of, 1998:238, 2001:70
sniper shootings, 2005:8
Snipes, Wesley, 2001:76–77
Snow, John W., 2004:34–35
Snow, Tony, 2007:4–6, 28, 37, 88
snowboarding
  as favorite Winter Olympic event,
    2002:36
soccer, 2004:44, 367–68, 489,
  2007:24
  as favorite sport to watch,
    1998:237, 2000:136
  as favorite Summer Olympic
    event, 2000:307
socialism
  as most important issue, 1999:195
social issues, 2004:50–51, 80,
  102–3, 470–71
  young voters on, 2003:389–90
Social Security, 1998:172, 195,
  240–41, 1999:125, 2000:183,
  2002:304, 2004:21, 147, 206–9,
  466, 2005:35, 160, 2007:208
  age and, 2005:5, 36, 64, 66,
    77–78, 156, 165–66, 239–40,
    470, 2006:261
  approval ratings, 2001:166,
    2002:91, 2005:15–16, 19, 27,
    59–60, 62–64, 68, 87–89,
    119–20, 130–31, 164–66, 194,
    239
  assessment of, 2006:408
  budget surplus and, 1998:4, 163,
    2000:318
  Bush, George W., and, 1999:81,
    2000:25, 85, 143, 196, 242,
    248, 258, 275, 309, 357,
    2001:22, 24, 105–6, 2002:27,
    2004:21, 29, 110–12, 420, 469,
    471, 2007:38

Social Security *(continued)*
Clinton and, **1998:**240, **1999:**44
Congress and, **1998:**194, 240,
2002:27, **2005:**3–4, 34–36, 63,
65–67, 130, 240, 412, **2007:**2,
16–17, 60–61, 90, 191–92,
237–38, 305
Democratic Party and, **1998:**194,
224, 240, **2001:**211, **2002:**17,
171, 291, 312, 336, **2003:**5,
2007:16–17, 61, 192
economy and, **2006:**216, 222
election of 2004 and, **2004:**
111–12, 420, 431–32, 469
election of 2006 and, **2006:**22,
25–26, 28, 266–68, 322, 455
expectations of, **1998:**195,
2001:112, 123
families and, **2007:**266, 349
Gallup analysis of importance of,
2000:322
geographic region and,
2005:156–57, 470
Gore and, **1999:**80, **2000:**24, 85,
143, 195, 242, 248, 258, 275,
309, 357
independents and, **2007:**16–17, 192
investors and, **2004:**40
Kerry, John, and, **2004:**111–12,
420, 469
maintaining, as biggest challenge
you face today, **2000:**192
as most important issue,
1998:60–61, **1999:**195,
2000:191, **2001:**59, 121, 255,
2002:10, 71, 116, 233, 360,
2003:25, 62, 86, 122, 155, 203,
284, 401, 443, **2004:**37–38,
155–56, 159, 467, **2005:**18, 35,
45–46, 72–73, 93–95, 98–100,
113, 148, 152–53, 174, 198,
213–14, 220, 223, 348, 366,
409, 421
in community, **2000:**190

as most important issue facing
nation 25 years from now,
2002:116
plans for, **2005:**31–32, 131, 240
political affiliation and,
2007:16–17, 61, 192
predictions for, **2007:**1–2
president and, **2007:**2, 16–17,
60–61, 90, 191–92, 237–38,
305
as priority, **1998:**235, **2000:**212,
428, **2001:**8–9, 229, **2002:**17,
130, 171, **2003:**4, **2007:**2,
16–17, 60–61, 90, 148–49,
191–92, 237–38, 305
privatization of, **2001:**23–24, 112,
2002:303, **2003:**392
race and, **2005:**46
Republican Party and, **1998:**194,
224, 240, **2001:**211, **2002:**17,
171, 291, 312, 336, 376,
2003:5, **2007:**16–17, 61, 192
satisfaction with, **2001:**29,
2004:21, 109–10, **2005:**20, 22,
40
State of the Union address and,
2001:49, **2005:**72–73, **2007:**38
tax cuts and, **2001:**39, 61
as voting issue, **1998:**217, 225,
1999:68, **2000:**18, 72, 242,
280, 356, **2002:**291, 312,
2003:338–39, 416, 454
social work
recommend as career for young
man, **1998:**238
recommend as career for young
woman, **1998:**239, **2001:**109
society (position in), 2004:66–67,
129–30
See also opportunities
soil
worry about contamination of soil
by toxic waste, **2002:**77, 81,
113

solar power
favor spending more money on
developing, **2002:**73
**Solid Foundation Skate Park,
2004:**359
Some Like It Hot (movie), **1998:**187
Sorenstam, Annika, 2003:174
Sosa, Sammy, 1998:155, 226,
2000:289, **2001:**83, 142,
2003:198, **2005:**115, **2007:**261
Souter, David, 2005:176
South Africa, 2001:44, 84
South America, 2000:186
South Carolina, 2002:160
South Dakota, 2002:340–41
**Southern Baptist Convention,
2006:**209
South Korea, 2000:380, **2002:**43,
52, **2003:**56, **2004:**100–101,
2007:508
"South Park," 1998:61–62
Soviet Union
and assassination of President
Kennedy, **2003:**413
breakup of, as most important
event in twentieth century,
2002:175
Spacek, Sissy, 2002:79
space program, 2004:20–21, 82
are there any U.S. astronauts in
space right now, **2003:**291
disasters in, **2003:**42–43, 62, 87,
291
should concentrate on unmanned
missions, **2003:**42
space travel common for ordinary
Americans by year 2025,
1998:222
spending on, **1998:**236, **2003:**42,
291
terrorism and, **2003:**42
value of, **1998:**148
See also NASA
Spacey, Kevin, 2000:99, **2001:**76–77

Spain, 2003:56, 99
special forces, behind enemy lines
favor women serving as, **2002:**3
special prosecutors, 2006:33
Specter, Arlen, 2006:198, 208,
2007:128
speed skating
as favorite Winter Olympic event,
2002:36
spending
age and, **2004:**460, **2005:**209, 435
Christmas and, **2004:**10, 459–62,
491–92, 507, **2005:**87, 434–36,
466, 477, **2006:**441, 485–86,
508–9, 534
on clothing, **2005:**86–87, 222,
367, 410
consumers and, **2004:**107–8,
110–11, 150–51, 185–87,
236–37, 254–55, 286, 379–81,
459–62, 491–92, 508
credit cards and, **2004:**157–58
on defense, **2004:**97–98
on dining, **2005:**86–87, 222, 367,
410–11, 482
economy and, **2004:**107–8,
150–51, 185–86, 452–53,
2006:216, 222, **2007:**297
employment and, **2004:**150
on entertainment, **2005:**86–87,
222, 367, 411
families and, **2007:**266, 349
finances and, **2007:**266, 349
on food, **2005:**86–87, 222, 367,
410, 482
gasoline and, **2004:**148, 150–51,
233, 235–37, 286, 492, 508
gender and, **2004:**461,
2005:86–87, 436
income and, **2004:**236, 254–55,
460–61, 508
interest rates and, **2004:**150
on Iraq war, **2005:**352,
2007:98–100, 185

spending *(continued)*
  as most important issue, **2005:**
    366, 409, 421, **2007:**349
  outlook for, **2004:**254–55, 373,
    379–81, 508, **2005:**181, 208–9,
    348
  outsourcing and, **2004:**110–11
  on poverty, **2005:**394
  preferences for, **2005:**162
  on prescription drugs, **2005:**458
  on recreation, **2005:**86–87, 367, 411
  taxes and, **2004:**150
  See also financial issues; financial
    situation, personal; government
    spending
spiders
  fear of, **1998:**238, **2001:**70
spirituality
  as biggest challenge you face
    today, **2000:**192
sports, 2004:43–45, 122–23, 144,
    367–68, 487–90, **2005:**53–55,
    311–12, 375–77, 422, **2007:**24,
    151–52, 385–87
  college, **2002:**89
  fans, **2001:**24
  favorite sport [list] to watch,
    1998:237
  as favorite way of spending
    evening, **1998:**237, **2002:**6
  greatest athlete active today [list],
    2000:289
  greatest athlete of century [list],
    2000:1
  hobby you are particularly inter-
    ested in, **2002:**6
  industry, overall view of,
    2001:201, **2002:**240, **2003:**
    289
  leagues, and parents, **1998:**190
Springsteen, Bruce, 2000:265
sputniks, Russian launch of
  as most important event in twenti-
    eth century, **2002:**175

Stallone, Sylvester, 2001:76
standard of living, 2004:10, 174–77,
    207, **2005:**73, 159
  satisfaction with, **1998:**137,
    2000:204
  worry about, **2002:**219
  See also cost of living
Stanford University, 1999:219,
    2003:299
Starr, Kenneth
  appropriate to call Monica Lewin-
    sky's mother as witness,
    1998:167
  appropriate to call Secret Service
    agents as witnesses,
    1998:73–74, 167
  belief in, **1998:**217
  blame on, **1998:**200–201, 215
  and Clinton, **1998:**167, 182
  and Clinton's testimony, **1998:**94,
    196, 234, **1999:**2–3, 9
  conclusions of, **1998:**208
  happen to see any of his testimony
    in congressional hearings,
    1998:234
  and investigation, **1998:**95, 170,
    182, 198, 234
  and leaks, **1998:**166–67
  Lewinsky's immunity agreement
    with, **1998:**94
  opinion of, **1998:**18, 28, 155, 215,
    234–35, 252, **1999:**46
  Reno and, **1998:**186
Starr report, 1998:114, 119–21,
    123–24, 130, 206–7, 209–14, 230
Star Wars (movie), **1998:**187
Star Wars: The Phantom Menace
    (movie), **1999:**262
state(s), 2004:2–5, 23–25, 251–53
  rights, as major issue in what war,
    2000:141
  See also blue states; geographic
    region; red states; swing states
State Department, 2006:514

state government, **2004:**163–64,
483–84
confidence in, **1998:**253–54,
1999:51, 158, **2003:**354
state governors, **2006:**519
honesty and ethical standards of,
1999:148, **2000:**388,
2003:422–23
as presidential preparation,
2003:375
State of the Union address,
2001:48, **2002:**29–30,
2003:35–36, **2004:**19–21, 28–29,
2006:40–42, 45, **2007:**28, 38
Steel, Danielle, 1999:267
Steele, Becky, 2004:109
Steele, Michael, 2006:416
Steinbeck, John, 1999:267
Steinberg, Judith, 2004:30
stem cell research, 2001:173–74,
190–91, **2004:**249–50, 329,
415–16, 471, **2005:**72, 195
morality and, **2005:**177, 192–93,
195
as morally acceptable, **2002:**150,
2003:159, 178, 218
political affiliation and,
2005:192–93, 195
religion and, **2005:**125, 131–32,
150–51
Stern, David, 2004:487–88
steroids, 2004:144, 487–88
Stevenson, Adlai, 2002:401,
2004:48, 96, 514, **2005:**482
Gallup analysis of gender gap,
versus Eisenhower, **2000:**159
Stevenson, James, 2004:263
stewardess
recommend as career for young
woman, **1998:**239
Stewart, Jimmy, 2001:76
Stewart, Martha, 2003:210–11,
2004:53–54, 271, 514,
2005:100–101, 483, **2006:**536

Stewart, Rod, 2000:265
stockbrokers, 2006:519
can be trusted, **2002:**199
honesty and ethical standards of,
1999:148, **2000:**389,
2001:265, **2002:**373, **2003:**422
stock market, 1998:116–18, **2000:**
152–53, 355–56, **2001:**64–65,
2002:191, 221–23, 344
assessment of, **2006:**407–8, 431
bought stocks based on environmental record of companies,
2000:122
concern for, **1998:**206, **2004:**147
confidence in, **2004:**451–52
economy and, **2004:**10, **2006:**216,
221–22, 429, **2007:**297
families and, **2007:**266, 349
income and, **2004:**453
investment in, **1999:**142–43,
2000:79–80, 152, **2001:**66,
196, **2002:**221–22
opinion of, **2001:**15
profitable, **2001:**196
thousand dollars, **1998:**177,
206, **1999:**143, **2000:**347,
407, **2002:**209
as most important issue, **2005:**45,
113, 152, 198, 366, 409, 421,
2007:349
oil and, **2004:**359
opinion of, **2001:**64, **2002:**209
person you most trust for information or advice about, **2001:**196
predictions for, **1998:**118, 205,
1999:143, **2001:**15, 268,
2002:142, 201, 209,
2003:23–24, 158, 243, 370,
2006:221, **2007:**1
put more money into market over
past week, **1998:**206
scandals and, **2004:**12–13
and Social Security, **1998:**195,
240–41

stock market *(continued)*
   stockbrokers and, **2002:**195
   volatility in, to be expected,
      2000:79
   See also investors
Stolberg, Sheryl Gay, 2006:352
Strauss, William, 2005:47
Streep, Meryl, 2000:98, **2001:**76–77
Streisand, Barbra, 1998:2,
   2001:76–77, **2003:**80
stress, 2002:1–2, 253, 347–48,
   2004:26, 181–82, 344,
   2005:382–84, 477
Strickland, Tom, 2002:340
stroke
   worried you will experience this
      illness, **2003:**424
students (age 13 to 17), asked of,
   1999:188–91
submarines
   favor women serving on, **2002:**3
Substance Abuse and Mental
   Health Services Administration,
   2004:270
suburban areas
   crime and, **2004:**478–79
   drugs and, **2005:**163–64
   economy and, **2005:**108
   euthanasia and, **2005:**179
   gambling and, **2004:**123
   guns and, **2004:**472, **2005:**141
   health and, **2004:**476
   Internet and, **2004:**109
   law enforcement and, **2005:**420
   prefer to live in city, suburban
      area, small town, or on farm,
      1998:238
   sex offender registries and,
      2005:212
   stress and, **2004:**182
   suicide and, **2005:**179
Sudan, 1998:201–2, 204
suicide, 2004:216–17, 249–50,
   280–81

age and, **2005:**179
Catholicism and, **2005:**131–32,
   150
church and, **2005:**179–80
community and, **2005:**179
gender and, **2005:**179–80
geographic region and, **2005:**179
ideology and, **2005:**179–80
as morally acceptable, **2002:**150,
   2003:159, 179, 218
Protestantism and, **2005:**151
religion and, **2005:**179–80
See also doctor-assisted suicide
Sullivan, Andrew, 2005:97
Summers, Lawrence, 2005:95
Sunset Boulevard **(movie), 1998:**187
Super Bowl, 1998:10–11, **2000:**30,
   290, **2001:**24–25, **2004:**43–44
   halftime show, **2004:**61–62, 361,
      471
   predictions for, **1998:**11,
      1999:252, **2000:**30
Supreme Court, 2004:169, 225, 306
   and abortion, **2000:**200
   approval ratings, **2001:**13, 145,
      2003:249, 325–26, 357,
      2006:404
   attentiveness to, **2005:**328, **2006:**32
   confidence in, **1998:**181, **1999:**50,
      209, **2000:**209, 216, **2001:**3,
      149, **2002:**184, **2003:**205–6,
      2006:233–34, **2007:**269–71,
      418
   death penalty and, **2005:**456
   filibuster debate and, **2005:**239
   and Florida election controversy,
      2000:411–12, 416, 419,
      2007:212
   gender and, **2003:**205,
      2005:244–46, 259, 363,
      370–71, 400–401, 405
   and homosexuality, **2000:**199
   ideology of, **2005:**40, 238–39,
      246, 259, 363, 401

television *(continued)*
  hobby you are particularly
    interested in, **2002:**7
  See also media; television news
television news
  confidence in, **1998:**181, 254,
    1999:209, **2000:**209, **2001:**3,
    149, **2002:**185, **2003:**205–6
  accuracy of, **1998:**96–98
  filming coffin arrivals from Iraq,
    2003:409
  and Florida election controversy,
    2000:408–9
  how often do you get your news
    from [sources], **1998:**191–93,
    2003:2
  impeachment hearings on, **1998:**243
  liberal or conservative bias in,
    1998:170
  political conventions on, **2000:**225
  show more crime and violence
    now than five years ago,
    1998:229
Temple, Shirley, 2001:77
tennis, 2004:44, 367–68, 489,
    2006:135, **2007:**24
  as favorite sport to watch,
    1998:237, **2000:**136
  professional, fan of, **2001:**81
Teresa, Mother, 1998:2, **1999:**249,
    2000:264, **2002:**400, **2004:**514,
    2005:483, **2006:**536
terrorism, 2002:262
  Afghanistan and, **1998:**201, 204,
    2007:274, 340–41, 349
  age and, **2005:**66, 470, **2006:**373,
    2007:47
  airplanes and, **2005:**273
  approval ratings, **2002:**91–92,
    260–61, **2004:**134–35, 167–68,
    188, 197, 258–59, 267, 389,
    450, **2006:**54, 92–93, 154–56,
    187, 240–41, 243–44, 303,
    309, 348, 422

  assessment of, **2006:**50, 101–2,
    241–43, 348–49, 387–89,
    408
  bioterrorism, **2005:**431–32,
    2006:481–82
  blacks and, **2007:**316
  and budget deficit, **2002:**22
  Bush, George W., and, **2002:**27,
    91–92, 260–61, **2003:**172–73,
    315, **2004:**20, 29, 104, 111,
    124, 134–35, 144–47, 167–68,
    171–72, 188, 197, 219,
    258–59, 267–68, 301–2,
    321–22, 325–26, 351–52, 358,
    374–75, 381–84, 389, 397–99,
    402, 418–21, 432, 437–38,
    444, 450, 469, 497–99
  civilian responses to,
    2001:242–43, **2002:**78,
    2003:81–82
  Clinton, Bill, and, **2004:**134–35
  Clinton, Hillary, and, **2005:**301
  confidence on, **1998:**169, 198,
    2004:167–68
  Congress and, **2002:**130,
    2005:3–4, 65–67, 130, 334,
    412
  Democratic Party and, **2002:**17,
    2003:4
  Democrats in Congress and,
    2002:27, 171, 291, 312, 336
  economy and, **2006:**216, 222
  election of 2004 and, **2004:**31, 33,
    111–12, 115–16, 124, 145,
    170–72, 197, 258–59, 267–68,
    299–302, 321–22, 325–26,
    352, 358, 374–75, 381–84,
    389, 397–99, 402, 418–21,
    431–32, 437–38, 444, 447,
    469, 497–99
  election of 2006 and, **2006:**21–22,
    25–26, 28, 266–68, 322,
    388–91, 426–28, 448–50, 455,
    460–61, 467

election of 2008 and, **2007:**46–48,
50, 255, 329–31, 336–37,
432–33, 479–80, 527–28, 543
embassy bombings, **1998:**198
Europe and, **2003:**39,
2004:244–45
first responders and, **2003:**81–82
foreign affairs and, **2005:**73
gender and, **2006:**8
geographic region and, **2005:**470
government and, **2001:**241, 249
confidence in, **2001:**216,
2002:78, 154, 168, 261,
2003:82, 313
surveillance, **2006:**82–84,
198–99, 393
Hispanics and, **2007:**316
independents and, **2007:**14,
16–17, 54–55, 192, 367, 411
intelligence system and, **2006:**413
investors and, **2004:**260–61
Iraq and, **2005:**445–46, 467, 471
Iraq War and, **2003:**147, 384,
2006:110, 240–41, 244–45,
295, 388–89, 517, **2007:**184,
199–200, 274, 350, 394
Kerry, John, and, **2004:**111–12,
171–72, 197, 258–59, 267–68,
301–2, 321–22, 325–26, 352,
358, 374–75, 381–84, 389,
397–99, 402, 418–21, 432,
437–38, 444, 469, 497–99
in Lebanon, **2004:**231
mass transit and, **2005:**273
military and, **2001:**216, **2006:**393,
413
as most important issue,
1999:195, **2001:**255, **2002:**9,
70, 116, 233, 323, 359,
2003:25, 62, 86, 122, 155, 203,
284–85, 401, 443, **2004:**20,
37–38, 112–13, 155–56, 159,
183, 239–40, 246–47, 381–82,
387, 414, 466–67, **2005:**18, 43,

98–99, 174, 213, 220, 251–52,
332, 348, 366, 421, 432,
2006:138–39, 162, 237, 279,
288, 338, 384–86, 434–35,
467, 479, 528, **2007:**37–38,
54–55, 123–26, 216, 255,
272–73, 315–16, 410–12,
442–43, 479–80, 501, 527–28,
543
as most important issue facing
nation 25 years from now,
2002:117
national security and,
2004:167–68, **2005:**334
and New Year's Eve, **1999:**247,
284, **2000:**2
orange threat level as serious matter, **2003:**73
Patriot Act and, **2004:**94–95
versus Pearl Harbor, a hundred
years from now, which event
will historians say had a
greater impact on the U.S.,
2001:266
perpetrators of
opinions on, **2002:**262, 302,
2003:313
trial and punishment of,
2001:216, 273
political affiliation and,
2004:15–16, 20, 37–38, 113,
115, 127, 134–35, 156,
167–68, 301–2, 352, 363, 375,
387, 431–32, **2006:**8–9, 16, 54,
101–2, 107, 125–26, 138–39,
155–56, 243, 245, 267–68,
303, 349, 370–74, 379–80,
385, 387–91, 393–94, 401–2,
413–14, 419, 426–27, 435,
448–50, 455, 459–61,
500–501, 528
predictions on, **1998:**79,
2000:176, **2001:**215–16, 241,
249, 266, **2002:**36, 77–78, 154,

terrorism *(continued)*
194, 260, 264, 302, **2003:**172,
312–14, 380, **2007:**1–2
better in year 2025 than today,
1998:219
president and, **2007:**2, 16–17,
60–61, 90, 191–92, 237–38, 305
prevention of, **2006:**102
versus civil liberties, **2003:**147,
314–15
as priority, **2001:**229, **2002:**17,
130, 171, **2003:**4, **2007:**2,
16–17, 60–61, 90, 148–49,
191–92, 237–38, 305
race and, **2007:**316
racial profiling and, **2005:**294
Republican Party and, **2002:**17,
2003:4
Republicans in Congress and,
2002:171, 291, 312, 336
responses to, **2001:**240
effects of, **2001:**240–41
State of the Union address and,
2005:72
Sudan and, **1998:**201, 204
suspects of, **2006:**393
swing states and, **2004:**374–75
taxes and, **2004:**153
teenagers and, **2004:**183, 414
as threat, most critical,
2004:100–101, **2007:**508
veterans and, **2004:**418–19
as voting issue
Congressional, **2002:**291, 312
presidential, **2003:**338–39,
416, 453
whites and, **2007:**316
who is winning, **2003:**146–47,
172, 380–81
worry about, **1998:**201, **2000:**125,
2001:215, 223–24, 232,
240–41, 248–49, 266, **2002:**36,
119, 264, **2003:**72–73, 127,
146, 312, 317–18, 378, 380,
2004:20, 64, 120, 126–27, 159,

362–63, 446, **2005:**18–20,
127–28, 136, 162–63, 170–72,
226–27, 251, 272–73, 293–94,
391, **2007:**126
See also September 11, 2001 terrorist attacks; War on Terrorism
Tester, Jon, 2006:364, 462
testing, 2004:376–77
Texas, 2000:34, **2002:**160
Texas A&M University, 2003:299
Texas Rangers, 2001:81
Thanksgiving Day
look forward most to eating [list],
2000:384
most thankful for [list], **2000:**384
Thatcher, Margaret, 1998:2, 154,
1999:242, **2000:**264, 431,
2001:278, **2002:**400, **2003:**455,
2004:513–14, **2005:**483
theater going
favorite way of spending evening,
1999:252, **2002:**6
hobby you are particularly interested in, **2002:**7
The Thin Red Line (movie),
1999:254
Third Day, 2004:358
third parties, 2006:382
vote, **2004:**87–88, 348–50,
378–79, 444
See also Reform party
"3rd Rock From the Sun,"
1998:61–63
Thomas, Clarence, 2003:252
Thompson, Fred, 2007:186–88,
239, 326, 346, 548
familiarity with, **2007:**225–26,
367–69, 388–89, 550
image of, **2007:**144–45, 155,
223–24, 226–27, 247, 256–58,
281–83, 345–46, 362, 397–98,
424–26, 452, 462, 541, 551
Thompson, Tommy, 2004:52, 331,
479, **2006:**531, **2007:**113–14,
222, 326, 344

Thorpe, Jim, 2000:1
threats, most critical,
　2004:100–101, 493–94,
　2007:7–8, 508, 542
　See also concern; issues, most
　　important
throat cancer
　think that cigarette smoking is
　　cause of, 1999:276
thunder
　fear of, 1998:238, 2001:70
Thune, John, 2002:340
Thurmond, Strom, 2004:88
Timberlake, Justin, 2004:61–62
time, 2004:7, 181, 2007:34–35,
　387–88, 449–50, 510
Time Magazine nerve gas story,
　1998:193–94
time of day, 2005:225
Time Warner
　merger with AOL, as good or bad,
　　2000:42
Titanic (movie), 1998:175
tobacco companies, 1998:177–78,
　185, 1999:277, 2000:221, 394
　See also cigarette smoking and
　　smokers
tolerance, 2004:70–71
"The Tonight Show," 2000:34
tornado
　ever personally been in, 1999:258
Toronto Blue Jays, 2001:82
torture, 2006:393
toughness, 2004:50–51, 80–81
towns
　prefer to live in city, suburban
　　area, small town, or on farm,
　　1998:238
toxic waste, 2004:141, 160
track and field, 2004:368
　as favorite Summer Olympic
　　event, 2000:307
Tracy, Spencer, 2001:77
trade deficit
　economy and, 2006:216, 222

as most important issue, 1998:60,
　1999:194–95, 2001:58, 121,
　255, 2002:9, 2003:442,
　2006:138–39, 237, 288, 338,
　479
as most important issue facing
　nation 25 years from now,
　2002:117
political affiliation and, 2006:
　139
traditional values, 2004:57, 447–48,
　470–71
　See also values
Traffic, 2001:73
traffic problems, 1999:259,
　2000:177, 179–80, 190
Traficant, James, 2006:4
transportation, 1998:137, 2005:273,
　356–57, 366, 409
travel, 2003:133
　hobby you are particularly inter-
　　ested in, 2002:7
　industry, 2005:311, 422
　overall view of, 2001:200,
　　2002:240, 2003:289
Travolta, John, 2000:98, 2001:76
trials, 2004:53–54, 209–10, 417,
　495–96
Trinity Church, 2005:134
Tripp, Linda, 1998:155, 188, 231,
　253, 1999:46
tropical rain forests
　loss of, worry about, 2001:90,
　　2002:77, 81, 113
trucks
　likely to buy or lease new or used,
　　1999:144
Truman, Harry S.
　admiration of, 2002:400,
　　2004:230, 514, 2005:482
　approval ratings, 2004:17, 229,
　　231, 247–48, 265, 437, 444,
　　450, 2005:26–27, 118–19, 263,
　　320, 392–93, 417, 2007:25–26,
　　100, 166, 312–13, 400

Truman, Harry S. *(continued)*
    averages during seventh quarter as president, **2002:**322
    Gallup analysis of, in December of last year in office, **2000:**422
    quarterly averages for, **2002:**111
    yearly job approval average above 70%, **2002:**322
    as greatest president, **2000:**58, **2001:**44, **2003:**163–64, 413, **2004:**233, **2007:**76
    image of, **2004:**233
    political affiliation and, **2004:**229
    re-election of, **2004:**265
    World War II and, **2005:**292
    as worst president, **2000:**59
Trump, Donald, 1999:47, 89, 99
trust, 2004:163–64, 205, **2006:**14, 91, 397–99, 514–15
    in American people, **2002:**199, **2005:**359, 378
    in Bush, George W., **2005:**425
    in Clinton, Bill, **2005:**425
    in Congress, **2005:**359, 378, **2007:**415
    in government, **2005:**378
    in judicial system, **2005:**359, 378
    in local government, **2007:**415
    in media, **2005:**359–60, 378
    political affiliation and, **2005:**360
    in presidency, **2005:**359, 378
    in public, **2007:**415
    in public officials, **2005:**359–60, 378
    in state government, **2007:**415
    See also confidence; honesty
Tsongas, Paul, 2007:355
tsunami disaster, 2005:8–10, 15
tuberculosis, 2006:521
Tuch, Stevan A., 2007:421
Turkey, 2002:54, 134, **2003:**39, 56, 99
Twain, Mark, 1999:267

twenty-dollar bill, new, 1998:233
Twenty-sixth Amendment, 2004:438
"20/20"
    how often do you get your news from, **1998:**193
    trust accuracy of news from, **1998:**98
Twin Towers memorial site
    what should be built in addition to the memorial, **2002:**262
Tyler, Steven, 2000:265
Tyson, Mike, 1998:226

U

U2, 2000:265
Udall, Morris, 2004:42
Ueberroth, Peter, 2003:279
Ukraine, 2005:79, 128
understanding, 2005:119–20, 148, 371–72, 403
    See also familiarity
unemployment
    benefits
        approve of allowing unemployed people to continue to receive benefits that ended in December, **2003:**7
        extending benefits will help the economy, **2003:**6
    Bush and, **2002:**27, 92, **2005:**3–4, 155
    Congress and, **2002:**27, 291, **2007:** 3; 60–61, 191–92, 237–38, 305
    Democrats and, **2002:**27, 291, **2003:**5
    economy and, **2005:**108
    employer has laid off employees in past six months, **2003:**287
    families and, **2007:**266, 349
    finding a job as biggest challenge you face today, **2000:**192

United Kingdom *(continued)*
  opinion of, **2000:**380, **2001:**35,
    43, 84, **2002:**52, **2003:**56, 99,
    2004:73
  possession of nuclear weapons
    as threat to U.S., **1998:**180
    as threat to world peace,
      1998:79
  religion in, **2004:**405, 415
  respondents in
    approve if British military
      were involved in air attacks
      on Iraq, **1998:**29
    if Americans and British launch
      air strikes against Iraq, then
      risk of dangerous chemicals
      and bacteria, **1998:**166
    if Saddam places Iraqi civilians
      at attack sites, U.S. should
      attack anyway, **1998:**166
    Iraq crisis as serious, **1998:**166
    Iraq under Saddam represents
      threat to world peace,
      1998:165–66
    objective of military action in
      Gulf should be removal of
      Saddam, **1998:**166
    possible to destroy Iraq's
      weapons by using air
      strikes, **1998:**166
    resolve Iraq situation through
      economic sanctions or air
      strikes, **1998:**165
    United Nations should con-
      tinue economic sanctions on
      Iraq until Saddam complies,
      1998:166
  royal family, **2002:**163
  smoking in, **2004:**79–80
  stem cell research and,
    2004:415–16
  traditional values and, **2004:**57
United Kingdom Stem Cell Bank,
  2004:415

United Nations, **2004:**101–2, 117,
  177–78
  approval ratings, **2001:**74,
    2002:333–34, **2003:**316
  and Iraq
    been too tough in dealing with
      Iraq, **2002:**277
    Clinton should accept UN agree-
      ment and reduce U.S. mili-
      tary forces in Gulf, **1998:**33
    confidence in UN ability to
      handle situation in Iraq,
      2002:334
    continue economic sanctions
      on Iraq until Saddam com-
      plies, **1998:**166
    favor UN agreement with Iraq
      worked out by Annan,
      1998:33
    relieved that military action in
      Iraq was avoided by UN
      agreement, **1998:**33–34
    trust will make right decisions
      regarding Iraq, **2002:**384,
      2003:32, 46
    use diplomacy and economic
      sanctions to pressure Iraq
      into compliance or take mil-
      itary action (air strikes),
      1998:20–21, 31, 168–69
    view of, since they did not sup-
      port invasion of Iraq,
      2003:316
  postpone release of videotape of
    Clinton's testimony because of
    his UN speech, **1998:**214
  role of in world affairs today,
    2001:57, 74
  on sending investigators into
    Palestinian refugee camp, take
    side of United Nations or
    Israel, **2002:**134
  U.S. should increase funding of
    the United Nations, **2003:**316

United States *(continued)*

put too much pressure on Palestinians to settle Middle East conflict, **1998:**178

as respected throughout world as eight years ago, **2000:**13

independents and, **2007:**28

and Iraq

should not attack Iraq unless attacked first, **2002:**307–8

should send ground troops to Iraq only if United Nations supports that action, **2002:**277

should wait how long for diplomatic efforts to be effective before invading Iraq, **2002:**334

Iraq and, **2000:**174, **2004:**117, 262–63

Iraq war and, **2006:**111–12, 244–45, 295, 514, 517

and Korean War, **2000:**194

and Middle East

take Israel's or Palestinians' side in Middle East conflict, **1998:**178

takes fair positions in conflict between Palestine and Israel, **2002:**58

think U.S. supports Israel too much, **2002:**61

most important issue in, **2004:**20, 35, 37–38, 84–85, 100–101, 107, 112–13, 116, 125–26, 155–57, 159, 239–40, 246–47, 334, 340–41, 381–82, 386–87, 414, 466–67, **2006:**2–3, 36, 68–69, 138–39, 162, 196–97, 206, 237, 279, 281, 283, 288, 320, 336–39, 384–86, 430, 434–35, 467, 479–80, 528, **2007:**37–38, 54–55, 123–26, 216, 219, 265, 271–73, 315–16, 319–20, 349, 410–12,

442–43, 500–501, 508, 532, 542 [list], **2001:**58–59, 121, **2002:**359–60, **2003:**203

and Muslim countries, **2002:**59–60

and Islamic values, **2002:**58

think notion that Muslims believe the following major reasons they view U.S. unfavorably [list], **2002:**62

unfavorable views of the U.S. by Muslims based on what U.S. has done, **2002:**60

national defense in, **2007:**87

NATO alliance makes U.S.-Russia relations better, **1998:**171–72

partisanship in, **2005:**27, 29–30, 37, 39

mood of country influenced by partisan orientation, **2003:**326

political affiliation and, **2007:**28

population of, **2004:**244–45

power of, **2005:**1–2

predictions for

involved in full-scale war by year 2025, **1998:**220–21

likely that terrorists will explode nuclear bomb in U.S. within ten years, **2000:**176

likely that U.S. will be attacked by country using nuclear weapons in ten years, **1998:**79

likely that U.S. will be attacked by country using nuclear weapons within ten years, **2000:**176

likely to become involved with Arab countries in full-scale war, **1998:**221

likely to become involved with China in full-scale war, **1998:**221

likely to become involved with Iran in full-scale war, **1998:**221

likely to become involved with Iraq in full-scale war, **1998:**221

likely to become involved with Middle East in full-scale war, **1998:**221

likely to become involved with Russia in full-scale war, **1998:**221

1999 as year when America will increase its power in world, **1998:**251–52

outlook for next twenty years as optimistic, **2000:**339

Republican or Democratic party likely to keep U.S. out of war, **1998:**229

will be at war with Iraq by end of the year, **2002:**246

will get into nuclear war within ten years, **2000:**176

priorities for

establish peace in Middle East or overthrow Saddam Hussein, **2002:**231

important for it to be number one in world economically, **2000:**204

important for it to be number one in world militarily, **2000:**171–72, 205

Republican Party and, **1998:**229, **2007:**28

role of, **2004:**244–45

in solving international problems, **2001:**56

in world affairs as presidential election issue, **2000:**19, 72

satisfaction with, **2004:**19–21, 68–69, 112–13, 124–25, 130, 156–57, 187, 205, 239, 246–47, 316–17, 341–42, 355, 386–87, 451

opportunities to get ahead in, by working hard, **2001:**28

overall quality of life in, **2001:**28

position in world today, **2000:**171, **2001:**56, **2003:**65, 106, 132

role in world affairs, **2001:**29

state of, **2003:**27–28, **2005:**10–11, 39–40, 69, 98–99, 112–13, 173–74, 213–14, 281, 320–21, 384–85, **2006:**80–82, 112–13, 120, 162, 175, 196, 236–38, 288–89, 337, 375–76, 432, 465–66, 468, 528

way things are going, **1998:**25–27, 141, 251, **1999:**47, **2000:**12, 203–4, 367–68, 378, **2001:**25, 122, **2002:**141, 173, 359, 382, **2003:**25–26, 29–30, 106, 154, 203, 326

should not attack another country unless attacked first, **2002:**307

should strengthen our ties with Western Europe, **2001:**139

United States v. Bullock, **2004:**505

university/college rankings, 2003:299

University of Arizona, 2003:299

University of California at Berkeley, 2003:299

University of California at Los Angeles (UCLA), 2003:299

University of Iowa, 2003:299

University of Michigan, 2003:299

University of Minnesota, 2003:299

University of North Carolina, 2003:299

University of Pennsylvania (Penn), 2003:299

University of Southern California (USC), **2003:**299

University of Tennessee, **2003:**299

University of Texas, **2003:**299

University of Virginia, **2003:**299

University of Washington, **2003:**299

University of Wisconsin, **2003:**299

Unknown Soldier

favor attempt to identify Vietnam soldier buried in Tomb of the Unknowns, **1998:**178

upper class

wealthy would benefit from Bush's tax cut plan, **2000:**288

wealthy would benefit from Gore's tax cut plan, **2000:**288

you belong in, **2000:**288

upper-middle class

you belong in, **2000:**288

urban areas

creationism and, **2004:**463

crime and, **2004:**478–79

drugs and, **2005:**163–64

economy and, **2005:**108

euthanasia and, **2005:**179

gambling and, **2004:**123

guns and, **2004:**472, **2005:**141

health and, **2004:**476

Internet and, **2004:**109

Kerry, John, and, **2004:**442–43

law enforcement and, **2005:**420

marriage and, **2004:**223

movies and, **2004:**89

race and, **2004:**223

safety of, **2004:**448–50

school, confidence in, **2004:**305

sex offender registries and, **2005:**212

sprawl, worry about, **2000:**316, **2001:**90

stress and, **2004:**182

suicide and, **2005:**179

USA Today

how often do you get your news from, **1998:**191

as important source of news about Florida election controversy, **2000:**408

news reported with liberal or conservative bias, **1998:**171

trust accuracy of news from, **1998:**96

Utah, 2002:160

utilities, 2005:311, 422

V

vacation, 2005:195–97, 474–75

changes in stock market have made you consider canceling, **1998:**117

expect to take, during Christmas holidays, **2000:**429

for how many days, **2000:**429

satisfaction with amount of vacation time you receive, **1999:**136

state you especially would like to vacation in [list], **2002:**160

state you would least like to vacation in [list], **2002:**160

summer

plan to take this summer, **1999:**269, **2002:**159

total days you plan to take on vacations this summer, **2002:**159

during what month or months are you vacationing this summer, **2002:**159–60

where you'll probably go this summer on your vacation, **2002:**160

taken any, away from home six nights in row, **2000:**5

vegetative state, **2005:**116–18,
121–22, 180
See also Schiavo, Terri
Ventura, Jesse, 1999:84, 89
opinion of, **1998:**155, **1999:**47
veterans, 2007:179–80, 369–70, 391
are you a veteran of the Armed
Forces, **2001:**129
have you received the respect and
thanks you deserve for serving
in the Armed Forces, **2001:**129
honoring, as reason to celebrate
Memorial Day, **2000:**165
which of the four branches of the
Armed Forces is the most pres-
tigious, **2001:**129
will be going to veteran's cemetery on Memorial Day,
2000:165
veterinarians, 2006:519
honesty and ethical standards of,
1999:148, **2000:**388,
2003:422–23
recommend as career for young
man, **1998:**238
VHS watching
favorite way of spending an
evening, **2002:**6
Viagra, 1998:67–68, 179
Vice President, 2004:124, 126,
272–74, 287–88, 311, 313–14,
353–54
know name of, **2000:**34
video games
amount of violence that children
are exposed to in, **1999:**202
controlling, could prevent another
incident like Littleton shootings, **1999:**192
enough information for children
about violence content in,
1999:203
government should do more to
regulate violence in, **1999:**179

Vietnam
as ally or enemy of U.S.,
2000:175
opinion of, **2000:**380, **2001:**44,
84, **2002:**52, **2003:**56
Vietnam War, 2005:315–18, 426,
2006:72, 310–11, 479, **2007:**
37–38, 185, 216, 299, 349, 352
Bush, George W., and,
2004:76–77, 83–84
CNN and *Time* nerve gas story,
1998:193–94
defense spending and, **2004:**97
election of 2004 and, **2004:**76–77,
82–84, 444
versus Iraq war, **2004:**166–67,
240–42, 258
Johnson, Lyndon, and,
2004:240–41
justness of, **2004:**228
Kerry, John, and, **2004:**76–77,
82–84, 345–47, 351, 444
as mistake, **2003:**241,
2004:166–67, 241–42, 258
as most important event in twentieth century, **2002:**175
as most important issue,
2004:155–56
Nixon, Richard, and, **2004:**240
Vilsack, Tom, 2005:468, **2006:**66,
235–36, 477, 531
violence, 2005:99, 136, 162–63,
170–72, 174, 213
age and, **2004:**61–62
blamed for Littleton shootings,
1999:192
crime and, **2004:**50, 445–46, 478
entertainment and, **2004:**61–62
find graphic violence in movies
offensive, **2001:**126
as most important issue, **1998:**60,
1999:194–95, **2000:**191,
2001:58, 121, **2002:**10, 71,
116, 233, 323, 360, **2003:**25,

Wall Street *(continued)*

as important source of news about
Florida election controversy,
2000:408

news reported with liberal or
conservative bias, **1998:**171

trust accuracy of news from,
1998:96

Walters, Barbara, 2004:514,
2005:483, **2006:**326–28, 536

admiration of, **1999:**242,
2002:400, **2003:**455

interested in watching her interview of Monica Lewinsky,
1998:235

Walters, Elizabeth, 2004:490–91

war, 2004:227–28, **2006:**72, 310–11,
479

fear of, **1999:**195

as most important issue,
2001:59, 121, 255,
2002:9, 70, 116, 233,
323, 359, **2003:**25, 62,
86, 122, 155, 203, 284–85,
401, 442

as most important issue facing
nation 25 years from now,
2002:116

predictions on

full-scale war by year 2025,
1998:220–21

more peace or conflict among
nations in year 2025 than
today, **1998:**222

Republican or Democratic
party more likely to keep
U.S. out of, **1998:**229

See also Iraq War; War on
Terrorism

Warner, John, 2006:444

Warner, Mark, 2005:300, 468

War on Terrorism, 2001:239,
252–53, **2004:**244–45, 325–27,
363, 400, **2006:**153, 241–45,

348–49, 387–89, 413–14, 517,
2007:96, 273–74, 340–42, 350

in Afghanistan, **2001:**224,
226–27, 232, 239, 251–52,
261, 267

approval ratings, **2001:**226, 254–55,
269–70, **2002:**67–68, 261, 301

versus diplomatic and economic
pressure, **2001:**252

in Iraq, **2006:**244–45, 517

favor taking direct military
action in Iraq, **2001:**224

if U.S. goes to war in Iraq, it
will be as successful as the
efforts in Afghanistan,
2001:272

opinions on, **2001:**224–27, 261,
2002:24, 68–69, 183, 194

as success, **2001:**252

who is currently winning,
2001:267, **2002:**10, 67–68,
166, 183, 194, 323

will be difficult or easy one,
2002:286

will be long or short one,
2002:286

predictions on

likely further terrorist attacks
in U.S. over next several
weeks, **2001:**227, 272

optimistic about, **2002:**23

as priority for Congress, **2002:**130

Republicans and, **2002:**376

satisfaction with

U.S. military progress in, **2001:**
252, 261, 272, **2002:**68

way things are going,
2002:261, 301

support for, **2001:**224–25,
2002:68

taxes and, **2006:**153

understanding of, **2001:**252

who is winning, **2001:**232

worry about, **2002:**166

weight *(continued)*
  children and, **2004:**385
  current, **2002:**367–68, **2003:**294,
    418–19
  diet and, **2004:**294–95, 331–32, 385
  gained weight over past five years,
    2003:293–94
  a lot, **2002:**203
  gender and, **2004:**331–32,
    486–87
  health and, **2004:**331–32, 468,
    476, 482
  how often you feel discriminated
    against because of your weight,
    2003:275
  ideal, **2002:**368, **2003:**420
  junk food and, **2004:**191, 385
  like to lose, **1998:**158, **1999:**272,
    2001:258, **2002:**368, **2003:**419
  morality and, **2004:**331–32
  perceptions of, **2004:**485–87
  teenagers and, **2004:**148–49, 191,
    385
  trying to lose, **1998:**158,
    1999:273, **2001:**258,
    2002:368–69
    seriously, **2003:**420
  worry about, how often, **1999:**272
  your weight situation,
    2002:202–3, 367,
    2003:274–75, 418
  See also obesity
Weinberger, Caspar, 2007:115
welfare, 2004:37–38
  Bush, George W., and, **2005:**156
  economy and, **2006:**216, 222
  as most important issue, **1998:**60,
    1999:195, **2000:**192, **2001:**59,
    121, 256, **2002:**10, 71, 116,
    360, **2003:**25, 62, 87, 155, 203,
    285, 443, **2005:**45, 99, 113,
    152, 174, 198, 213, 348, 366,
    421, **2006:**237, 288, 338, 480
  in community, **2000:**190

as most important issue facing
  nation 25 years from now,
  2002:117
reform
  as issue to be addressed by
    next president, **2000:**212
  as priority for Congress,
    1998:236
Wellstone, Paul
  likely to support, **1998:**66,
    227–28, **1999:**72
  opinion of, **1998:**66
West, Kayne, 2005:346
western countries, opinions on
  care about poorer nations,
    2002:58
  eager to have better relationships
    with Muslim countries,
    2002:59
  people are free to control their
    own lives and futures, **2002:**
    59
  respect Islamic values, **2002:**58
  take fair positions in conflict
    between Palestine and Israel,
    2002:58
  take fair positions toward Muslim
    countries, **2002:**59
  think better understanding
    between Western countries and
    Muslim countries will occur
    soon, **2002:**60
Western Europe
  U.S. should strengthen our ties
    with, **2001:**139
  what happens in, as important to
    U.S., **2000:**186
West Nile Virus
  worried you or someone in your
    family will be exposed to,
    2002:299
White, Jason, 2004:487, 489
Whitehouse, Sheldon, 2006:416,
  462

women *(continued)*
    marriage amendment and,
      2004:86–87
    Medicaid and, **2005:**14
    Medicare and, **2004:**38–39, 110,
      2005:14
    in military
      favor women doing combat
        jobs [list], **2002:**3
      should be required to partici-
        pate in a draft, **1998:**183,
        2002:3
    money and, **2005:**162
    morality and, **2004:**215, 250
    news and, **2005:**369
    nuclear energy plants and, **2005:**161
    nuclear weapons and, **2005:**292
    parenting and, **2004:**182
    Patriot Act and, **2004:**94
    patriotism and, **2005:**62, 267
    pay and
      favor increased enforcement of
        equal pay laws for, **2000:**43
      feel you are paid less than a
        man (asked of women),
        2000:43
    Peterson, Scott, and, **2004:**54
    political affiliation and, **2004:**5–6,
      130
    politics and, **2000:**85
      country governed better if
        more women were in politi-
        cal office, **2001:**4
      country will have elected
        woman president by year
        2025, **1998:**222
      would vote for woman for
        president, **1999:**54, **2001:**4
    position of, satisfaction with,
      2005:20, 22, 39
    prefer to work for man or woman,
      2001:10, **2002:**138–39
    pregnant, crimes against,
      2001:108

    presidential elections and,
      2004:95–97
    reading and, **2005:**203
    religion and, **2004:**70, 120, 506,
      512, **2005:**132, 234, 447, 463
    Rice, Condoleezza, and, **2005:**
      116
    rights movement
      agree with goals of, **2000:**120
      and policies, **2000:**119
      right to vote as most important
        event in twentieth century,
        2002:175
    satisfaction with, **2001:**146–47
      position of in the nation,
        2001:29
      treatment of, **2001:**158,
        2003:360
      your community as place to
        live, **2001:**146
    smoking and, **2004:**79, 307
    Social Security and, **2004:**110
    society, position in, **2004:**129–30
    spending and, **2004:**461,
      2005:86–87, 436
    sports and, **2004:**44, **2005:**54
    stress and, **2004:**182
    suicide and, **2004:**281,
      2005:179–80
    Supreme Court and, **2005:**259,
      363, 370–71, 400–401, 405
    taxes and, **2005:**67
    think few black people dislike
      whites, **2003:**220
    tolerance and, **2004:**70
    as veterans, **2004:**418
    weight and, **2004:**331–32,
      486–87, **2005:**296, 305–6,
      440
    World War II and, **2005:**292
    See also gender
**Women's National Basketball Asso-
ciation, 2004:**367
Woodruff, Bob, 2007:193

Woods, Tiger, **2000:**34, 108–9, 289, **2001:**41–42, 142–43, **2004:**367, 480, **2007:**1–2
woodwork
hobby you are particularly interested in, **2002:**7
work
importance in your life, **2003:**1
workers
corporate mergers as good or bad for, **2000:**42, 360
deserve most credit for good economy, **2000:**262
increased trade between U.S. and China would threaten U.S. workers, **2000:**154
working class
tax cuts and, **2000:**288
you belong in, **2000:**288
workplace
ban cigarette smoking in, **1999:**277, **2001:**182
know anyone capable of violence at your, **1999:**216
set aside areas for smoking in, **2001:**182
worried about violence by co-worker in your, **1999:**216
WorldCom
as major problem, **2002:**190
World Health Organization (WHO), 2004:79–80
World Series, 2001:24, 82, **2002:**250, **2004:**44
See also baseball
World Trade Organization
China and, **1999:**150, **2000:**92, 124, 153–54, 162
World War I
as most important event in twentieth century, **2002:**175
World War II, 2004:227–29
difficult or easy (asked Dec. 12-17, 1944), **2002:**286

long or short (asked Dec. 12-17, 1944), **2002:**286
as most important event in twentieth century, **2002:**175
wrestling, 2004:44, 489, **2006:** 135
as favorite sport to watch, **1998:**237, **2000:**136
professional, fan of, **2001:**81
writing
hobby you are particularly interested in, **2002:**7
Wye River peace accords, 1999: 214

Y

Yale University, 2003:299
yard work
as favorite way of spending evening, **2002:**6
Yeltsin, Boris, 1998:155, 206, **1999:**183, **2000:**3
Y2K computer problem
cause major problems for you personally, **1998:**85–86
computer mistakes due to year 2000 issue will cause major problems, **1998:**84–85, **1999:**156, 245
computer mistakes due to year 2000 issue will cause major problems for you personally, **1999:**156, 245
concerned about, **1999:**245–46
confident that foreign governments of developed countries have upgraded computer systems, **1999:**159
confident that foreign governments of Third World countries have upgraded computer systems, **1999:**159

situation handled by Clinton,
2000:333

U.S. made mistake in sending
troops there, **2003:**240

See also Bosnia; Kosovo situation

Z

**Zaharias, Babe Didrikson,
2000:**1

Zellweger, Renee, 2002:79